THE FIFTH HOUSE OF THE HEART

ALSO BY BEN TRIPP

The Accidental Highwayman (young adult)

Rise Again: Below Zero

Rise Again

THE FIFTH HOUSE OF THE HEART

A NOVEL

BEN TRIPP

GALLERY BOOKS
NEW YORK LONDON TORONTO SYDNEY NEW DELHI

Gallery Books
An Imprint of Simon & Schuster, Inc.
1230 Avenue of the Americas
New York, NY 10020

This book is a work of fiction. Any references to historical events, real people, or real places are used fictitiously. Other names, characters, places, and events are products of the author's imagination, and any resemblance to actual events or places or persons, living or dead, is entirely coincidental.

First Gallery Books trade paperback edition July 2015

GALLERY BOOKS and colophon are registered trademarks of Simon & Schuster, Inc.

Designed by Jaime Putorti

Manufactured in the United States of America

10 9 8 7 6 5 4 3 2 1

Library of Congress Cataloging-in-Publication Data is available
Tripp, Ben, 1966–
The fifth house of the heart / Ben Tripp. First Gallery Books trade paperback edition.
pages cm
1. Vampires—Fiction. 2. Antiques dealers—Fiction. 3. Quests (Expeditions)—Fiction. I. Title.
PS3620.R569F54 2015
813'.6—dc23

2015019234

ISBN 978-1-4767-8263-8
ISBN 978-1-4767-8264-5 (ebook)

For the Agéd Crone

Present Day

PROLOGUE

NEW YORK CITY

Asmodeus Saxon-Tang knew the French Napoléon III clock to be an authentic piece with a sound provenance; the same could not be said for the blonde bidding against him. Like the clock, she was all porcelain and gilding. But she had neither the authority of age or the freshness of art about her. She was a piece of work. He thought he could detect tool marks.

Sax inclined his catalog with an imperceptible twitch of the wrist, raising his bid another hundred dollars. She flicked her paddle, swatting his bid away like a fly. Number ninety-six, the paddle proclaimed. Sax required no paddle; he was *known*. Impatience nipped at him. He should have eaten lunch, his figure be damned. Low blood sugar influenced his mood. He was bidding with his emotions, not with the great brass-bound Turing's Automatic Computing Engine inside his head. What mattered was determining the margin between an object's value and its cost, then staying well within that range. A few hundred calories could make the difference between a moment's petty triumph and an excellent deal. But there was something more to add to the calculation this time.

The ormolu clock, in excellent condition, was shaped like a footed funerary urn, in blue enamel with wheat, laurel, acanthus, and fruit mountings, wreathed and beribboned, all gilt; its eight-day movement was by Hazard and the face was from a much older piece, signed by Antide Janvier. It was created in Paris in the year 1895. All of this made it a worthwhile object.

There was something else that made the clock what the vulgarites would call an *extraordinary find*. The magic of good provenance, the biography of the piece itself. Sax knew through an intimate connection that the clock had been owned not only by Jean Cocteau but also by Sergei Diaghilev, founder of the Ballets Russes; the latter gentleman had given the clock to the former as an affectionate token for his services in writing *Parade*, the 1917 ballet—designed, pleasingly enough, by Pablo Picasso, with music composed by Erik Satie.

A handful of clients with exquisite taste, sharing Sax's relish for beautiful objects enriched by time, would desire this clock. They understood its significance. Great men, great talents in the vibrancy of their youth, had gathered before it, cast their reflections upon it; they had set their watches by it, their voices had reverberated against its gleaming belly. The clock was witness. God knew *what* it had witnessed: Cocteau and Diaghilev were a couple of outrageous queens, Picasso would fuck anything that moved, and Satie was an inveterate masturbator with an umbrella fetish.

Somehow, the blonde must have got wind of this delicious intelligence as well, because the damn clock wasn't worth fourteen thousand euros without the detailed provenance (which was absent in the auction catalog). It might, however, sell to the right collector for upward of eighteen thousand, if the anecdote could reliably be attached to the piece. Which it could, if one had read the letters of the author Raymond Radiguet and knew that the "golden egg, clucking its opprobrium" in Cocteau's room, mentioned in the epistle dated December

12, 1920, precisely three years before his death, could be no other object than this clock.

These letters of Radiguet's had never been published. Therefore, the blonde had access to the contents of some private archives to which Sax did not think she was qualified for admittance. Therefore, she was acting as an accomplice for someone else, someone within a small circle possessing the requisite access. That someone was unknown to Sax, further reducing the diameter of the circle.

Sax knew something else that was not common knowledge: Radiguet was certainly murdered by a vampire.

That being the case, there was an outside chance the blonde was working for the very fiend who had slain the young poet. Against this possibility, Sax estimated, it would be well worth the premium to win this clock, regardless of price, humiliating though it might be in the jaded eyes of the auctioneers. *Has Saxon-Tang lost his nerve?* they would wonder over their sandwiches and whiskey after the sale. *Is the old dragon becoming sentimental after sixty years of ruthless trading in aged and beautiful things?*

Despite the loss of face, Sax knew he must persist. He scented prey. He twitched his catalog again, the price ascended past fifteen thousand, and as the blonde raised the bid yet again, it occurred to Sax that he had somehow traded beauty for age himself. Never mind. At least he didn't dye his hair.

The clock went for 20,200 euros, a third again what it was worth, anecdote or no anecdote. A slack-faced Japanese businessman had entered the bidding at 16,500, apparently trying to impress the blonde. He exited at 17,200 without eliciting so much as a glance. The three dozen other auction-goers in the room were breathless, hushed, as attentive as the crowd around a baccarat table in Monte

Carlo watching two fortunes in a cockfight. The telephone proxy bidders at the back of the hall, professionals themselves, fell silent, their clients on the other end of the lines squawking audibly for information. The auctioneer, Samuel J. Wesson III, kept up his steady uninflected patter, but his voice rose an octave in pitch toward the end.

The blonde had apparently been given a ceiling of twenty thousand, which she surpassed by only a single bid, most likely because anything above her limit would have come out of her cut or salary. Despite her flinty poise, she had also been feeling the rush of acquisition by then, the brute force of money against money. But that was the danger of auctions: Every bidder can stake a fortune. Only the winner loses their money.

The winner being Sax in this instance, he affected the most neutral demeanor possible, kept his eyes slightly hooded so the auctioneers might think he knew something they didn't, and sizzled with shame at his madcap bidding performance while the room buzzed and breathed again and heads shook in wonderment all around. The blonde, slightly flushed, a lock of pale hair clinging to her smooth, moist brow, spared a single look past her shoulder at Sax, then made her way to the bar downstairs. She hadn't any further lots to bid upon. Sax did, but he'd lost interest in the remaining trifles on the block.

He forced himself to stay in his seat, lamenting the muttering of his empty stomach, picking through the archives of facts and trivia with which his ample brain was crammed, looking for an association of one piece of ephemeral information with another that could inform this strange incident with meaning.

If his theory was correct, he had just unearthed the first part of a glittering trove of artifacts that was buried within the material world of ugly, everyday things, like hidden treasure. Such treasures he had found before, to his incalculable profit (although he had attempted the calculation, naturally).

It had been many years since the last one. The price of its retrieval was paid in terror, blood, and death.

Sax had never entirely recovered his health following that adventure, and he was much older now, his walking stick no longer an affectation. Yet there was no greater triumph than the liberation of one of these fortunes, rich with history and art—and incidentally worth the kind of money upon which empires were founded.

Well worth the risk, if you didn't end up in an open grave with your still-beating heart shoved up your ass.

Sax paid for his auction items and sent word to his warehouse to come pick them up, then took a late luncheon at Écrevisse, served by a provisional waiter unfamiliar with his habits. Still, it was twenty minutes past the end of the midday seating, so Sax knew he should be grateful the staff accommodated him at all.

He tried not to think about the wretched blue-bellied clock of which he was now the owner. It would be in his office at the warehouse when next he showed himself there. He would open the clock, and perhaps inside it would be stuffed with rubies or a sketch by Picasso, thus justifying the price.

He picked through a tuft of escarole, followed by shellfish ragoût with thin slices of polenta and a soft-boiled quail's egg in a tiny footed porcelain cup that reminded him, unfortunately, of the clock. To accompany the light meal, a glass of Dom Pérignon provided by the house. He was at the table less than an hour, then made his way abstractedly back out onto the pavement.

The weather that day was warm in the sunlight, cold in the shade. It had been a terrible summer in Manhattan, humid and wet; now the autumn was dry but feverish, with skies that seemed somehow the wrong color, lurid, like old nickel postcards of New England scenes. Winter would come eventually, and it would be ferocious.

Sax wondered, without much emotion, if he would live to see the spring.

1

MUMBAI

The yellow air was thick as feathers, stuffed with dust and smoke and exhaust fumes and the stench of the river Mithi. There had been no monsoons that year to flush away the filth.

Mumbai, an island city ten times the size of Manhattan, with twelve times its population, relied on the wind and rain of the monsoons. They washed away millions of tons of industrial waste, excrement, and refuse for which there was otherwise little infrastructure. Without the weather, the city became a stinking pressure cooker. People prayed for rain and hoped they wouldn't get war. The god Indra was associated with both.

The sky hung low and overcast, but there was no rain.

This had no effect on business. Despite the ongoing malaise in the major Western economies, India continued to expand as a commercial power. Its motion picture output, particularly, was becoming more popular every year, with vast audiences in Britain, Germany, Eastern Europe, and even South America. It dwarfed Hollywood.

Bollywood, as Mumbai's entertainment industry was wryly called, was becoming the dominant power in storytelling around the world.

If you wanted to succeed, if you wanted billions of fans and not mere millions, you came to Mumbai. The squalor and the hustlers and the noise and the foul air were nothing—merely the grime that collects on well-fondled money.

The only thing success could not relieve was the accursed traffic. However many country villas one could afford, however fine one's automobile, getting to the former in the latter was nearly impossible. Even the burgeoning helicopter business was little help—it was still a drive to the airfield.

Neelina "Nilu" Chandra was an item girl. She had started out as an extra in the innumerable crowd scenes called for in Bollywood movies. Eventually she became a dancer, performing choreographed routines alongside several dozen others in the background behind the stars—item numbers, these musical interludes were called.

Now Nilu had the lead in an item number of her own, in a production called *Kaun Hai Woh Pagal Ladki?* She was playing the part of an anonymous club singer; her job was to dance and lip-synch a *filmi* song that echoed the hero's emotional condition as he pined for the heroine (the "*pagal ladki*," or "crazy girl," of the title). The stars would be involved in the number. Nilu had no fewer than five routines to perform with the hero in the course of the song.

The heroine was supposed to be sitting alone at a table in the club, ignoring all romantic entreaties, so Nilu wouldn't have to compete with her for screen time. It was an ideal opportunity that could result in more item numbers with Nilu as the lead dancer, which could bring about a proper dramatic role with dialogue. From there, it was in the audience's hands. If they liked her well enough, she would become a star.

Nilu had some good features, she knew. Aside from her body, which was the result of good genes, dancing, and not eating anything containing ghee, Nilu also had the nose of Kareena, the brows of Kajol, and eyes that were all her own. She couldn't sing particularly well, but that meant nothing; neither could any of the stars. The songs were always dubbed by voice-over specialists called playback singers. So Nilu had a fair chance.

The problem wasn't what she did on-screen, but what she didn't do offscreen.

There were certain trapdoors built into the entertainment business. Some were shortcuts to heaven, some to hell. The price of access was one's honor. None of the most successful actresses had fallen into that trap (or at least, none had confessed it), but the temptation came to them all. A girl could do very well in this town if she gave up a little pride and a lot of chastity. The question was, would such compromises keep her from the very top? The Indian press thrived on scandal, and the public feasted on it. An actress was easily ruined.

So far, Nilu had been careful. There were forces, however, conspiring against her better judgment. Tonight she would confront one of those forces in the guise of the film's producer, Mallammanavar Jagadish.

His nickname, "Jag," was appropriate, as it suggested the supreme being. Which, in cinema, Jag certainly was. He was a second-generation filmmaker and also produced television commercials. In commercials, his specialty was working with professional athletes. When it came to film, his specialty was actresses. Jag's affairs were conducted with perfect secrecy. His discretion was legendary. *I do not hunt tigers for their skins*, he once said.

The problem was not him or even his household or familiars, but the diabolical skill of scandal hunters for the tabloids. They could deduce a romantic connection merely by observing who disappeared, and when, and for how long. The parties involved need never be seen together. Verification came from studying the credits of Jag's next film; when it came to women, promotion was a sure sign.

Nilu had made sure to let several people know where she would be that evening and who would be there. That way, the tabloids could only unearth facts with which Nilu herself would agree. The problem was that Jag was notorious for ending a dinner party early, clearing an hour or two in the evening to study the latest script or budget. During that time, a woman might find herself delayed, perhaps to discuss an upcoming role. Upon such hours entire careers might hinge. Nilu had a feeling her hour would be tonight, and she didn't yet know what she would do when it arrived.

The afternoon shoot went well. Nilu spent the entire morning warming up and doing her routines alone; the rehearsal was a single run-through, and then she was on camera, singing and dancing with Sunil Kumar. He was a professional and got everything right. Nilu kept up. She was nearly an inch taller than him, but he had shoes for that.

By the end of the day they had filmed the entire dance number, except for some insert shots of the actress brooding at her table in the club. Nilu had not spared a moment's thought for the evening until an hour after the shoot was wrapped. She was changing into her civilian clothes, fashionable distressed jeans and a backless frock of pistachio-green chiffon. The green was especially suited to Nilu's skin, which was a few shades darker than the current pallid mode. Bangling gold at throat and ears, a cascade of gold bracelets at the left wrist: enough. She was ready. Sexy, but not brazen, she hoped. She tucked her feet into a pair of cork platforms and strode out of the communal dressing room she shared with eight other dancers. Maybe in a few months, she would have her own dressing room.

Maybe in a few months she would disappear, as so many girls did, back to their home villages, another starstruck hopeful ravished and sent away in shame.

Nilu wondered what had happened to some of the girls she had known. For example, a very pretty dancer named Deepa, with whom she had been fairly close. Although Deepa was her competition, Nilu liked her. It helped that Deepa wasn't as good a dancer, of course, but she was also quite charming. She seemed vulnerable in a way Nilu could only pretend to be. Deepa had a way of looking at people that suggested she was waiting for an approving word but didn't expect it to come. This quality vanished once she was dancing on camera, however, and she was just another sexy silhouette, the same as all of them.

Had Deepa been able to harness that vulnerable quality for her performances, she might have become known. As it was, Deepa had gone on some dates with film executives and above-the-line people—a director, an executive producer—but never had she been invited to dine with Mr. Jagadish. Someone had gotten through her defenses, in any case, because after one of these dates, Deepa was not seen again. Speculation in the business was that she had become pregnant during a previous encounter, confronted her lover with the news, and that very night was sent packing back home. As with so many people in Mumbai, where "home" was, nobody knew. Mumbai was home enough for the whole world.

Nilu splurged on a taxi to the corner of the block on which Jag lived, then walked the rest of the way to his gate. Several fine automobiles were parked on the gravel inside the palm-forested compound of his three-story house. The wrought-iron gates were geometric in design. There were no photographers or strangers lurking about anywhere on the street. She took half a dozen deep breaths, then went to the small gate set into the wall beside the main gates. There was a guard at the gate in a red peaked cap. He ushered her through, and she went up the illuminated path past a glowing blue fountain and into the mansion.

The evening went by in a whirl of moments. Jag himself answered the door. He was a very handsome man, and taller than most. He had a long, structural face and perfect teeth. He radiated strength. His house was enormous and brand-new. The entrance hall was the size of Nilu's parents' house, with a cantilevered staircase in African slate curving up to the second and third levels. A chandelier like a vast bursting firework hung in the center of the space, glittering in the icy-dry breath of the air-conditioning. The décor had all been assembled by a professional—it was impersonal but rich, with acres of bone-colored walls enlivened by slabs of abstract canvas and broad, baronial timbers. There seemed to be dozens of lamps in every room, so no matter where one stood, the light was flattering to the skin. The interior didn't suggest anything of Jag's personality. It merely said he was a man of enormous wealth and taste enough to hire a good decorator.

There was a variety of people at the dinner, held in the wintery-white dining room: Nilu recognized a couple of aspiring actresses who had entered the business through the dramatic side, rather than dancing. Junior artistes, such people were called. Seated opposite Nilu was a retired judge, who now held large tracts of working farmland, and his wife, once an actress who had worked with Mallammanavar Jagadish's father. Beside them were a noted architect and his spouse, a fashion designer who had made a fortune in prewrapped, fitted saris for Westernized *desi* girls.

A big, white-haired Russian with a diamond wholesale business in Surat sat to Jag's right. At the opposite end of the table was a director of photography who was known for his action sequences back in the 1970s and whose memoir had been quite successful. He was a very funny man—it turned out he'd once been a comedian in films, then discovered he preferred life behind the camera.

It was an interesting party, enlivened by Jag's impeccable skill as host. He knew how to keep things moving along. The popular image of the film producer as a demanding boor was entirely out of place with him. His sense of etiquette and propriety could not be faulted. Nilu thought she detected the mode of his sexual conquests: he was so equally interested in everyone that the other two young actresses were competing for his attention. Even Nilu found herself doing it. They all wanted to shine just a little more than the rest, collecting laughter and smiles from the party like gambling chips scooped up from the center of the gleaming mahogany table. It wouldn't take much before one of them carried the competition to the bedroom.

At some point, Nilu realized the formula for success in this setting. Concern for her reputation had kept her from throwing herself completely into the "brightest young thing" contest; the taller of the two actresses was winning that category, as it happened. But it was precisely Nilu's reserve that caught the eyes of them. She observed it was the girl who least often jumped into a conversation, and spoke only thoughtfully, who most fascinated the men. At first she wasn't certain how to amplify the effect: after all, a girl who is *too* quiet will come off shy or stupid. But Nilu found she didn't have to speak so much as listen.

If she nodded her understanding of the perils of land management when the judge spoke, Jag and the Russian watched her instead of the actresses, who could scarcely feign to be listening at all. But to really make an impression, she couldn't just listen—she must speak. However, she knew little of the subject.

She scoured her memory for something and recalled an article she had read on a bus the previous year. Something about women's rights and the system of village governance. Yes! So she asked a pointed question about the *panchayati raj* system and land ownership for women, and the judge went off into a lengthy, fairly technical explanation of the issue. Although in truth Nilu had very little idea what he was talking about, the fact that she had composed an informed-sounding question earned her admiration all around.

Eventually Jag announced he was going to have to break up the party earlier than he wished; there was a script that needed revising and Jag had paid the writers enough already. He would do the work himself. Nilu's heart beat faster. If there was to be some kind of assignation, it would be soon.

The party lingered awhile. Nilu watched Jag for signals. She didn't know what they would be, or how she would respond. She wasn't a virgin, but neither was she particularly experienced. She didn't know how they did these things in the swinging world of real players.

The judge and his wife left first; shortly afterward, the fashion designer towed her architect away, although he had been hoping for more drinks. The rest of the party retired to the great room with its vaulted ceilings and tall, stacked fireplace of rough stone.

Jag poured cognac for the Russian and the young women continued on with their Californian white wine. He made a whiskey and water for himself. They sat at intervals on the white leather sectional, which formed the margin of a conversation pit set lower than the rest of the floor. Nilu admired everything, smiled and laughed as the others did, but she was still afraid. She felt like a contestant in a game show she wasn't certain she wanted to win.

Jag checked his ashtray-sized Panerai watch and clapped his hands together.

"Another few minutes," he announced. "Then we must part ways."

To her surprise, Nilu realized the Russian was observing her closely. She hadn't paid much attention to him; he seldom spoke throughout the evening, and when he did, it was with an impenetrable accent. Apparently she had made an impression. She studied him with brief glances as the conversation fluttered around in its last phase.

His name was Andronov, which he pronounced *yendronew*. His eyes were dark gray, and even the whites of them were gray, as if there was a shadow that fell eternally over them. His hair was white and stiff, like cats' whiskers, and swept back over a monumental skull of such strength that his features seemed merely to have been draped over it. His face was complex and mobile, shifting with expressions that Nilu could not read.

It was as if she was seeing him through slightly rippled glass. He had large, hard hands with thick fingernails. She could not guess his age. In some moods, he appeared to be around fifty; in others, he could have been a hundred years old. There was something ancient about his eyes. When he looked at her, he caught Nilu staring. He smiled, just a little, and seemed almost to light up from within. Nilu wanted him to smile at her again. He was so masculine, his face more expressive even than that of the actor Sanjay Dutt. She had danced once with "the Deadly Dutt." He was tall, but not as tall as the Russian.

It might have been the wine, but Nilu found herself less wary than she had been all night. She was still on the alert for trouble, but she believed now that trouble could be handled. It could be shaped. She could stop things whenever she wanted. There was more to be discovered tonight.

The junior artistes twittered and cooed and the short one all but asked if she might stay behind. Jag dismissed them both, and the old director of photography went out with them. Nilu felt light-headed but well. She made her good-byes, knowing the next move was not hers to make. Jag glanced at Andronov. The Russian was staring fixedly at Nilu. Jag turned his eyes back to her.

"You made a good impression," he said. "Please stay a few minutes longer. I am interested to hear what sort of a career you have planned."

Nilu felt like she had leapt off a cliff and soared into the air and flown upward toward the sun. Tonight it was all happening, that moment when things would go right. For most people, that moment never came. For those few who got such a chance, some were not ready, or not paying attention, or didn't have the courage to proceed; they would wake up ten years later to discover they had not realized their dreams. Nilu felt blessed: She was aware. Now her life could truly begin.

Jag smiled at her and she smiled back, although the smile somehow missed Jag and landed in the Russian's cognac.

"I'll go get the latest sides for the new show," Jag said, and put his glass on a console table. He walked out of the great room, leaving Nilu and Andronov alone. Neither of them spoke until the ice stopped turning in Jag's glass.

"You are an item girl," the Russian said. Nilu blushed.

"Only a dancer. But I want to take dramatic roles," she said. Her ambitions suddenly seemed very small in her mouth.

"It's a competitive industry," he said. "Even with diamonds, it's nothing so competitive. There are always so many more diamonds than people believe. There are thousands of tons of them in warehouses all around the world. They're common."

He removed a ring from the small finger of his left hand and tossed it to Nilu. She caught it in both hands, slopping her wine. It was an enormous flashing stone in a plain gold mount; the thing had looked petite on his finger but was as big as a door knocker now that she held it. She noticed the metal was cold, although he'd worn it all night.

"Talent," Andronov continued, "is far more rare than diamonds."

Nilu offered him the ring back. He dismissed it with a puff of his lips. "Keep it," he said.

Nilu was ashamed of her own suspicious mind: now she wondered if he was offering her the price of her body. It wasn't unreasonable to be concerned about such a thing. She didn't know what to do with such a valuable gift. She couldn't keep it. It would be seen to influence whatever else happened.

She found the Russian hypnotic. In fact, she wanted him to have her for nothing. He excited her. Fifty? He was in his midforties, seething with virility. He looked older because he was so pale, as Europeans were. She wondered if his body was like his face, a powerful frame harnessed with muscle, and if he was so large everywhere as he was in the hands.

The blush sprang up her face again. She was thinking immodest thoughts. She might joke about such things with the other dancers concerning an especially fine male specimen amongst their colleagues, but it was only coarse talk, without the heat of desire. They never spoke in that way about the leading artistes, the stars with whom they danced, or about strangers, for that matter. Now she was experiencing real lust, her mouth flooding with it. A ridiculous fear caught her off guard: What if the Russian could tell what she was thinking? Could he see her thoughts reflected in her eyes? He would see himself naked, then. Nilu laughed aloud in spite of herself.

"You look happy," Andronov said.

"I feel happy," Nilu said, and knew it was idiotic. She carelessly set the ring aside.

She laughed again, abandoning her nagging self-observant monkey mind. An aching orb of pleasure was swelling inside her, honey flowing in the nerves of her belly. Laughter and light was the thing. Touch and spill and tangle. Her joy flew into a million glittering fragments. She could hear tinkling bells somewhere above her, a golden tintinnabulation that matched the sparkling light of the room, waterfalls of gold. Diamonds. It was the sound of diamonds she heard. But she saw gold, flowing in bright rivers.

• • •

It was blue dark and quiet when she awoke. Her body was sore, her groin so tender she could hardly move her legs. Her breasts ached. Even the light satin bedsheet abraded her nipples. There was a throbbing in her womb. She remembered some of it now. The Russian, Andronov. He'd taken her. His skin was cold and hard as stone, corded with veins. Pale and translucent. His mouth was cruel.

He had done more than violate her—he had made her *want* it. She remembered begging him to defile her, but it wasn't desire she felt then. Only fear. He had taken her, teasing unwilling orgasms from her like a magician with a volunteer from the audience: an endless supply of climaxes, from here, from there, from anywhere he chose, until Nilu was weeping with exhaustion and the pleasure had turned to agony. Wave upon wave of profound sexual release, electric spasms crashing down upon her until it was the same as drowning. It came from outside her and rushed into her. It was terrifying, like snake poison. She felt herself dying, draining away. Her strong dancer's muscles were torn and bruised, cramping from the paroxysms of release that flooded through her body.

She was in ruins. He had literally fucked her half to death.

Nilu rolled on her side and was sick on the floor. She'd been drugged, certainly. She had no idea where she was. A bedroom. She didn't know where. There were shutters on the windows. Faint light crept between the slats. She could hear distant traffic sounds. She was still in the city. Perhaps still in Mallammanavar Jagadish's mansion.

Andronov was not there. She felt his absence. There was a power that radiated from him when he was around. It left behind a stale note, like ozone, when he was gone.

It occurred to Nilu that he might return. Panic strobed in her mind. She tried to get out of the bed and fell to the floor instead, the sheets clinging to the vomit on the cool marble. She needed to find her clothes, or anything at all she could cover herself with. She was getting out of here, away from danger—wrapped in a curtain, if need be.

She crawled to the wall, where the dark rectangle of a doorway loomed in the shadows. She pushed herself up the wall and her fingers found a switch. The room lit up behind her. Suddenly she knew *he* would be there, sitting naked in a chair with a drink in his hand, waiting for her. Then he would begin his attack again, and soon she would be dead.

She spun around. The room was empty.

There was the ring, sparkling on a side table. She stumbled across the floor on trembling legs and snatched up the bright circlet. It smelled like the Russian. *Like the ocean*, she remembered. *Like wet earth.* His mouth tasted of cold flint. Nilu cast the ring on the floor.

There was a wardrobe against the wall. She made her way to it, lurching from one piece of furniture to the next, and was afraid to open it. Andronov was inside, waiting for her. She opened it despite her fear. A long white terry-cloth dressing gown hung inside, and wire hangers in paper jackets. She pulled the gown over her naked body, her arms sore and protesting as she thrust them into the sleeves.

Nilu staggered, and sometimes crawled, and eventually made it outside. She was not in Jag's palatial home; it was a private bungalow on the grounds of a large hotel she didn't recognize. There were a dozen such cottages arranged at discreet distances from each other in a densely landscaped part of the property, a hundred meters removed from the main bulk of the hotel.

There was a doorman beneath the brightly lit porte cochere of the hotel proper. Nilu thought to beg his help, but even now she held some faint hope that she could salvage her future. If she sought aid, she would be identified. She would become a sensation. The public would sympathize with her plight, a poor beautiful item girl drugged and raped by a foreign madman. But it would also label her a whore. Then she would have to remember where her home was, because it would no longer be Mumbai. She would have to live in what little of her past she could reclaim. The future would be gone.

High walls surrounded the hotel grounds. There was night traffic beyond them. Nilu pulled the dressing gown tight around her and left the hotel by the driveway entrance, her bare feet slapping on the pavement.

The police found the young woman lying in the street at three in the morning, dressed only in a white cotton robe. They transported her to Saint Mary's Hospital near the Victoria Gate. She was not a beggar or a slum dweller. She was too well maintained, her hair handsomely cut. So they took good care of her at the hospital and placed her in a semiprivate room, in case her family should turn out to be wealthy.

Nilu lay in her hospital bed and listened to the din of the Mumbai traffic coming in at the window. It was daylight. The room smelled of exhaust fumes and phenyle cleaning solution, a sweet tarry stink. Without turning her head, she could see an old-fashioned glass intravenous bottle on a chromium stand rising up on the right side of her bed, some sort of beige electronic machine on a cart to her left. There was a green curtain on a rail and a ceiling fan overhead. She couldn't see the window itself, except as a bright patch beyond the flexion of her eyes. She couldn't turn her head at all. Her neck had become stiff.

Because there was nothing else to do except listen to the traffic in the street below and stare straight ahead at the wall, Nilu reassembled the events of the previous night and studied them in her mind. It was as if she had memorized individual pieces of an enormous jigsaw puzzle, their shapes and the fragments of pictures upon them, but the puzzle would not remain in its finished form. Each time she wished to examine the picture, it had to be rebuilt. There were pieces missing. She yearned to conjure them up but also feared them.

The picture was ugly and terrifying, worse than the vividly painted tableau of the goddess Durga Maa she had found so fascinating when she was a child: opposing an army, the many-limbed deity sat astride a lion, her fists full of bloody weapons, the battlefield littered with dismembered corpses spewing gore that flowed like long hair.

A nurse stepped into the room and the puzzle flew apart again. The woman crossed through her field of vision, small and dark in a white half-sleeved smock and starched cap. The traffic noise diminished as the nurse closed the window and latched it. Nilu shut her eyes against a wave of pain from trying to turn her head. When she opened them, the nurse was gone. She hadn't heard the door close. The blades of the ceiling fan were turning now, stirring the warm air. The darkness came then, and swallowed her up. She dreamed of hard, white bodies and probing fingers and long, snakelike tongues. She itched and burned. The Russian sucked at her flesh and she felt her soul draining away.

It was nighttime again when Nilu returned to consciousness, flailing through slimy folds of nightmare back to the stifling-hot hospital room.

Andronov was standing at the foot of her bed. Fear flooded her veins. His face was impassive, the flesh lifeless except for his eyes. He seemed about to speak but thought better of it. Instead, he glanced toward the door of the room, then stepped around the foot of the bed until he stood beside the chromium IV stand.

Nilu was terrified, but she made no move or sound. He had come to kill her, she knew. She could not resist. Her life was his to take. Now he would finish the project.

He stretched out his large, waxen hand and touched Nilu's face, kneading the flesh like a doctor palpating for hidden flaws. Then he bore down, and the cold fingers became hard, and Nilu's neck screamed with pain but there was no voice to it. Water spilled from her eyes. He had his cool palm across her nose and mouth. She began to suffocate. He stared into her eyes, and what she saw there was more terrible than hatred or glee. It was boredom. She forced her arms up and clawed at his fingers, but they were as unyielding as stone. Bursts of light filled her vision. Her empty lungs burned.

Then there was a loud, sharp *bang* and a flash of light that leapt up yellow along the underside of Andronov's jaw, his nostrils, the hollows of his eye sockets. He stumbled backward. Nilu gasped for breath. Her neck scissored pain, but she had to breathe.

The same nurse emerged from her place of concealment beneath the bed. She was holding a sawed-off shotgun. She was a tiny figure compared to the enormous Russian now pressed up against the wall. He was clutching at his groin, and from there a vast crimson stain was spreading. He raised his bloody hands and bent them into claws, snarling at the nurse. She cocked and fired the weapon all in one convulsive gesture. The Russian's face imploded, his nose and jaws gone, blown into the back of his head.

But he didn't die. He threw himself at the small woman instead. She fired the gun again and a dark red peacock's tail leapt out of the Russian's back, all over the walls and ceiling. Then the Russian collided with her and both figures fell on the bed, bearing down suddenly on Nilu's legs. The intravenous bottle toppled and shattered on the floor. The pain was such that Nilu thought her head was tearing free of its foundations; she wanted to die.

The combatants rolled off the end of the bed, and Nilu was slipping toward the floor. She gripped the sheets and hung at an angle, as afraid as if she might fall ten miles, not two feet.

Shoes clattered in the hallway. People were coming. There was another bang, another flash. The Russian rose to his feet and roared, a gurgling cry of rage and pain made shapeless because he had no features, no lips to make the sounds, only a single rolling eye beneath his tattered forehead. The woman had shot him point-blank in his face a second time. He swung his head, drunk with wounds, first at the door, where fists hammered on the other side of the panel, then around to look with his single red eye at the window.

The nurse was on her feet, now injured herself, swiping a hand at the braid of blood that spilled from her nose. She got her back against the wall and shoved herself along it, away from the Russian. She pulled a second weapon from its concealment behind the green curtain, a long-handled bludgeon with a spiked hammerhead. The Russian saw this thing and lurched for the window.

The nurse charged with a hiss of rage and swung the weapon. Nilu could not see it strike the Russian from her skewed, upside-down angle. He hulked on the edge of her vision as a blur of struggling darkness. But she heard the brutal spike go into his back, and she heard his bubbling scream of agony. The window shattered. The Russian ripped the entire sash out of its frame and flung it into the room, tearing the curtain down. Traffic noise clamored in again, and exhaust fumes.

Andronov was gone through the window. The nurse leaned out to see down into the street below. One of her feet rose into view as she flipped it up for a counterbalance: she was shod in military canvas boots with toothy rubber soles. Not proper footwear for hospital personnel. Then she was looking down into Nilu's face, a finger to her blood-jellied lips.

Silence, the gesture said. But Nilu understood what was really meant: *Say nothing*. Nilu saw that the woman was North Asian, Chinese perhaps, or Japanese. She had lost the small, stiff nurse's cap. Her black hair was cut short.

Moments later, the nurse crossed to the door and opened it, and doctors and orderlies rushed in. Questions were flung around, arms waved. A tremendous cacophony of voices filled the hot, blood-stinking air. Several pairs of hands found Nilu at once and worked to stabilize her on the bed; through the gaps in the crowd she saw the nurse, bloody faced, against the wall, shaking her head as a doctor demanded to know what had happened. Then the crowd shifted, there was confusion, and when Nilu could see again, the doctor's attention was elsewhere. The nurse had gone.

2

New York City

Sax paid Wesson's Auctioneers a visit, then Sotheby's, Craine Bros., Swann Galleries, Christie's, and a couple of others. It took him the entire day. He could have telephoned or sent e-mails, but his business was entirely based on personal relationships, upon which he sometimes put considerable strain. So he never missed an opportunity to appear in person, accepting a drop of tea or a splash of spirits, depending on the venue.

The awful days when all the young, overgroomed assistants would ply him with bottled water were thankfully past now. Besides the cellular telephone and saddle shoes, Sax thought there was no more unpleasant accessory than water in a plastic bottle. Especially the bottles with pop-up nipples on the end. Ridiculous, a nation of adults suckling at polyethylene tits. What with the economy and the discovery that bottled water was identical to tap water, this indignity had fallen out of vogue, and he could get proper beverages again.

Sax's final visit of the day was to Woodbride, Barron Auctioneers, who specialized in European and Japanese collections. He was ushered in by an obsequious young fellow named Stoate dressed in horsey tweeds, a spotted ascot, and saddle shoes. One of those creatures that affected homosexuality to advance his career but would be frightened out of his wits at the touch of a real mustache. Tragic, Sax thought, but at least it would keep him out of the gene pool for a while.

He followed Stoate down the dim corridor that ran along the upper floor of the Woodbride, Barron warehouse, past rows of dark, glass-fronted offices with Victorian racing prints on the walls. Business was terrible these days. Twenty years before, every one of these offices would have been occupied by valuation specialists, schedulers, insurance experts, and all the rest; now most functions were handled in the front office, into which Stoate ushered Sax.

The place used to smell of cigars and leather. Now it stank of copy machine toner. The water cooler glugged dismally and the shaded ceiling lamps gave off a hospital light. None of the employees looked up to note who had arrived. It was as subdued as a library. Sax hated to see the business in this condition, but the whole antiques trade had suffered. Sax himself had taken to stockpiling entire estates he'd bought for the price of haulage with a single bid, knowing that someday, when times were richer, he could portion it out a piece at a time for obscene profit. Probably to the Indians or the Chinese, whoever gentrified first.

His old friend and sometime rival Jules Amies emerged from a corner office with his hand extended. Jules, a distant relative of the famous British haberdasher Sir Hardy Amies, was a tall, thin man, gray of face, suit, tie, and hair, with heavy black plastic spectacles that appeared to be bolted onto his nose. His one element of plumage was a brilliant scarlet pocket square. Jules had dozens of the things in every imaginable color and pattern. His usual loud greeting was this time muted, affected as he was by the somber atmosphere. Still, Jules shook Sax's hand and clapped him on the arm as they retreated into his office.

Sax took the green leather guest's chair. Jules sat in his incongruous new Herman Miller chair, one of those modern contrivances that appeared to be made of baling wire and showgirl's stockings. Stoate brought them bottled water, then departed with a bow. Jules opened the bottom drawer of the desk and produced a pair of pony glasses and a liter of Cragganmore whiskey.

"Sax," said Jules.

"What's left of him," Sax agreed.

"Ratio? Business to pleasure?"

"Half each, dear. It's my pleasure to come see you—call it an excuse—but there is a matter of some interest I wish to discuss."

"Who have you already talked to?"

"Don't be vulgar," Sax said. "You're always top of the list." And then, "Everyone. They think I'm mad."

"You *are* mad," Jules said, without humor.

"Still, I do have fun. Listen, Jules. I've come up against a buyer. European, I think. Works through proxies. Bids outrageous sums for things. Been active the last few months here in New York."

"Does this have to do with that clock of yours?" Jules was interested. His drink hung in the air halfway between desktop and lips.

"That bloody ormolu? Yes. Talk of the town, I know. Cheers."

"Twenty thousand, I heard."

"Twenty thousand two hundred. Salt the wound, Jules, salt the wound. I have my reasons, as you know."

"Everyone has his reasons."

"Not often. But *I* do. Here's what I want to know: Who wanted the thing so much? And don't tell me it's that dreadful acquisitions person from Daimler or the Barclay's woman. It's nobody I know, you know? But it's someone who knows what I know, if you know what I mean. A player."

"Someone inside your own network?"

"Someone that shares the same network," Sax said. "But unknown to me."

"Or someone familiar to you who has decided to remain anonymous, of course," Jules said.

Sax shook his head. There was a hand-colored steel engraving of a long sausage-shaped horse running across the wall behind Jules's head; the jockey was as small as a monkey, and the horse's legs were stretched out fore and aft as if it was diving into the sea.

Sax said, "Most of the people in the, ah, network or circle I'm talking about are either dead, retired, or enjoy the notoriety. Anonymous just isn't their style. And I should think after about a million years in the business, I could detect the fingerprints of someone known to me. One comes to recognize their appetites. This person, this *nemo incognito*, has entirely new and eccentric tastes, in my experience. I have here a list of purchases attributable to this party—and it's eclectic, to say the least."

Jules swirled the fluid in his glass.

"I don't know," he said.

"You don't know who it is? Or you can't tell me?"

"It's a favor."

"Yes yes yes," Sax said, impatiently frothing the air with his hand.

"I didn't tell you," Jules added.

"I was never here," Sax said, in jest. But Jules, it seemed, wanted to hear the words. His shoulders relaxed and he tossed back his drink, exhaled, then leaned across his desk conspiratorially.

"A woman," Jules said.

"That narrows it down," Sax replied. The last thing he needed was a slow reveal.

"Her proxy bidders are always attractive young women, right? There's a blonde, and a gorgeous brunette with legs like a Queen Anne console."

"Spoon foot or ball-and-claw?"

"Don't joke with me, Saxon. I'm telling you what I know."

"You haven't told me her name."

"I don't know it. It's just shop talk. We've seen the weird buying pattern, too. It was the blonde that bid against you for the clock. Twenty grand for that thing—nothing personal, but Jesus Christ. We think there's also a redhead working for the mystery woman, which has a certain symmetry to it. London side of things, sometimes Italy. I know a guy at Brunelli Casa d'Aste—he picked up on the same pattern. Incredibly high prices for good stuff, but not great stuff. Real random kinds of things: sometimes art, sometimes furnishings, glass, ceramics. No common theme. We figured there must be some provenance we don't know about, right? Like that fake Holbein that went for two thousand pounds a while back, and turned out to be a real Holbein worth millions."

"Don't remind me." Sax had been at that auction, looking for porcelain, and had failed to spy the masterpiece, a portrait of the Dutch scholar Erasmus. He studied Jules's face and decided he should give something up, see if it yielded further information.

"If you *must* know, I had some information about the clock," Sax confessed. "It has a bit of history that wasn't in the catalog, if one knows where to look for it. But it's not worth an extra six thousand, of course. I kept bidding because I must know who this mystery buyer is. I was hoping she'd make me a better offer out in the hallway, or try a gazump, to be frank. I didn't want to pay the money. But now I'm stuck with the thing, and I'm determined to find out who my rival is."

Gazumping was a practice that originated in real estate auctions—the fine art of making a better offer to the seller after a deal had ostensibly closed. Sax knew it was too much to hope. He could then have initiated a lawsuit and found out who his opponent was. He didn't think the unknown bidder often found herself on the losing end. It was disappointing that she gave up so readily.

"You may be the first person to outbid her," Jules said, startling Sax. They had been following identical trains of thought. "She might yet approach you."

"One hopes as much, certainly," Sax said. "So: The buyer is a woman, and her familiars are known. A Neapolitan selection of ice queens—vanilla, chocolate, and strawberry. So far, so good. I have admitted to you that the clock, at least, had some value beyond its book price; in my researches today I've identified a few other pieces that probably went to the same party. Also at outrageous prices."

"The girls write checks against different accounts," Jules said. "Always from LLCs or holding companies. The checks are always good. No personal paper. Dead end there. But I can tell you a couple other things. The companies are in Europe, for one. French, English, and Swiss. And the stuff we know about, all the stuff she's bought, has one thing in common. Every single piece disappeared during World War Two, then showed up again in the nineteen sixties. So there's this gap. That's everything I know." Jules leaned halfway across his desk. "Anything else you find out, let *me* know. Because she sure as hell got the attention of us hammers."

Sax turned his steps toward the New York Public Library on Fifth Avenue. The shadows were deepening; the sun had already sunk to the bottom of Forty-Second Street. There was only an hour until closing time. He moved reverently between Patience and Fortitude, the stone lions sculptured by Edward Clark Potter, and passed beneath the familiar portico into the building. He knew the library well and referred to it as his "personal Internet"; in fact, a vast quantity of written matter had not yet—and would never be—transcribed into digital form. With thirty million volumes in the New York City library system, plus another hundred million documents, he could find things recorded there that mere digerati could not hope to discover. It was all in knowing how to refine the search, and to do so swiftly. Besides, he loved the spicy smell of old books.

Sax could have called the library's telephone reference system, but he didn't trust intermediaries. Better to find the thing oneself. There was instinct in it. The right information might not be the thing he sought, but the thing next to it on a page. It was almost a matter of echolocation, like bat flight.

He made his way through the recently renovated stacks, first pulling certain volumes of general reference. Consulting these, he jotted down the names of some histories and biographies. Those books yielded further subjects for discovery.

After fifty minutes of diligent exploration that left him perspiring and weak, he had what he needed. It was dreadful being so old, Sax thought. Everything was tiring. Even enthusiasm. He could scarcely carry the few books he checked out for closer study. What had happened to the strong young man who carried walnut armoires on his back down stair and street? Even his bones lacked the spring they once had. A fossil, that's what he was. A fossil engaged in archaeology. Queen of the Stone Age. Ridiculous.

The taxi back to his roost overlooking Gramercy Park cost ten dollars, including the peak-time surcharge and tip (Sax was generous with tips, to be fair). The distance covered was precisely one and one-third miles. It required two left turns and two rights to make the trip. Sax didn't know how people of ordinary means survived in the city. Everybody walked or took the bus, certainly, even Sax, but *everything* was that expensive. His sparrow's luncheons cost fifty dollars, even without wine. He couldn't get a shirt laundered for less than two dollars, and he possessed dozens of shirts. In 1973, when he bought his apartment—or, to be precise, the building in which his apartment was located, although the other tenants didn't know the old bird in 301 was also their landlord—it was because owning was cheaper than renting. Now the place was worth an astronomical sum, despite its narrowness and unimproved character. Even with vacancies in every commercial building in town, people still had to live somewhere. Sax told his friends the only reason he kept his key to the residents-only Gramercy Park was so that he could grow potatoes when he ran out of money. Not that he would ever run out of money. He just didn't like it running.

Sax ate dinner in, something he usually avoided, and alone, which was worse. But he needed to finish his project. His meal was a simple one: tinned *foie gras aux truffes* from Harrods, spread thickly on crisp, dry toast. A few lambs' ears of endive with herbed salt, balsamic vinegar, and pumpkin-seed oil. Champagne to clear the palate, an '88 Veuve Clicquot. Lean, with a substantial structure. Hint of spice in there, dried fruit, flowers; some toast in the nose, then off to an assured finish with smoke and mineral, amongst other things. *Toast in the nose*, Sax thought, sieving a mouthful through his teeth. The more rarefied a thing became, the more absurd. The language of wine, for one thing. Himself, for another.

He swept the crumbs out of the books and filled pages of a calfskin diary with notes. Details of alliances and betrayals during World War II. Which distinguished continental families suffered, and which didn't. Who was in sympathy with Axis or Allies, and what they did about it. Fortunes that vanished and reappeared, or vanished entirely. The movement of wealth. The allegiances of title and privilege with brute power. Something Jules Amies said had gnawed its way into Sax's calculations—that everything the mystery bidder sought to buy had disappeared around the time of the war, then came back into circulation. Of all the random bits of information Sax had gleaned, that was the most important.

Two factors came into play with every antique: quality and time. A masterpiece was valuable the day it was created. Add five hundred years, it became even more valuable. If it could be known what happened to the masterpiece during the intervening half millennium, and it was a jolly good story, the value reached whatever maximum the market would bear.

Sax wrote out a list, consolidating his notes into a thesis. Here he had an unknown collector, probably European, believed to be a woman. Sax hadn't asked Jules how that was known. Presumably one of the proxy bidders had used the feminine pronoun when speaking of her client—if they spoke of their client at all. He would have to take Jules's information as given, for the time being. *Desires to remain anonymous. Why? Many collectors so inclined. Any reason out of the ordinary? Consider possibilities. Meanwhile: objects sought after appear to be unconnected.* Those of which Sax was aware, at least, didn't seem to come from a common source. Sometimes that was a factor, as the newly prosperous descendants of fallen, once-great families attempted to reassemble their patrimonies. *Tilting at windmills, that lot. Bless 'em.*

The objects the mystery buyer had accumulated were from all over the place, of all periods, no apparent common thread. Prewar history identified amongst perhaps half of the pieces in question (such as Sax's ormolu clock), the rest, origin unknown. Purchased by proxies in Europe and the US, possibly with additional buyers elsewhere, as yet unrecognized. It seemed like an entirely random event.

There were only two common elements: price was nearly no object, and everything had dropped briefly out of sight during the war.

Sax underlined the last part again and again until the paper was wet with ink. That was the key—the war gap. He belched champagne gas and his eyes watered.

Many of the great families had lost everything when the Germans made their play for a thousand-year empire. Italy, France, Poland, everywhere but Switzerland and England had seen a great churning up of the sediments of heritage. It had settled back down like so much sand deposited by a swift tide, in entirely new places, creating a new landscape. What did that suggest? How did that inform the particular interests of Sax's unknown collector?

Sax made himself an espresso with the ominous black Italian machine his niece Emily had given him for Christmas the previous year. It was simple to operate: water in here, coffee in there, batten the hatches, and press the button. It made a terrifying noise and dispensed the brew with explosive force. There was a steam-emitting milk-foaming attachment as well, which Sax would under no circumstances attempt to use.

He fetched his woolen motoring rug and moved his operations into the living room, which was ample and magnificent. He spread the rug over his knees, his slippered feet propped up on the Art Deco Wolfgang Hoffmann coffee table that he irrationally despised but that so perfectly suited the room that he couldn't get rid of it. Then he continued working at the problem, filling pages in his notebook. Three times he scorched himself another tiny espresso, once with biscotti to tamp down the rebellious pâté, which seemed to be in a revolutionary mood despite its bourgeois origins.

Rummaging amongst the books, he was able to narrow down his list of possibilities until he had something like a theory. The linchpin of the idea had to do with the postwar period. Great private collections suffered twin indignities during the wartime era: First, the collections were broken up, sold, hidden, or appropriated, reflective of the misfortunes of the original owners. Second, the objects from the collections were liberated from their new possessors, mostly Nazis. Precisely the same breaking up, selling, hiding, and appropriation was visited upon them again. As nobody wanted to be accused of looting, provenances were fabricated by the thousands. Forgers made expert during the war were then out of jobs; they turned to fake letters, receipts, and other documents created to support the false provenances. It was a disaster, from a historical perspective.

Sax had known all of this in a strictly professional way; he would frequently play both sides of the fabricated-documentation issue, sometimes passing the provenance off as authentic when he rather suspected it wasn't, and other times exposing the faked papers in order to get a better deal. It was a part of his moral code that he never attempted to tamper with an authentic provenance. He had been an infant when all this collection-bashing and forgery was originally going on. Consequently, the details of the period had always been of less interest to him. It was within his lifetime, but not the bits with which he had any personal associations.

But now that he was putting together a picture of the people and events that precipitated the chaos, those years became much more vivid in his mind. As usual, he best witnessed human affairs through the objects amongst which those affairs were conducted. This crash course in midcentury events made things downright exciting. However, the suspicion he'd had at the auction at which he had procured Cocteau's clucking golden clock was borne out by what he'd discovered. This disturbed him.

He began a new page of notes. At the top he wrote:

VAMPIRE

Then he scratched out a timeline. Vampires might live indefinitely, so he could assume a single individual was involved throughout the period in question. Sax's original idea was that someone was reassembling an earlier collection that had been looted during the war. Now he thought the truth was something far more repulsive. The vampires had prospered during both twentieth-century European wars (as in every war), attaining high rank, feeding with impunity, amassing tremendous material wealth. They did especially well with the Nazis, who had the kind of mind-set the vampires could best use—and one closest to their own way of thinking. Sax had heard this long ago from another collector, one who knew his vampires.

What must have happened, as Sax indicated on the timeline, was a reversal of fortunes for one of the vampires. Its hoard had been liberated. Right after the war, from 1945 through around 1949, and long afterward, in some cases, zealous survivors of the conflict had searched out every hiding place in Europe, determined that no malefactor should prosper by evil. Even the vampires, some a thousand years old, could not resist such resources flung against them. Not all of them were discovered, but those that were lost everything—often including their un-lives.

Sax thought he knew what was happening now. One of these creatures had recently emerged after what—to a thing that measured time in decades, not days—was only a sensible interval of eighty years or so. During that period it had amassed a new fortune, as vampires easily do. With this wealth, it was attempting to reassemble its old glory. Such monsters, after all, might have acquired a piece from Napoléon Bonaparte himself, or Queen Nefertiti, for that matter. There were memories attached to such artifacts. It was the memories they cherished.

Vampires dwelled in the past. It was one of the things that most distinguished them from human beings. For a vampire, the future is nothing, despite the centuries they can expect to survive. For men, the opposite is true: men live always for the future, of which they may claim so little. Robbed, as a vampire would see it, of its rightful trove of mementos, the creature would work diligently to reclaim every last piece. And for a vampire to work at all was a terrible sacrifice for it. They were lazy creatures, dragons content to sleep on their hoards. It was a compelling motive, Sax believed.

So it might be a vampire. On the other hand, it could just be some reclusive nouveau riche Chinese tycoon buying up a mansion's worth of clutter to make it look like he had a pedigree. It all came down to the ormolu clock, and whether or not that poor young fellow Raymond Radiguet—poet and novelist, friend of Great Artists—had been killed by a vampire.

Sax had found a book to address that issue as well. *Lives of Paris*, it was titled. Radiguet got half a page, including a eulogy written by Jean Cocteau that Sax thought rather lachrymose. Cause of death was typhoid. Which, of course, could be a misdiagnosis, or the doctor might have cited typhoid to spare the deceased's loved ones the indignity of a less flattering illness. But Cocteau's words held a clue. In the eulogy to Radiguet was a quote from the poet's deathbed, spoken in a fever:

There is a color that moves and people hidden in the color.

Victims of systematic vampirism died in a fever, boiling with lymph, bleeding within, their flesh broken out in poxy rashes. And hallucinated toward the end. Sax had witnessed it with his own eyes. It would look much like typhoid. Radiguet was only twenty, too dreadfully young, Sax thought. *A color that moves.* Sax ran the words through his mind. *People hidden in the color.* He knew something about that.

Despite the woolen rug across his legs and the lusty clanking of the steam radiators beneath his windows, Asmodeus Saxon-Tang felt a chill spread over his flesh. It was the damp cold of newly turned earth in an autumn graveyard. He felt terribly old and weak and tired. He knew his wild conjectures were right. He might be the only man alive who could put together the scattered bits of information to discover what he'd found.

There was no vanity behind the thought. In his cleverness, he'd made a fool of himself, and possibly a target. He had exposed himself to the vampire when he outbid the blonde for that accursed clock.

What was it Nietzsche had said? *When you gaze long into the abyss, the abyss gazes into you.*

Sax could almost feel the eyes upon him, out there in the darkness beyond the brittle panes. He shivered. The telephone rang. Sax leapt at the jangling noise, the convulsion of his buttocks popping him a foot into the air. He clawed the instrument to him and clapped the handset to his ear.

"Saxon-Tang," he gasped. His heart was pounding.

"It's Barry, Mr. Tang. I'm sorry about the late call, but . . ." It was Barry Lions, Sax's foreman in the New York warehouse.

"But what?" Sax prompted when Barry failed to continue.

"Somebody broke in," Barry said. "The night watchman?"

The night watchman what? Sax urged in his mind. *What?* Barry was obviously beside himself; he couldn't seem to get through a sentence tonight.

"The night watchman what?" Sax prompted at last.

"He's dead," Barry said. "I mean *real* dead."

The police were out in force with their flashing bubblegum lights and barking radios, milling around examining the ground. A detective with very dark skin introduced herself to Sax as Millicent Jackson. She had one of those faces that Edward Hopper would have painted: enduring boredom with a patience born of hopelessness. Sax suspected she had never laughed in her life. She didn't seem to believe his name was real.

"Asmodeus Saxon-Tang? Sounds like a sports drink."

Sax found himself babbling out his brief cocktail-party speech on the subject: "Saxon is my father's surname, the *Tang* being an embellishment at my mother's insistence—it was her family surname. From *Étang*, French for 'pond' or 'bog.' It sounds better in French. Don't ask about the Asmodeus part." He handed her his passport, as he lacked a driver's license.

She nodded without looking convinced, walked away, and made him wait.

Sax detested the police for every possible reason. And no reason at all. He just didn't like them. Putting aside the fascistic tendencies, the aggression, authoritarianism, paranoia, vendibility, and fear, they were also the only people in the world who could make a uniform look bad. Even the UPS man looked dynamite in a uniform. *Is that why you became a cop? Because you didn't look good in shorts?* The phenomenon applied worldwide. London Metropolitans dressed as tram drivers with glans-shaped helmets. The Parisian flics with their elastic-cuffed tracksuits and oversized pillbox hats. Italian carabinieri kitted up like hotel doormen, Tokyo cops who ought to be delivering mail. The only exception Sax could think of was the Royal Bahamas Police. They turned out with smart white tunics and pith helmets and had the jaunty look of an Edwardian marching band. Sax realized he was letting his thoughts run away. He was anxious.

At last, the detective came back and ushered him beneath the crime-scene tape stretched around the front of the warehouse. It was past two a.m. The warehouse was in Yonkers, not far from the Amtrak station. It was an area of industrial decay where men were dwarfed by big machines, a landscape of heavy, grimy things that beetled along amongst ugly cavernous buildings like the carcasses of beached whales. To step inside the warehouse, as Sax now did, was a revelation. He always enjoyed the effect of it. Always except tonight.

Detective Jackson walked at a funeral pace into the warehouse ahead of Sax, eyes on the floor, and spoiled the grand entrance.

It was a wonderland in there. Sax allowed very few of his clients to see this place, preferring the presentational control his local shop provided. Nothing here was cleaned, staged, or dressed for sale. It was exactly as it had been found.

The ranks of priceless and beautiful things rose up all around them for three stories, a treasure worthy of the Smithsonian or some great European museum, but all for sale. Cabinets, cupboards, beds, chairs, tables, mirrors, desks. Acres of carved paneling. Church fixtures, including a Christ on the cross at least twelve feet tall in brutal, wet-wounded polychrome. Fifteenth-century German, of course, writhing on the nails. An entire manor's worth of Louis XIV furniture in ebony and gold. A forest of candlesticks in gold and stone and wood. Windows, doors, medallions, and milled trim of every style. In one far reach of the place, it always appeared to be raining: here hung the dozens of crystal chandeliers that couldn't be safely put away in crates.

There were workshops at the back nearest the docks where restoration and repair were done, and offices at the front. An enormous walk-in safe near the offices, once a bank vault, contained objects of uninsurable value. Opposite the safe was a climate-controlled room for storage of paintings, paper, textiles, and other fragile things that required fresher air than the HVAC could provide. The river was a liability in warm weather, and Sax had been forced to spend a great deal of money on antihurricane measures as well.

Detective Jackson led Sax past the offices. Barry Lions emerged from the last one in the row, mewling.

"Thank God you're here," he said. "I'm losing it, man."

Sax liked Barry. A large, seal-like man, Barry knew the business and how to take care of people and things, and he liked to stay organized. This tendency was only a liability if you had a dead man in the warehouse. Barry was falling to pieces now, a plainclothes cop following him as he hurried to Sax's side.

"They asked me if *I* did it," Barry said.

"Which you did not, I presume?" Sax said.

"Damn straight I didn't. He owed me money on the football pool."

The attempt at bravado failed completely. Barry was frightened, not least because he'd had to wait for the police to arrive and was alone in the warehouse for half an hour with the corpse.

They approached the locus of police activity: halfway down the central aisle of the warehouse beneath the old-fashioned bulbs (fluorescent light was terrible for antique finishes), sprawled at the foot of a mahogany William and Mary hutch *écritoire* with a double-dome cornice, was the night watchman. He lay facedown on the concrete. His blue uniform was soaked with blood that ran from beneath his chest, across the floor, and down a drainage grate. His name was Alberto, and prior to tonight he had looked very well in uniform, unlike the police. There was a small flashlight on the ground beside the body, a ring of keys, and Alberto's baseball cap, turned up to the ceiling as if to accept pocket change from passersby. Each item had a small yellow evidence tent beside it.

Sax hated the sight of death. He'd seen it before, death in peace and in violence. Hard to avoid at his age. The watchman looked vulnerable, one half-closed eye visible, his cheek pressed to the floor. It occurred to Sax that Alberto had become like everything else in the warehouse: a relic of past life, something precious in its workmanship. He had a provenance as well. Barry wouldn't get closer to the corpse than fifteen feet and couldn't bear to look at it. Sax approached, waving away a couple of uniformed men who closed in as if to stop him falling across the body in his grief.

"Please," he said. "He worked for me."

Sax stooped stiffly beside the body under the watchful eye of Detective Jackson.

"This is Alberto Robledo?" she said.

"Yes," Sax replied. He straightened his back and stepped away from the body. "If this is an opportune moment, I'll tell you everything I know. Alberto's shift begins at nine. There's an alarm. It sends a call to Mr. Lions's home in addition to yourselves. I received a telephone call from Mr. Lions tonight, stating he had received the alarm and driven straight over from his residence, which is relatively near. He phoned me from his office here. To the best of my knowledge, there shouldn't have been anyone else present with Alberto. I have a staff of twenty-three people who work here full- or part-time. If you wish to inquire into their activities this evening, I can provide you with the necessary information."

Jackson recorded this statement with a finger-sized device. Then she raised it to her own lips and added Sax's name and the time of the statement.

"Thank you, Mr., um, Saxon-Tang." She made a sound like there was something else she wanted to add, but she didn't add it; instead, she took a new tack. "Can I ask if there's anything you see missing? I mean there's a lot of stuff, but I assume this was a burglary."

Sax made a slow turn where he stood, looking up and around at his stock of beautiful artifacts. Robbery made no sense, not in the warehouse. This stuff wasn't jewelry. One would need moving trucks, dollies, and a dozen men to carry off a worthwhile haul, and selling it would be nearly impossible. The market was too small. Everybody knew everybody else. Although he kept rejecting the idea, there was only one individual object he could imagine might have led to this tragic circumstance. Sax considered not mentioning it. It would complicate the plans forming in his mind. But there was death here. He couldn't obstruct whatever efforts might be made to solve the crime. Still, he hesitated. Who knew what his ideas would lead to? An open case, detectives—complications.

"Sir?" Detective Jackson was staring at him. He stared at her. Her lower lip projected in a furrowed bow like the shell of a Brazil nut. She looked tired because the outside corners of her eyes were lower than the inside corners. And because she *was* tired. Sax decided to do the decent thing, however inconvenient. If by some remote chance God was waiting for him, upon his own death Sax could point to this moment as a mitigating factor when it came time for sentencing. He took a long breath.

"Let's have a look in my office," he said.

As he suspected, the ormolu clock was gone.

3

NEW YORK CITY

The apartment appeared to be the aerie of a woman three times Emily's age, albeit one of good taste. Emily lived on MacDougal Street in Greenwich Village, in one of the brick buildings with a fire escape on the front façade. There was a Tibetan imports shop and a café on the ground floor. Emily occupied the fourth-floor front apartment.

Asmodeus Saxon-Tang made his way slowly up the stairs of the building, wheezing, clutching a gift box. Emily was not waiting at her door, as that would have been vulgar; Sax preferred his struggle with the stairs to go unobserved. Once he had caught his breath, Emily answered the door at the first knock and ushered Sax in with a sincere hug. She put the kettle on for tea.

The apartment was furnished with nondescript antiques, mostly knock-around brown Victorian pieces, the floors covered in worn Persian rugs. Mismatched bookshelves occupied every available wall, old family photographs peering out from the gaps in the books. In wet weather, the dowdy tufted chairs smelled of horsehair. It was the kind of place that ought to have a Manx cat slithering around the ankles, but

Emily had never possessed a cat. It was a thrifty, genteel space, such as a set decorator might conjure up if called upon to create an elderly music teacher's flat.

Asmodeus Saxon-Tang proffered the gift box to his niece. She wore a sheath of rough oat-colored silk, belted with a broad, knotted *kamarband* of magenta cotton, a gold circlet on her left wrist, and on her feet, Greek-style goatskin sandals. The simple outfit perfectly suited her rosewood-colored skin and black, softly rumpled hair. Emily accepted the box, turning it in her hands. She knew her uncle's ways. A gift from him was never shaken or manhandled. One never knew: it could be a battery-powered alarm clock he'd bought in the street from a Haitian costermonger, or it could be a Fabergé egg. Emily had received both from her beloved uncle. Everything came in the same sort of stout white cardboard boxes he used to pack things at his shop.

"It's heavy," she observed, winging up her black brows.

Emily was not a prompt riser. The gift alarm clock had gotten her through many sleepy mornings. The Fabergé egg had gotten her through graduate school. It was, her uncle had said with the sidelong wink of the born thief, one of the eight missing imperial eggs. He knew it for a fact. Unfortunately he couldn't admit he knew it for legal reasons, so he gave the thing to Emily, and with his blessings she sold it without its extraordinary history for a tenth what it would otherwise have realized at auction. The tenth she *had* gotten was quite sufficient.

Emily was the only thing in the world Sax trusted, besides gold. She knew it and didn't make anything of it, and that was half of why Sax trusted her. In addition, she found him charming, rather than amusing, which was the scourge of a mincing old creature like himself; of all the family, it was she who understood and accepted his self-invented scruples. Uncle Sax had a moral code as rigid as that of the Puritans and as heartfelt as godfaith, insofar as his interests were concerned; it was just that 90 percent of his interests ran counter to popular standards. Besides, he and Emily were the outsiders in their old, brittle family. Exotic and demure, like the subject of a Gauguin painting, and not a bit Saxon looking, she was a *love child*, always spoken in italics; he was anything but.

The box was square, wrapped in crisp Japanese paper with a chrysanthemum pattern in red and gold. Exactly the right size to hold a human skull, a two-slice toaster, or a handbag.

"May I open it now?" Emily asked.

"You might as well, I suppose," Sax replied with studied indifference. Emily relished his show of unconcern. It concealed a love of giving, or more precisely, of distributing things to their right places. Sax had been alive for too long, and in the game of antiques too long, to harbor any illusions about possession. To give, to receive: merely an addition to the object's provenance. For him, the joy of giving was in seeing the object suitably disposed. If useful, better yet. But so many old and wonderful things were useless. In that case, they were called "art," and thus became useful again.

"It's won't be useful, I hope," Sax added, because Emily was taking too long stripping the paper off the box. He preferred the way she did it as a child, greedily ripping through paper and box alike with small fingers, but he knew she now liked to save the paper to make jackets for her softcover books. At last she got the paper off, primly folded it on the tea table at her elbow, and gave the box another turn in her hands. Her fingers were long, arched, with unpainted nails as thin and bright as a salmon's scales. Sax crossed and uncrossed his legs. She was rather overplaying the opening business, he thought. Toying with him.

At last she pried up the interlocking ears of the box top, revealing the nest of springy pine shavings in which he packed everything: he got the stuff in bales, sold as horse bedding. Emily rested the box on her knees and carefully wriggled her fingers into the shavings, looking not into the box but at her uncle's face.

Sax beamed indulgently. Emily's expression became quizzical as she felt the object inside, then drew it up from the ruffled pine. It was silver, or skinned in silver; its weight, five or six pounds, suggested a core of iron inside. The thing was nine inches long, shaped somewhat like a sharp stub of pencil. The end corresponding with the eraser appeared to be the face of a mallet, its surface dimpled and rough as if used to drive spikes. Emily saw there was an oblate hole through the shaft, so the object must indeed be the head of some kind of large hammer. The pointed end was octagonal in section, tapering to a bright needle tip; the entire length of the point was deeply notched, so that if it were driven into something, it would make a star-shaped hole. Throughout the piece, the silver was richly chased with what looked like Aramaic characters and decorative motifs, though much blurred by time and use.

"A war hammer," Emily said. "You shouldn't have."

"Yes, I probably shouldn't," Sax agreed, his anticipation giving way to concern.

"It *is* a war hammer?"

"Twelfth century," Sax said, almost with regret. "French Crusades. Probably made by a Palestinian craftsman on commission." His chin had sunk to his chest and he pinched it between thumb and forefinger. Emily waited for some further explanation, but her uncle was off in a cloud of thought.

"Uncle Sax? Why did you give me a war hammer?" Sax blinked and returned to the present. Emily was amused, it irritated him to observe.

"It's not strictly a war hammer," he replied. "I mean that's what it's thought to be, what I insured it as, and certainly one could use it for that sort of thing, knocking people off horses and poking holes in their armor. But that silver, of course, is too soft for martial use. It would smash to bits the first time you stuck it up somebody's cuirass."

"Really, Uncle Sax."

"Don't be coarse. A cuirass is the breastplate in a harness of armor."

"So it's just a parade weapon, then," Emily said.

Sax leaned forward, his elbows on his knees, and his hands mimed what he spoke. "Except as you can see," he said, "it's had considerable use in the last eight hundred years, yes? The bludgeony end has been beaten into lumps and the pointy end has been sharpened. So it's a war hammer, not intended merely for display, or for use against an armored opponent, the customary purpose of such an article. Therefore," he said, and then stopped.

"Therefore," Emily concluded for him, "it's for use against an unarmored opponent."

"Precisely."

"It's lovely," Emily said. "Thank you, Uncle Sax." She leaned forward and kissed his cheek, spilling horse bedding on the threadbare Sarouk carpet.

"Don't you want to know what it's for?"

"You said it's for bashing unarmored opponents," Emily said. "I'll have a handle made for it and keep it by the door." Sax suspected she was deliberately being obtuse. Normally she indulged his penchant for the dramatic reveal. He might as well get it over with.

"It's for killing vampires," Sax said, and sat back again, to observe the effect of his pronouncement. It was suitable. Emily's brow crinkled and she stopped rotating the hammer in her hands, then sat up straight, hands and hammer resting on the edge of the gift box.

"Vampires?" she said. "Like Dracula?"

"Dracula wasn't a vampire. Listen. I don't think it's of any use to you. I certainly *hope* not, as I said. Unlikely, but possible."

"Explain," Emily said sternly, as if Sax had committed a conversational faux pas.

"It's one of a dozen made at the same time; they are called the Twelve Apostles. This one is Simon. Peter, Thomas, Judas, and a couple of the others are lost. James Alphaeus is in the Tower of London. John and Thaddeus and possibly Philip are in the Vatican. Grasping swine, those Romans. Matthew is in a private collection in Switzerland. They're all legendary for killing vampires. Real ones, I mean."

Emily sat stock-still, as she had done since childhood: her uncle Sax had conjured up these mad tales of old things and the long, comet-like tails of history that trailed after them. He had never lied to her before, always marking conjecture from established fact. Theodore Roosevelt's hobbyhorse from his childhood home. The ring of a Plantagenet. A faience *wedjat* from Egypt's Third Intermediate Period. Now he spoke of vampires in the same way.

"When the Crusaders claimed the Holy Land, they split open an ancient order of things, like a spider mound. Within that place, where the desert sun never reached and the cries of Christian and Saracen could not pierce, there were vampires." Sax saw the astonishment on Emily's face and hurried his narrative along. He needed her to listen, not wonder if he'd gone mad.

"These weren't as you think of them, sexy fellows with widow's peaks and hypnotic eyes, but *proper* vampires—diseased old shapeshifters with cold breath and the smell of decay on their skin. The Europeans were entirely incapable of handling this new threat to their ridiculous venture. It wasn't until the Third Crusade that they got a system sorted out. These little fellows"—here he indicated the silver hammerhead in Emily's hands—"were instrumental in wiping out much of the coven. According to legend, the one you're holding, Simon, was wielded by Conrad of Montferrat. It slew the vampires Abbas and Myrion, amongst others. No proof of any of it, naturally, but the slaying aspect is genuine enough. Someone I know quite well used this very instrument to put a great big hole in the vampire Corfax in 1965, eighteen years before you were born. I assure you, it does work."

"Are you serious?" Emily asked, her brows risen almost to her hairline.

"Deadly serious, if I may," Sax replied. "I'm not sure how to explain this. Bear along. Vampires are real, of course. Not like elves or fairies or anything of that nature. It's sheerest vanity we humans imagine ourselves to be the dominant species just because there are so many of us. Sheep may entertain similar delusions. Like all predators, the vampires are few, but extraordinarily successful and dangerous. And they look like us, more or less, so one might never know. But they're not the same. They take on the appearance of their prey. A thousand years ago, half of them were more wolf than man. Not so easy to spot now.

"I've discussed them with scientists, you know. The few that are aware of them. Vampires come from something different from us. They're a different form of life. That's the main thing. All monster myths may descend from them. They're the living clay from which nightmares are shaped."

As if regretting the mad horror of his words, Sax chuckled.

"Forgive my mood. I don't anticipate *you'll* have any, ah, difficulties, but they are also damnably clever creatures, and if one of them detected my relationship with you—"

"Uncle Sax?"

"Yes, Emily."

"How do you know—?"

"Well. That's a very long story."

"But for now."

"For now," Sax said, and shrugged an apology for being mysterious, "consider this a bit of insurance. I have the handle to it at the shop, but the box was too big to carry. It's as long as my arm. Keep it by the bed, I suppose. Seriously. I don't think there will be any difficulties at all, but if there were, they would wind up on your doorstep, I'm afraid."

"Vampires, you mean."

"Yes."

"I think it's time we discussed putting you in a home."

1965

Europe

I

The new Canadian flag had just been introduced. Sax's gentleman friend at the British Museum described it as "*gules a pale argent, charged a feuille d'érable,*" which seemed hilarious at the time, probably because Sax was at the zenith of his snotty phase and found all things Canadian to be parochial and dreadful.

Martin Luther King marched on Montgomery, Alabama; Malcolm X was assassinated in Manhattan. The Voting Rights Act had been proposed to Congress by President Johnson and a cosmonaut had walked in space. *My Fair Lady* was deadlocked with *Mary Poppins* to sweep the Oscars; Sax had wept openly at the premiere of *The Sound of Music* at the Rivoli theater in New York City, and two weeks later, on March 16, he saw a pop combo called the Rolling Stones perform at the Granada Theatre in Greenford, England, and struck up an acquaintance with the drummer, Charlie Watts. Sax knew their manager, Andrew Loog Oldham, having sold him some good Regency pieces for the offices of Immediate Records, in addition to meeting him socially in the back of Mary Quant's shop. Meanwhile, 3,500 American combat troops had been deployed in Vietnam.

In those days, Sax was spending half his time in Manhattan and the other half touring the restless world in search of what he called sound articles. He traveled by ship and plane, depending on the destination and the extent of his purchases. His shops in London and New York did excellent business, as his particular taste happened to coincide with the newly wealthy youth culture's fascination with Victorian, Gothic, medieval, and Asian antiquities; he had a sure sense of the grotesque. He understood the power of symbolic imagery. He supplied George Harrison with Cambodian stone Buddhas, plied Grace Slick with ebonized mirrors adorned with demons and saints. Bob Dylan was photographed for an album cover sitting on an Art Deco settee belonging to Sax.

He was one of the fascinating people on the periphery of the Scene, someone who knew everyone, peppering his speech with amusing Polari slang he'd picked up in London's theater district. It didn't hurt that Sax had been dressing in Victorian velvet long before it was fashionable. And queer was in.

And at twenty-five, he was only just getting started.

That year, Sax left New York in March, then abruptly departed London in April, when his casual relationship with a gentleman at the British Museum turned serious for the gentleman but not for Sax. He fled to the South of France and his quaint pied-à-terre in the Dordogne Valley in the midst of a walnut orchard. There, much to his surprise, he found a young Beat poet he'd met in New York, a friend of Allen Ginsberg, waiting for him. This was back when Sax was virile and promiscuous, of course; he took such developments in stride, in those days. But the poet soon bored him. When the telephone rang, Sax eagerly answered the call, hoping it might be a summons to somewhere else.

"Saxon-Tang," he said into the mouthpiece. The phone was in the front hall beneath a mirror. Sax checked the Look as he spoke. An open-chested ethnic vest in embroidered wool, a gift from his acquaintance

Givenchy; ruffled linen shirt with bloused sleeves; wine-colored velvet trousers; and black coachman's boots. Hair in his eyes and swept back on the neck. Well enough for getting on with, certainly. He escaped coming off as an utter ponce because of his rugged face, which was an accident of birth. Nothing to do with him, who slept on silk and got ten hours of sleep a night when he wasn't on the job. If only he could master walking like a proper man, with his elbow out instead of in! All of this went through his mind in an instant, and then a stranger's voice spoke on the other end of the line.

"We've met," the voice said, narrowing the field to about half a million people. "I am told you are not averse to adventures."

The voice was male, deep and dry. A smoker in his fifties, French. The meaning was clear enough, if one knew Sax at all: he could not resist an opportunity for enrichment, regardless of the peril or moral implications. He was known and hated for it amongst his rivals. They thought he had a taste for danger, a rare attribute in the business, and was a scoundrel as well (less rare). Both Sax and his ex-boyfriends knew he was, truth be told, an abject coward. What people took for bravery was in fact avarice so intense it overcame his keen sense of self-preservation. It was only his lust for acquisition that sent him into the literal and figurative jungles of the world.

"What sort of adventure?" Sax replied. He ought to make sure this wasn't just a lewd proposition, although he wasn't averse to those, either.

"There's a château on the Loire, entirely furnished in the original. Survived the revolution and both wars. Guests, verifiable by letters, *cartes de visite*, notes, and so forth, include Napoléons *une et trois*, Marie Antoinette, Cardinal Mazarin, several of the Frondeurs—"

"Yes, yes, all very interesting," Sax interrupted, trying to sound as if he had something better to do. In fact, he was salivating.

"The present owner of the château is a lady of indeterminate age,

Madame Magnat-l'Étrange. I am told she is ill. She is intestate. The contents of the property could fall to the hammer, but it is more likely the government will intervene and make a collection of it all."

Sax detested when governments made collections of things. Sticking paper labels on beautiful objects and subjecting them to inventory inspections. Taking them permanently out of the market. Other sins. He felt the urgency of the situation. He had swallowed the hook and he didn't care.

"Mmm," he said, allowing himself the minimum expression of interest.

"Perhaps we can discuss the matter *en mains propres*," the voice said.

Two hours later, Sax was on the Bordeaux-Périgueux-Paris train.

There were other advantages. Foremost, Paris was a suitable distance from his cottage in Dordogne. At first, it was primarily the distance he was concerned with—the Beat poets were past their prime, and this particular specimen, although beautiful in a wispy-bearded, postadolescent way, wrote miserable poetry. Worse, he read it aloud, interrupting himself to make scribbled revisions on scraps of paper. The escapade suggested by the voice on the telephone was riddled with omissions and lies; of that, Sax was perfectly aware. But the extended description of the Loire estate was convincing. If he got so much as a pair of good chairs out of the deal, it would pay for the trip. Sax tossed the house key at the poet and told him to clear out in a week if Sax didn't come back. Then he cleared his own calendar for two weeks.

Once Sax was on the train for Paris, he could properly consider the odd assignation toward which he was rushing. *You may bring confederates*, the smoky voice had said. Accomplices, he meant. Sax had a few of those, and considered his options. Gander, his beefy assistant manager from Liverpool, might do for a start. The London branch was staffed primarily with willowy, oversexed shopgirls Sax recruited from Liberty, Laurent, and similar retailers, because they were attractive and hip. The real work, however, was done by the assistant managers.

There were others in Sax's stable. Marco the Italian was strong and unscrupulous but prone to panic; this job seemed to have elements of a burglary about it, and Marco's anxiety might get the better of him, regardless of how well he looked with his shirt open and that wealth of dark curls bursting out.

The Pole, Szczepan (whose name, disappointingly, was pronounced merely "Stefan"), was an immense, powerful man with a devious mind, but Sax didn't trust him—Szczepan remembered too well the bread-lines and hunger back in Poland. Sax didn't doubt the man would take the prize for himself if he thought he could get away with it. Which he couldn't. But he might try.

There were a couple of lads in London and the German Krunzel brothers, but Sax hadn't seen any of them in a while. After some consideration, he settled on Gander. Nigel, an effeminate, cunning, hand-dry-washing buyer's assistant, could keep the shop in Gander's absence.

Gander looked like an apprentice butcher, with huge red hands and ears and a low forehead surmounted with blond, bristling brush-cut hair. He never seemed to blink, his small blue eyes peering out uncomprehendingly from a wealth of pink face. Appearances deceive. Gander was extremely intelligent. He had been a specialty furniture remover before Sax recruited him; Gander had spent several years standing by at auction houses, soaking up along with tea and cigarettes the details of period, quality, and style that defined historical objects. Gander's mates didn't care what they were moving. It was all weights and measures to them. Gander alone took note.

He knew something of art, furniture, and ceramics when Sax spotted him at a lythcoop, or estate auction, at a North Country mansion; since then, he'd learned a great deal more. Gander's recent affinity for three-piece pinstriped suits with high lapels was ideal. He looked honest and disinterested to Sax's customers, who expected to deal with someone effeminate and cunning who dry-washed his hands when he spoke. Consequently, Gander, who appeared incapable of haggling, could often realize prices that made Sax blush. In addition, he had heard Gander enjoyed tremendous luck with the willowy shopgirls. The brute was probably hung like a Brazilian pack mule.

At the dreary, cinder-blown *gare* in Poitiers, Sax descended from the train and found the bank of coin-operated telephones inside the station. He fed a pocketful of francs into an instrument and got the London shop; apparently, Gander was at the warehouse in Tilbury. Sax rang the warehouse and an unfamiliar cockney voice answered. Moments later, Gander was on the line. Sax outlined his plans, omitting certain details, and asked if Gander was available to assist. He was. Gander would meet Sax at a café in Boulevard St.-Germain, not far from the Sorbonne, the following afternoon.

"It might be a little risky," Sax added. He thought Gander had agreed too quickly. Perhaps Sax hadn't made the circumstances sufficiently clear. "Possibility of intervention by the gendarmes."

"Right," Gander said, and rang off.

Paris in 1965 was enjoying a jazz renaissance no less influential, within its sphere, than the rock and roll of London during the same year. Sax wasn't particularly interested in music for its own sake. He went to a great many concerts of all kinds, but for him it was a social function, not an aesthetic one. He liked his arts to be durable, to occupy space.

Music was something to fill the air around the artifacts. Still, he found he rather liked jazz. Not the big-band stuff, but the intimate trios, quartets, and quintets with their playful yet urgent interpretations of standards, the original compositions that leapt and flickered like fire. Thelonious Monk, Sonny Rollins, Wes Montgomery, Dexter Gordon, and Bill Evans—they were all in town that year, not to mention the bigger acts. Dizzy Gillespie had performed at the Olympia in November. Duke Ellington played the Théâtre des Champs-Élysées.

Besides finding the music tolerable, Sax also liked the men who liked jazz. They were usually older, more complex. The rockers wanted to get theirs and get out. The jazz aficionados tended to be filmmakers, writers, diplomats, and attachés, people with interests that extended beyond racketing about in the counterculture, taking amphetamines, and rogering each other. This crowd found Sax interesting, too. He was a curiosity on the scene, which trended toward narrow lapels and black neckties. It wasn't easy to stand out in the circuslike Mod world; it was hard *not* to stand out amongst the deliberately understated jazz people.

Sax had the evening to himself. He would meet the voice on the telephone the following day at 1300 hours for a cup of coffee and a nice conspiracy. He decided to take the night off, enjoy a set of music in a club, and then, refusing any romantic engagements that might arise, he would dine alone and sleep in monastic solitude at L'Hotel, on the Left Bank.

This proved to be a difficult if virtuous plan. The first flaw in the strategy was L'Hotel. Sax knew the manager, Guy Louis Duboucheron. The place attracted flocks of the rich and famous. Guy planned to renovate it soon, and Sax's furnishings figured in those plans. So whenever Sax was in Paris, Guy had a good room for him at half price. When Sax tiptoed down to the snug little bar, he was astonished to discover his recent acquaintance Charlie Watts of the Rolling Stones sitting at the end, drinking Coca-Cola. The Stones were in town for a concert at the Olympia.

Things deteriorated from that point. Sax never made it to the jazz bar. He went with Charlie to a sort of artist's cooperative instead, a hotbed of Trotskyites and radicals and bearded youths trying to overthrow the tyranny of the paintbrush by making dreadful pictures without it. Andy Warhol was there, amongst some other interesting people; he said he was going to retire from painting. There was a certain amount of drinking early in the evening, then smoking of grass, which always rendered Sax completely helpless. He spent at least an hour talking to a most extraordinarily beautiful woman with skin like porcelain, who knew all about antiques and claimed to have the best private collection of Caravaggio paintings in the world, mostly studies and sketches, but including the lost masterpiece *The Magi in Bethlehem*.

She must have been as stoned as he was. Sax was under the impression he was talking to one of Warhol's people, Edie Sedgwick or Baby Jane Holzer—he didn't yet know the habitués of "the Factory," although he would later spend a fair amount of time with them. Someone eventually told him the woman was a countess from Germany, the Gräfin von Thingummy Somethingorother, a title as long as Hindenburg's *pimmel*, in any case. Events went by in a colorful, noisy rush. He met the real Edie Sedgwick, who rearranged his kerchief. Sax was content. He was in the middle of things again, a party to the happening, a happening to the party. Still, he was ashamed of himself. It was supposed to be a quiet evening.

The next morning (with five minutes to spare before the noon bells rang), Sax crawled out of bed and drew a lukewarm bath. If it was hot, he would fall asleep in it. He despised himself. The carousing he could live with. That was the price of being an attractive, interesting person with such notorious friends. What brought out the real, hundred-proof self-loathing was what had happened afterward. He'd picked up a young Arab in front of an all-night *tabac*; the lad, prodigious in his endowments, applied himself to his host *avant et arrière* until well after dawn, then stole the contents of Sax's wallet on his way out of the room.

Despite a detour to the bank, Sax arrived at the café precisely on time. He was freshly dressed in a trim bespoke suit from Millings in Great Pulteney Street. Unfortunately he was trembling and greenish in the face, and the circles around his eyes looked like cigar burns. A more obvious hangover would have been hard to effect. Sax sat at a table on the sidewalk, placed several of the brand-new silver ten-franc pieces on the table to keep the service brisk, ordered a glass of tea, and begged a cigarette from the waiter. Business attended to, he sat and smoked and brooded on his own shortcomings with such concentration that he was startled to discover a man standing at the other side of his table. Sax rose.

"You look just like that actor," the man said. He was broader than Sax, and shorter, with brief, iron-colored hair. The man's suit was double-breasted, cut in the postwar style, the color of river water. Brown shoes. Trilby hat. He wore a cream cashmere scarf around his thick neck. The overall effect, Sax thought, was part gangster, part bank teller. In other words, he looked like a man who had spent time in prison.

"Thank you," said Sax, entirely uninterested in which actor. He wanted to be ill on the sidewalk. *Must resist that, if only for professional reasons.* "Asmodeus Saxon-Tang," he added, and held out his hand.

"You'll pardon me if I identify myself only by my Christian name," the man said. "Jean-Marc. I feel like I'm back in the Resistance, but there it is. Discretion is of the uttermost importance."

Jean-Marc ordered a glass of wine and smoked foul SNTA cigarettes from Algeria. He said he had become addicted to them during his time there. He did not say what he had done in Algeria, besides smoke. There was little small talk in him.

"Allow me to describe the property first," Jean-Marc said. "Property is my business in some ways. The château is built directly on the river Loire. There is a tunnel beneath the walls for boats, built in the nineteenth century. In this way, one can enter the château from the water. It makes a mockery of the fortifications, naturally. There is a gravel carriage path up to the front of the property, and a dirt track that leads along the river's edge, interrupted by the structure itself."

Warming to the subject, Jean-Marc began to diagram the house with his fingertip on the tabletop, an incomprehensible mass of strokes.

"It's a bit like Château de Chenonceau, but the place doesn't extend out into the water. Or Montreuil-Bellay, if you know it. A cross between the two. Medieval structure with Renaissance improvements. Riddled with secret passages and hidden rooms and tunnels. The château is built on three levels, exclusive of the cellars and attics. The main entrance is in the center, salons on either hand, dining and music rooms behind, kitchens beneath. Upstairs the usual bedrooms, parlors, suites, and so forth."

"Monsieur," Sax interrupted. "You describe the place as if we were planning a . . . What is the word. Christ. *Un vol qualifié*, if I have that right. A burglary." Sax didn't like the sound of this. He needed to know the prize before he learned the obstacles.

Jean-Marc broke off a small piece of a laugh and chewed on it. "How can I describe what is inside the place if you cannot imagine the place?" he asked.

"I am not sure you should describe what is inside."

"Very well. You know it's most valuable; I'll skip to the meat of the matter. The property is owned—"

"By a lady of indeterminate age, Madame Magnat-l'Étrange. She is ill. She is intestate. I remember," Sax interrupted.

Jean-Marc raised his glass. "My apologies. You are not the first I have approached. The speech has become a habit. You remain interested?"

"Strictly for conversational purposes."

"Naturally. Madame Magnat-l'Étrange is a formidable character, by the way. Erase from your mind any image of an ancient, trembling skeleton in a bath chair. She is a mystery."

"In what way?" Sax asked, and flagged a glass of beer from the waiter.

Jean-Marc rubbed his hands together as if to start a fire. "There's no record of her existence."

"Pardon?"

Jean-Marc tapped the tip of his own nose. "I have some interest in real estate, as I say. It's all a matter of documents. There isn't a patch of earth in all of Europe that isn't carpeted with documents. Every bureaucrat has his little rubber stamp in the desk drawer next to the scissors and string and the gift for his mistress. He puts the little stamp on a document in the morning. He goes to lunch. He puts another little stamp on another document in the afternoon. Millions of bureaucrats for a thousand years have been doing this. And me? To get my feet on a single patch of honest dirt, I must first dig through a layer of documents as deep as oak leaves in the forest."

Jean-Marc finished his wine and wagged the glass for a refill. Sax sipped his beer and tried not to look as interested as he was.

"Oak leaves," Jean-Marc said again. "I was looking into the potential of just such a patch of ground two years ago for a little project near to my heart, and in the course of my investigations I noticed there was a lack of paperwork associated with the land across the river. By which I mean, not a single document had been filed in regards to Château Magnat-l'Étrange—although that is not its formal name—in over one hundred and thirty-five years."

Jean-Marc pronounced *thirty* with an initial *F*, an accent Sax associated with Paris. Local boy, then. "The family hired solicitors," Sax said. "They retreated behind a legal curtain for reasons of their own. Incorporated."

Jean-Marc shook his head. "You're not understanding me. When I say nothing, I mean that they have opened no permits to build, asked no permissions. Installed no gas. No water, wiring, or telephone. The taxes on the place are paid automatically by a blind trust, at a rate fixed in the year 1812. How can this be? What happened to the socialist government with all its"—here he made a swirling motion with his hands—"its redistribution of wealth? The twentieth century has frowned on entitlement, monsieur. How has she escaped it?"

"In the same manner her ancestors did, presumably," Sax replied. "Kept her head down, left the place unimproved. It's probably listed as a ruin in the local government's books by now."

"I said no records whatsoever, did I not?" Jean-Mark said curtly. "Two years, I searched. Listen to me. You must. There were no births, no deaths, no marriages. There has only been one name on the deeds to that château in all this time, never changing hands."

"Surely you're not saying this Magnat-l'Étrange woman is one hundred thirty-five years old?"

"Of course not. I'm saying she died a century ago, or more. And since then, certain persons have been . . . We have the same word in French, it's borrowed from the English. Squatters. *Squatters illégaux.* I suspect a local family discovered the original Madame Magnat-l'Étrange dead, or killed her, when they learned she was alone, and since then they have been living by cunning on the value of the property, perhaps selling pieces from it now and then for cash: bottles from the cellar, furniture, and so forth. For seven generations, they've been at it."

"Incredible," Sax said, meaning *ridiculous.* Surely the man didn't believe this himself?

"Yes, incredible," Jean-Marc said. He was caught up now, breathless with his enthusiasm. "I suspect the servants, myself. Their families. They found the madam of the house dead, they realized the next owner of the property would bring his own servants, and so they hid the tragic event. And with all the wars and chaos in Europe since then, they got away with it. Until now."

"So what is your idea? Purchase the property by some kind of law of adverse possession?"

"No, that's what these squatters have done. All statutes long since expired. They may very well be the legal owners now, in the strictest sense of the idea. But they can't make any noise about it, or God only knows what sort of tax bill they could end up with. And the property is unimproved since a hundred years! It will be condemned."

"So what's the plan?"

"We walk in and take everything."

II

There was genius in it, Sax had to admit. Gander sat beside him in the back of the prewar touring car, smelling of armpits and cologne in his old furniture-moving clobber of cloth cap, breeches, waistcoat, and shirtsleeves. He looked like something from D. H. Lawrence. Sax was wearing an army surplus coverall in denim and a shapeless Derby hat. Jean-Marc sat in the jump seat with his back to the engine, facing Sax. He was dressed in a much better suit than the one he'd worn in Paris, gray mohair with a seal topcoat, kid gloves on his blunt fingers, a silvery gray Eden hat resting on his knees. The bank teller look was gone, the gangster predominant; of prison, there was no indication. He appeared prosperous and unreliable. They all smoked continuously.

The driver, Rollo, was one of Jean-Marc's men. The back of his short neck was riddled with blackheads and deeply creased. He wore his hat jammed down low on his ears. Behind the touring car were three removal vans, ex-military box trucks repainted gloss black and picked out with thin green stripe. *Déménagements Toulouse* was lettered on the sides in crimson. At the rendezvous point where they'd met that morning, a motorist's café and fueling depot a few kilometers south of Paris, Sax had heard Jean-Marc reminding his men not to touch the paint, as it wasn't thoroughly dry. No half measures with him. There were ten men in the trucks, most of them old mates of Jean-Marc's.

Sax was frightened out of his wits.

He hid it as best he could, but his mouth was ashy and his heart fluttered inside his rib cage like a little yellow bird. His spine was wet with sweat. It was all very well, these great big thugs going about stealing things—and it *was* stealing, no question, even if the rightful owner had been dead a century and a half—but Sax was an up-and-coming, reputable dealer in sound articles. A stretch in a French prison was nothing to these other men, who might as well wear fraternal rings, being so obviously graduates of the penal system. But for Sax, prison would not be a place to make professional contacts. It would be hell on earth. Real homosexuals placed behind bars were doomed. It was the straight arrows who survived, gritting their teeth against the forced submission, the humiliation, their manhood stripped away, again and again brought to their knees for the brutal—

Sax realized he was getting an erection.

"Alain Delon," Jean-Marc said.

"Where?" Sax said.

"The actor you look like. Alain Delon."

"Mmph," Sax said. He could imagine what short work an alpha male like Jean-Marc would make of him in a prison setting.

And yet, despite his fear, Sax could not possibly turn back. This adventure could be the making of him. He had competition with just as much taste, flair, and beauty as he commanded. Some of them had titles as well, or large family fortunes. Sax's father was a wealthy patrician, a naval officer during the war; his mother was French and English. There was money in the family, but Sax had been disowned at the age of nineteen.

What he needed was a big score, a haul of extraordinary objects that would form the foundation of his career. He was already successful, yes. But it depended entirely on what he could find one week and sell the next. When he was away on his buying expeditions, the stock in New York and London waned perilously low. When he returned there would suddenly be an enormous surfeit of things he had to sell cheap, just to make room. A mother lode of quality pieces would erase the cyclical aspect of his business, give him depth of range—and yield him a fortune, practically for free. Unless, of course, he paid for this escapade with ten years of his life.

They drove through long stretches of rolling hills with fallow mustard fields and quilts of winter spinach, Swiss chard, onions, and wheat, bordered by hedges and copses of trees. Villages with roofs of gray slate and red clay tile were nestled in valleys and clustered around hilltop churches. Sax recognized Orléans and Blois, large towns, but the convoy bypassed them, taking smaller roads to avoid the urban centers. The trip covered some 250 kilometers and required nearly seven hours.

In a fast car, they could have made the distance in less than half the time, but the trucks were strong, not swift, and lunch required two hours of the afternoon. Jean-Marc's crew sat on the bistro patio for the meal, ate bread and sausage, and drank twenty bottles of cheap red wine, trading stories and filthy jokes in the rough argot of men whose entire lives had been marked by crime, conflict, and the main chance. Sax pretended his French was poor, but he understood well enough. He caught a few references to his sexual preferences, Oncle Bénard, Monsieur Môme, and so forth, but nothing any worse than the obscenities with which they abused each other. Following a collective piss on the wall that could have cleared the Augean Stables, they piled back into the vehicles and rumbled on.

Their destination was not far from the Château de Chenonceau, in the part of the Loire marked by grand fortified houses at every turn in the river. There were more than three hundred châteaux in the Loire Valley, and at least as many manor houses only slightly less imposing. Hundreds more had been destroyed during various wartimes and the French Revolution. The valley was the cradle of the modern French language, high culture, and the French Renaissance. Its beauty never failed to lift Sax's spirits, and in the spring it was so gorgeous it made the heart ache. Such luscious green everywhere, ancient trees and bountiful fields, all punctuated by fairy-tale castles and senescent, rambling towns. The scent of new flowers and ripening leaves filled the air. The late-afternoon sunshine teased and dappled the road before them. Even now, obsessed as he was with the prospect of incarceration, Sax could enjoy his surroundings.

The château, gilded by the setting sun, was a handsome Renaissance structure with a much older conglomeration of walls and turrets at the west end, the remains of an eleventh-century fortification with a massive stone tower. From the east end projected a handsome late-baroque addition with tall, airy windows. The asymmetrical massing on each extreme of the firmly symmetrical main building gave the place a lively silhouette. The river Loire flung bright golden glints through the trees that flanked the château; the garden and lawns had been laid out on the side facing away from the river, because that was the formal approach.

Sax sat on a fallen tree beside Jean-Marc, their backs to the glorious sunset. They traded a pair of ex-military binoculars back and forth, discussing the disposition of the château. They were at the top of a hill that rose above the forest a couple of kilometers from the house, with a narrow view all the way to the river's edge. The wall that surrounded the property was at the foot of the hill in front of them. It had once been inset at intervals with wooden doors bound in iron, placed for the convenience of hunting parties; these doors had mostly rotted away, so the wall was no obstacle to foot traffic. One such opening was near their lookout.

The château grounds were overgrown now, lawns turned to meadows, trees that might once have been neat hedges crowding the façades. Despite its size, the building was well camouflaged by ivy up to the roofs. Scattered around the grounds were carriage houses, barns, and outbuildings, a village's worth; most of these appeared to be falling to ruin. There was a steep Gothic chapel by the edge of the woods with a small burial ground, its tombstones ranged in the shaggy grass like a flock of gaunt gray sheep. There was no sign of current human activity. Not at the château itself, not even in the far distance. There were no roads nearby, no villages, no farms.

If ever a very large property were to escape notice for a century or two, this was the one.

Jean-Marc pointed out that there was a wall directly at the river's edge, which would discourage idlers in boats from clambering around the place. The only effective approach to the property was the direct route, straight up the front carriageway to the grand entrance. If there was going to be a confrontation with whatever scoundrels were keeping the place to themselves, it would be then and there.

"I don't expect there will be any blood spilled," Jean-Marc said matter-of-factly.

"I shouldn't think so," Sax replied nonchalantly, but about two octaves higher than his usual speaking voice. His anxiety was at a fever pitch. The château was, after all, a castle. They were going to storm the damn thing. There could be land mines or savage hounds. Dungeons full of hapless furniture dealers lured to their dooms. Sax imagined himself in some lightless pit beneath the foundations, shackled to the wall, surviving on bread and water. Or worse, American breakfast cereal. His captors would discover he despised the stuff and he would subsist on Wackies banana-flavored cereal until his demise.

Sax was gibbering inside his head, he realized. He needed to pull himself together. He focused his mind on the problem before them.

"You spoke of this Magnat-l'Étrange woman as if you'd met her," Sax said. There were several aspects of the adventure nagging at him. Chief amongst them was the possibility that there was indeed a rightful heir to the property. "You're absolutely certain she's an impostor?"

"I haven't met her," Jean-Marc said. The sunset was in its decrescence now, reddening, the light becoming vague as it lost its grip on the earth. The river no longer shone gold.

"You said she was a formidable woman," Sax prompted.

"So I've heard. There are anecdotal encounters, you know. Locals have run into her. She keeps them from . . . snooping, if that's the correct word. They assume her to be the lady of the place; I've spoken to a couple of farmers and some fishermen I met during my scouting expeditions, and they confirm there is such a person on the property, very pale and sickly in appearance—they almost sound like ghost stories, to hear them tell it. Avoid the place at night and that sort of thing. In any case, she has never introduced herself, you understand. Not by name. There is an assumption being made that she is the great-great-great-granddaughter of the last Madame Magnat-l'Étrange to leave behind a piece of documentation. I am absolutely certain that assumption is false. You will see I am correct."

They made their way down the back of the hill. The color was fading from the sky. The planets winked through the atmosphere. Soon the stars would come out. The shadows in the forest gathered strength with startling speed, the riotous green canopy becoming dim and gray. The men stumbled over bracken and molehills, hurrying back to where the touring car and the three trucks were parked by the side of the road. By the time they reached the vehicles, it was dark.

The party spent the night at a secluded farmhouse; Jean-Marc had rented the place for a week, no questions asked, for seventy new francs, the equivalent of fourteen dollars in American money. Gander fell in with the workmen and played cards all night, although he spoke almost no French; Sax spent the hours in silent worry. Once the contents of the château were offloaded into the farmyard, it was Sax's problem to shift the spoils to wherever he wished to store them. By that time, Jean-Marc would be back in Paris, preparing legal documentation to take possession of the house and grounds.

Jean-Marc's scheme hinged on the place's being demonstrably uninhabited when at last he brought it to the attention of the authorities. His 20 percent of Sax's future profits on the furnishings was a token. He didn't care about this revenue particularly and assumed Sax would cheat him anyway. What mattered was the real estate, which, transformed into a luxury resort for the nouveaux riches, could net him millions. So the place had to be empty. The reason Jean-Marc needed a dealer of Sax's exceptional cunning was to ensure the furnishings were introduced into the market in a manner discreet enough to avoid attracting the attention of Interpol or the French authorities.

The entire scheme sounded excellent to Sax, except for the insistence that he be directly involved in the removal process. But it made sense: If Sax didn't participate in the risk, he might not take it seriously. Or worse, he might rook his partners. This way they all went down together, if something went wrong. It inspired diligence. And terror.

III

They rolled out of the farmyard at nine in the morning. Preparations had been completed, equipment checked and rechecked, and all the men had been briefed as to their roles in the proceedings. Very few of them saw anything unusual in the project. It was a job moving furniture out of an old house, he reminded them: valuable bits and pieces, treat it with care. Don't let anything fall into your pockets. Might be a little extra by way of a *pourboire*, or tip, if everything made it out in top condition. Lift with your knees, boys, some of this old stuff is heavy.

It was explained by Jean-Marc that Sax and Gander would be going around the place after the fashion of an advance party with a couple of the lads doing an inventory; then they'd pack everything up tidy and cart it into the trucks. Every last candlestick and spoon. They'd do it in relays, heaping the loot at the farmhouse, until the château was empty.

While the men were piling into the vehicles, Sax found the opportunity to speak to Jean-Marc alone for a few moments. He lit his third cigarette of the day with a trembling match flame.

"You seem to have a fair idea what's in the place," Sax said. "I thought you'd never been inside." Jean-Marc leaned in and lit his own smoke with Sax's match. Sax found this incongruously erotic. The sex drive never rests.

"I haven't," Jean-Marc said. "I've spent months climbing every damn tree for leagues around, squinting through those binoculars, studying every room I could see into."

"No, you haven't."

Jean-Marc's brows went up. Sax threw his half-smoked cigarette on the ground. He hadn't slept for a single minute that night, and the previous evening he'd played the role of the Knights Templar to that Arab youth's reenactment of the fall of the Krak des Chevaliers, so he was irritable. He wanted to lash out.

"The shutters, man," Sax said. "The house has shutters on the windows. You can't have seen in."

Jean-Marc allowed himself his bullfrog chain-smoker's laugh. Sax hadn't accused him of lying before now; it didn't seem to offend him.

"Perhaps I once entered the house, then. But only to use the telephone. No one was at home."

"They haven't got a telephone. You knew that." Now Sax was being self-righteous. He couldn't help it. He wanted one last moment of being right before he spent the rest of the day investing heavily in being wrong. Jean-Marc laughed again, this time with genuine amusement.

"They haven't a lavatory, either, so I urinated in the fireplace."

It was inevitable. Greed won over cowardice and Sax climbed into the touring car next to Jean-Marc. He felt he would choke in the stiff, musty coveralls. The vile hat was crushing his brain. He was probably having a seizure, and there being no telephone, he would die twisting in the straw in front of the château.

Inexorably, they drew closer to their destination. Sax considered hurling himself out of the moving vehicle. Or he could pretend to go blind. Surely there was some way to extract himself from this rendezvous with larceny. He watched Gander fall asleep, his head lolling with the rocking of the car. Impossible. Sax was positive he must be pretending. How could a man doze off at a time like this? Sax dozed off.

When he awoke, the château loomed above him. They were braking to a halt directly in front of the stone steps that swept out from the formal entrance, the tires grumbling on the toothy gravel of the drive. Sax was disoriented. He felt this must be a dream.

Things began to happen at great speed.

The drivers angled the trucks until the tailgates hung over the steps to the house. The vehicles' rear doors burst open and planks clattered out across the gap to form wooden bridges. The men spilled out of the trucks, marching over the sprung wooden boards, each carrying his gear like it was the Normandy landing: ropes slung across chests, arms laden with boxes and crates, blankets and tools. Two men bore a ladder. Not Normandy, Sax decided. A siege. Medieval sort of operation. Gander yawned and scratched and joined the activity, towing a pair of dollies after him out of one of the trucks.

The first wave assembled at the château's front doors, immense oaken things with crystal panes set into them, intended to be seen flung wide for highborn guests. There was a moment of quiet as Jean-Marc strode amongst them, a ring of lock-picks twirling on his finger.

This was it, then. Sax was certain he would faint. Jean-Marc stood back to survey the doors, coughed economically into his fist, then stepped forward. He examined the keyhole. Then he grasped the handle of the door and pushed.

"*Elle n'est pas verrouillé*," he said. *It isn't locked.* They stepped inside the château.

Sax caught his breath. Now was the time to run. Now was the time to get away from this whole rotten scheme. Jean-Marc couldn't cut him out now; Sax could be five miles away in a café drinking himself stiff and it wouldn't make any difference. But if the local gendarmes showed up at the château when they were in the midst of the operation *avec leurs mains dans le sac*, it was all over.

He could smell the musty air from within the château, now, a cool, dry scent of old dust, stone, and the exhalation of ancient wood.

It was an odor Sax loved. It was the smell of ancient beauty, of things that needed bringing back to life. Gentle cleaning, damp sponges, white vinegar, beeswax and oil, new air, new eyes to gaze upon them: time itself leaves a skin on things, the way the air leaves sulfur on silver, turning it black. When that obscuring film is removed, the light in the heart of things radiates. The beauty, like some princess in a story by Perrault, awakens after a long sleep. *An apt analogy*, Sax thought. *Sleeping Beauty*. After all, the French title was *La belle au bois dormant—The Beauty Asleep in the Wood*. He'd kiss the wood awake. And the marble, stone, ivory, gold, silver, wool, linen, silk, glass, porcelain, plaster, and paint, too. Shine and rise.

To his great horror, Sax found he had not run away but entered the château. It was too late. Like a cartoon dog beguiled by the phantom aroma wafting from a freshly baked pie, borne along on his nostrils with beckoning fingers of steam, Sax had crossed the threshold.

As his eyes adjusted, the other men crowding with their raw-onion sweat stink and cigarette breath around him, Sax saw he had crossed another threshold as well. He was standing in the eighteenth century.

IV

The first impression was of a deep and teeming coral reef. A blue, milky darkness hung in the air, crepuscular as the sea, churning with slow dust, relieved by thin straight fillets of sunlight that knifed through the broken slats of the shutters. These picks of light fell upon colors and forms of exquisite, mesmerizing beauty, bright as exotic fish peeping amongst the stones of a sunken temple. The rooms were cavernous, hung with heavy textiles; the marbled green walls rose up into murky heights from which gold winked on coiling baroque plasterwork. Crystal chandeliers caught what light there was like vast jellyfish trailing their poisoned limbs.

Sax expected a liveried footman in periwig and dog-skin breeches to pad across the room and thrust open the shutters at any moment, and then he would go mad with the glory of it all. If this was some sunken treasure in a cave beneath the sea, Sax was going to need an air supply; already he was unable to breathe. And this was *just the first room*. His fear was forgotten.

"Blimey," Gander said, putting it all in words. "We're fucking made, mate."

V

Jean-Marc propelled them into motion. He had a fistful of legal-looking forms on a clipboard in case anyone happened by and would handle the confrontation if the impostor lady of the house showed up to argue with them. Nonetheless he wanted to get moving as fast as possible.

Despite the avarice that consumed Sax, he felt a rare tug of guilt, as well. This ought to have been a national historic site, despite his loathing of such conventions. It was a time capsule, perfect in every detail. This interior was in absolutely original condition, as if shut up on a July afternoon in 1830 when word came from Paris that *les misérables* were rising up in arms again, and the noble family of the house decided to toddle off to Austria until things quieted down—never to return.

Every single thing here was valuable. The modern age had imposed no mass-produced rubbish. It was all crafted by hand.

That didn't stop Sax beckoning a couple of men to follow him. They moved into the dark depths of the immense rooms, looking for case goods that might contain anything of value. They wheeled hand trucks laden with flattened cardboard boxes from piece to piece, starting in the two gigantic salons on either side of the entrance hallway.

First, they would empty the rooms through which one must pass to get to other rooms. It reduced breakage. The rest of the men fanned out through the mansion on their various missions, Jean-Marc barking orders in his tanned smoker's voice.

Sax was beyond fear. Maddened with lust for every single object that passed before his eyes, the value of all of it together ringing up ever higher in his mind, he knew that he could die in this place and they would have to pry his fingers from whatever object he fell across on the way down. He wanted to take it all with him. He didn't want to sell it. He wanted to *live* here, the queen of the castle, sprawling amongst silken pillows with the music of the sparkling Loire outside.

The first of the heavier pieces went out the doors, an Italianate console from the entrance hall, parcel-gilt ebonized mahogany, three thousand dollars, the down payment on an average American house at the time. There was a mirror to go with it, and two golden wall sconces, and a brace of Louis X fauteuils, gilded, with richly embroidered upholstery that had to be original to the chairs. Meanwhile Sax and his assigned laborers, Grigor and André, had emptied out a Napoléon I secretary and a couple of chinoiserie bombé chests filled with packets of ribbon-bound letters, mostly dated from the reign of Louis XV.

When they took down the tapestries in the entrance hall, quantities of thick, choking dust filled the air. The men had to open several windows, despite the increased possibility they might be observed. When the sunlight streamed in, the place lit up like a silver bowl full of fire.

It was simply too much opulence. Sax knew what he was. A Visigoth or Hun set loose in a Roman treasure house. An invader, obscene in his lust for wealth, ignorant of value, thinking merely of price. He required only a bloody sword and a belt of human thumbs to complete the picture. He hated himself. But he wouldn't hate himself once the sale of this stuff began.

Sax entered the grand salon. Above the fireplace, which was a marble fantasia large enough to park a sports car inside, there was a portrait in a golden frame chased with cherubs and serpents. Sax thought he had seen the likeness somewhere before.

The style of hair and dress placed the picture around 1650. He might have been looking at an original Sébastien Bourdon; it had very much the same transparent brushwork and crisp color Sax associated with the French master. Bourdon was a contemporary of Rembrandt and Vermeer, amongst others. It was a great age for portraits.

The painting depicted a woman, beautiful, cold, and pale, her cobalt-blue dress wrapped loosely around her bosom, shoulders exposed beneath a tissue of lace; her hands lay in her lap like pet doves. The piled-up white hair did not appear to be a wig—too white for such a young face, but not out of keeping with the eyes, which were like pools of ink. A hint of the abyss in them, watching.

Sax thought the artist had feared his subject in some way: there was haughty menace in the posture of the head. The woman stood beside a stone balustrade; the landscape behind her was chilly and leafless. There was a plate in the frame of the picture. Sax approached to read the legend. He was looking at Therese Minette Vrigne du Pelisande Magnat-l'Étrange.

Sax's reverie was interrupted by a strangled cry from upstairs. All activity stopped, the workmen frozen in place. They listened for another sound. When nothing came, Jean-Marc hooked a thumb up the grand stairs.

"Sounds like Hector met with an accident," he said.

Two of his cronies thumped up the stairs to investigate. At this moment, Gander emerged from the salon opposite Sax's, crossing the echoing marble floor. Sax had resumed emptying cabinets; his hands were full of two-hundred-year-old letters. This was no time for a chat.

"Pardon me, Mr. Saxon," Gander muttered in his thick Scouse accent. "Summat up."

"Yes, yes, yes," Sax said, impatient to get on with the looting. He was beginning to understand how the Mongols felt when they reached Europe. So much pillage, so little time.

"Shegeezer's 'mongst the premises, reckon," Gander said, whispering slightly.

"Speak English, you great melon," Sax hissed, impatient to get on with the work.

"What I mean to say, sir, things has been gone through, like. *Recent habitation*, as might be." Gander was cutting his eyes around now, as if there were unseen lurkers watching them. "We ain't alone."

Sax looked all around, irrationally expecting this would be the moment some rogues chose to leap out at them.

"Look, Gander. I thought we'd established that several persons, families perhaps, have been selling this stuff off in small amounts for a very long time. Of course somebody's disturbed things. They've been picking it over."

"Not like that, sir. I found a letter on a desk in there. The ink was *fresh*, sir."

"How fresh?"

"Wet, Mr. Saxon."

"O sweet-bosomed Jesus on the tree," Sax said. Adrenaline sprayed into his bloodstream like nitrous oxide into an engine. His heart hit ninety miles per hour in under a second.

"We ain't alone," Gander repeated, meaning *someone was home.*

VI

Jean-Marc picked up the letter Gander had found and peered at it in the dim salon, angling it toward the entrance hall doorway, from which most of the light came. He touched the ink with his finger and rubbed the finger on his thumb.

"It *is* fresh," he said. Sax and Gander stood shoulder-to-shoulder with him, huddled around the desk on which the letter had lain. The penmanship was exquisite, light and swirling but firm. Distinctly old-fashioned. A feminine hand.

"We must have frightened her off in the middle of writing," Sax observed, unnecessarily. "She may have run for the police, don't you think? *Les flics?*" Fear had switched places with avarice. He was clammy with sweat, his coveralls humid. His fingers were trembling like aspen leaves, rattling the packet of ancient letters he still held in them. He thrust the letters into his pockets to conceal his fear. Jean-Marc was shaking his head.

"I don't think she's gone anywhere. We're not burglars; we're a removing company. She would confront us."

"Besides," volunteered Gander, "once the swag started going out the door, old bird should have come out wi' talons bared, like."

"Jean-Marc," Sax said, "I think we should abort the operation immediately."

"What have you got there?" Jean-Marc replied.

"Evidence of my guilt," Sax replied, withdrawing the beribboned envelopes from his pockets. Some of them bore unbroken wax seals, embossed with signet rings to ensure the privacy of their contents. He held them up, revealing his quaking hands. Then his eye flicked between the new letter in Jean-Marc's hand and the letters in his own. He fanned apart the old leaves of paper and plucked one out.

"Jean-Marc, observe," he said, and handed it to him. Jean-Marc held the age-foxed document beside the new one, and his eyes, too, sprang from one to the other.

"*Dieu! It's the same hand*," he said.

"Lumme," Gander said.

"I think what we have here is not an impostor. I think the lady of the house is the rightful heir, descendant of the originals," Sax said, his voice hissing like a kettle. "Handwriting runs in families, you know."

"No," said Jean-Marc. "I know my forgeries. Made them during the war. This is the same, identical hand."

Sax was not just terrified now. He was exasperated. "Then we're up against a very, very old woman indeed," he said. "Hundreds of years old. Ridiculous. Let's get out, shall we? The pieces we've already got will more than pay for this dreadful excursion, I think."

Sax turned on his heel and strode toward the entrance hall door, aiming for a decisive, masterful effect. He realized it appeared he was walking with an egg in his pants; he had simply never mastered manly striding. Shoulders sagging, he abandoned the attempt. Instead he looked back to Jean-Marc and Gander, who had returned their attention to the newly written letter and missed his entire performance. They were muttering amongst themselves.

"Please, can we go now?" Sax said.

"This letter," Jean-Marc said, "did you read it? It's written to a dead man."

"What?" Sax was rapidly losing his grip on reality. Only the sound of one of the laborers dropping something valuable in the hall kept him rooted in the world around him. If things could still bounce down the stairs, he was not yet insane.

"This is a love letter to a dead man, telling him what she did the past few days. She calls him 'my dear deceased.' Those other ones. Who are they written to?"

Despite himself, Sax turned the bundle of letters over in his hands. "This one . . . Alastor. Erm, Alastor this one as well. These are all Alastor. Now let's go away and we can discuss this over a nice bottle of wine each."

"There's a demon called Alastor," Gander said, unhelpfully.

"There's one called Asmodeus, as well," said Sax. "Namesake. My mother was mad. Let's leave, now."

Gander marched off flat-footed into the entrance hall.

One of the workmen entered the salon to report, in obscenity-laden French, that Hector, the one who had cried out upstairs, was nowhere to be found, and the other two men who went to look for him had also disappeared, and furthermore there was a nice old chair with the leg off that had gone down the stairs. Did they want to bring it to the truck anyway?

As far from Sax's mind as the original project was, he remembered to keep up the illusion and not to bark orders to the man in good French. Instead he told Jean-Marc in English to have the men assemble outside so they could come up with an emergency course of action. Jean-Marc told the laborer to go find the other men and he'd be with them in a few moments.

Nobody seemed to feel the same urgency Sax did. He was certain he could hear the police approaching down the drive. When he peered between the shutter slats, he saw only some pigeons looking accusatorily up at the trucks. Every moment that passed brought them closer to discovery. If the woman had simply confronted them at the door—but no, she'd done what any sensible woman would do when presented with a wrecking crew of ill-smelling *voyous*. She'd gone for help, and help would come. This couldn't be the first attempted raid on this place. It was impossible. So they were racing against the clock.

Jean-Marc was still standing there in the gloom, examining the specimens of handwriting. Sax didn't think he was taking the situation seriously. Then Gander returned with one of the cardboard boxes full of old correspondence from the chests they'd cleared in the other salon.

"All addressed to this bloke Alastor," Gander reported. He seemed now to be answering to Jean-Marc. Fine. Let the he-men gather and speak amongst themselves and exclude the *lapin pédale*.

Gander was pulling out random letters. "There's some dated with the Republican calendar, care of Alastor. Now here's to Alastor, March sixth, 1820. Alastor, January tenth, 1833. Alastor, June of 1841. All the same writing."

Jean-Marc, confused, looked to Sax. There was something uncanny before him that Jean-Marc could not grasp despite the evidence of his senses, like a creature born underground that sees the sky for the first time. The man couldn't believe that the same woman had been living in this house since 1835. Even an expert on forgery could be wrong; he must be mistaken about the handwriting. And yet—

Sax's impatience exploded. He marched over to Gander and knocked the box of letters down, spilling the thick pages across the floor.

"Damn it, man! Both of you! We're leaving. We're leaving *now*." Sax turned again for the salon door, and for once he walked with the steady gait of a cinema cowboy. He threw an angry glare over his shoulder and stepped into the foyer—just as a high, agonizing scream came whistling from the upstairs hall. Jean-Marc charged past, thrusting Sax aside, and Gander was close on his heels.

"You wait outside," Gander said to Sax on his way up the stairs.

If Gander hadn't said this, Sax might very well have gone outside on his own. As it was, he suffered a flash of pride. He wasn't going to be told what to do by his subordinate. He ran up the stairs after them, albeit whimpering out loud. It was dark upstairs. Broad archways led to long, windowless corridors stretching to the east and west wings of the house. Dust coiled lazily in the sepia gloom like cream at the bottom of a cup of strong tea. The air was fetid, as choking as a velvet rag.

There were boot marks in the dust in both directions. Jean-Marc had run east, Gander west. The rest of the men were clomping up the stairs. Sax followed Gander, plunging into the darkness after his assistant manager's fast-receding back.

VII

The darkness became impossible. Gander lit a wooden match and held it low to the floor, sweeping it back and forth. He hurried onward, burned his fingers, and lit another. Then he stopped, raising a hand like a slab of beef ribs to halt Sax in his tracks.

"Claret," he said. *Blood.* Gander held the match over a strew of glistening red beads in the dust. The boot prints they'd been following ended at a doorway. The blood was at the foot of the door, which was firmly shut. Gander hissed through his teeth and shook the match out. Rather than light another one, he reached for the doorknob. Sax's hand shot out and held Gander's in place.

"Don't," Sax said. At the other extreme of the corridor, which was as long and high as the aisle of a cathedral, the Frenchmen were bashing doors open at random and rushing into the rooms. A little light fell into the hallway then, but dim and blue, as though cast through a bank of snow. There must have been twenty bedrooms along the corridor, and innumerable smaller chambers between them; many of the doors did not open directly into the hallway but into secondary corridors that linked together suites of rooms. Sax wanted to shout to the others, warn them. But he didn't know of what. And he couldn't bring himself to raise his voice in that place, which was more tomb than house. Instead, he whispered to Gander.

"Do *not* open this door."

"But, sir," Gander said, and Sax felt the massive paw flex on the doorknob. Sax renewed his own grip.

"Don't. Something is going on."

"Aye, bloke's bleedin' to death on other side of this door," he said.

"Where the hell is everybody?" Jean-Marc shouted in French. Then he repeated it in English. Of his ten men, only five remained in the cavernous hallway. The rest were lost somewhere in the warren of rooms on either side.

"No one go into any of the rooms!" Sax shouted in French. No point in maintaining he didn't know the language—or in being quiet. "There's blood here. I think we're being attacked."

As if to punctuate Sax's statement, there followed a scream from one of the rooms—a raw, throat-tearing howl of fear and pain.

"There," said Jean-Marc. He drew a small, flat automatic pistol from his jacket. Two of the men beside him produced blackjacks from their pockets. The three of them ran to a doorway even farther down the hall.

Sax addressed Gander again. "Now: let's open the door slowly, and don't be standing in front of it," he whispered. "Someone must be in there. Secret passages and so forth, yes? We need to defend ourselves."

Gander ignored Sax and threw the door open. He and Sax pushed themselves back against the wall on either side of it, then Gander risked a look. There was only a narrow, empty hallway, lined with old portraits. They went farther in, leaving the noise of the French contingent behind.

Sight and sound were swallowed up. There was a scrap of light to the left. Gander went to it and found another doorknob. He twisted it and shoved this door open, jumping back so that he collided with Sax.

"Take care, you great oaf," Sax said, winded. They craned their necks around the deep frame of the door to look into the room beyond, from which murky daylight was leaking. There was more blood on the floor, and on the walls, and now they could see there was blood in the hallway at their feet—an explosion of it that had reached as far as the main corridor. There seemed to be no source, as if the victim had simply burst apart into liquid.

Gander emitted a low, descending whistle. Sax took in the spacious room without consciously considering it: all original furnishings, presumably, the carpet woven in imitation of the architectural ornamentation. That wasn't what impressed Gander.

Everything sparkled with blood. It made a disturbing counterpoint to the rich décor, as did the shattered remains of an enormous chandelier that had fallen all the way to the floor on its length of wrought golden chain. Crystal baubles were strewn across the carpet, mingling with the blood like diamonds with rubies. Both Sax and Gander assumed the victim was beneath the chandelier. But Sax saw nothing there except wreckage.

A hot, wet droplet fell on his cheek. He raised his eyes to the deeply coffered ceiling. There was something there in the shadows above them. Sax nudged Gander and pointed with his chin.

The ceiling featured two domes deeper than the rest of the ornamentation; from the farthest one had descended the fallen chandelier. The nearest one, only a few feet into the room, contained the mutilated remains of Hector, his limbs splayed out like some huge, gruesome spider crushed under a boot. He was caught in an immense four-jawed trap, springs of iron studded with long black teeth snapped shut around his remains. It was so powerful it had blown him to pieces. He was held together only by scraps of flesh and what appeared to be a sheet of canvas tangled up in the iron jaws. His eyes had popped out when his skull was crushed; they dangled now, straight down, swaying in a sudden rumbling vibration that passed through the structure of the building.

In unison, Sax and Gander took a step back toward the doorway. Gander knelt to look at the floor.

"Man trap," he said, expressing what Sax thought was so obvious it might as well have gone unsaid. Gander pointed out a deep impression on the rug shaped like a cross inside a circle, six feet wide, right in front of the sweep of the door. "That bit of canvas up there must have been thrown over it, like. Bloke steps in, puts his foot down amongst the folds, and snap it goes, like."

Sax swallowed. "Yes, and the chandelier acted as a counterweight to pull him up. My God." Something else occurred to him: "Gander . . . I think this entire floor might be littered with these things."

"We won't go barging into any more rooms, then."

"I mean, not just these. There could be all sorts of, ah, mechanisms, knives in the walls, trapdoors."

"Oh."

"Let's retrace our steps, shall we? Perhaps we can wait outside for the other gentlemen."

With that, Gander was ready to agree. They made their cautious way back into the bedroom hallway, then to the main corridor. At first Sax thought the excitement and fear had confused him and he'd gotten turned around somehow, or possibly they had taken a new route and were in another, previously unseen space. It ought to have extended westward for a great distance. Instead, there was only a blank wall.

"Have we gone the wrong way?" Sax said.

"No," Gander said. "New fuckin' wall. Our foot marks come out from under it."

"Did you notice that sort of vibration thing a minute ago?"

"Must have been this."

"Somewhat of a mousetrap situation."

"A maze for rats," Gander observed. He didn't seem much excited by this bizarre turn of events, but his voice had taken on a funereal quality. "I suppose we'd better find an alternative way out, then."

"I expect," Sax said, "that is exactly the intention of our captors. However, I fail to see what else we can do."

"We could go out the window," Gander said, his voice brightening. "Knot some of those hangings together and shin down the front, like."

"I'm not going back into that room," Sax said. "How do you know there isn't something else lying in wait for us?"

"Some other room, then?"

"I fail to see the difference. We're in mortal danger, Gander. If you want to go dangling from the windows, that's your prerogative, but I have a suspicion that anyone who took the trouble to engineer man traps and portcullises inside the building will also have thought of that rather obvious method of egress, don't you?"

Sax's face was hot. He was not only very frightened but angry. What was needed was the assistance of some proper brains, not this precocious product of a North Country secondary school. Hurling oneself out of windows seemed like an obvious solution to the present dilemma. Sax wanted it to be that simple. It wasn't.

Gander thoughtfully pinched the bridge of his nose. "I think the Nazis put all this in."

"Focus on the problem at hand, shall we?" Sax said, his voice getting higher in pitch. "Defenestration is not the worst idea. It can't be more than a thirty-foot drop from that window to the stones below. Otherwise, we can go that way"—here he pointed down the length of hall that led deeper into the building—"and hope there's some way out. There could be a secret passage of some sort, for example. It all depends on time."

"What do you mean?" Gander said, staring at Sax in the darkness with eyes like tiny blue marbles.

"Whoever arranged all this . . . do you imagine they're just going to let us roam around in here? They'll come for us. Then we're really for it. We have to get moving."

Sax and Gander came to another doorway like the one in front of which they had first seen the blood. Gander opened it, both men prepared to spring out of the way. Instead of an inner hallway, it opened directly into a large salon, with communicating doors that led to bedrooms at either end. The salon was exquisitely appointed, as with every room in the place. There was a spinet piano by one of the two large windows. The floor had no shrouded traps in it that Sax could see, no lumpy heaps of canvas lying about as if forgotten by a careless workman. That simply meant the danger was better hidden.

"I hate to suggest this," Sax said, sincerely, "but I think perhaps we should throw the Louis XIII chair just to your left—yes, that one, very fine piece—into the center of the room and see what happens."

Gander didn't do things by halves. He kept his mass back in the doorway, picked up the chair, and bowled it into the room. It tumbled and bounced and knocked over a small tripodal gueridon table. Nothing else happened. Gander grunted and tiptoed halfway across the room until he reached the chair. Then he picked it up and threw it again. Still nothing occurred.

"Don't get killed," Sax recommended. He remained firmly in the doorway. Gander had reached one of the curtained windows now. He picked up the chair again; one of its arms had broken and hung by a length of bullion trim. Gander wrenched the arm free and used it to hook open the ponderous curtains that obscured the window, keeping himself as far from the opening as possible. Again, nothing happened, except the curtains parted. The window behind them was eight feet tall from stool to head jamb. It consisted of a pair of diamond-pane casements that could swing out on hinges. The shutters outside would prevent the casements from opening, but the shutter latches were on the inside; there didn't appear to be any impediment to escape. Gander rubbed his hands together.

"Don't you move!" Sax barked. Gander's arms froze in midreach. His back hunched as if he'd been struck. Sax risked advancing a few feet into the salon, sweat running freely down his neck. "Come back here. Bring that poor chair."

Gander did as he was told, watching Sax's face as if expecting to be punished. When Sax said nothing, he turned to face the window and they both stared at it, yearning to get out into the sunlight that glowed through the shutters. Sax took the arm of the chair from Gander and threw it at the window. The arm bounced off the glass.

"You throw like a little girl," Gander observed. With that, he raised the remainder of the chair above his head and launched it. It crashed through glass and lead alike, and punched out several slats in the shutters. The shutters remained closed. The chair sagged in the ruins of the window but remained suspended there above the floor.

"We seem to be in the clear," Sax said.

An instant later, there was a rapid thumping sound as of an anchor chain running through a hawsehole; the top of the window casing split apart, and an enormous iron blade came roaring down out of the wall. The guillotine slashed through the chair, splitting it in half as if it were made of cake. With a deafening *crack*, the blade sank into a channel in the windowsill. Where moments before there had been an opening to the outside world, there was now an iron plate that completely sealed the frame. The room was dark and the air filled with fine, choking dust.

"Cor," said Gander.

"Let's not bother with the windows," Sax said.

They moved down the hallway, now keeping their shoulders against the walls so the middle of the floor remained clear. Death could come from anywhere: a cloud of poisoned arrows or scythes in the ceiling. There was a suit of armor in a niche. Gander was almost forced to carry Sax past it, because Sax was absolutely convinced it would attack them.

When they got by unscathed, Gander returned to the effigy and wrenched the halberd out of its gloves: a stout, pole-handled combination of hook, spear, and ax, it would make a fine deterrent to anyone except a gunman. There was a sword suspended from a frogged belt at the armor's waist. Sax dragged the weapon from the scabbard. It was heavy. He felt no safer with the notched old blade in his hand; in fact, he felt grotesque. There couldn't be a man on earth less likely than Sax to give someone a prod with a sword. Still, he could use the weapon to poke around for further booby traps. He followed Gander and his poleax into almost total darkness.

Sax's mind was calculating all the while. His fear, his anger, were all laid on at the surface. Down below, the imperturbable thinking machines were hard at work, and they were starting to show results. As the companions groped their way along the hall, Sax considered the maze they were in. He knew what the building looked like on the outside and had a fair idea of how many windows there were, the thickness of the outer walls, the height of the stories, and the dimensions of the overall structure.

Downstairs the layout was simple enough, and he understood that. The big, open rooms and high ceilings precluded certain arrangements of hidden chambers or stairways; there was a limit to what one could achieve within a stone-and-timber structure. The main salon was beneath their feet, if Sax was figuring their position correctly. He had no confidence in this whatsoever, but it would have to do. If he was correct, the corridor would pierce a load-bearing wall just ahead of them. The portcullis that blocked their access in the opposite direction had come down out of a similar wall.

There was a good chance they would be crushed like beetles by another of these when they passed through the bearing wall, or by some other evil trap hidden within the thickness of the masonry. Bearing walls in a building of such size could be eight feet thick or more: plenty of space to conceal all manner of death-dealing machinery.

Sax thought of the blade that descended from the window frame. He was certain no local ruffians had built that thing. It was part of the original design of the château. He considered how amusing a family of high blood would have found it to employ the guillotine, that weapon of the common people, to execute would-be trespassers in their domain. These defenses might have originally been built to foil an external attack mounted by the peasants. It was clever: make the architecture do the work of a defending army.

All of which suggested to Sax that there had to be a concealed passage somewhere close at hand. What good were such brutal, automated defenses, if not to buy time for the inhabitants to flee? It was some small comfort to consider that he and Gander might find an escape route—not outward, but inward, into the heart of the place. He prayed to his unconvincing notion of a deity that it might be true.

They flung themselves through the space demarcated by the thickness of the bearing wall. Wood paneling clad the piers; there was only the slightest intrusion of architecture into the hallway—an arch overhead. When no traps sprang and killed them, Sax ventured to explore the woodwork with the point of his sword. Gander lit a fire with a match and a scrap of tapestry he tore from the wall. Sax was almost, but not quite, at peace with the destruction they had so far wreaked on the contents of the château. It was a terrible loss, even the chair Gander had been chucking about. But Sax could not erase from his mind's eye the hideous shape of the man pulverized by iron jaws up in the ceiling of the bedroom. He didn't want to meet a fate like that. Or any fate.

"If there's a secret panel," Sax said at last, "I can't find it." They had pressed and pushed every knob in the carved paneling, twisted the nearest sconces and candlesticks; Gander had even stumbled his way back through the darkness to manipulate the suit of armor, in hopes some switch might be concealed within it. Nothing changed. They stared at each other in the smoky, red light of the fire. Gander had wrapped the tinder around the end of the halberd for a torch. It threw frantic shadows on the walls, like ravens mating in flight.

"There *has* to be a secret way out of here," Sax said, and believed himself for once.

Maybe the space was concealed not in the transverse wall they were examining, but in a bearing wall that ran parallel to the corridor. That would mean the gimmick was in either the left-hand or right-hand passages alongside the main corridor. Sax was reaching the limits of his frustration. The disaster had begun less than an hour ago; an hour before that, they had started loading furniture into the trucks. So it was not even noon, and the situation had become one of murder and destruction. When night fell, would he and Gander still be creeping around dark passageways, or would they have been killed by some hidden rat trap scaled up for human victims? Or would those who knew the place steal through the secret ways behind them and slit their throats in the darkness? Sax needed to stop thinking, but he could not. He tried to focus his mind on the problem at hand.

"Gander," he said.

"Gorn," Gander replied, his pink face wobbling in the firelight.

"Have you any cigarettes?"

"You smoked 'em all yesterday, sir."

"Terribly sorry. Gander?"

"Sir."

"I'm sorry about all this, really."

"Can't be 'elped," Gander said. Sax was grateful. If their positions had been reversed, Sax might have strangled himself by now. He took a long breath and let it out slowly, the air shuddering between his lips.

"Right," Sax said.

They sat in silence, backs against the wall. The château was quiet around them, but it was the muffled quiet of massive enclosure through which sound cannot penetrate, not the silence of empty space. The important distinction between a tomb and a graveyard, Sax thought. Then—

"Douse the light," Sax whispered, gripping Gander by the meat of his upper arm. Gander wrapped the burning rags in his cap, snuffing them out. The stink of scorched wool made Sax want to cough, but he held his breath against the leaping of his diaphragm. He dragged his assistant into an alcove.

There had been a sound.

It was now absolutely dark where they crouched; the faintest pallor showed the way they had come, but to eyes not adjusted to the darkness it, too, would have been invisible. Sax was clutching Gander's arm with such force his fingernails ached, but he didn't let go.

There it was again. A high, thin squeal, the sound of wood on wood. Somewhere back the way they had come, someone was opening a door.

A light glimmered beneath one of the doorways halfway along the right-hand side. The door eased ajar in careful increments. A glow of candle flame was cast through the opening, yellow and oily. The light hung there, warping. Then a slender arm emerged, bearing up a candlestick. It hovered in the air, then drifted forward.

A woman emerged. It must have been a trick of the light, but Sax could have sworn he was looking at Therese Minette Vrigne du Pelisande Magnat-l'Étrange from the portrait downstairs.

She turned her head slowly upon its axis, like an automaton. But her eyes were active, glossy and black. Her nostrils arched. She was sniffing at the air. Her eyes studied the shadows in which the men were huddled.

She didn't see Sax or Gander, apparently, because she turned away. Her floor-brushing dress swayed down the corridor in the opposite direction, the old silk rustling with the sound of dead leaves. Moments later, she pressed her ear to another door. Satisfied, she opened it, again with great care. She disappeared into the space behind the door, and the yellow, fatty light went with her. The door closed and it was dark again.

Sax released Gander's arm. Something convinced him the candle was made of human fat.

They had to do something. The woman might come back. They could dash out her brains, Sax supposed, or flee in the opposite direction.

Or—they could exit the way she had entered.

Half a minute later, feeling along like blind worms, they found the door through which the woman had arrived. Sax located the doorknob and turned it and the latch sprung quietly. He knew the trick for opening creaking doors without the creak, because he hated that sound, and old cupboards always creaked. He pressed one hand against the hinge side of the door and lifted up on the doorknob; pressing and lifting, he swung the door open silently. He took Gander's wrist and led him into the even deeper darkness, where the veins inside the eyes lit up for lack of sight. If there was a trap inside the space they entered, they would die of it; there was nothing else they could do.

Sax stretched out his arms and found that, at the extent of his fingertips, there were walls. He reached through the darkness and touched Gander's sleeve and took hold of it, then felt his way down the wall of what he now knew was one of the smaller connecting passages of a suite. He was following the smell of hot candle wax, stronger this way, dissipating in the other direction. He followed the soapy reek until his outstretched hand met an obstacle. He touched it, his fingers describing a tall wooden panel. There was a candle stand mounted just above the height of his shoulder. It was a dead end in the hallway—but if his estimation was right, the space terminated at the bearing wall they had been exploring in the larger corridor.

His heart was racing. There might, after all, be a way through. He would try the candle stand: if there was a secret lever to operate a door, it would be concealed inside that.

Sax gave the thing a firm pull. It came off the wall, fell into two pieces, and toppled with a tremendous clash of cymbals to the floor. The very darkness vibrated with the noise. Sax cringed. Their presence had been announced.

"Gerrahtavit," Gander said, and pushed Sax aside. There was a splintery thump in the darkness, then a second, and with the third kick Gander knocked the panel clean out of the wall and into the cold, stone-dank space beyond.

A door slammed somewhere out in the broad hallway. They were seconds from a confrontation with the woman, who might or might not be physically dangerous. Sax didn't want to know.

He squeezed around Gander, who was panting fragrantly in the dark, and stepped through the broken paneling into a cool current of air that came from somewhere far below. He felt with his feet and found a step; his fingers met a coarse rope suspended along the wall through metal rings. Sax guided Gander's fist to the rope. Both men took hold.

The air was whistling through Gander's nose, the first indication that he was in any way alarmed by the situation. Sax took heart. He didn't like to be the only frightened person in a crisis.

He started down the stone steps, and once his feet had the rhythm of them, he all but ran, pitch blackness or not. The stair descended a long way.

They came out into a big, dimly lighted space with a groin-vaulted ceiling borne up on stout stone pillars. It had to be the cellars beneath the house; they had certainly come down far enough, four switchbacks in the dark before the first gleam of light showed them the doorway below. The door itself, when closed, was disguised as an inset cupboard. Gander swung this shut, then jammed an oaken chest up against it.

The floor of the cellar was of well-trod flagstones. Broad deal tables were ranked in the center of the space, where long ago the kitchen staff would have prepared enormous banquets. There was a hearth at one end of the room, corresponding, Sax guessed, with the foot of the fireplace in the salon where the portrait hung. Dust-dimmed copper pots and pans lined the walls and there was a legion of serving dishes along the shelves of deep cupboards built between the columns. Nothing had been touched, it appeared, in decades, if not centuries: a thousand knives had quietly turned black with rust in their wooden slots, ten thousand implements, whisks and rolling pins and sieves and ladles and every conceivable manner of tool for the preparation of food, rotting quietly in their pots and jars.

"Just like my mum's kitchen at home," Gander said, puffing breathlessly. Winded and half doubled up, he crossed to one of the racks of knives and drew out a carver with a fourteen-inch blade, the edge worn hollow with sharpening. He had left the halberd in the narrow corridor upstairs. Sax still had his sword, though, and now he realized the armaments weren't properly distributed: he liked right things in their right places. So he offered Gander the hilt of the sword. Gander took it and smiled at it, his eyes glittering. He in turn handed Sax the knife.

"Fair enough," Sax said, and they hurried toward a broad doorway at the top of a short flight of stone steps.

Jean-Marc's description of the place suggested there was at least one further level below this one, of storerooms and cellars, where the riverboats could glide right under the roots of the château to deliver goods and presumably shuttle lovers to their assignations unobserved. They were halfway up the steps when Sax paused, catching Gander by the sleeve. He eyed the ample doorway and didn't like the look of it.

"Gander, can you swim?" he asked.

"Course I can, my brothers was always drowndin me," Gander replied, offended. He lurched his weight forward to get to the top of the stairs, but Sax pulled him back.

"Only I'm not too keen on stepping through there," Sax said. "Look at the ceiling."

Gander followed Sax's eyes. Just beyond the doorway at the top of the stairs was a low, plastered ceiling, instead of the intersecting concave barrels of the groin vaults found throughout the rest of the cellar. There were slots cut into the plaster, the size and shape of a bay leaf. Dozens of these apertures punctured the ceiling in a grid pattern.

"It's nothing," Gander said, desperate to get out of the place, into the real light and air of the world again.

Sax held up a finger of warning. "Indulge me."

There was a wooden cask at the foot of the stairs. Sax hefted it. Something the consistency of mud sloshed inside. Sax moved past Gander to the topmost step, prayed nothing would happen—because if nothing happened, he was going to beat Gander to the front door upstairs by ten seconds at least—and lobbed the cask into the middle of the landing at the top of the stairs. The response took less than a second from start to finish. There was a kind of grunt that came from a hollow beneath the flagstone upon which the cask landed; the small barrel wobbled on its belly like an American football. There was a metallic *thwack*, very much like a huge trigger releasing. Then a forest of heavy iron spears dropped through the slots in the ceiling, struck sparks from the floor, and transfixed the cask. The little barrel burst into kindling and the red-black sludge within it ran down into the cracks between the flagstones and dripped into the hollow space beneath.

"Lumme," Gander said.

The spears, their shafts and tips barbed, formed an iron gate twenty rows deep. Sax and Gander were alive—but their way was blocked.

The cellar had rung with the din of the spears striking the stone; now, in the silence that followed, they could hear echoing footsteps, coming closer. Down the secret stairs.

"We wait for the woman and we kill her," Gander said, a murderer's smile on his lips. He'd have been stuck full of rusty spears, pinned to the floor, if not for Sax. That much he knew. He wanted revenge.

"Do you really imagine she's alone?" Sax implored. "I think she may have been sent up there for this very purpose, to draw us out—perhaps even down here where we'd be trapped, or killed by that ghastly portcullis."

"So . . . we take her prisoner and use her as a hostage," Gander said. He was revealing an unexpectedly agile mind for criminal solutions. Sax would have to remember that, if he survived the day. He shook his head, pulling urgently now at Gander's clothes.

"This way, I think," he said, and made the biggest gamble of his life to date. There was a low doorway beside the stairs, itself reached by a flight of four or five steps sunk down into the floor. The door stood open. He dragged Gander by main force toward the stairway into the earth. Gander resisted, throwing a red-faced, angry scowl across the kitchen at the cupboard concealing the hidden stairs. He clearly wanted a chance at that witch. But Sax was right, and starting to whimper.

The approaching footfalls clattered toward them, magnified by the stone passage so they sounded like the iron shoes of the devil himself. Sax and Gander ran down the steps, deeper beneath the château, beneath the earth.

VIII

Sax had a feeling he'd made a fatal mistake. He'd hoped this subterranean way had been abandoned for centuries. But there were lamps burning in the tunnel through which he and Gander descended. Somebody frequented this place. They might be waiting just ahead.

The oil-fueled lanterns, archaic but functional, were spaced at intervals of twenty feet, their mantles radiating reeking heat. Narrow openings in the stone overhead drew up the smoke. After four of these lanterns, the tunnel became another vaulted room. The chamber was mostly in shadow. Only two lamps burned there, hung beneath tall iron tripods. Immense barrels, gutted by rot, stood in the middle of the floor. The walls were entirely lined with racks, and the racks entirely filled with bottles. This was the wine cellar. Despite everything, Sax had a tremendous urge to see what vintages were stored there. Two-hundred-year-old? Three hundred? Bottles for long-dead kings might be glinting amongst those cobwebbed rows.

In one corner, the lamplight found a simple chair, soggy with mildew, and beside it a crooked table with legs that had rotted half away. On the table stood a stemmed glass of cut crystal, webbed and opaque with dust. It was like something from the *Mary Celeste*: in happier times, the butler had come down for a drink in the cool quiet. He'd been called away. He never returned.

"We need another way out," Sax said.

Gander was poking into the shadows with his sword. "You better block that door, sir," he replied.

Sax spun around. Of course—the woman was right behind them somewhere. She would come bursting through at any moment, no doubt with twenty armed men behind her. The idea of the men didn't frighten Sax, though; it was the woman with her black, lightless eyes. The way she scented the air, nostrils flared, like a wolf. The fact that she had no fear of two big men but came after them implacably. He could almost believe she was the creature in the portrait after all, still waiting. A ghost, avenging the desecration of her resting place.

These thoughts swarmed in Sax's mind like angry bees; meanwhile, in a blind panic, he was running around looking for something to block the opening. Gander clapped a hand on Sax's shoulder and guided him aside, then muscled a tall barrel, oval in section (Sax hadn't seen one of those in ages—a lost art, making barrels like that) into position. He shoved it until it tipped over, its narrow end wedged into the doorway. Anybody who wanted to get past it was going to have a hell of a squeeze, and given the purposeful way Gander retrieved his sword, Sax thought they wouldn't make it halfway through.

"There," Sax said, and pointed at the back of the room. Behind the stacks of barrels was a large door on rails, like a barn door, but immensely thick and studded with iron nails. Three massive padlocks of rust-black iron depended from chains coiled through rings in door and wall. There was no getting out that way. Sax fancied he could hear the subterranean river lapping just beyond the damp-swollen wood, but it was only the pulse in his ears.

Gander took up the bail of one of the lanterns, burning his fingers. He wrapped an immense plaid handkerchief around the wire and held the light aloft.

"There," he said, and pointed to the darkest corner, where a doorway had been cut into the living rock of the earth, only five and a half feet high and very narrow.

Behind them came the footsteps, flat and sharp in the confines of the tunnel leading down to the wine cellar. They negotiated the labyrinth of kegs and ducked through the small, dark doorway, heading yet deeper into the ground.

They ran, bent low, down the burrow that ran crookedly beneath the ground. It was cut into bedrock. Water leaked from the walls and snickered at them from channels cut into the floor, outrunning them. There were rats, hunchbacked and bristling. Sax despised rats: they were amongst the enemies of old things hidden away in attics, shitting little vandals with chisels for teeth. Gander's lantern carved a small pit of light from the darkness around them.

They had gone as far as Sax could run without gasping for breath, a fair distance but not as far as he would've liked to have gotten—he was thinking Minneapolis—when there was a tremendous crash from the wine cellar. It would have taken dynamite to smash the barrel Gander had jammed into the doorway, but it sounded like that had just occurred. Men with hammers, perhaps. He suddenly had a vision of the white-haired, black-eyed woman flying at them down the tunnel, arms outstretched, teeth bared, her feet dangling above the stone floor, borne toward them by supernatural forces.

Fear gave him speed. He shoved at Gander's back.

"Hurry, man! They're on us!" he cried. Gander redoubled his loping pace. The shape of the tunnel changed, becoming irregular and rough walled, now tall, now wide, the cut surfaces falling away into natural outcroppings of stone. The floor began to slalom up and down and twist between hulking carcasses of rock. They had entered into a natural cavern to which the tunnel was connected.

Their feet splashed through icy puddles and pools. The rock was slimy now, limestone slick with calcium secretion. Droplets of water bitter with minerals slapped at their faces. This was a true labyrinth. There were caverns and fissures coiling out in all directions. If they went wrong in here, they might as well starve as be captured, or plummet into some bottomless pit in the darkness.

"Oh, sir," Gander said, and stopped running.

"Don't stop for anything," Sax said, but also halted. Gander raised the light.

The cavern was full of human skulls.

There were thousands of them, heaped like cannonballs, slowly merging into the slime of the stone. The two men stared, and then, at the same moment, they ran onward, feet flying.

There was light ahead, the cloud-colored glister of daylight on wet stone. It was above them. They charged along the poorly sketched path, stumbling and clambering. Gander threw his lantern aside and the light flared up and died with a clatter amongst pale spires.

They were climbing now, as much with their hands as their feet. Sax's eyes ached in the unaccustomed light that grew above them. There was a square opening up there above the bright-lit rims of jagged stone. Their feet found rude steps cut into the rock. Gander went first, hauling up his exhausted bulk with difficulty, so that Sax was leaping with terror below him, shoving at Gander's backside, sure that skeletal claws would reach up at any moment and drag him with the strength of evil back down into the inky dungeons of raw stone.

After an eternity of slipping and grabbing their way up the steps, they reached an iron-framed opening and tumbled through. The light was unbearably bright, vivid with tall figures that glowed like jeweled gods, their heads surmounted with blazing golden suns. Sax knuckled his streaming eyes and stumbled across a smooth, dry floor of laid stone. He blinked away the pain, looked again, and found himself in a chapel. The gleaming figures he'd seen were icons set into the stained glass of a dozen magnificent church windows. Gander was retching, totally out of breath, his hands on his knees, his knees on the floor, head drooping. He had dropped his old sword on the stones and almost appeared to be praying over it.

"We've got to get to the trucks," Sax said, and was racked with coughing. If he survived this, he was going to quit smoking.

He crossed to Gander and grabbed him by the collar, pulling the big man to his feet. They were both filthy and soaking wet, with rivulets of clean skin showing where the water had run. Sax shoved Gander toward the doors of the chapel, then just as quickly pulled him back.

There was the scrape of a seldom-turned lock, the boom of an iron latch, and then with a juddering groan the doors swung open. A woman was standing there, her features plunged into shadow by the bright daylight that spilled across her white shoulders.

Madame Magnat-l'Étrange had arrived.

Sax was frozen. It was Gander who burst into motion. He scooped up the sword and, in the same gesture, rushed at the woman in the doorway between the rows of medieval pews. He was shouting obscenities in a half-nonsensical stream, the weapon held out before his chest at the full reach of his arm. Then his sword hand swung back, and he was two strides from her, propelling his weight into his arm to slash her head off her shoulders, the blade whickering through the air like a striking snake.

With a speed that Sax's eyes could not follow, the woman's own slender arm shot out and Gander jerked in his tracks, his feet flying up level with his head on their own momentum, and he slammed to the floor, unconscious. Blood burbled from his broken nose as if from a spring. The sword tumbled through the air and whacked into one of the pews, where it quivered grip upward, swaying.

The woman stood there, her hand still outstretched, the palm outward as if in benediction. There was a rosette of blood there. She put her hand to her mouth and kissed the blood away with a thick purple tongue. Sax's heart was beating at frightening speed and with nearly unbearable force.

"How dare you," said Madame Magnat-l'Étrange. She spoke without anger. It was merely a question to which she did not have an answer.

"I'm terribly sorry," Sax said in a faint, strangled voice that sounded like it was coming from the end of a drainpipe. "You see, I was misinformed. I thought—"

She stepped fully into the chapel. Her skin was so pale that the whites of her eyes were undifferentiated; the black irises shone like chips of obsidian set into a marble bust. Her white hair, brows, and lashes and the absolute tranquility of her features increased the effect. She was a thing of white stone, draped in a rust-red silken gown, staring at Sax without blinking.

"My letters," she said.

"Who is Alastor?" Sax asked, randomly picking the question to keep her talking. He was racing through escape scenarios in his mind, none of which were the least bit plausible. If this woman knew judo or whatever she'd used on Gander, Sax was no match for her at all—nor would he have been in any case, he admitted to himself. He tried to appear calm, even amused, as if he had another trick up his sleeve that would end this game at the time of his choice. The effect didn't seem to be working.

"Alastor is here," she said. She pointed past Sax into the back of the chapel.

Madame Magnat-l'Étrange's voice was hypnotic, like the sound of the ocean carried on the wind. It sounded, Sax realized, like she only exhaled, all her words flowing from a single, endless breath requiring no inspiration of air. The breeze that soughed from the mouth of a cave.

She was drifting imperceptibly closer, passing over Gander's prostrate body like a mist. But she was real enough—she'd smashed Gander's face, and she cast a long, black shadow.

Sax cringed. He dared a glance away from the woman, following her outstretched finger, and saw there was something on the altar behind him. A coffin. The box was carved of some blasted, ancient wood, bound in intricate bronze turned green with age. It had been wrapped in animal skin of some kind, of which only gray tatters now remained.

Sax was startled to see that in the brief moments he'd looked back at the coffin, the woman had narrowed the gap between them by half.

"You write him letters," he said, conversationally. He took a few steps along the floor, in any direction but toward Madame Magnat-l'Étrange. The motion brought him closer to the coffin.

"He will require to know what has transpired while he sleeps," she said. "He sleeps . . . he sleeps."

"Rather deeply I should say," Sax remarked, and then regretted it. *No time for flippancy. Not a cocktail party. Death in the face and so forth. Keep her engaged. Find a weapon or something.* He'd long before lost the kitchen knife. Senseless in any case. He couldn't use a weapon—he'd never struck anyone, except as a boy when it was a matter of flailing fists to keep the bullies from bashing out all his teeth.

He watched her face. She was looming closer, slow as sunset, inexorable. Sax had his back against the altar now. He could smell the stale wood of the coffin.

"You told no one of your journey here," she said. It was a declaration, but Sax thought she was asking a question.

"Lots of people," he said. "My assistants and Jean-Marc's people, he has lots of people, very alert, I—*we*—were told this property was vacant and the contents, you understand, and well—I mean we came right to the front door, and nobody told me there would be this unfortunate mix-up, ah, of course the police and so forth, the, er, ah, accident, the accident upstairs with that sort of flytrap device, I mean there will be inquiries—"

"No one knows," she said in a dreamy voice, as if Sax had confirmed her thoughts with a simple affirmative.

"Lots of people," Sax said again. "Everybody knows. People could be arriving, you know. This minute."

His fingers found the deeply carved paneling of the altar and crawled lizardlike along it. There were heavy silver candlesticks on either side of the coffin. Sax might be able to defend himself with one of those, or at least beat his *own* brains out before Madame reached him. He was so very tired, so very afraid.

She had now crossed two-thirds of the chapel without appearing to move at all.

The coffin rested on a corroded altar cloth of linen worked with gold thread; the linen was so ancient it hung in filaments, like the webs of weary spiders. It was fear alone that made Sax wind his fingers into the brittle fabric. He had no plan, no results from the good old calculating engine in his mind. He was just a trembling animal before the wolf. Even now he wasn't sure why the woman frightened him so. It was something that flowed from her, like cold air. He only knew he was afraid almost beyond endurance, and for the first time in his life, he could imagine death as an alternative to living anymore. He wanted this to end without pain, without horror. It didn't seem to be shaping up that way.

And then she was before him, close enough to take his hand, if she wished. He didn't see her move. She was simply there.

He could see her perfectly now, her translucent skin stealing what little color it had from the glow of the stained-glass windows. There were no tiny veins in the whites of her eyes, no dabs of red at their corners. She was pale as the meat of a fish, without pores or the fine vellus hair that softens human skin.

Sax's mouth went dry. His ears roared with undifferentiated noise, his limbs light and hollow.

"I have had visitors before," she said. "None have come so far as you. These are new times. I shall have to . . . adapt."

"I think we can be reasonable," Sax squeaked. "I'll turn myself in, if that helps." He knotted his fingers in the altar cloth, clinging to it. Without it, he might fall.

The coffin shifted its weight. Hope flashed in Sax's mind like a new coin catching the sun. Behind Madame Magnat-l'Étrange, Gander had rolled facedown, shaking his thick neck, trying to clear his head. He was regaining consciousness, dragging his heavy limbs under himself.

The coffin shifted another tiny amount.

"There are enough of you for my Alastor. I shall bathe him. We shall bathe together in your blood. Your filthy blood, that tastes of ashes and fat. It nourishes but does not refresh."

"Come again?" Sax said, his voice tremolo. At that moment, he realized two things.

First, she was not speaking to him, not really; he would be dead soon, but it was likely her habit to say aloud what was in her mind. Her thoughts had been, for ages, the only voice she heard.

The second realization was this: *She's a vampire.*

"*Ego sum lamia, cruoris et letum comedo,*" she whispered. Latin. Sax knew that much. Her hand rose again, describing a serpent's path through the air toward him. Sax was panting with fright. He felt as if he was shrinking.

"*Hominum tepidus refrigero*," she breathed, as if in a dream. She spoke with a lilting accent like Italian, and the fraction of Sax's mind that was still working wondered if he was hearing Latin as it was pronounced two thousand years before. He would remember her words for the rest of his life, all thirty seconds of it.

Her breath fell upon his face, cold as dew, scented with the crypt. A string of saliva spilled from her mouth and hung from her chin. Her lips parted. Thick webs of mucus stretched between them. Her dark tongue stirred between fine, chisel-thin teeth—not fangs, but razors. A gout of clear fluid poured out of her mouth and spattered the floor between them, and now Sax could see the veins and tendons in her throat rising up, bundles of cords squirming beneath the skin. The black of her eyes contracted until the white showed all around them.

Sax understood that he was not looking at a human being, not even a thing that had once been human. This was a beast clothed in human features, and he was nothing more than prey.

Her fingers stole across his face, and now the brilliant light that swarmed through the church windows was turning gold. Sax could hear bells, or laughter. The white face before him seemed golden, illuminated from within. There was joy in it, joy for him, and for herself, those seething wet jaws stretching not only to drink but to share delight. Sax felt a hysterical bubble of laughter within himself. He was grinning, he knew. He could feel it, and his heart was as light as a feather. The world was a glittering golden fountain and they were the source of all the light that shone. This was the woman of dreams, the lover of all lovers, bright as fire, fresh as sunlight. She was desire incarnate, Helen of Troy.

All his fear was gone, and before him there was this glorious beautiful color, behind which moved the woman. All the woman mankind had ever sought.

But Sax—Sax liked *men*.

He yanked on the altar cloth with all his strength, and it was enough. The cold, black eyes flicked up and the world of gold vanished in an instant, the bells were silent, and now in the gray stone room there was a harsh, grating noise and the coffin, dragged along on the disintegrating cloth by Sax's straining arms, teetered on the edge of the altar, then fell. It lurched down into the open arms of Madame Magnat-l'Étrange and drove her to the floor.

She screamed. Sax's ears nearly burst with the piercing sound, then the coffin struck the floor and cracked and vomited out a geyser of stinking, sapropelic filth. The lid to the box, unsecured, clapped loudly on the stones. From within the coffin slid a thing so unspeakable that Sax's brain could not give name to it.

It was a shriveled effigy of bone and flesh, the colors of butchery, hairy with pale filaments that branched and branched again, seeming to root in the reeking liquid, to draw substance from it in silvery, translucent sheets that coalesced into an obscene caricature of a man. It could not be alive, and yet, as it sprawled across the struggling Madame Magnat-l'Étrange, its limbs contracted, its spine writhing with something like will.

The woman spat and hissed. There was a silvery object jammed between the raw thing's ribs, bright and heavy. Madame clawed herself free of the monstrosity, her whiteness smeared with dark slime. The hideous remains flexed once more, then lay still while the blood-dark sewage pooled outward around it.

The horror of what he'd seen propelled Sax backward. He thumped against the altar and slid down it until he was sitting on the floor with his knees up in front of him, his hands flat on the stone beneath him.

Madame Magnat-l'Étrange followed his progress with her white-rimmed eyes, lips drawn back from her teeth to such an extent that the glistening, violet gums were exposed to the root of her cheeks, her mouth now yawning wide as a python's.

There was nothing human there at all.

From her throat came a bronchial hiss, a reptile sound. The corpse-thing lay on its side, the front of its skull turned toward Sax. There were gelatinous tumors in its eye sockets. Its facial features were indistinct, built up from scraps of tissue. The homunculus did not look decayed; it looked unfinished. Sax saw that the silver instrument that had plugged the hole in its chest had slipped partway out, the blunt end now resting on the stone. It was a tapering, star-shaped maul of some kind, razor-edged and cruel, streaming with glutinous tissue from within the chest of the cadaver. A dim notion made it through the shock that had descended to muffle Sax's mind.

He shifted his weight and the woman rose to her feet, seeming to gain in height until she towered in the lofty chapel. To Sax, the box was of no more consequence than the cask of spoiled wine he'd thrown at the top of the kitchen steps, a vessel with something unwholesome inside. To her, it was a holy relic. He would pay for this desecration.

"Alastor," she spoke. Her voice came from somewhere sulfurous and ice-bound. Then her head turned toward Sax, eyes blazing cold like the moon.

Sax lunged forward, straight at the unfinished corpse on the floor, his belly skidding in the putrid flesh-liquor. His fingers found the silvery weapon tangled in the bowels of the monster, and he gripped it with both hands and twisted himself around.

The creature that he knew as Madame Magnat-l'Étrange, but which must have had some more ancient, evil name, was suspended in the air above him, or so it seemed, hanging there, eyes fixed upon him. But time caught itself up again and she was hurtling down toward him with her jaws screaming wide, her fingers bent into meat hooks, the dark dress billowing up around her, a thundercloud from which was descending the angel of death. She struck Sax, crushing him to the floor, her teeth jammed deep into the flesh of his neck—and she did not move again.

Sax lay there, senseless, and only dimly understood that Gander had returned. Gander with a mustache of blood that curled up past his ears and a swollen purple nose like a clown's. Gander lifted the heavy corpse away from Sax. Her head dangled on its pale neck, white hair streaked with blood and filth, and the half-lidded, blank eyes seemed even in death to see him for what he was, and disapprove. Gander made a noise of disgust and dumped Madame Magnat-l'Étrange beside her cadaverous mate.

There was a star-shaped puncture in her exposed bosom. Sax had killed her with the strange weapon. Or rather, she had killed herself by Sax's hand, her own momentum driving the silver lance into her heart.

Gander dragged Sax outside into the air, and Sax looked upon a fleecy sky and green leaves. He smelled fresh grass and the scent of damp soil—clean, honest dirt. Gander looked down at him, his bloody face bent with concern. Gander was feeling his pockets now, looking for something. He produced the little box of matches from his waistcoat.

"Half a moment, sir," he said, and returned to the chapel and set it on fire.

Present Day

4

NEW YORK

"I am a monster, feasting on blood and annihilation. Warm man, I make cold. Those were the words she spoke in Latin. I looked it up."

Emily sat beside Sax in the twilight on her dowdy old sofa. He held a cold cup of tea perched on a mismatched saucer, which he didn't recall picking up.

There was a buzz on the door intercom and Sax startled, sloshing tea into the saucer. Emily sprang to her feet and smiled at him.

"Thai delivery," she said, and went to answer the door. Sax was so immersed in the past, he hadn't even realized she'd ordered it. He put the cup aside on a little Moroccan inlaid table next to the sofa. Or rather, he put the cup on top of the books on the table. Books covered most surfaces in Emily's life.

Sax took a few deep breaths and his fingers sought his sagging, wattled neck. He felt the soft skin there, and remembered the terrible wounds that had taken so long to heal. That was when he'd added ascots and kerchiefs knotted at the throat to his look, which became, it flattered him to recall, something of a fashion craze amongst the

Beautiful People. Even with the few lovers he took in those days, he kept something on his neck. They thought it was a kink.

He showed no one except trusted medical specialists the purple weeping scars that wouldn't knit. He lacked vigor by then; his youthful energy was gone, driven out by not only the injuries but the horror of what he'd seen.

It was exactly one thousand days after the ghastly adventure at the château, at a time when he was on holiday in a modest villa in Umbria, when he awoke in the morning and found he was ravenously hungry and had an erection like a *salumi Calabrese*. He sprang from bed and examined himself in the bathroom mirror. His throat bore only some raw, pink patches, shiny and smooth—it had healed overnight. These marks faded over the course of the next few months and eventually could not be seen at all, unless he failed to shave. The beard never grew back in those places.

The tale, as Sax had told it to Emily, had been much briefer than these memories that flooded back upon him. For her, he made it as simple as he could, leaving out details of scene and conversation. The thing he most scrupulously omitted was his own abject cowardice. He could scarcely confess to Emily what a quivering, helpless infant he was that day. Even so, the sun had been high when he arrived, and now there was only a faint stain of light in the sky, with the windows of Greenwich Village lit up below it. The ceiling lights came on and Emily bustled back in with a fragrant paper sack. She extracted white cartons from it and the air was tropical with the smell of lime and chilies, coconut and shrimp. Sax realized he was still holding his throat where the vampire's teeth had torn into him.

"What happened then?" Emily said, eating the pluralistically included fortune cookie first, as was her custom. "'Soon life will become more interesting,'" she read on the slip of paper inside it.

"I think you've got mine by mistake," Sax muttered. Now that he had described the events of that long-ago day in France, he found he had no desire to pursue the mysterious woman who had bid against him for the beastly ormolu clock. If his theory was correct, he was setting himself up for an equally dreadful calamity, only this time he was old, feeble, and much wiser.

Then he remembered poor Alberto, his dead night watchman. Sax hadn't started it this time. It was self-defense. And retribution. He'd see this thing through, neck or nothing. A reason to die, at least, besides sheer decrepitude.

"The rest is anticlimax, I'm afraid. We found Jean-Marc out in the driveway, frightened out of his wits. And when I say 'we,' I mean Gander, you understand. I was quietly bleeding to death on the lawn. When the police did finally show up as a result of the chapel fire, there was a search party organized. Two of the workmen were still alive, hiding in upstairs rooms. The rest . . ." Sax tossed his fingers and shrugged. "There were all sorts of traps in that place. A policeman lost his foot before the end of the afternoon."

"Terrible," Emily said. Sax couldn't tell if she was criticizing his tale or lamenting the loss of life and foot.

"In the end," he continued, "it was all perfectly legal. Jean-Marc's documentation turned out to be accurate in content, if not in fact: the place was not legally owned by anyone, including, by a loophole in the laws at that time, the state. As Jean-Marc asserted possession, the whole mess went to him. Once the death-traps had all been cleared out, I had the contents of the place removed, donated half of it to the Musée du Louvre, and sold the rest at a cataclysmic profit."

"Did you ever give Jean-Marc his twenty percent?" Emily asked, looking sidelong at Sax. She was spooning the steaming food onto plates.

"Oh, nearly," Sax said airily. "The point isn't your uncle's cunning. The point is that it's a true story, every bit of it. If you don't believe me I'll grow out my beard and you can see the bald patch. It looks just like a shark bite."

"I believe you," Emily said, without conviction. She licked her fingers thoughtfully. "Is that the same vampire hammer—" she ventured, pointing an elbow at the gift box.

"No, it isn't," Sax said. He poked at his plate of food as if searching for a cufflink. "You know, I still had the thing in my hands when the ambulance came? They couldn't get it out of my fingers. It was the one called Thaddeus, and those bastards at the Vatican came along and took it according to some law or other they'd had on the books since before the bloody papal schism of 1378. I got this one here, yours now, quite by chance when a museum of arms and armor in Connecticut went out of business, back when Carter was president. Paid thirty dollars for it. Mine has been a mad life, even without the vampires. They're real. You have been warned. Heed me, my girl."

Emily was an economist. Her field was the intersection of money and politics. To her credit, she was accustomed to dealing with unthinkable, hypothetical, once-in-a-million-years situations that seemed nonetheless to come true about every decade. So she knew especially well there are three categories of information: what we know, what we *know* we don't know, and what we *don't* know we don't know. The third category was infinitely larger than the other two. Could vampires fit into that realm? Not according to her rational mind. But the irrational was not always wrong. And her uncle *was* rational. He lived a mad life in the sanest of ways. She had to give the yarn credence. But still.

"So what about crucifixes and garlic and all that, Uncle Sax? I never heard of silver hammers."

Sax shook his head. "Vampires are pre-Christian. These hammers used to have the handle sticking out at the top and were cross-shaped, that's all. Gives that little bit of metal some perspective, does it not? A whole myth rising up from that very object. *Allium sativum*—that is to say, garlic—will work, but not just great lumps of it. What's needed is diallyl disulfide, which you get from garlic, and allicin, the same. Foams up their blood. Fatal in thirty seconds."

"Would Gander back you up on this?" Emily asked.

Sax's first instinct was to respond with irritation. How could she doubt him? Would he make such patent nonsense up? But he let his annoyance go. It was no good scolding the woman. She was an adult with her own life. Making himself disagreeable wasn't going to improve her chances of survival if things went hellishly wrong.

"Gander died of cancer," he replied after an interval. "About nine years ago. He wrote it all down, but his family has that now. Three charming daughters, you know. One is your age, exactly."

Emily took Sax's hand and looked him straight in the eyes.

"Uncle Sax . . . what are you up to? What are these 'difficulties' you're worried about?"

"I'm going to be out of town for a while. Bit of a buying trip."

"That's not a real answer. What are you planning?"

"I can't say," Sax said.

He had asked himself the same thing: What *was* he up to? What was driving Sax out of his comfortable Manhattan nest into God only knew what sort of trouble? He had wrestled with this question, wanting to believe it was simple greed, or perhaps a mixture of greed and pride. But there was something else. He had walked into the warehouse, repository of all his vanity, and found a man dead upon the floor. There would be more deaths. The vampire was aware of him now, and must have suspected he was aware of *it*.

Even over a matter as trifling as that silly, gauche clock, such a fiend would measure out its vengeance by decades, merely to pass the time. What else was there to do with all eternity but litter it with corpses? God Himself had set that example.

Sax had never experienced a scintilla of religious feeling, but he did believe there was something within him that answered the description of a soul. If the monster came for him, it would come for him *last*. First it would destroy those whom he loved. Emily would die. Others as well, people completely innocent of the business. Alberto was only the first and no wergild would repay his death.

Incredibly, and certainly out of character with himself, Sax found that his real motive in undertaking what would probably be his final, fatal escapade was not self-enrichment at all.

He had caught the attention of death incarnate. Now—if he wanted to save his soul, and countless others—he was going to have to hunt the devil down.

5

MUMBAI

Nilu felt unwell long after she was released from hospital. The sickness went beyond the trauma of the assault following Mallammanavar Jagadish's dinner party, and beyond the minor injuries she'd received during the bloody conflict in her hospital room. Her neck remained stiff, but she could turn it without discomfort. However, she was altogether too weak to return to dancing. She'd been forced to cancel her next engagement, a minor speaking role in an action movie starring Shahrukh Khan—a wrenching professional setback. No word of what happened to her had reached the tabloids, for which she was grateful to God, but she had not heard anything from Mr. Jagadish, either. He was aware, Nilu had heard through an intermediary, that she'd left his house under unusual circumstances but apparently thought she had merely become drunk, and his Russian acquaintance, Andronov, had escorted her to a taxi.

Through the intermediary, she had requested a further conversation with Mr. Jagadish. On this point, there was some confusion: they seemed to think Nilu wanted to discuss her career, when in fact she wanted to learn what the omniscient Jag knew about the Russian. He would be dead; she knew that much. A man didn't survive being shot several times through the head and body, then stabbed, then precipitated out a third-level window. Had she been connected to the incident in any way other than as a bystander? Had anyone identified the assailant as Andronov? She did not know. In fact the man's body had never been found.

He wasn't admitted to the hospital while she remained there. Of that she was quite certain. If a huge, curd-white man full of bullet holes had been found on the street beneath her window, she would have heard about it. So the Russian had, against all odds, gotten away. His corpse must have been rotting within a few hundred meters of the hospital. But it had not yet been discovered.

As to Nilu's career, she was rethinking her ambitions. What difference did it make if she was famous and wealthy and adored? Had she the right sort of character for that kind of notoriety? She was attractive and fit and still had her good manners. She could find a fine husband with plenty of his own resources and be happy with her children and her spacious home with a refrigerator that dispensed cool filtered water from the door. Her husband would say with indulgence, *This is my wife, who used to be an item girl*, and she would blush appropriately, and his friends would be envious, and she could eat ghee and grow plump. Then again, every time she saw a film poster up on one of the innumerable hoardings of Mumbai, she would experience the needle of envy for even the artistes with the least impressive billing. *Their* faces were up there, however small in comparison to the major stars. Nilu herself was nobody, and had been terribly used—if she quit, it was all for nothing.

In addition to the malaise she couldn't seem to shake, there had been a strange side effect from Andronov's savage abuse of her body. She now found herself obsessed with sex. It was the very opposite of what she would have expected. Desire would lance into her belly at any time, unbidden, and rankle there like a stain that couldn't be scrubbed out. It was a kind of lingering itch that tickled and drove her mad.

Before now, she was prey to the ordinary flashes of love and lust. She had always craved intimacy, too, in the usual way; the thought of a good man in her life, in the bedroom as elsewhere, was appealing. Now she cared nothing for intimacy—Nilu just wanted to feel hot fingers crawling over her skin, a strong body pressed against her, and the mindless beating rhythm of animal coupling. It made her mouth water. She remembered the paroxysms of physical ecstasy that had nearly consumed her, and she wanted more, afraid as she was of what it might do to her. The madman had made an addict of her.

Nilu was nine days in the hospital, and the doctors at first could not determine why she was fading rather than getting better. There was nothing outwardly wrong, once the bruising went down. Her stiff neck was a complete mystery. But her vital signs were growing weaker. She hadn't been able to speak and remained unidentified.

After six days, when the administrators of the hospital were becoming concerned that she might die before she was known, her condition abruptly improved. The fluttering eyelids that showed crescents of white beneath them, the constant sweats, and the thin, fast pulse relaxed. Nilu slept, her heart beating strongly.

That same day, Ghauri, a fellow dancer, saw Nilu's photograph on a message board in the hospital's emergency admissions department, where Ghauri had gone for a broken toe. She got her visitor's pass and limped upstairs. She was not surprised when Nilu begged her to remain silent about her condition, and when Ghauri returned to the studio where they worked, she said nothing except to explain Nilu had been called away suddenly and would be back soon.

Three days later, Nilu was out in the street wearing some clothes a friend had gathered from her digs in the south part of the city.

She went home and slept some more. Her flat, in a 1930s-era *chawl*, was in the crowded Chira Bazar area, which had once been considered middle-class, populated mostly by Maharashtrians; now it was all jewelry shops and Gujarati immigrants. The landlords were always talking about redeveloping the building, but it never happened, and because they were always about to redevelop the building, no improvements were ever made. Nilu shared a single room with a very tall, thin teacher of mathematics, Sangeeta, known as "Geet," who worked at the tutoring school next door. When Geet saw the bit of gauze taped to Nilu's inner elbow and the dim bruises on her face, her hands flew to her mouth with horror.

"I thought you were dead!" she cried in her very high voice.

"I fell," Nilu replied.

She spent two more days sleeping, stirring mostly at night when it was a little bit cooler and the noise in the street was less. She would let herself out quietly, easing past snoring Geet with her long, bamboo-knobbed limbs drooping over the sides of her cot and her mouth open in a breathy O. Then Nilu would go out down the corridor past the quiet rooms with their lumber of humanity locked inside, restless babies and clattering fans, stepping around the rows of cheap sandals and milk bottles by the doors. Outside in the acrid night she would walk, feeling the soreness in every muscle of her body, but also filled with a need to prowl, to keep moving.

She didn't fear bandits or lonely men. She feared nothing, it seemed. Nilu's anxieties were all focused on something she couldn't even identify, something that seemed to lie on the other side of that strange, bright universe she'd encountered that night at Jag's mansion. What was beyond that place had seemed like heaven but was only a sparkling curtain of golden bells between this world and another.

There was someone there. People were moving through that glowing place, through the color.

They were waiting for her. She decided to find them.

Min Hee-Jin still could not believe the squalor here in India. Even in the hospital, of all places, it had been that way. She remembered lying in wait beneath the bed of the girl and under there were dead flies and dirt and a surgical glove, rumpled up like a used condom. The locals seemed immune to it all. Everything was coated in grime and thick with fine, poisonous dust that stung the sinuses. Nothing was permanent, and nothing was worth saving; no surface met another with a clean strong joint, but was shoved together to keep the rain out for one more day. Weeds sprang up in improbable places, growing from windowsills and rooftops and the ever-present piles of obscene rubbish heaped up against everything. Only the filth seemed immune to decay. It grew every day, and spread, and the lean bony cows that wandered the streets would eat the garbage and shit it out again in yellow-green streams and from the shit it appeared more garbage would spring up overnight.

And what nights they were. Whole families huddled asleep on pavements that Min wouldn't touch with her bare foot, let alone allow children to sprawl upon. Those children—skeletal brown waifs with huge tragic eyes like pools of rusty water and their hair wild and tawny from a lifetime spent in the sun. Their hands were always reaching. Their faces were always filthy. The young ones carried the infants. The infants had noses crusted like the condiment bottles in a cheap café.

It was repugnant to Min, but she knew it was not India that was at fault for all this, but herself. She came from South Korea, where there was a tremendous sense of collective responsibility for everything. In Korea, a person without a home, a child in the street, constituted a rebuke to everyone. There *were* such people, as everywhere; Korea had more than its share of helpless drunks, for example. But they were not invisible. Here in India, with more than a billion people, it was necessary that hundreds of millions should starve, and sleep exposed to the dogs. In Korea, there were only fifty million people. It froze in the long winter. Things had to be built well and maintained properly. There were entire shopping districts constructed underground. Most people in the cities lived in high-rise apartment buildings, big uniform blocks with spacious, functional flats surrounded by mountains and forests and rivers. In contrast, she saw Mumbai as a dried-up sewer filled with human refuse.

These thoughts revolved in Min's mind. But they did so beneath the level of her awareness. On the conscious plane, she was watching. She stood in the deep shadow cast in an alley by a buzzing yellow streetlamp. The lamp splashed acid light across a wide dirt road with rumpled sidewalks and low mud-brick industrial shops where tires were retreaded and engines and electric motors rebuilt. Many of the employees of these places slept in the narrow yards in front, propped against a wall; there were a few of the tiny bumblebee three-wheeled taxis there as well, their owner/operators sleeping with knees drawn up inside. Probably a hundred people on the street within fifty meters, Min thought, but so dirty and shrunken that she appeared at first glance to be alone. And it was three in the morning. Nobody in their right mind was walking the street, let alone watching and waiting for someone to go by.

Then the young woman approached.

Min heard nothing, because the woman did not always bother with shoes, like many people in India. But Min saw a shadow roll across a distant wall and pressed herself deeper into the darkness, and a minute later, the young woman walked past, hurrying along as if to get somewhere quickly. But she wasn't going anywhere. Min had been following her ever since she was released from the hospital. Nilu was like a vision with her graceful, perfectly proportioned body and shining hair that flowed to her elbows. She was dark-skinned, darker than some Africans, but her features were Aryan, slender, the bones of her face arched in delicate bows. Min allowed her to pass, then stepped out of the alley, moving slowly.

Min was dressed in a sari of orange cotton, chosen without a glance from a pile of them that rose to the ceiling in the little shop she had stepped into when she arrived in Mumbai. She had paid five or six times the Indian price without attempting to bargain, handing over a fistful of grubby rupee-denominated bills; later she attempted to determine how to wrap one of the garments around herself. She got it all wrong. A local woman working at the hostel she was bunked in took pity on her and showed her the technique.

This was, although a typical Indian gesture of generosity, extremely difficult for Min to tolerate with good grace: she was always so impatient, straining at the leash of time, desperate to lunge into the next task. Perhaps that was why she spent 90 percent of her hours these days motionless, lying in wait for someone to come along. It was a lesson in patience. In any case, she was swift to learn the wrapping and tucking required to turn a six-meter strip of cloth into an entire costume. The woman had explained it as a *nivi* drape, the most common style. Min later modified it so it would better suit her fighting technique, but the fact that the cloth was loose around the legs and left the arms relatively free to move was an excellent place to begin. The pleats at the waist could also be made to hide a variety of weapons without showing a bulge. The length of the garment, extending to the ground, helped conceal her French canvas commando boots.

To make herself further invisible, she'd taken to wearing a rose-colored shawl thrown over her head. The color combination was hideous, but Min had very little interest in aesthetic matters. Her practicality started at the bone.

There was nothing in her life except what served her goals.

When the monster had destroyed her family, she had thought she'd lost everything that was precious to her; now she had come to understand she'd lost everything that was superfluous to her purpose. The monster had given her that purpose. It was not a fair trade, but fairness was a concept that had vanished in one bloody night from Min's universe.

She would hunt down and destroy every one of those creatures that raised its head from the darkness. Even if she had to wear a sari.

Min followed Nilu along the buckled pavement at the distance it would take her to run in ten seconds. This was a good interval to maintain because it would take that long to release the silver hammer from its holster at the small of her back and get the fiberglass handle—hung from a belt at her waist beneath the sari—locked through the eye. The sawed-off shotgun could be deployed in half the time, but it had a tendency to dispatch the victims as often as the villains, in her experience.

Nilu was striding along oblivious, as she was every night, to her surroundings. She moved very swiftly for a Mumbaikar, but nowhere near the kind of speed at which Min habitually moved.

Nilu sailed amongst the dogs as thin as hair combs, the dirt-dulled sleeping urchins and cardboard shelters and drifts of flyblown rubbish, without taking notice of any of it. Not that a local *would* notice, but she didn't even glance around her. This suited Min. She wasn't observed. And it was precisely according to the pattern of behavior Min expected to see.

Nilu would keep venturing out on these nocturnal expeditions for days or weeks until she found what she didn't know she was looking for, Min knew. She didn't think it would be very long. It had been nearly two weeks since the attack. The Russian would be starving, his damaged tissues screaming for replenishment. She had visited some catastrophic damage on him, that evening at the hospital. The Russian vampire, called Yeretyik in his own land, "Ерэтик" when written in Cyrillic lettering, as it was in Min's little black book, could not have gotten far. Not with half his head blown off. But she had failed to puncture the *Herzblutkammer*, the appendix-like organ that grew on a vampire's heart. It was a difficult target, unless the creature was in the act of feeding; then it expanded like a balloon and was easily burst.

Min had expected him to attempt a feed at the hospital. She had waited for three hours, hidden beneath Nilu's bed, for him to do just that; then he would have been helpless. Too bad for the victim, but not Min's concern. When Yeretyik opted to merely murder his quarry instead of draining her blood, things got complicated. That small black sac on the heart, bulging with veins, was the key to the vampire's survival. It was the reason for the legendary wooden stake: in the old times, they would have sharpened a stout green stick, then split the pointed tip lengthwise until it formed a tight bundle of individual skewers. Driven into the chest of the monster, the skewers would spread apart inside the body, and the odds of piercing the *Herzblutkammer* were greatly increased. In the early days, the Church organized the killing, and back then the organ was called in Latin *quintus domus cordis* —"the Fifth House of the Heart."

Min knew the entire history of vampire hunting back to front. It was all she cared about. Since the beginning of the sixteenth century, when the Vatican started hiring Swiss mercenaries to do the work, the language of vampire hunting had changed to German. In the modern age, it didn't matter where you were from. All it took was reflexes, no fear of death, and an insatiable appetite for violence.

Min cursed herself for not making the kill shot in the hospital, and further, failing to cause Yeretyik enough damage to keep him from going out the window; the blow from her silver hammer hadn't slowed him down, although it had certainly collapsed his lung.

Min kept Nilu at the edge of her attack radius and followed for an hour and twenty minutes. At no point did Nilu suspect she was being tracked. Min had leisure to wonder again at her own squeamishness when it came to things like whether the streets were clean and whether children slept in beds. She wouldn't hesitate to kill a child if it meant destroying a vampire. In theory, at least. The opportunity had never come up. But here in India, she found herself queasy all the time, afraid to eat the food, afraid to touch things, afraid even to breathe the air. It was a weakness in her and she would have to address it. After all, for the Indian people, this was normal. There were a hell of a lot more of them than Koreans. So on balance, *this* normal was *more* normal.

Min's thoughts took her focus away, so it was a shock to see another figure emerge from the shadows beneath a peepal tree and fall into step directly behind Nilu.

6

New York

"Asmodeus, my old friend, you've gone mad," said Pillsbury in his hushed, sacerdotal voice.

They sat in Pillsbury's office on the seventeenth floor of 1011 First Avenue in Manhattan, where most of the New York Archdiocese's administrative offices were located. It was an ugly brown building that resembled, to Sax's eye, one of those smoked-glass stereo cabinets from the 1970s.

Pillsbury was attached, due to some flash of gallows wit from a superior in the Catholic hierarchy, to the Calvary & Allied Cemeteries Office, in charge of the maintenance and operation of all Church burial grounds in the local area. In fact, he worked for an entirely different department. Pillsbury was the sole US representative of the Ordine dei Cavalieri Sacri dei Teutonici e dei Fiamminghi, Special Branch, one of those vestigial bits of the Church that had survived for many centuries because they had some obscure, fiddling responsibility that, being sacred, could never be extirpated from the Vatican payroll.

Pillsbury, being an apostolic protonotary diocesan priest, was entitled to a certain measure of respect amongst his peers, if not Sax, who sat opposite him on the laity's side of the desk. There was a tendency amongst the better sort of priests in the building to attempt to decorate their offices as if they were not located in this geometrical, bureaucratic hive, but rather a five-hundred-year-old building at Oxford, with linen-fold paneling and Italian Baroque furniture. To Pillsbury's credit, he had made no attempt to tart up his room. It could just as well have been an insurance manager's office in midtown.

Pillsbury was tall and thin and immaculately hygienic, with a stiff silver finger bowl of hair and a sallow face upon which were engraved lines of caution and concern. He was wearing his prescribed outfit of black cassock with red buttons and trim, a purple sash bound high up around his waist, and the usual white dog collar; he was entitled to wear a dashing purple cape, a *ferraiuolo*, as well, but was not wearing it now. Sax vaguely recalled there ought to be a fancy-dress hat included with the costume, but he'd never seen Pillsbury in one.

Sax realized that Pillsbury expected some kind of response.

"I suppose I have gone mad," he said. "But let us recall which one of us has made an entire career of this kind of thing. I merely dabble in it." Sax was referring to vampire hunting, which was the secret responsibility of the Ordine dei Cavalieri Sacri dei Teutonici e dei Fiamminghi, Special Branch. There weren't many Teutons or Flemings in the order any longer, and Pillsbury had never actually seen a vampire, let alone stuck anything in amongst its ribs. Sax suspected the man didn't believe in them at all, despite all the evidence to which he was privy. Generations of such men, perhaps afraid of looking foolish, had failed to sound the alarm to the world at large. Consequently, the general public hadn't the first clue what peril it was in.

Sax, on the other hand, fervently believed in vampires but not in

Pillsbury or the Catholic Church. The opinion of the vampires about either one had not so far been discovered, so it all came out even.

"This will be what, the third such dispensation for which you have begged my petition?" Pillsbury said, the pomposity welling up in beads and dripping from his voice.

"The second," Sax said. "Strictly speaking, I didn't ask for the first one, as you may recall, sir. You sort of laid that on me, as it were." Pillsbury was entitled by his rank to the honorific *monsignor*, but Sax would be damned before he used it. It would only encourage the man. It was *sir* or nothing.

"That was an indult after the fact, Asmodeus," Pillsbury said. "You had violated canonical law. The Roman Curia forgave you."

Sax rolled his eyes. "I didn't require forgiveness, though. Have I also been forgiven for being an unrepentant old sodomite?"

"What you do with your eternal soul is otherwise entirely your own business," Pillsbury said, his brows raised like a pair of hands praying over his nose. What Sax found most peculiar was that Pillsbury seemed to genuinely like him, in spite of everything. All the condescension and disapproval in the world couldn't hide it. Sax wondered, not for the first time, if Pillsbury was secretly light in his loafers.

"Yes, well, God forbid, if I may use that expression in this most sacred of office buildings, that somebody should do in a vampire without the Pope's permission. Leave it to you lot to come up with paperwork for a thing like that."

"The vampire," Pillsbury said with an implied sniff of disdain, "is an emissary of evil. That makes it Church business. As you very well know, there are matters of cleansing and so forth. Disposition of remains."

"You took my vampire hammer," Sax said.

Pillsbury delicately pulled his right earlobe as if it contained a switch to trigger his memory. "You're not still upset about that, are you? It was what, forty years ago?"

"Blink of an eye for a vampire," Sax grumbled. The real reason he'd given half of the contents of that château on the Loire to the Musée du Louvre, other than sheer largesse, was so the Vatican wouldn't get its hands on the stuff.

The Church had a fairly self-enriching policy when it came to the property of vampires, as he learned shortly after the events at the château. His Holiness's emissaries, a couple of ordained lawyers, had visited him in the hospital with the details of the Church's monopoly on vampire hoards. In order to hang on to as much loot as possible, Sax had been forced to generate some favors in the Catholic-dominated French government, and fast. Did the Louvre need a few bits and bobs?

It worked, and while the little rubber stamps were coming out, he was able to get a large quantity of the remaining furnishings out of the country through notorious dealers such as the Wildensteins. The silver hammer called Thaddeus was not so easily retained. It might as well have had *Property of the Vatican* engraved upon it.

"So you've found another one," Pillsbury said, steepling his hands in prayerful imitation of his eyebrows. "Where?"

"I don't know," Sax said. "That is to say, I know there *is* one, and I think I can find it, but I haven't found it. So I thought it best to come 'round here right away, rather than . . ."

Sax batted his hand vaguely in front of his face. He had no interest in the spiritual aspect of an ecclesiastical warrant. Vampires lived or died according to man's deeds, not God's decree. But it would save him a great deal of official difficulty afterward, should he chance to survive the escapade.

However, there was something else Sax would need. In the past he'd been young and hale. These days he could hardly get out of bed.

He was going to need assistance.

"Very wise," Pillsbury agreed. "So. Is that it? I think we can handle the matter within a week or two."

"There's one more thing, now you mention it."

"I see."

"Your head office is in Rome, is it not?"

Pillsbury sat back in his chair, wary now, the lines around his mouth forming a parenthetical moue. "At the office of the church Santa Maria in Campo Santo Teutonico," he confessed.

"I rather wonder," Sax said, "if I might get an introduction."

7

Rome

It was a dry November in Rome as well. It should have rained. The nights were cool, the days hot. Sax arrived at the very end of the month, having secured permission to leave the United States from the assorted police agencies connected with the case of his murdered night watchman.

Alberto Robledo had been stabbed in the heart with a woodworking chisel, according to Detective Jackson. A single blow. The coroner thought it might have been delivered from behind, by someone reaching around Alberto's shoulder. The intruder, Sax realized, must have been waiting behind that handsome mahogany escritoire for Alberto to walk past. Definitely not the work of the vampire. It would have been a familiar, doing the work of immortal evil in much the same way lickspittles from celebrity entourages did all the car-parking and cocaine-purchasing their idols couldn't be bothered to do themselves.

To murder someone for an overpriced clock, however, was beyond the pale. Sax wished he had opened the damned thing immediately upon receipt, but there was no key, and for twenty grand he wasn't going to pop the clock's lock with a butter knife. Whatever had been inside it, he wasn't going to find out unless he found the creature that had ordered it stolen. There had to be something concealed inside, he was absolutely sure of that. He'd racked his brains (and his archives) for evidence that such a timepiece had some other intrinsic value. A fine clock, certainly. Beautiful craftsmanship. Not inherently worth killing for.

Ormolu, from *or moulu*, French for "pulverized gold," was a beautiful material but obsolete. It was deadly stuff to make: the gold was mixed into a mercury amalgam and applied to a metal foundation, and then the mercury was cooked off, leaving the gold thermoplated to the surface of the object. It was electroplating before there was electricity. Sax's lost clock wasn't ormolu in the strictest sense; the true ormolu process was discontinued in the first half of the nineteenth century, as the mercury vapor killed all the craftsmen. By the time Sax's clock was manufactured, all the mounts were plated by electricity, but the use of gilded bronze mounts continued to be called ormolu. Had the thing been older, created by some workshop where all the artisans suffered from phossy jaw and mercury poisoning, perhaps its value might have been a trifle greater. But there was no other rationale that would increase its worth more than a fraction. Even sentimental value could not extend desire as far as murder, Sax thought. Not even for a vampire.

Those ancient creatures, it was understood, wished more than anything to dwell in their exquisite pasts, gazing upon some object their lover touched and remembering those glorious days. That much was true. Madame Magnat-l'Étrange had been doing it for centuries in that dusty museum-home of hers, even going so far as to keep her lover's remains in that stinking coffin, neither dead nor alive, as a token of history. But then again, it was usually the vampires that killed each other. For all their romanticism and yearning for past glories, they were worse than black widow spiders when it came to slaughtering their mates. It was always a matter of territory and food supply. When things got tight, out came the razor-edged teeth or the heart-bursting weapon thrust home in the dark.

Sax's taxi stopped in front of the hotel and he allowed himself and his luggage to be handed into the lobby in a flutter of euros. It was a good hotel, not an interesting one; it had once been the palace of a cardinal and was located within steps of Vatican City. The room was small in the European way, and the bathroom microscopic. The service was suitably obsequious. Furnishings all contract stuff in imitation of the original. Sax took a shower, then attempted to get his cell phone service working; it was one of those SIM card things that was supposed to operate in any location at all, requiring only the insertion of a small bit of gold-printed plastic—a modern-day version of ormolu—into the phone. He had done something wrong, apparently, or more likely, it was Italy's fault. There was probably another strike.

Sax left the hotel and walked toward the vast bulk of St. Peter's Basilica, majestic seat of the Church on Earth, but hooked a left through the sweeping colonnade that reached out from the basilica to cradle the ellipse of the piazza. He reached a narrow street, crossed a parking lot, and arrived at an undistinguished ochre-plastered villa with a red clay roof. Sax paused to dab the moisture from his brow; even a brief walk would wear him out these days. And it was damnably hot for this time of year. He had brought a silver-headed cane on this trip and was glad to lean on it until his heart stopped thumping.

He was standing before Santa Maria della Pietà, a modest church (especially compared to its gargantuan neighbor) by Roman standards. There was a high wall around the patch of grounds attached to the building; this enclosed the cemetery that had lent Pillsbury's order its name. It was a burial ground for Germanic people, dedicated by Charlemagne for that purpose. *Ordine dei Cavalieri Sacri dei Teutonici e dei Fiamminghi* translated to "the Sacred Order of Teutonic and Flemish Knights"; a fair number of those fellows were buried here, and quite a few of them had died fighting vampires.

Sax went in through the familiar public lobby, where a butch young Italian in a well-fitted cassock sat behind the desk. Sax identified himself, then sat on the long bench opposite, where he could keep an eye on the young man's strong Roman profile and clean, brown hands with the thick black hair along the metacarpals. A potted palm tree nodded by the doors, tousled by a fan bolted to the cornice below the ceiling. There was an electric wall clock that ticked and hummed. Sax felt jet lag soaking into his brain like opium fumes. He struggled to not fall asleep and failed, his cheek resting on his hands, which were folded across the handle of his cane. He awoke in confusion when, half an hour later, Fra Paolo Muscarnera, canon of the order, gently shook him by the arm.

Sax was mortified to discover he'd been drooling. He creaked to his feet, rubbed his moist sleeve on his other sleeve, straightened his jacket, and harrumphed.

The man before him wore a black cassock as well, unrelieved by any other color, and his hair was closely cropped in the monastic way. He was a dark, handsome fellow, over six feet tall, with a strong, shining, blue-black jaw and a single black brow above serious eyes the color of ripe green olives. If Sax had been a younger man, he would have done everything in his power to get this handsome piece of classical statuary into his bedchamber; as it was, he merely experienced a stab of greed, which was what he had left of lust.

Fra Paolo unexpectedly embraced him and Sax nearly dropped his cane.

"Good heavens," Sax said.

"The famous Asmodeus Saxon-Tang," Fra Paolo said. "Welcome to our humble home."

The clerk at the desk, who had essentially ignored Sax until now, except to smile patronizingly at him once while he was falling asleep, was now on his feet, hands clasped in front of him. He came around the desk and spoke to Fra Paolo in Italian, of which Sax knew only a very little. But Fra Paolo answered, "Yes, he is," and the young man curtsied and touched his brow, head lowered.

"Oh, come on," Sax said.

"We seldom get to meet the old vampire hunters," Fra Paolo said, without guile. Sax was offended anyway, but he knew what the man meant to say.

"That's because most of us don't get old," Sax replied. It was a standard kind of exchange: fatalistic, macho, and heroic by turns, and entirely false in Sax's case. "I've only done it twice," he added. Falling off a bicycle twice didn't make one a stunt man, after all. And on the second occasion, the creature had been debased, mindless.

"Most do it only once," Fra Paolo said, and to Sax's amazement he actually cast his eyes heavenward and pressed his fingers together in a brief gesture of prayer. This canon was either the most honest and faithful servant of Christ in Rome, or an unutterable charlatan. Sax hoped it was the latter. True believers could get you killed.

Fra Paolo took Sax gently by the arm and steered him past the marble stairs that dominated the lobby, toward a deep architrave with a black-painted door set into it. The clerk resumed his post behind the desk. On the other side of the black door there was another desk, this one manned by another handsome youth in cassock and wooden beads; he was lean as venison, with yellow hair, blue eyes, and a nose like the nasal of a Viking helmet. If everyone who worked for the Ordine dei Cavalieri Sacri dei Teutonici e dei Fiamminghi, Special Branch, was this good-looking, Sax thought, maybe he should take divine orders himself. He might look well in one of those little red hats and a lacy surplice.

They settled into Fra Paolo's office on the ground floor. It was taller than it was wide, with two narrow windows set into shining pale pistachio-colored walls. There was a framed photograph of the Pope about eight feet up one wall, a bronze crucifix opposite that, and a calendar pinned up behind the desk. These articles, plus three identical wooden chairs and a wastepaper basket, made up the contents of the room.

Fra Paolo offered Sax refreshments. Sax accepted a coffee, brought in by the lean yellow-haired man: a German, Sax learned. The coffee was ferocious. Apparently the order did not frown on all stimulants. Fra Paolo explained that little had changed since Sax's last visit, thirty years before, except obviously the staff. The brothers who operated the place then had been, for the most part, long since promoted—or had died. The brotherhood's work remained the same. Mostly they assisted German Catholics seeking the graves of their ancestors, arranged funerals for newly deceased dignitaries, and did administrative work.

Now and then, they also slew vampires.

"I am told by the monsignor in New York that you wish to assemble a team," Fra Paolo said, after what he gauged to be a decorous interval of polite conversation.

"Yes," Sax said. "A sort of motley crew. I don't know if you customarily do that sort of thing. I feel silly even asking."

Fra Paolo crooked his ermine brow and nodded gravely. "It is distressing, though," he said. "We bring people together, they go out into the world, and we bring them back sometimes in small boxes. We come to feel responsible."

"You needn't feel responsible. This is my junket entirely," Sax said. "I wouldn't trouble you to begin with, except for the bureaucratic aspect of things. And I do need some introductions, of course. What happens after that can hardly be your fault."

Fra Paolo opened a drawer in his desk and retrieved a daybook. He leafed through it. Nailed an entry down with his square fingertip.

"Here," he said. "Yes. You see, Mr. Saxon-Tang—let us speak to my superior. He will explain."

Five minutes later they were standing inside the cool, echoing nave of Santa Maria della Pietà, which looked remarkably fresh—it had been bombed during World War II, and restored more than once since then, so it lacked the usual patina. The newness of the finishes made the sculptural motifs of dancing skeletons attended by fat marble putti all the more bizarre. Very German. Nero's bloody circus had stood in this same spot. The soil beneath the floor was soaked with the gore of early Christian martyrs. The Vatican's phalanx of archaeologists had developed a theory that the wolves to which some of these victims were thrown may actually have been lycanthropes; that is, they were vampires in bestial form. Sax wouldn't put it past a chap like Nero. Then again, it would have been something to attend those parties the late emperor threw.

Fra Paolo introduced Sax to a very short, stout German prelate named Achenbach who wore a black zucchetto, or skullcap, and old-fashioned steel spectacles. There was an awkward moment in the introductions when Sax failed to do something that was expected—kiss his ring? Lick his shoe? Sax had no idea what it was. His heathen status now established, the conversation went straight to business.

"You seek a demon," Achenbach said.

"For lack of a better word, yes." Sax rapped his cane on the floor for emphasis and it made an unexpectedly loud report like a gunshot. He winced.

"You do not know where presently it is."

"Yes," Sax said. "That is to say, no."

"But you have on two occasions," Achenbach said, his pale, folded features struggling to hold back an expression of disbelief, "these creatures found?"

"One of them found *me*, strictly speaking. But yes. I was much younger then."

"You will be killed," Achenbach said, and smiled in a compassionate manner. Fra Paolo stood by with his muscular hands clasped in front of his groin, head tipped back in an attitude of listening.

"Yes yes yes," Sax said. "I've thought of that myself, you know. I didn't come all the way here just to be told I'm a bloody fool, Your Honor. I came here—"

"Yes," Achenbach interrupted. "I understand. It is curious. That is all. You are a peculiar individual."

Sax turned to Fra Paolo and wagged the cane at him.

"Young man, we must have a linguistic barrier. In German or Italian, if you please, explain. I was hoping, you see, for some assistance. This gentleman can either help me or he cannot. I wish to know immediately. I can't be wandering from church to church all day—I've got work to do."

Before Fra Paolo could respond besides turning deep red, Achenbach spoke.

"I was told you were . . . *iconoclastic* was the word. I understand it now. You defy all emblems of power but your own free will. You fear authority figures. You dislike men who wear the mantle of office. You dislike Mother Church, which claims authority not just over this treacherous world, but the souls within us all. I accept that this is your way, and I pray for you that someday you will discover forgiveness for the world, and seek for your own self forgiveness. The Church here is always. When you renounce your sins and seek to be cleansed of spirit, the Church here is always. Her arms open to you are always."

This speech caught Sax off guard. He had thought this was going to be a straightforward case of some old reprobate with a fancy hat telling him he was a very naughty sinner and to remember to fill out the forms after he'd slain his vampire and hand over anything of interest (meaning value) to the Church, for which of course he would receive absolution for any violation of Christ's law during the struggle to subdue the fiend incarnate, and a tax-deductible receipt. That's what had happened the last time. Now they were handing out offers to join the team. It would be coupons for the Vatican gift shop next. Sax grunted, because words failed him. Achenbach was staring at him, his moist, faded eyes dim behind the spectacles.

"It may surprise you to know, Mr. Saxon-Tang, that you do have friends here. It was to me a surprise to learn who they were. You go with great blessings. Mighty blessings."

Sax inclined his head by way of thanks. He couldn't quite say *thank you* aloud, but he wasn't immune to blessings, spurious as they might have been. As an inveterate name-dropper, Sax was very curious to know how high up in the hierarchy his surprising friends in the Church might be. Achenbach had bent his eyes in the direction of St. Peter's when he mentioned it. It would goose the hell out of old Pillsbury if Sax turned out to be pals with the Pope himself. But he didn't ask. Even Sax occasionally deferred to the gravity of a moment, if only for variety's sake.

"So go you with God," Achenbach continued when Sax had been silent longer than usual.

"Yes," Sax said, realizing the interview had ended. "That's all very well. But along with God, who else am I going with?"

"Oh," said Achenbach, and waved a small pink hand at Fra Paolo. "Him."

8

Rome

After his interview with the prelate, Sax had gone straight back to his hotel for a nap. He was to meet Fra Paolo at six o'clock that evening, which gave him three hours. Sax slept heavily until the knock on his door signaled the young man's arrival.

"You keep waking me up," he said, and ushered Fra Paolo into his room.

Fra Paolo looked extraordinarily well in his priest's clothing. He had been given dispensation to wear something more practical than the fitted, ankle-length cassock for the duration of this adventure, so he now wore black trousers and a short-sleeved shirt with a postage stamp of white collar at the throat. His arms, freed from the stovepipe sleeves of the cassock, were strong, veined, and richly furred. None of these garments were equipped with pockets, which Sax presumed was something to do with being a monk. Instead he carried the small black purse on a wrist strap favored by European men.

Sax found himself fervently desiring to be young again. He'd show this beautiful bit of Italianate ornament a thing or two. One thing, at least.

Fra Paolo was chatting happily about inconsequential things: how strange it was to be wearing ordinary clothing, and how well the interview with Achenbach went, and what dry weather it was. After a few moments, when the sleep and prurient desire had been cleared from his brain, Sax erected a finger to signal he wished to speak; there was something important to say. Fra Paolo shut up immediately.

"I am," said Sax, "pleased to have you along."

"Thank you," Paolo said. "The honor is mine. You are a famous man in our field."

"Now, hang on. I wasn't done. You'd better sit down. Have an Orangina from the fridge. Here's the thing. I am, as is obvious, a homosexual. That is the least of my disqualifications, but it does cause the narrow-minded some discomfort. But there's more to me than just that. I am, in addition, an unscrupulous, greedy, spiteful coward—with the scruples of a jackal and the reliability of a Renault 9. I'll betray anybody for a profit. Judas wouldn't have stood a chance against me; I'd have been down at the Pharisees' office with a copy of Christ Jesus's driving license for thirty pieces of copper, no questions asked. Any stories you've heard about some dashing vampire killer are absolute rubbish. Look at me. I can scarcely get across a room without widdling myself, let alone bung a spike through some bloodthirsty monster. Every single bit of the hard work on this job will be done by others. I won't do a bloody thing. And afterward, when everyone else is dead, injured, and infected with plague, I'll shove everything worth having in a couple of suitcases and off I'll go. Not a glance backward. *That's* who I am."

"Yes," said Paolo. "So I was told."

Sax was terribly offended. But at least he'd made his case. He'd gotten it all out there. Now Fra Paolo could bow out of any personal involvement, find Sax some proper assistants—meaning sociopathic mercenaries—and Sax could get on with the job.

Sax found he was sweating. He fumbled out his handkerchief and wiped his face.

"I see," Sax said, when Fra Paolo failed to add *just kidding*.

"I was told you are a bad man for this job. I was also told you are the *only* man for this job."

Apparently, Fra Paolo's dispensation amounted to a free pass. His usual existence was constrained by Church regulations, and what he wore was the least of it. There were rules and obligations accreted around every imaginable aspect of the monastic existence, the result of fifteen hundred years of trying to outwit the devil or defeat human nature, depending on one's point of view. The idea, hatched apparently in the Vatican itself, was for Fra Paolo to blend in, at least as far as a man dressed as a priest can do so. It would get more difficult the farther they got from the Vatican.

When Sax suggested Fra Paolo take him around to some antique shops in the immediate area so he could see what worthless brummagems they were trying to pass off as sound articles, Sax got some insight into what a life of avoiding sin—as opposed to seeking it out, which had been his own approach—was like. It was misery, from Sax's point of view. Fra Paolo was forever second-guessing himself, hesitating, and deciding he'd better not. And that didn't just apply to the obvious things.

In one of the shops there was, Sax had to admit, a very nice ebony crucifix with delicate ivory mountings. It was Victorian, distinguished because it was a common object crafted with uncommon skill. Worth relatively little. Fra Paolo picked it up, examined it, and then put it down with a little guilty jump as if he'd been caught shoplifting the thing down the front of his trousers. When Sax had asked him, in an entirely conversational way, if he liked the object, Fra Paolo had responded, "No, I couldn't."

"You don't, or you can't?"

"I couldn't."

"I only asked if you liked it, not if you wanted it. Is that against the rules?" Sax genuinely wanted to know. He was fascinated by people who denied themselves, as they were so alien to him.

"It is an object made by men. To worship the material, the craftsmanship—"

"Yes, well that's what you do already with that dangly thing round your neck, for that matter," Sax said, indicating the small silver cross Fra Paolo wore on a long chain.

"This? It's a symbol only. I don't think of it, only what it represents."

"So you've gotten used to it, in other words."

"Yes," Fra Paolo said, and shrugged with great force.

"In that case," Sax said, picking up the ebony cross, "would you not get used to this nice bit of workmanship here? As you say, it's just an object."

"But to become accustomed to an object of such beauty would be an act of pride."

"Pride? Because you had something nice on the wall?" Sax found himself pressing the tips of his fingers against his forehead, as if to keep it from falling off until they could reach a hospital.

"Yes," Fra Paolo said, shrugging with less force this time.

"But," Sax said, aware that he'd gone down a rabbit hole with no bottom, "you can see the dome of bloody Saint Peter's out your office window!"

"So?" Fra Paolo looked even more worried now, his big dark eyes wide with alarm.

"Do you ever look at it?"

"Yes," Fra Paolo said, as though admitting he was addicted to cough medicine.

"And you've never felt a little tickle of pride at that?"

"No. Perhaps, Mr. Saxon-Tang, you do not realize Santa Maria della Pietà is not located within the margins of the Holy See. We are across the street. When I look out my window, I am looking from my humble outpost in the secular world at the very threshold of heaven. It is a kind of penance, to my way of thinking." Fra Paolo shook his head mournfully and extracted the cross from Sax's fingers. He placed it back on the little wire stand that held it upright, and they went out into the street.

From that time forward, Sax no longer called the man Fra Paolo; he would now be only Paolo. To stick a title on the front of his name was only encouraging the poor fellow. And he had a little side project to occupy the empty hours when they weren't after the vampire. Paolo was afraid of his own mortal weaknesses, it was clear. So all Sax had to do was to find which weakness Paolo had the least control over and exploit it. That would be jolly good fun. There were many ways to seduce a man.

That night, Sax felt quite lively. Paolo was allowed to drink, apparently, and showed no special hesitation at doing so, which demonstrated that wasn't his weakness. After an aperitif in the hotel bar they repaired to a small *osteria* with which Sax was familiar. Sax was gratified that Paolo had never heard of this place, less than a ten-minute walk from his office. Of course Paolo, being the austere type, probably ate nothing but peanut butter and jelly sandwiches.

Sax was energized, he suspected, by the simple act of making something happen. Not everyone, after all, got the Vatican's blessing to go out and loot a vampire's hoard, and was given a piece of Italian beefcake to go along with it.

9

MUMBAI

It had to be Yeretyik who was following Nilu.

He was too big, his movements too drunken as he walked, to be anyone else. And he had wrapped himself from head to knees in tattered blankets so that only one long, pale hand was visible, clutching the fabric together; there was a slit where his eyes would be. People would mistake him for a leper. His wounds were still fresh and even if he'd drained fifty dogs and a few beggars of blood to stay alive after his escape from the hospital, he would be extremely weak and hampered by his injuries—vampires healed quickly and could regenerate any part of their bodies, but regeneration took months or years, not days.

Min adopted a shuffling, hesitant gait and hunched her head over her chest, as if she were very old. The blanket-wrapped figure that had emerged from the darkness ahead of Min looked around furtively, saw her, but did not mark her as important. Just another shrunken peasant in the sweltering night, two blocks behind. Min didn't even know if the Russian could see her at that distance. He only had one eye, and it wasn't likely to be working as well as it had before Min blew his face off.

Min kept herself hunched over but increased her stride, closing the distance between herself and the quarry. The vampire was intent upon Nilu. He was moving fast. Nilu's steps slowed, and she stopped moving, as if in a trance—which she probably was. Yeretyik halted, and there was some kind of invisible communion between them. Nilu turned as if to run away, but she moved in slow motion. In her mind, she probably thought she *was* running—vampires could do that, make their victims lose all sense of the passage of time. Min was acutely aware of time. She had another few meters to go before she would be within attacking distance, the critical intersection of how long it took her to draw her weapons and how fast she could run.

Her steps picked up speed. The vampire had not observed her, still fixated on his victim. Nilu had crossed the street and now she was leaning against a building, rocking her head back and forth as if to deny Yeretyik's existence. He threw the blankets aside and seemed to grow in height, expanding at the scent of his prey so close.

He was about to attack.

Min bolted flat out, the scarf falling from her head, and she had her silver hammer and the shotgun in her hands. It would be five or six seconds before she could reach the vampire. She might be too late.

Then there was a whirl of blackness against the caramel night sky. Something soared down from one of the rooftops above Min and caught itself on the rotting Art Deco façade of an apartment house, hanging there for an instant, appraising Min, who skidded to a stop, pulling back against her momentum.

It was a second vampire, a female, its white face and hair gleaming in the bilious light of the streetlamps. Min had never seen anything like this. Even vampire couples hunted alone.

The creature bounded off the wall of the building a split second after it alighted, its black hooded robe luffing behind it, whirling through the air. Min's heart was racing. She wanted to kill this new creature and the Russian as well, but the threat was too great. She had lost her strategic advantage. The female vampire hit the pavement on churning legs, catching up with its own speed, and before Yeretyik had time to react, they collided.

Min's shotgun split the thick night air. She was running again, and in full motion she fired three times. Hit nothing.

The new vampire threw Yeretyik over her shoulder, and in a rattle of robe tails she was gone into the shadows, carrying the Russian down an alley with a swiftness and agility that defied the laws of physics.

Nilu collapsed. There were street people on their feet now, pointing at Min, who was racing to Nilu's side. No use pursuing the monsters; they would be gone by now, or waiting in ambush.

Min knelt beside Nilu; the girl was perspiring, her eyes wide and bewildered. The trance was broken. She was present for what was happening now.

Min didn't care how many witnesses there were. She was nobody to them.

She pressed the barrel of the shotgun against Nilu's head. Better to blow her brains out before the inevitable vampire infection took her over.

Nilu grasped the barrel in her hands, but she hadn't the strength to push it away. She was begging in Hindi.

Min didn't care. She was about to squeeze the trigger when it occurred to her that she now had something Yeretyik wanted. Vampires didn't leave half-finished victims behind them. Yeretyik had risked destruction to find Nilu again. He would keep trying as long as the girl lived. Wherever Min took her in the world, the monster would track Nilu down. Min could set up an ambush on her own terms. She'd kill the second vampire, too, if they both appeared. The advantage would be hers next time.

She depressed the safety, shoved the shotgun back into its harness, and caught Nilu beneath her arms. Min hauled the girl upright, then propelled her away into the night, ignoring the jabber of excited onlookers.

10

Rome

"What is the Italian for *peanut butter?*" Sax asked.

"*Burro di arachidi*," Paolo said. "Why?"

"I enjoy learning new things."

They had, as it was Sax's ambition always to do, dined well. So well that Paolo nearly wept. Sax did the ordering, with the assistance of the owner of the place, Angelo, who remembered Sax from his last visit. How long had it been? A year or two? Sax was always struck by the power of recall that restaurateurs seemed to possess—but then, he could remember every chair he'd ever sold, and how much he'd made on each deal. What one remembers best is whatever one specializes in. Angelo's specialty was returning customers.

For *l'antipasto*, Angelo recommended a simple bruschetta—crusty bread with a coarse salsa of onions, tomatoes, garlic, olive oil, and balsamic vinegar spooned atop it, garnished with fresh leaves of basil and crumbs of bright salt.

"*O, tanto aglio*," Paolo said, in purely secular ecstasy. *So much garlic.*

"*Ammazzavampiri*," Angelo said.

Paolo jumped in his chair and dropped his napkin. Angelo laughed, and Paolo laughed a moment later. Sax waited patiently for an explanation.

"He says it will kill vampires," Paolo said, laughing. "Vampires!"

If it were only that easy, Sax thought. He didn't find it funny.

Sax had a single bite of the tangy bruschetta. It was enough. He savored it. An old man must pace himself. Paolo, however, consumed the rest with the appetite of a man rescued at sea, exclaiming over every mouthful. Sax admired the way the olive oil ran down Paolo's chin and fingers and the black pepper reddened his lips. *Extra virgin*, Sax thought, his mind strictly on the oil.

Angelo was apologetic. He was supposed to be creating winter dishes, but it was like summer outside. So he would be mixing the seasons a little. For the fall, the first course (*il primo*) was a soup that Sax had never encountered before, the primary ingredient being rare *agnolotti del plin*, tiny hand-folded ravioli no bigger than a fingernail. Angelo had gotten them fresh from his cousin in Piedmont. He prepared these in a broth of vegetable stock flavored with a few scraps of thinly shaved black truffle. Sax was unable to resist eating his entire portion; it was a time for truffles, it seemed. Paolo raised his bowl to his lips with both hands and drank, moaning. Sax felt a note of triumph: He had found Paolo's weakness. Seduction by gluttony.

They ordered a good Carmignano wine on the recommendation of Angelo. Paolo enjoyed it immoderately, becoming ever more voluble concerning the food and life in general.

"I have some people for you to meet," he said, abruptly breaking his concentration on the meal.

"Ah," said Sax, not sure what people Paolo meant.

"They have themselves experience in the business of—" Here Paolo made a *crick* noise from the side of his mouth and ran an oily finger across his throat. "The things we hunt," he added, when Sax still didn't comprehend.

"Oh, *that*, Sax said. "Those. Yes. Yes yes yes. I have some specific requirements we should discuss first, but I'm not sure if this is the correct . . . *venue*, you understand." Sax looked around the small, whitewashed stone room with its beams and yellow parchment lamps, the little flock of tables crammed together so the waiters might tiptoe through. Sax's plans included bloodshed and evil hearts bursting beneath silver hammers, screaming and dying and fire. Better if the other customers thought he was merely some old sinner taking his confessor out for a meal, not a cross between Quentin Crisp and Torquemada.

When *il secondo* arrived, in the form of *ossobuco alla Milanese*, a rich winter dish, Sax ate a few slow bites of his own portion, then offered the rest to Paolo, who consumed it after he had finished his own. Even with the sparing amounts Sax allowed himself to eat, he was still sweating by the end of the course, overwhelmed by the food.

"There is a woman," Paolo said. Sax's grizzled eyebrows knotted themselves into a frown. "I know. You do not wish to speak of business. But I cannot enjoy such a meal unless I am paying for it in some way."

"You'll drive yourself round the bend with that sort of talk, young man," Sax said. "Even a priest must get the occasional evening off, must he not?"

Paolo shook his head, splashing more wine into their glasses from the pigeon-breasted decanter that, like so many things, mocked Sax with its faint resemblance to the accursed ormolu clock.

"It is not a job in that way. It is the same for artists, I am told. They are never free from their vocation. It is their calling. It is part of them and with them always. The artist cannot look at a landscape and merely see it; he bears witness to it, he interprets it. My calling as well is that way."

Sax nodded. He knew the feeling. He was not himself an artist, but he was certainly alive to the arts, a disciple. He lived in a world not of objects but of creations, and in each he saw reflected the skill and context and the act of creating it. Sometimes he yearned for a table to be just a table. Then he could get rid of that beastly Art Deco Hoffmann in his living room.

"Yes," he said.

After their labors at the table, the two men rested, refreshing their palates with a cold glass of tart *limoncello* made on the premises. Angelo approached them almost apologetically, his hands clasped in supplication, and had to tease Sax into accepting suggestions for *il dolce*—the dessert; Paolo did not hesitate, bold and valiant in youth as he was, and also at his ideal body weight. Out came bleeding wedges of Roman cherry tart, dashed with a reduction of cherry liqueur and chocolate. "Christ in heaven," Sax breathed, and Paolo did not chide him for it.

"Right," said Sax, when at last they left the *osteria* with loud promises to return. "To business."

He was pleased to see Paolo was no longer enthusiastic about the prospect of discussing work; the rich and plentiful meal had taken the edge off his customary appetite for business. Everyone had a sin; the trouble with gluttony was Sax couldn't keep up with it.

They did need to talk things over, and there was some urgency to it. But every activity had a right time, just as everything had a right place, unless it was do-it-yourself Scandinavian flat-pack furniture, in which case it had neither. Sax knew just what Paolo needed—he took him to the first busy bar they encountered on the walk back toward the hotel, where they consumed thimble-sized espressos like rocket fuel.

"I require only a few assistants for this matter," Sax said, once they had resumed their stroll, Paolo now sufficiently restored for the purpose. Sax's cane tapped along like a stork seeking frogs.

"We recently sent a team of seven men to Finland," Paolo said. "They are not all back yet. One of them is missing. So we are less of staff." He said this in a confessional manner. Sax guessed it had been Paolo who'd sent them on their way.

"I want as few people as possible," Sax said. "Consider me the brains of the operation, seeing as that's all I have left. I'm not keen on having you along, but I suppose that's none of my business. Still, you can handle the coordination and so forth, see to that side of things. I will also require the most seasoned burglar you can get your fine muscular hands upon, preferably with experience in this kind of project; he should fear death and dismemberment only sufficiently to make him cautious, and he should bring his own tools."

"That will require recruitment outside our usual resources," Paolo said. He looked thoughtful.

"And—" Sax said, and paused.

He intended no aposiopesis, but there was a bit of food under his dental bridge. He greatly desired to pick it out. His vanity, however, overcame the irritation. If he could just conceal his disgusting weaknesses and deformities for a few days, perhaps Paolo would come to see him in an avuncular light, as did Emily. Then, if they survived the adventure, Sax could invite Paolo to his most recent villa in France and all of Sax's old friends would assume the worst and burst with jealousy. He gave up attempting to suck the morsel out from under the superstructure holding his tooth in place.

"And," he said, resuming, "I need at least one proper vampire killer. A sociopath would be ideal, but not a psychopath. It is an important distinction."

"I have just the person," Paolo said, brightening.

"What a treat," Sax replied. "I'll need in addition one chap with extensive special operations training. The sort that goes down ropes on cliffs and swims across rivers with a knife in his teeth and so forth. That should do the trick. We're going to keep this fast, violent, and quiet."

"What is your plan, Mr. Saxon-Tang?" Paolo asked. There was a note in his voice Sax didn't like. It was admiration, he thought. The sound of trust. It was something Sax seldom heard, unless from Emily in unguarded moments.

The name *Tang* was like a withered limb in Sax's estimation. "Please call me Sax," he said. He mentioned this primarily to gain some time to compose his answer to the question: in truth, his scheme was vague at best. He would begin with the background and maybe a proper plan would emerge.

"This vampire. I've collected some information about her. Female, yes. Wealthy, as they usually are. Most of the pieces she's bought are European, which of course suggests she's spent at least the last couple of centuries here. Also, she was in Europe during the Second World War, because it was directly thereafter that most of these objects appeared, which tells me she lost them during the festivities."

"Brilliant," Paolo said, failing to see what a tissue of conjecture it all was.

"Indeed," Sax muttered. "Now, I became aware of this creature when I won at auction a clock with an interesting history, at least up until 1939. It was owned by Jean Cocteau, the great dramatist and filmmaker. Cocteau dropped out of sight for two years, and the clock as well, and after that, he no longer had it. It turned up again after the war in a respectable American diplomat's household in New York, and remained there until recently, when the diplomat's effects were auctioned off, his heirs having fallen into, ah, reduced circumstances, as seems to be the vogue."

"So what is the plan?" Paolo said. They were now strolling down one of the avenues that led to the Piazza San Pietro, lined with handsome apartment buildings and occasional small palaces with their own wooded grounds, mostly converted into *condomini*.

"Getting to that," Sax barked. Only Emily knew how to listen. "I was able to determine where the diplomat was stationed during the war and his whereabouts after that while he was still in Europe. I've got that narrowed down to Wolfsburg, in Lower Saxony. Where they make Volkswagen automobiles. The diplomat was sent there to oversee conversion of factories from wartime production to civilian stuff that could be exported to the United States on the cheap. He made use of his dollar salary, his connections to the U.S. Army, and Germans in need of many favors. He ended up with a great deal of what one might call the spoils of war, if *pillage* is too strong a word."

"Shameful," Paolo said.

"Shameful? The man was a genius."

"So you know where she is," Paolo said, betraying a whiff of impatience. He stopped walking, as they were now close to Sax's hotel, and rested his haunches against a raised triangular plot of grass in a stone bed, presumably some relic of antiquity. Lovers and tourists in various combinations were strolling past at the uniquely Roman pace, like snails.

"I know where the monster *was*. In 1945, at least. Or where she probably was. None of this is certain. Listen. A lot of things flowed through Wolfsburg then on the railway lines. It's only a clue: her location was connected to that city. So it's a point on the map. Her location is connected to these objects as well. They may have been purchased with mechanisms to keep the buyer secret, but they all had to be shipped somehow. And shipping agents are less discreet."

All in a moment, the complete plan appeared in Sax's head. He now knew what to do. And at the same time, he wasn't going to tell it to Paolo. Not because it was disagreeable in any way, or stupid, or dangerous, although those were all aspects of the thing. Rather, it was because *nobody* was discreet—possibly including Paolo. It wasn't in the human genetic code.

Vampires, though, were discreet by nature, and very good listeners indeed. Sax's fiend would already know he was in Europe, for example, although given his frequent travels, she might not have known why. But it wouldn't take long. Then all he would have to keep himself and his team alive long enough to get to the source of things, the only real advantage, would be—

"Do you know what a secret is?" Sax said.

Paolo looked confused. "A secret? Something kept from knowledge?" he suggested valiantly.

Sax shrugged. "A secret is a baby conspiracy. It's an infant when one man knows it, a child amongst two men, and when three men know it, it's old enough to make its own way in the world. I'm not going to tell you my plan. Not yet. Not until I'm prepared for the vampire to know it, too."

The next day, Sax's reticence concerning his brilliant plan paid off early. He sprang from his bed at the crack of ten, and an hour later was sufficiently awake to proceed across the way to the church where Paolo had his office.

Paolo had not been idle. He was, as Sax had suspected, in constant communication with his superiors. This didn't make him underhanded; it was an aspect of being a part of the Church hierarchy that one had no secrets from one's betters. Their response upon hearing that Sax would not reveal his scheme wasn't, as Sax assumed it would be, to wish him the best of luck and withdraw Paolo from the operation. Instead, good old Achenbach opened an expense account for Paolo, from which he could draw cash for whatever contingencies might arise. Sax's list of contingencies quadrupled in an instant upon hearing this news.

Paolo had made his inquiries and tracked down the people Sax would need to retain, insofar as he was able. Sax sat in one of the puritanical chairs on the other side of Paolo's desk and listened to him talk on the telephone and clatter away at his computer keyboard. Sax drank a series of coffees relayed in by one or another of the monks of the Ordine dei Cavalieri Sacri dei Teutonici e dei Fiamminghi, Special Branch. Sax thought pleasantly that they should pose for a calendar someday, hairy chests coyly apeep beneath their vestments, doing monkish things like treading grapes in bare feet or scrubbing floors with their bottoms in the air. It could raise a fortune for orphans and the like. Monks on every wall; have you seen Fra October? What a *bel figo*! Sax realized he was daydreaming, almost asleep despite the coffee.

"The personnel files are coming," Paolo said, interrupting the reverie.

A moment later, the door opened, and a monk with curly auburn hair entered with a stack of file folders of the type that close with a flap and red string. Paolo extracted dossiers from them and slipped glossy black-and-white photographs across the desk to Sax. He fanned the pictures out: his first hand of cards in the game.

"This is Min Hee-Jin, from South Korea. She is our vampire killer," Paolo said.

"Is she not a trifle too small for the work?" Sax asked.

"The bigger ones are all psychopaths, which you said was no good. She is very good," Paolo said, as if enticing Sax to sample a morsel of cake. "She may be only this tall, but she's killed four vampires."

"*Four* of them?" Sax thought she might be *too* competent for his purposes. He didn't want a mass murderer to deal with.

"Miss Hee-Jin is on her way back from India, where she has been hunting down a Russian vampire. There were complications. In fact, she may not arrive. She didn't say what the complications were, you see. The last time we were informed of complications, the individual involved turned out to be infected. Not Min Hee-Jin, of course."

This sounded inauspicious to Sax. "Has she killed anybody else? Other than vampires?"

"One or two have died, but it was not her fault."

"What a relief. Who's this brooding fellow?"

The man in the next file was Gheorghe Vladimirescu, a Romanian burglar who also did bank heists, conducted strong-arm work for the Russian Mafia, and occasionally performed as a street acrobat. He was available because he happened to be in Italy under an assumed name, avoiding a conversation the Romanian authorities wished to have with him. The Vatican had better contacts than the police. Gheorghe was rough carved, pale, and black haired, with dark circles around deep-set black eyes that had the cold gleam of porcelain electrical insulators.

The next candidate was the paramilitary sort.

"Did you find this chap at Central Casting?" Sax asked. The photograph revealed an umber-skinned man with immense muscles. His head was shaven and his skull had a rippled surface that telegraphed the convolutions of his brain. Manfield K. Rocksaw was his name, which Sax assumed had to be some kind of joke, and he had been with Special Forces in the United States Army. He was a Green Beret, or had been. Then he went freelance, following a disciplinary action when an examination of the details of the recent unpleasantness in the Middle East revealed he'd made some decisions contrary to the word, if not the spirit, of certain international treaties and conventions. He made no attempt to defend himself during the proceedings except to say, as was noted in the file, *Shit rolls downhill.*

The only person missing from the equation, at this point, was the bait. Sax hadn't mentioned the bait. It could be anybody attractive with a fair amount of blood inside them. It was difficult to sort out this aspect of the plan ahead of time, because vampires generally hunted by gender: males killed males, females killed females. There was a biological reason for this. Vampires did not themselves have fixed genders, or even anatomies, for that matter, and gradually took on the form of their prey. The transitional period between male and female could be awkward. The transition from human to beast (or vice versa) was worse; witness the early-medieval period when so many loups-garous were slain as they made the transition from wolf to human prey, wolves having grown scarcer than men. These days, the lower order of vampires ate mostly dogs, and so weren't werewolves but *hundings*—essentially were-dogs.

Sax thought his bait should be female for this reason: assuming the vampire was female, the odds of attracting it would be better. They tended to drain the blood of the gender they occupied, to avoid slowly metamorphosing into the other. Unless they wished to switch. Vampires sometimes did. For this purpose a female victim offered better odds.

Of course, the bait might not be required at all. Sax didn't want any more innocent people hurt. Forty years earlier, he had fervently believed there *were* no innocent people, only those before whom opportunity had not yet appeared. Since then he had come to know there were genuine innocents in the world, and they ought to be protected. Paolo, unfortunately, was probably one of them.

Sax wondered if there would soon be even more blood on his hands.

11

Paris

Sax and Paolo took the train to Milan, then the Frecciarossa night train from Milan to Paris—a seven-hundred-mile journey. The overnight was interrupted only by the customs check in Switzerland, which was not a member of the European Union. They passed through the Alps and some of the world's most ravishing scenery in the dark. Sax had booked a private compartment, which they shared. Paolo, accustomed to the constant company of men, was unashamed to march around the compartment in his briefs while he prepared himself for sleep, although he donned a modest muslin nightshirt before retiring. Sax had thought he would suffer an embolism if the man bent over the washstand one more moment performing his ablutions with his latissimus dorsi catching the light just so, but the crisis passed and the lights went out and there was only the deep rattling metronomy of wheels on track, surging through the darkness.

At nine a.m., they reached Paris, where Sax saw a striking redhead step down from the train, one car farther back from the engine, at the same moment he did. The redhead, in a slim white sweater and green kilt, looked around as if she'd lost someone, caught Sax's eyes, and stopped looking. That she went from interest to disinterest so suddenly aroused Sax's suspicions, but he dismissed the concern. There were plenty of redheads on trains. Twenty minutes later, he and Paolo arrived at Sax's latest favorite hotel in the city, a place so narrow it had only two rooms per floor.

It was vertically constrained by the Haussmannian height restriction of twenty meters to six floors, thus yielding a total of a dozen guest rooms, including the retrofitted pair in the attic. Sax secured the two rooms on the third floor for himself and Paolo, informing the concierge that if Paolo got lucky he would need the privacy. Paolo empurpled, and the concierge was scandalized. Paolo was, after all, dressed as a priest.

Sax himself opted for a pale gray suit, combined in a fit of daring with a mauve shirt, sea-foam-green ascot, and yellow lisle socks in buckskin oxfords. A dotted pocket square in yellow and purple completed the look. The overall intent, spiteful as it might have been, was to inform passersby in no uncertain terms that he was unaffiliated with the Church, despite his companion.

Their first stop was the Louvre. Their second was rather mysterious; they were to collect the Korean vampire killer, but Paolo was evasive on the subject of why they had to meet her at some abandoned hospital on the outskirts of Paris.

At the great museum, which itself had once been a palace, Sax and Paolo crossed the featureless pavement of the Cour Napoléon, which led to the glass pyramid in the forecourt, and then, instead of descending into the pyramid beneath the ground to the museum entrance, they continued on past it to the original entrance of the palace—Pavillon Richelieu, a grand pile in the style of the Italian

Renaissance. While not on the scale of St. Peter's, its architecture was muscular enough to support a freight of allegorical stone figures and an oxide-streaked mansard roof of lead and slate. They crossed under the arched portico and passed along the Passage Richelieu, once a coach entrance for grand events to keep the wigs out of the weather, and turned to the right.

They went up some steps, Sax plying his cane with vigor on the stone, and passed through one of four doors of oak and ironwork pierced with great oval oeil-de-boeuf openings. On the other side of the doors, a guard in complete camouflage fatigues, black beret, and scowl stepped toward them; Sax produced from his breast pocket a laminated card. The guard lowered his submachine gun and shone an ultraviolet penlight on the identification, then nodded, mollified, and spoke into his radio. Sax made a campy little salute. The guard took a second look at Paolo, decided he was a real celibate and not a freak in a costume, and waved them on down a long, echoing stone hallway.

Sax was preoccupied, but not so much that he couldn't observe from the edge of his eye that Paolo was impressed. *That's right, young man: the old girl* knows *people*, Sax thought. A door halfway along the passage opened, and a gentleman with white hair in a dark blue pullover beckoned them inside the room from which he had just emerged. He was smiling.

"Saxon," he said in a Cambridge accent. "*Quel plaisir.*"

They entered a communal office space that had needed refurbishment in 1940. The radiators clanged like competition blacksmiths. The white-haired gentleman was Eric Rohmer—the curator, not the film director, as he was quick to point out to Paolo, who had never heard of either one. Sax owed Eric a long luncheon soon, he asserted. Sax felt free to promise the event would happen without fail; given what they were about to face, he didn't expect to live long enough to have to endure the occasion. Eric was a kindhearted, enthusiastic, and conscientious fellow, in love with life and his occupation—consequently, a crashing bore.

It was Sax's donation of half the contents of the château owned by the vampire Madame Magnat-l'Étrange (or Corfax, as she was known in the ancient annals) that had secured Eric a position at the Louvre. Sax had been looking for a youngish, naïve sort of person who wouldn't think too much about provenance and would think a great deal about pedigree when it came to an enormous haul of questionably secured antiques. Eric Rohmer was ideal because he was also new to the French system of museums, being at the time a mere teaching assistant on loan from the history department at Cambridge. He managed the paperwork and documentation of the sound articles, made a name for himself as a "good egg," or *bonne oeuf*, and continued to believe he owed Sax quite a lot.

Paolo and Eric got along splendidly, both being entirely decent, well-meaning human beings with snowy consciences who hadn't done anything shameful in their lives. This irritated Sax.

At the Louvre, Eric had at his command most of the shared resources of the European museum world, from the smallest private collections to the panthemic hoards found in such places as here and the British Museum. Sax described what he was looking for to Eric, scrupulously avoiding the strong tea with which they were provided, as it would render him incontinent. Eric nodded, deeply interested if mystified.

When he began to suspect Sax's request was slightly immoral, possibly even a whiff illegal, Sax mentioned coincidentally that his latest junket might result in a bounty similar to his first for the museum. This seemed to calm Eric's conscience. Besides, with a priest along for the ride, how bad could it possibly be?

Sax had within his calfskin notebook the list of items he knew had been purchased by his mysterious antagonist's female proxies. He had an additional list of antiques once in the possession of the deceased American diplomat. Further, he had indexed which items fit into both categories. The ormolu clock was one of these. There were others as well. A silver samovar with gold fittings, for example. A harpsichord. A figurative candelabra. A painting by Jacob van Walscapelle from around 1700. A few other things.

What Sax was looking for couldn't be determined just through auction houses and sales listings. He needed the authority of the great cosmos of museums with their permanent collections—always ebbing and flowing, *permanent* merely referring to a state of ownership at any given moment, as opposed to loaned items and temporary exhibitions. Not everything the vampire wanted would be for sale or in private hands. Some of it would have found its way into museums. That is what he claimed to be after to Paolo and Eric.

It would be useful to know what was out of circulation, of course. But Sax was hunting for something else, about which Eric would resist telling him if he knew that Sax was interested. Sax hoped to identify objects that seemed to come from nowhere, entering history as if out of the clear blue sky. *Those* items, Sax thought, were the ones the vampire would have acquired firsthand. A Rembrandt that had been in the continuous possession of a single individual since the paint was still wet would have no provenance at all.

Determine what such mystery objects had in common—country of origin, age, style, circumstances of discovery—and he could guess quite closely where the vampire had lived just before the war. If he could do that, he knew he could find where it had gone to ground afterward. Then the game was afoot. That was one of the few disadvantages vampires had: all the muck they collected was very hard to move.

It was a bit of a ruse, but he didn't want Eric or some similar well-meaning dupe to give away what he was up to. Even Paolo could be a liability. They both argued Sax's approach was confusing and roundabout, but they weren't looking in the correct direction, just as Sax had intended.

No mention was made of the ultimate purpose of Sax's mission: Eric had not been informed of the vampire aspect of things and thought the whole project was an attempt to consolidate some objects that would be worth more together than in disunion. A fair enough objective, had it been even remotely true.

There was a great deal of file carrying from distant paper archives, and Eric's latest intern spent an hour typing at her computer keyboard. The conference table became too small and the effort migrated up on top of the flat files, where they could spread things out, after empty cups and staplers and heaps of museum memos on blue and pink paper were shoved out of the way.

Things were proceeding at a satisfactory pace. Sax luxuriated in not being too involved in this boring part of the project that looked uncomfortably like work. Instead he examined some of the museum catalogs and gazed out the window at the handsome camouflage-clad guards who sauntered cocksure and hard-eyed through the tourists, like bulls amongst sheep.

The research was not halfway to completion when Paolo called Sax over to his pile of documents. He'd been working on the provenance of the samovar with Eric's gentle guidance. Now Paolo spoke softly, removing any excitement from his voice. Eric was across the room with his assistant, poring.

"There was a candelabra on your list," Paolo said.

"Silver gilt, figure of Neptune holding a hydra above his head, one of a pair," Sax confirmed.

Paolo slid an Interpol bulletin across the work surface to Sax. It was in French, English, German, and Spanish, repeated in sections.

"Theft of articles from a significant collection . . . Museum of . . . Ah, I see." Sax maintained his composure with a skill that had been earned at a thousand hammer sales. Even poker players could not compete with the stone face required to win auctions, Sax believed. He could be bidding on an object of incredible worth, an unrecognized gem that would net him the kind of profits that drove competitors to suicide, and yet he would betray no more excitement than the corpse at a Calvinist funeral. It was this same detachment he summoned now.

According to Interpol, the thief that had stolen a variety of objects from a museum in Chemnitz, Germany, had been apprehended in Schönbrunn only fifteen days ago, and was currently being held in a Chemnitz jail. The stolen goods had all been recovered except for a silver gilt candelabra depicting Neptune holding the hydra aloft; further description of the object and its hallmarks was provided, along with a very poor photograph from the museum. The candlestick was grotesque, the proportions unbalanced. Early nineteenth-century English. More money than taste back then, Sax thought.

But although he amused himself with his prejudices against the silversmiths of George IV's brief reign, his real thoughts, deeper down where they couldn't cast any influence upon his features, were racing along the rails at top speed, billowing steam and coal smoke. Sax maintained his cool to such a degree that Paolo, having watched Sax read the bulletin from Interpol, was crestfallen.

"I thought it was a clue," he said. "So it's not important?"

"Nothing to speak of," Sax said—and meant it.

They were to appear at l'Hôpital Poulenc in the Eighteenth Arrondissement around seven o'clock in the evening. Sax was not fond of the *banlieue* area. Quite aside from the gangs, drugs, and poverty that ruled the streets, it was also unattractive: home to ugly municipal apartment gulags, near the commercial docks, and seamed through with train tracks.

Sax felt something peculiar, despite the surroundings. He was almost euphoric. Things seemed vivid, his senses alert to sounds and scents. Colors leapt out at him. His mind was working well. He remembered things, details of conversations, items he'd seen or bought forty years before. Names, faces, what he ate, what he did on days he'd forgotten he ever lived. He wondered at this.

Paolo sat beside him in the dark backseat of the cab with blocks of yellow light sliding across him from the streetlights moving past the windows, slipping across his face, around the back of his head, then darkness until the next one came along. Sax could smell the clean male scent of his companion. He could smell the ghosts of cigarettes in the headliner of the cab, too, and his own stale old-man smell masked with a bay lime cologne he ordered handmade in a shop in Manhattan, because he always thought that is what old men ought to smell like, even when he was young.

What was this feeling he had? It was even in his veins. His limbs and skin felt nourished somehow, as if his very blood had gotten sweeter. He mused on this, and as the great idiot hulk of the abandoned hospital rolled into view down the avenue, he thought he knew the answer.

It was just life paying him a rare visit. He felt *alive* for the first time in years.

Several tracksuited youths shouted vulgarities at them as they exited the taxi and walked the last couple of blocks; the thrust of their imputations revolved around the relationship of the two men, speculations insulting to Paolo and flattering to Sax. Paolo walked through the unsafe streets with the ease of a beachcomber, without an apparent care in the world. He was simply too unconcerned with worldly dangers, smiling at every young brute who scowled in their direction. Sax wondered if Paolo thought there was protection in that dog collar of his.

Paolo shrugged. "The French," he said, as if heckling was merely a national custom.

The hospital was a huge carcass rotting in the flotsam of the neighborhood: it had been abandoned for over ten years. There was a tall hurricane fence around the weedy, trash-deep lot. The structure was a relic of the postwar period, a way station for the wounded. It had no role to play in wellness. Pollution, vandalism, and cheap materials had conspired to make it a blight in an already blighted place. Sax felt as if he were in the presence of a vast, blind, mindless thing that had been forgotten but still lived. His grip on his cane was tight enough that he had to switch it from one hand to the other to rest his fingers.

The broken glass of the entrance doors crunched beneath the ferrule of the cane. They stepped into the darkness gathered under the portico and entered the lobby, where the fixtures had been stripped from the walls and what remained had been smashed.

He remembered the château of decades before, the darkness inside that place with its shutters and windowless halls. Now the same icy lizards stole down his spine. His brief fit of good spirits had decisively fled.

On their way out of the Louvre, following extended hand-wringing farewells from the faithful Eric, Sax had purchased a souvenir flashlight adorned with a decal depicting the *Mona Lisa*. Its light was strong and blue—even the cheapest flashlight was powerful these days, now that LED technology was ubiquitous. Paolo followed its beam through the hospital. Sax stayed by the entrance to the lobby. He simply hadn't the courage to penetrate the gloom inside that decaying place. It reminded him too much of his past adventures in vampire hunting—and too much of what might lie ahead. He told Paolo he would stay there and rest his old legs, but it sounded like bluffing, even to himself.

He stood in the lobby and listened to the hooligans, or *keupons*, as they called themselves in their durable Verlan slang, turning words inside out to obscure them. *Apache*, they would have been called a century earlier. Their lives revolved around drugs, antiestablishment sentiments, and music, and in that way, though they considered themselves self-invented outcasts, a force new to the world, in fact they represented the most venerable of all traditions. They were conservatives, their outlandish style and manners notwithstanding. They adhered to rigid codes of speech and behavior that precluded any true originality. Sax had been no different, in his youth. His rebellion was identical to that of his peers, if slightly more interesting only because, as a homosexual, he was part of a subculture within the subculture. It would never change.

Sax was sunk in thought along these lines, and so was startled to discover that others had almost reached him, their footsteps zinging off the naked concrete walls. He rose from his seat on the edge of an overturned steel cabinet, pressing his weight into his cane. He didn't feel so alive now. He felt very old and tired.

"They were in the cafeteria," Paolo explained. "Way down that end."

Two figures resolved themselves out of the gloom behind him, one propelling the other into the reluctant light, and Sax's plans went awry.

Min was immediately recognizable from her photograph, although she had aged five years since it was taken. She was long bodied, strong, her center of gravity low. She had a way of settling into a stance with one shoulder dropped, arms slightly bent, her brows creased in evaluation, as if she was a climber studying a difficult face of rock—the attitude of Michelangelo's sculpture *David*. There was a stream of blood running out of her left arm.

The woman beside her was taller, classically proportioned, a Hindustani with dark, ripe features and sleek limbs. Her hair flowed like black oil. There was something in her face that Sax was not happy to see. The shadows around her eyes were tinted with green and the highlights on her cheeks and jaw had a bloodless, stretched look. She might have been a junkie, except there was no hunger in her eyes, no calculation. Only fear. And one other detail: her mouth was thickly finger-painted with smears of blood.

"Did she bite you?" Sax asked of Min. "Who is she, for that matter?"

"Nilu," Min said. Sax couldn't tell which question this was supposed to answer. She spoke it like an obscenity.

Nilu stared into the light, distant and hopeless, pupils failing to properly contract.

Paolo cleared his throat, seeking words. "You see . . . ," he said, and stopped as if that would do it. Sax waited. Paolo continued, "I asked the same question. She—that is, Min—thought she could do an experiment to see if Nilu, that young lady, was interested in drinking blood. She made a hole in her arm and blood came out, but Nilu did not show interest. When I got there she was trying . . . Min was trying to *make* her drink the blood."

Sax ran his fingers through his hair, a futile gesture given the scant plumage.

"Young lady," he said, addressing Min. "This will not do. You're here because of me, at my behest, if you will. In my endeavors, as a matter of policy, I absolutely forbid anyone involved to force anyone else to drink their blood. Do you understand?"

"Yes," Min said, shielding her eyes against Paolo's light with her bloody arm.

"We observe the Geneva Conventions, particularly the fourth."

"*Go-ja*," Min said, impatient with the lecture. *That* was clearly an obscenity.

"As for you," Sax said, turning to Nilu. He didn't say anything else because he was at a loss. Paolo was frankly staring at the woman. She was extraordinarily beautiful; Sax could see that much. It occurred to him he could still, even now, revert to pleasantries.

"I'm Asmodeus Saxon-Tang, but you can call me Sax," he said. "And your name is?"

"Neelina Chandra," Nilu said in a small voice. "Nilu."

"And you are Min Hee-Jin, and this is Paolo," Sax said. "He's a monk, in fact, not a priest as his costume suggests. The, ah, Ordine dei Cavalieri Sacri dei Teutonici e dei Fiamminghi, which I assume I have horribly mispronounced, Special Branch. He's with the Vatican—he works for God."

Paolo bowed but did not offer his hand.

"So," Sax added. "So."

Nobody volunteered to speak. Sax tapped his cane on the floor. He framed his questions.

"Young lady," he said, addressing Min. "You come highly recommended, of course. And you're welcome to bring friends along. It's a free country, if expensive. However, I suspect there's more to this"—here he gestured in Nilu's general direction with the cane—"than meets the proverbial eye."

Min nodded. "She got bite from a Russian in Mumbai. The vampire got away and"—here Min switched her attention to Paolo—"I want know if we kill or not kill."

"*Che cosa*—" Paolo was flabbergasted. Sax put a hand on the Italian's arm.

"How did you get her here?" Sax asked.

Min pointed at Paolo. "The Catholic people arrange everything."

Sax fixed a most murderous hairy eyeball on Paolo, who took it badly.

"We arranged to get this girl on a hospital plane," Paolo said defensively. "She was supposed to go to our hospice in Nimes, not this disgusting place. *She* changed the plan." He pointed at Min.

Sax shook his head. This was his problem now. "So she was kidnapped. I see. And drugged, by the look of her pupils. Happens to the best of us. Has she shown any hunger? For blood, I mean?"

"He was only feed, not recruit," Min said. Now she was comfortable. Shop talk for her.

"And you interrupted him in the sort of feeding routine."

"I almost kill him but I did not."

"And you have personally," Sax said, in the tone of a doctor discussing a patient's medical history, "the usual story of a family savagely murdered before your eyes, you sworn to vengeance, and so forth."

Min dropped her gaze and nodded at the floor, agreeing with it. "Yes."

"*Condoglianze*," Paolo said.

Sax pushed his face at him, irritated. "You mustn't start speaking Italian every time you're the least bit upset, or we'll have to carry phrase books around."

"I am sorry for you," Paolo amended.

"We have," Sax said, "a problem. Paolo, you shiftless bastard, you must have known Ms. Hee-Jin had whatever Nilu is, a hostage, a prisoner. And you didn't tell me. Here you've been splashing your virtue around like holy water, and meanwhile keeping an important secret from me. I'm the only one allowed to have secrets on this mission."

"I am sorry," Paolo said. "I'll see she's taken into the care of our people here."

"You will not," Min said.

"They are experts," Paolo said, smoothing the air between them with his hands. "You brought her this far. Now I take her to our hospice where we look after such people, and we proceed with Mr. Saxon-Tang's mission."

"She doesn't leave my eyes," Min said. "You tell me bring her, I bring her. But she is not safe. You don't ever let one with bite away from your eyes. That is a rule in stone."

Throughout this conversation, Nilu stood beside Min, her eyes moving from one speaker to the next, but otherwise without reaction. Sax couldn't tell if she was even following the words. She might not have spoken English, for all the response this discussion of her fate aroused. Though, of course, she'd been drugged as well. The drugs were so much better now than in his heyday, when it was all grass, amphetamines, Valium, or LSD—or in other words, up, down, or chaos. Now you could go sideways, backward and forward, do spirals—maybe it was time to start taking drugs again.

It was chilly inside the abandoned hospital, but Nilu didn't seem to feel it despite her bare arms.

"Now, look," Sax said, aiming for a reasonable tone of voice, which came out petulant. "I don't care what you do with this girl. It's none of my business." Even as he said the words, he knew they weren't true. If she was in Paris, Nilu was his business, no less than avenging Alberto the watchman or keeping Emily from harm. "Paolo here has a great big organization at his back that I'm sure can deal competently with this kind of thing. But let's be clear. Vampire bites lead to four outcomes, am I right? I mean, nothing has changed in the last few decades."

"Recovery, death, infection, or false vampirism," Min said, bobbing her head with each careful word.

"I was infected myself," Sax said. "I recovered. She's not well, but she needn't die. So false vampirism is the main problem before us, yes? She can't turn into a proper vampire or anything like that. They're another species."

"My family—" Min said.

"I'm talking about here and now. This young lady beside you. She didn't attack your family, is that correct? She hasn't attacked anybody else. So the question is, will she develop the hunger and start killing people, and that's why you don't want to let her out of your sight."

"I did not kill the one that got her," Min added.

"And?" Sax said, feeling rather thickheaded.

Paolo was looking thoughtful, an index finger curled around the point of his chin, elbow supported by the opposite hand. "I see what the problem is," he said. "The vampire, the Russian she said, is still out there. They can always come to their prey, yes? So he will come to this one. No matter how far she runs, he can find her. If he came to the hospice at Nimes—"

Min struck the air with the edge of her hand. "I did not tell you the bad part," she said, and began to pace through the broken ceiling tiles that littered the floor. "The reason I not kill the Russian is because a second vampire come and take him away."

"But vampires hunt alone," Paolo said. "Even mates hunt separately. They can't share prey."

"You see why I am worry," Min said. "The second vampire not want the victim. She want the Russian."

"She?" Sax said, the icicles once again forming on his vertebrae.

"It was a female," Min said, and shrugged. It meant nothing to her. Sax, however, had a terrible feeling it might mean something to him.

There was no time to waste. To conceal his alarm, he started toward the front doors, where the streetlights cast pale stripes across the floor. "We need to get moving. Paolo and myself have discovered something of interest that will require a day or two of our time."

"We have?" Paolo said, brightening.

"That Interpol bulletin was a stroke of genius."

"I knew it," Paolo said, then quickly added, "It was all your doing," because he heard the pride in his own voice and pride was sinful.

"In the meanwhile," Sax said, "you ladies will please repair with us to the headquarters I have established in the countryside for this operation. I want no further bloodshed, self-inflicted or otherwise, and if you, Min, kill this young lady, no excuse will prevent me turning you over to the authorities. Are we clear?"

Sax was half-wild with the urgency of their mission by the time they left Paris. He had a near-magical key to the vampire's location, in the form of some petty criminal sitting in a German cell. It was a miracle the man hadn't yet been found with his neck mysteriously broken. Every minute might mean the difference between a dead end and the true beginning of the adventure.

On the other hand, once the vampire's location was discovered, the bullet was out of the gun. There was no calling it back. Whether it was aimed at the monster's black five-chambered heart or Sax's own more typical specimen would be a matter for fate to decide.

Sax had purchased the farm in Petit-Grünenwald in the 1980s, when French real estate was nearly worthless and the American dollar had some buying power. He owned a dozen properties around the country from the same period of his life. They were all good holiday rentals and he never lost money on them. He had found this property during a whimsical trip with his boyfriend at the time, a handsome Nigerian doctor, to see what a nearby town called Bitche looked like. Sax fancied having an address in Bitche, if only so he could forward all his mail there. *Asmodeus Saxon-Tang, Bitche, France.* He liked the sound of it. In the end, it was tiny Petit-Grünenwald that caught his eye. The village had been part of both France and Germany at various times in history, and the local culture offered a fascinating blend of both heritages. Best of all, his farm was precisely in the midst of the Maginot Line.

France had reinforced its border with Germany between the world wars with a mighty rampart of gun emplacements, walls, minefields, and antitank barricades, naming the whole thing after the minister of defense, André Maginot. The gauntlet was as much as twenty kilometers deep and ran five hundred kilometers in length, from Switzerland to the Belgian border, where Belgium had its own fortified line. The whole thing turned out to be a bust, but it was a valiant enterprise. Germany had simply bombed the Belgian bit of the line from the air and gone around the back way into France.

Besides lending its name to any military defense that didn't work at all, the Maginot Line had also left behind masses of impressive fortifications of concrete and steel that still studded the landscape in the region. Sax's farm, in addition to its attractive riverside cottage, main house, and barns, had a *petit ouvrage* located on the hilltop above the fields. This was a small, bunker-style fort, its bulk sunken beneath the ground, from which protruded a concrete eyebrow of gun emplacements surmounted with steel turrets. The guns were long gone, but the fortification remained, and would be there for another few centuries. Children loved the *petit ouvrage* and, despite halfhearted signboards forbidding entrance, spent all their playtime there, making shooting noises while they gunned down the Germans and punctured themselves on rusty bits of metal. For this reason, Sax called it Château le Tétanos—Castle Tetanus.

Min liked the farm accommodations at once. The cottage had heavy doors and small windows. Easily defended. However when Sax pointed out the *petit ouvrage*, Min was in heaven. She took her bedroll up to the hilltop fortress, towing Nilu along. Nilu had regained her ability to think independently, but Sax had not yet seen any indication of her personality. She was still in a daze. The vampire infection was probably working on her as powerfully as the drugs Min had administered; Sax well remembered the feeling. It was like living inside an old-fashioned diving suit. Sensations all registered in the brain at a slight remove, almost secondhand, muffled and narrow. He hoped she would live, despite Min's nursing.

Sax aired out the cottage and the big house beside it, the *maison de maître*, with its four good bedrooms. Paolo went off to one of the bedrooms and spent some time in prayer, then more time on the phone with his masters in Rome. A van arrived to deliver groceries at two o'clock in the afternoon, exactly in accordance with Sax's instructions. At three o'clock, a second rental car joined the first in the yard. It was a small vehicle, which magnified the scale of the enormous man who emerged from it.

This was Manfield K. Rocksaw. He had with him an ex-military duffel bag and was dressed in jeans and a sweatshirt. He was enormous, three inches taller than Paolo and a hundred pounds heavier. He spoke always in a whisper, but the depth of his voice allowed it to carry without projection.

"Nice tie," were his first words to Sax. As it happened to be Sax's favorite, a Dior paisley on cream, Sax instantly liked the man.

"Mr. Rocksaw," he said.

"Call me Rock."

At 5:50, an hour after the long, slow sunset of a northern winter, Gheorghe Vladimirescu arrived in a cloud of smoke astride an old Ural motorcycle, his worldly goods in a canvas backpack strapped to the seat behind him. He was two hours and fifty minutes late. Rocksaw had been on time to within the margin of error of the various watches involved. Five points for him, five points off for Mr. Vladimirescu, Sax thought.

"I must piss as racehorse," were Gheorghe's first words.

The farm, nestled at the dark foot of the hill with its mellow lamps and cheerful cotton-print curtains at every window, looked like the sort of place hobbits might turn up. How many peasant weddings and holidays had it seen, ringing with glad voices as the red-cheeked farmers set barn doors on trestles to make tables and the women in aprons and kerchiefs came bustling out of the kitchen door, laden with country cooking in stoneware dishes and crocks?

Sax savored the nostalgic charm of the place. For him, nostalgia was nothing more than a fondness for a past one didn't have to suffer through oneself. In truth, on such a simple farm in times past, Sax himself would have been beaten from the dooryard the first time he was caught with another country boy. He could imagine that scene just as well as the merry times, guilty youths tumbling down the hayrick ladder and out the door, dragging up their homespun trousers. And then of course there were the Germans, twice in the last hundred years marching through this peaceful landscape across the fields and lanes, leaving thousands of homesteads like Sax's empty because everyone who had lived there was killed.

They ate that evening together, even Min and Nilu, in the combined dining, living, and kitchen area of the cottage. The team was gathered around the long refectory table Sax had gotten from an abbey in the mid-1970s. The chairs didn't match, and they were of various heights, not necessarily arranged according to need. Rock was in one of the taller chairs, Nilu in a shorter one. They didn't appear to be the same species, the chairs or the sitters.

Sax knew he had to break the ice quickly; he was dealing with as ill-assorted a group of misfits as ever he had met, except possibly the Kinks. He was at a further disadvantage because the Kinks, frequently at each other's throats, were a rock band, while his group was going to have to defeat a monster with its own more lethal interest in throats.

Luckily, if there was one thing Sax knew well, it was breaking the ice. The trick was food and drink.

The meal was of that extemporized type that people accustomed to impromptu entertaining are adept at assembling. There was a pile of baguettes, fresh, tender bread with a sharp crust from the local *boulangerie*; a huge slab of butter in butcher paper; olive oil in a flask; pepper in a mill; sea salt in a dish. On a plank, big pieces of local cheese, white and yellow, at room temperature so they were fragrant and soft. A dish of fruit and nuts. White Alsatian wine in mismatched bottles without labels, straight from the local farms. Cold beer.

Sax fried sun-dried tomatoes in olive oil with pine nuts, garlic, butter, and a fistful of dried herbs grown on the property, and tossed this into a big pottery mixing bowl full of hot, toothy *strozzapreti* pasta, served with Parmesan cheese grated reverently by Paolo.

In the same pan, Sax seared chopped peppers, onions, and mushrooms in butter, glugged in a good measure of white wine, lowered the heat, and laid perch fillets and sprigs of thyme over the top of the vegetables. He allowed the fish to steam beneath a heavy iron lid, then brought it directly to the table in the pan with the steam billowing up under the basket lamps that hung from the beams.

It was very little real effort to prepare all this food—he could serve anything from five to twenty people with it. Best of all, it impressed the hell out of Paolo, who stood by wanting to help the entire time, all but salivating on his priest's collar. The seduction was proceeding apace. Sax wore his frilly Provençal apron to the table. Let them laugh. Let them! He wanted to establish who was the boss, and that his mincing ways nowise detracted from the seriousness of their purpose. He bade everyone eat.

"Smells good," Rock said. But nobody started eating; it was as if the internationally accepted signal to begin had been forgotten. The hesitation was made even more uncomfortable by Paolo's aspirated prayers with head bowed and hands clasped. Nilu sat staring and motionless in her chair beside Min—although Min had kidnapped her, she was also the only familiar thing in the universe right now from Nilu's standpoint. Min surveyed the smoking dishes before her with suspicion.

It was Gheorghe who broke the silence. "Does anybody but Father here"—he pointed at Paolo—"know what name is this kind of pasta?"

"It's *strozzapreti*," Sax said. "Why?"

"Is mean 'strangle priest' in Italian. Ahahahaha."

Gheorghe's laugh sounded mechanical and entirely mirthless, like the clanking of the Louvre's radiators, but he seemed to enjoy it. He heaped his plate with food.

"I will be sure to chew carefully," Paolo said.

Sax was gratified to see Min start to eat. She began with the fish, which was at least a familiar ingredient, and once that failed to kill her, she ate an astonishing quantity of pasta. Eventually she pushed herself back from the table, folded her arms across her belly, and puffed her cheeks out with a *phoo*, as if she had just accomplished some feat requiring athletic effort. Her breath blew the fringe of hair up off her forehead.

Nilu, taking Min's cue, attempted to find anything she was familiar with to eat, settling on the walnuts and fruit. She had little appetite, probably hungover from the tranquilizers, but she did nibble. Sax was glad to see that. He hadn't had any appetite during his period of vampire infection in the 1960s, and lost so much weight people assumed he was a junkie like most of his friends.

Conversation began in earnest about halfway through the meal when the subject of vampires, inevitably, came up. All of them had experience with the creatures and knew they existed. That tiresome argument did not need rehashing.

But their experiences were varied, and they described them.

Min explained Nilu's presence, she the silent, shell-shocked victim with the vampire's poison in her blood; of her own background, Min said only that of her family, she was the last one left to fight. Rock revealed a philosophic nature, describing his own role as a soldier of fortune who had finally found an enemy he could fight without the complication of shifting moral sands. Men were no less deadly, but vampires were fair game. He wanted a "clean win"—the destruction of a vampire was all good.

Gheorghe didn't want to discuss anything. Rock urged him on, tossing a loose volley of banter across the table. There weren't any lawyers in the room, right? No cops. Gheorghe (or George, as they anglicized his name) was amongst friends, unless he tried to steal Rock's shit from his room. Gheorghe smiled and laughed his gallows laugh and eventually drained a glass of beer (even the roughest Europeans would pour beer into a glass, Sax had observed), and wagged his hand from side to side to stop Rock's flow of patter.

"*Bine*. You know the *zmeesc*, the dragon, yes? One time, I steal the eggs from inside the dragon's nest. After that, I go back to men shooting with guns. Is safer. Ahahahaha." He poured himself another glass of beer but only watched the bubbles rise. He did not drink it for some time.

It was Paolo's turn. The monk explained simply that he was a servant of God, and it was his job to defeat the evil ones. It was only his specialty, like missionary work or beer brewing.

As Paolo's story lacked much interest, all eyes were bent upon Sax.

At any other time, Sax would have basked in the attention like a cat under a heat lamp. Tonight, it was less comfortable for him. Their lives would be marked by his ambitions. The reasons he gave, the story he told this evening, would have to carry them into the darkness that waited. He considered telling them of the second time he had met a vampire. On that occasion it had been deliberate, which made it a model in some ways for the present escapade. But if this operation went as badly as that one had, they were doomed.

1989

Czechoslovakia

I

Sax bravely marched into the deadly cave when his hired thugs were afraid to move a muscle. It was all downhill from there: the cave and his good fortune.

The jump across the Czechoslovakian border had been unnerving, but not due to any real physical danger. Sax had already developed his acute loathing for bureaucrats, and with the Velvet Revolution in full swing, Warsaw Pact governments were toppling like dominoes—so there were a great many bureaucrats looking for something to do. In addition, there was a heavy NATO presence on the Western side, with a lot of commanding officers who had risen through the ranks during the Cold War now deeply concerned the tide of freedom would rise up high enough to wet the shoes of their jobs. They were bureaucrats, too, but with tank battalions.

Luckily the borders were chaotic, and many stretches had been stripped of barbed wire and left unguarded, so Sax's primary team was able to enter the country through West Germany without much difficulty. Bribes were paid, of course. But Sax was accustomed to that.

And they had all sorts of forged documents in case anyone required them.

They met with the secondary team, the local men who would be doing the physical work, outside Prague, and then the convoy headed into the deep country in three ex-Soviet trucks—it seemed that surplus war materiel and vampire hunting went well together.

"Right, those of you with guns and things, you go in first. I'll keep lookout," Sax commanded. He was standing at the mouth of the cave, pale December sunlight at his back. Nobody moved. "I hired you lot to do the heavy lifting," he added. When the rest still didn't move, he swore under his breath. Then he fixed them all with his manliest gaze, one after the other. It was clear they weren't going into the cave without their feckless leader. He must act. He could almost smell the precious metals. So Sax marched into the chilly darkness, bold as pink buttons.

In an ironic twist of fate that was the only amusing thing about the entire debacle, when rumors of the ensuing exploits leaked out, the story always began with how Sax had marched fearlessly into the deadly cave when his hired thugs were afraid to move a muscle. In fact, the reason his head was held stiffly up and his shoulders were thrown back square and proud was because he was semiparalyzed—so petrified, he couldn't move his spine. *Fifteen paces*, he'd told himself, *and I turn around and scamper back*. But he'd sorely miscalculated how far fifteen paces would carry him, particularly with the defiant stride he'd affected. He was all the way to the slab in front of the crypt before the countdown ended. It was too late. Now he must pray the men followed him, or he'd have to treat them to the sight of a man soiling his trousers just as fast as he could run.

The slab was an immense chunk of rough-hewn stone, devoid of workmanship, but hacked from the living cave wall in a very big hurry some six centuries before. The crypt surrounded the slab, and a very nasty one it was, too. According to Sax's information, the cave was shaped like an hourglass lying on its side, wide at the entrance and innermost depths, and very narrow in the middle. The crypt had been formed by erecting a wall of cyclopean stones across the narrow part of the cave, with an entrance in the center of the wall about five feet high. The entire surface of the crypt had been carved with a crude motif of snake-tongued demons dancing around a ten-foot-tall satanic face, the mouth of which corresponded with the entrance. Some wag had even made the pupils of the devil's eyes into lamp niches.

The folktale Sax had found, and which had led him to this place, said that the crypt had originally been equipped with a proper oaken door bound with iron. When the subject of the legend escaped, it burst the door apart "as easily as a clay pot." When the monster returned, the opening was sealed with "a mighty stone tablet," which certainly described the one Sax was looking at. But he couldn't look at it any longer. The entire congregation of devils carved on the wall was obviously laughing at him, eager to witness his fate if he stepped another inch closer.

So Sax turned around, radiating imperious irritation, and glared back at the cave entrance. The men shuffled and looked at their feet.

"Bring your tools," he barked in a faint whisper.

Despite the lack of authority in the command, it worked. The men picked up their iron bars and shovels, their backpacks full of vital equipment like rope, hammers, and vodka, and started picking their way down into the cave. Some of the big box torches flared on, and now they could properly see the interior. It was a massive cave, broad and tall, and did indeed taper like an hourglass, at least on this side. The rock was black, dry, scored with fissures. The fine dust in the air tasted of match heads.

"Just get this slab aside, here. Lean it up against the wall with those pieces of canvas behind it. I don't want to damage the carvings. No sense upsetting the archaeologists." He was back in charge. As the men moved in and began arguing over the easiest way to shift the stone, Sax rather elaborately realized he was in the way, and that one of his bootlaces needed tying, and so ended up off to one side and somewhat closer to the exit than anyone else, in roughly the pose of a sprinter at the starting blocks.

As it transpired, the slab was moved with relative ease, grating against the wall with a tooth-grinding sound. The lower part of it had been cut in an arc, so it rolled like a wheel until an opening was exposed that a man could fit through without difficulty. Sax noticed that the men who weren't applying wrecking bars to shift the slab were instead shining their lights on the ever-widening gap, making it bright as the moon. They wanted to see as far into the crypt as possible, as early as possible, so they'd know to run for it in good time. This meant the men with their shoulders to the stone were completely blinded and had to stop for a few minutes to let their eyes readjust to the darkness.

That wait was when Sax's previously formless concerns began to take coherent shape. While the others passed around vacuum flasks of lukewarm instant coffee, he paced about as if impatient to get moving again, not just to hide how badly his limbs were shaking. He recalled how he had vowed never to dabble in the supernatural again after the adventure in France. Then the inevitable erosion of will had occurred. He heard whispered stories of treasure hunters who had met terrible creatures and prevailed, to the great benefit of their bank balances. He had thought, *I am one of those!* But as the fortune merged into his other fortunes, as the last of the sound articles from that time passed into the hands of his clients, he began to pine for another such big score.

Then, hanging about with the Roman brass, he'd learned a few things about vampires that only encouraged dangerous thinking. He learned there were many kinds of vampire, including *weak* ones. And the odds were, when you heard about a vampire, it was probably bullshit to begin with. So he'd talked himself into it. He could handle a weak vampire, especially if it was imaginary.

The truth was, in the old legend he'd found, there was a lot of nonsense. There was a better-than-even chance the whole monster aspect of it was rubbish concocted to keep out treasure hunters and curiosity seekers. But now, for the first time since he began planning the exploit six months before, he saw the story in a different light.

He'd expected to find the crypt had already been looted. The cave was all but unknown; he'd found it mentioned in a handwritten fifteenth-century manuscript that had likely never been copied. The approach to it was unmarked by footpaths; it stood in a part of the countryside which was unprofitable for farming and too far from paying work to be worth living in. But people got everywhere. A landless peasant seeks shelter from a storm, or some teenagers want a place to screw in privacy—a big, dry cave would never go unexplored. Although the entrance was choked with bushes through which the men had been obliged to hack a path, it wouldn't always have been so.

So his first reaction on seeing the crypt was still sealed was delight. Tempered with fear, but delight nonetheless. The crypt, if it had been disturbed at all, had been entered and exited with care. That might mean there would still be artifacts inside—if the story had any truth to it, that is. An entire mansion's worth of furnishings, and a fortune in gold packed in cedar chests. The cave was so dry that anything behind the crypt door should have been beautifully preserved.

But once the spike in hope wore off, he started wondering about a couple of things. As he paced, the questions got more alarming. The bushes—there hadn't even been a fox path through them. And there was no animal dung, no bird droppings, no bones inside the cave. No bats. Not even any beetle shells. Why did nothing live in the cave? And why was the crypt still sealed? Had there really never been anyone in there to discover it in all those centuries? He hoped it was something to do with carbon monoxide or radioactivity. A good old not-supernatural form of death.

The men were ready to proceed. They collected their gear and shone lights into the crypt.

"Have a look," Bobek said. He was the foreman of the laborers—or gang leader, depending how you thought of it.

Sax didn't want to look, but he would have to do so if he was going to hang on to any shred of respect from these brutes. He had a second team some three miles away at the narrow lane that ran nearest the cave; they were men he'd known for years and were well prepared for mutiny. That's why they were with the trucks. Nobody got out of that place with the loot unless Sax was stepping alongside, whistling cheerfully. *Actually* whistling. It was a signal: if he didn't whistle, there was a problem. He wouldn't trust these local men with a plug nickel. He was thinking of the second team, and wondering why he hadn't brought at least one of them along to give him courage, when he stepped up to the exposed slice of the entrance and peered inside.

He expected a great shaggy claw would spring out of the shadows and tear off his face, but there were no shadows. "Hand me that light," he said, and pointed the nearest torch down the tunnel behind the slab. It must have been the thickness of the wall—ten or fifteen feet deep, the tunnel was, a low passageway that led straight back to a square of absolute darkness, no matter how he moved the light about. The back wall of the cave must have been considerably farther in. So the inner chamber was deeper than the outer one.

Something about that darkness—it chilled his guts. The way it soaked up light, no dust or mineral glinting in it.

"Who wants to go in first?" he asked the men. He already knew the answer to that.

It was a curtain. That's why the light hadn't been able to find anything deeper in the cave. Across the far end of the passageway, hung from a wooden rod, was a curtain of very brittle black velvet. It turned to dust in his fingers when he shifted it aside. He choked on the minuscule, prickly fibers whirling in the air, and waved a breathing space through them, and shone the light into the crypt itself. What he saw almost took his fear away. It certainly gave his avarice a substantial boost.

The legend was exactly correct, and had even left some interesting details out. The cave hadn't just been furnished like a mansion—it had been *walled* like one. There was wooden paneling over the walls; the floor was of marble and the ceiling had been plastered and painted with heraldic designs. All around the perimeter walls there were windows carved directly into the stone of the cave. They were fitted with leaden frames. But instead of looking out on mountains, fields, and forests, they stared back into the cave: the windows were glazed with mirrors, not clear glass. All the mirrors at eye level had been smashed, revealing coarse stone behind them.

The interior of the cave was divided into rooms, the walls arranged between the massive pillars that held up the ceiling. They corresponded in plan with a great house of the period in which the crypt was built, featuring small rooms arranged around large ones down the center. There were three large rooms, the first at the end of the passageway, the second at the back of it, and the third at the back of the second.

Once Sax was through and hadn't been attacked by the Toad King, the men poured down the tunnel after him, competing to see who could find something valuable first. They had strict orders not to touch or move anything, but in all the excitement they had apparently forgotten this.

"*Pasti vraždy*—booby traps!" Sax shouted as the men began ducking into the small side rooms and he heard things falling about. All of the men emerged again; a couple of them had copper basins and candlesticks in their hands. They set these carefully down. Sax had memorized a few phrases he thought might be useful.

"I told you what happened last time," Sax continued. "There's the same feeling here. Search the place, but move carefully, and report anything you find that looks unusual. Remember, everything in here is valuable, even the paneling. If you treat it with care, you might not get killed. Everybody wins."

According to legend, there was once a prince in Bohemia who loved buried treasure. Křesomysl was his name. So obsessed was he with finding the buried hoards that many farmers were recruited to the work of digging instead, and so many fields went fallow, and many villages went hungry. But Prince Křesomysl did nothing to relieve their suffering, saying instead that the men must earn their bread by bringing up not barley from the ground, but gold. Although the men toiled and delved until their muscles cracked, they found nothing, and many of their families starved to death during the cruel winter.

Then one of the men, hardly more than a boy, was digging deep beneath the soil when his pick broke through the floor of the tunnel beneath him. When he lowered his rushlight into the opening, he saw great riches there. The young man rushed up out of the mine and told the master who oversaw the work, and the master told Alezh, an officer of Prince Křesomysl. The officer told the master delver to show him the man who had discovered the treasure, and told the man to show him the treasure itself. Once they were all down the tunnel, Alezh slew both master and youth, and placed guards at the entrance to the mine. Then he went to fetch the prince.

• • •

They moved as a group, pushing deeper into the cave-mansion. Nobody touched anything now. Sax didn't know if they'd merely gotten lucky so far or if vampires weren't in the habit of turning their homes into weapons—it might only have been Madame Magnat-l'Étrange who went in for that sort of thing. But the less that happened, the better he liked it—and the more worried he became. It had been too easy by far. The doubt still nagged him: Why had nobody broken in here in all the centuries since the crypt was sealed? Why were there no rats?

He hated rats, but there ought to have been rats. For some reason he thought *There ought to be rats* to the tune of "Send in the Clowns," the Sondheim number. He was becoming hysterical. So far, he'd managed to carry himself in front of the other men, simulating a leader fairly well, but as they approached the back of the second great room, his fear became too intense. He considered pretending there was something wrong with his shoe, but he was concerned they'd stop to wait for him and he'd end up in front again. So he feigned to take an interest in the architecture of the ceiling, which required he stand back a little way for a better view. A brilliant plan—Sax was dead last when Bobek reached the final door. The trouble was, there were only ten men, so if something came galloping through it, Sax didn't stand a chance of escaping.

"If the treasure is here, it's in there," Bobek said, unnecessarily. Sax thought *he* might be stalling as well.

"I haven't seen any indication of traps in here," Sax said, as if disappointed. "My primary concern now is the state of the ceiling. It doesn't look as if it's properly stuck on anymore. We had better proceed with caution."

Nobody argued with that, particularly the men who didn't speak English. Everyone got the general idea. Bobek and another man stood at the sides of the door and pretended to be worried the ceiling might come down; all the rest moved back, creating a broad open space in the middle of the floor.

"Right-ho," Sax said, and Bobek depressed the heavy iron latch on the door. It swung inward on croaking hinges and a different kind of atmosphere wafted out like ghost shrouds. A damp, bilious exhalation. The men were breathless, tense, holding themselves rigid. All lights were aimed at the opening, so when the door swung out of the way there was a clear view beyond. It wasn't another paneled room, but what amounted to the backyard of the subterranean house—the stone walls there were raw, unmarked by tools. It was the rear of the cave as nature had formed it. In the middle of the undressed rock of the floor stood a stone well, from which issued the sound of flowing water.

Prince Křesomysl did not lose a moment once he arrived at the mine. He took up the rushlight and strode deep beneath the soil, down the tunnel the young man had dug. At the bottom he found the pick, and took it in his hands and smote the stone floor with all his might. Again and again he swung the pick, and soon had made an opening large enough to admit a man. Alezh cried for him to be cautious. The prince allowed a rope to be tied about his middle but would not otherwise delay, and in his greed would admit no other man to the hidden chamber. So he descended into the hole and out of sight. Only his rushlight could be seen, glinting off the long-forgotten hoard of gold. For a long while, there was no sound but the occasional cry of delight as the prince discovered some new wonder in the cavern below.

Then there was a terrible scream, and the din of a struggle. The officer Alezh bade his men pull up the rope. At first it jerked and dodged like a fishing line with a prize catch upon it, but at last they hauled up the prince, who was covered in blood and senseless, so that they feared him slain. He was conveyed up to the surface and laid out in a nearby cottage, where the doctors despaired of his life, for an animal had cruelly bitten him in three places, and the wounds would not heal.

The prince, however, didn't die, and claimed that he could not do so until he had lived with the great treasure in his possession for long enough to satisfy his heart. Instead he remained between life and death for a long while, and only recovered his strength in small degrees. But he was never the same. His appetites changed, and his character, and soon the people of his court were so concerned they ordered the cavern of treasure explored, to find what animal had attacked him.

A team of soldiers went down into the cavern, which had hitherto been sealed, and explored the treasure chamber. Amongst scattered riches upon the stone floor they found a thing of indescribable ugliness, which the prince had run through the heart with his sword; the blade still stood in its ribs. The soldiers who found the monster were terribly afraid, and did not remove the sword from its body, but conveyed the monster into the sunlight, and burned it there beside the entrance to the mine, and it is said that the smoke of the fire choked them and they perished. It is also said that the prince ordered them murdered because they had set eye upon his hoard of treasure.

By this time, the prince was eating a dozen toads at every meal, and would touch nothing else.

They lowered one of the battery torches down into the well. Sax was no longer at the back of the party—he had some sympathy for the legendary Prince Křesomysl, whose greed had led him to destruction. But the prince had been brought up with that medieval sense of self-sufficiency and probably believed in God, so he'd gone it alone. Sax was grateful to have plenty of strong arms at his back. He himself lowered the lamp on a rope until they could see, about thirty feet below the floor, that there was black water at the bottom. Not still water, but agitated, bubbling.

"Give me a bit of paper or something," Sax said, and dropped the proffered cigarette wrapper down past the lamp. The wrapper alighted on the water and swirled in place for a moment, then was sucked away and disappeared through a gap in the foot of the well. "There's a channel down there. Bobek, have you the map? See where this might flow. I have a feeling this tomb isn't sealed off after all."

"There's a *bažina*, a swamp, half a mile to the south of here where the ground is low. Half a mile of water is as good as half a mile of rock. Nothing to fear there; fish can't climb wells."

Sax, who had put a great deal of time into researching vampires since the French adventure nearly twenty-five years ago, realized he didn't know if they could survive underwater, and if they could, for how long. It also occurred to him that the creature reputed to haunt this particular cave was described as an amphibian. He was not encouraged.

"Let's close the door back up and make a proper survey of the contents of this place. Set up the camera and make photographs. If there's no treasure here, it's worth more as an archaeological site . . . damn it."

There was no treasure.

Some excellent late-medieval furniture, including a couple of items Sax couldn't identify—one might have been a sort of primitive bidet, in which case it was a unique survival, to his knowledge—but nothing worth the price of the expedition. He might have to resort to plan B and write the whole thing off on his taxes. The museum this stuff ended up in would be well pleased, though.

Once the photographs had been made and an inventory written up, Sax discreetly examined the men, and thought a few of them had rather heavier pockets than before, but he didn't want to press the point. Let them nick a few trinkets. It might satisfy them enough so they wouldn't try to steal the petrol out of the trucks before the expedition was back in civilization.

He'd been watching them for a couple of minutes when he noticed that one of the men was missing.

"Where's the tall one with the mackintosh?" he muttered to Bobek.

"He is pissing in the well," the man said, as if this was a folk custom.

"When did he go back there?"

"Minutes ago."

"Unless he's got the bladder of an elephant, he ought to be back by now. Go check, will you?"

Sax had almost forgotten he was afraid; now it felt as if ice was melting down his scalp and into his collar. Bobek stumped back through the mansion, indifferent.

Then Bobek didn't come back, either.

"Chaps, somebody go see what's happened to the rest of the party," Sax said, his voice wobbling. "Not just you," he added when one man turned to go. "Bring three."

Now the fearful glances went around again. He could see the concern on their faces. What did the American *teplouš* think was happening? His mood was contagious. If something had happened to Bobek, it would be up to Sax to set the pace. The pace he had in mind was a three-minute mile. The men picked up their iron wrecking bars and headed for the back door. They returned quickly.

"Gold," said the one with side whiskers. "Found gold."

The strange appetites of Prince Křesomysl could no longer be concealed. At first, only the closest of his officers and courtiers knew of it, but there are no secrets where there are servants. Someone had to catch the frogs and toads, and someone else had to put them on a covered dish. Nor could the change in the prince's appearance be hidden. He no longer rode out across his lands, or appeared at the gates, or even at the door of his hall. Rumors flew on whispering wings across his domain. Some said he had contracted gangrene from his wounds, and others that he had leprosy, and others said he'd been cursed. None guessed how terrible his affliction really was.

To make matters worse, the prince's cruelty was not forgotten, although since the treasure was found he had ceased to compel the peasant farmers to dig beneath the earth, instead of planting barley upon it. The death of the young man who had discovered the treasure was a subject of much speculation; none knew what had happened to him, or to any of the men whom the prince had slain to protect his secret. A hungry winter had sharpened many appetites, not just for nourishment, but for justice as well.

One night, the prince was discovered outside his castle by the trusted Alezh, who had shown him the mine. The prince was senseless upon the ground, smeared with blood. Alezh helped him into the hall and bathed the prince with his own hands, although it filled his heart with horror to touch the flesh of his master. He burned the prince's garments in the hearth. The next morning, a peasant child was reported to have been torn apart by wolves, and her entrails devoured.

At last, it was clear that something must be done. The prince himself knew that he was beyond help, and for the first time, he was afraid for his mortal soul. He ordered a suitable cavern to be discovered, far from the knowledge of men, and a palace to be built within it suitable for a prince, with a vault spacious enough to hold a vast treasure. According to the stories men told, not one laborer or builder who undertook this project remained alive, but all met with accidents, or were beset by thieves, or died in one way or another. Then the prince left his hall, and his castle, and dwelled in his cavern, where only the officer Alezh knew him to be, and there he lived for many years, and his domain was ruled by his son, who was young enough that he knew not what had befallen his father.

Then the peasants of the villages in the region of the cavern began to die, some torn apart by animals or sickened by a mysterious pestilence, and others simply vanished. The loyal Alezh, now old and heartsick from the burden of his own sins, knew he had one more task to complete before his duty to the prince was over.

• • •

In hindsight, Sax had always known the mission would end up somewhere even worse than a cavern. Bobek showed him a gold coin with some unknown king stamped upon one side; it had been half buried in the dust, and the man had discovered it while peeing down the well. Bobek had an idea then, and had lowered his light down the well until the lens of the lamp was touching the water. It lit up the water from within, and they could see the bottom. It sparkled with more coins.

With all the men present, they lowered the smallest amongst them on ropes until he was waist-deep and standing in the water. The man had to be offered an extra two shares in the reward in order to convince him to go down there, but once he was in the water, he lost his fear, scooping up double handfuls of black silt studded with gold coins, like the muck along a shoreline is studded with clams. But he couldn't find more than this. A treasure, perhaps, but a minor one.

"You know, Bobek, I think we might want to learn precisely where this comes out. I think our little hoard may have moved itself."

II

The light was waning as they pushed the flat-bottomed skiffs out into the stream. They ought to have waited for morning, but the men were nearly frantic to go on, and Sax didn't want to wake up to discover they'd already sought out the sedimentary delta formed by the outlet of the stream and absconded with the loot.

Most of these men had lived their entire lives behind the Iron Curtain, so they hadn't seen the classic Universal horror pictures of the 1930s. Otherwise they'd have recognized the signs immediately: The black, unwholesome water belching beneath the poles as they pushed the boats along. The twisted limbs of the drowned trees. The rank fog that flowed down from the uplands and blotted out the rotten reed beds around them. The warning croak of a lonely raven. Sax had seen these pictures; he knew. The scene lacked only Boris Karloff.

Still, they punted along through the rustling reeds, navigating the twisted waterways of the swamp. It was full dark, and their lamps were casting a mournful glow in the fog, when Sax's boat (regretfully the one in front) grated on sand. They had found the silt deposit carried to the swamp by the underground stream. The men let themselves over the sides, careful because the gooey muck underfoot wanted to swallow them, and they wallowed upstream for a hundred yards, poking the slime with sticks and pry bars.

They found a low arch in a brow of exposed stone, right at the top of the swamp. The water babbled from it as if excited to have completed the long journey beneath the rock. Now the men formed a line and began jabbing at the silt in earnest—if anything was to be found, it would be here, where the gold was piled up against the sediment. Sax was in the middle of the pack, as eager as the rest—it was only a swamp, after all. Karloff had been dead for twenty years. This very thought was in his mind when his own stick sank into something rather more rubbery than expected. There was a great frothing burst of gas from beneath the silt, and the monster rose up, screaming.

Alezh paid Prince Křesomysl one final visit. The prince did not know him; his soul had gone. He was unrecognizable now, so hideous in mind and body that even Alezh knew him not. Alezh did not tell his master of his intentions but left a cauldron filled with squirming toads and frogs and efts to occupy the prince's attention, and to serve as his last feast. Then Alezh went out of the buried mansion and ordered that the great wall be built across the cavern, and the stout door framed in the entrance. His men cut mighty stones and placed them there, and all the while the prince did not show himself, nor make any sound, so that they thought the banquet of wet creatures had been poisoned.

But it was not so. When the work was finished, Alezh went into the cavern to pay his last respects, for the mansion was now truly a crypt in which Prince Křesomysl must sleep forever, with no way out. He knelt before the ironbound door and wept, and it must have been that the prince heard his cries, for the door was suddenly burst apart, and so the men at last saw what their ruler had become. The prince fell upon his loyal Alezh and cruelly slew him, and the laborers drove the monster back into the crypt with their torches and sealed the entrance with a stone too large for any creature to breach, however monstrous.

Each man described what he had seen in his own way, but all of them agreed that the thing that had once been Prince Křesomysl was now a giant toad with human limbs, and that his white-fleshed mouth was so large it could bite off and swallow up the head of a man with one gulp—for indeed, that was what happened to Alezh.

Sax wet himself, but immediately fell backward into the swamp, so nobody noticed.

When he had still been researching the legend safely back at home, he had suspected there were grains of truth in the story of Prince Křesomysl—the treasure, for one thing. But the monster, for another. The beast in the story sounded very much like a description of the most debased form of vampire, those that lived in isolated places where their only food was low creatures whose form they would gradually take. So it was: this creature had obviously subsisted on frogs, fish, and other slimy things. For many centuries, if it was the prince himself, which Sax did not doubt.

Scholars of vampire anatomy with whom Sax had conferred said such a malnourished vampire was not very dangerous, as long as you kept out of its mouth; they generally lacked the reflexes of the canine or humanoid versions and were completely without intelligence. Only the latter part proved to be accurate. This thing had the strength of a bull. The men, stuck as they were in the sucking silt, couldn't flee, so instead they beat the apparition with their iron bars and broke branches across its back. It clawed and struck them, and knocked more than one man senseless, but they opened many wounds in the tissue-thin skin of its flanks.

Bobek took the opportunity to slosh his way back to the boats; Sax thought he was trying to escape, and found himself outraged at the cowardice of it. *Nobody* escaped, if it wasn't he himself. But Bobek returned with a bottle of vodka, stuffed his cloth cap in the neck of it, and set it alight. The flaming missile hit the monster squarely and exploded. It burst into flames. The warty skin bubbled and split, the huge yellow eyes rolled wildly and turned red. The monster bellowed like an avalanche, and then turned about and hurled itself down the waterway beneath the stone, the water hissing as it sank below the surface. The fire was extinguished, but not before they'd seen the thing churning away down the tunnel at tremendous speed.

As it wasn't possible to flee the swamp on foot, they had all retreated as far as the boats. Not that they'd offer much protection from Moby-Frog if it came back for more.

"Have we got blasting caps?" Sax asked as a couple of men picked him out of the mire and dumped him into the boat with the injured.

Bobek rummaged around and found a tin box with a skull and crossbones on it. "Here."

"I hate to risk destroying any treasure that's drifted this far," Sax muttered, "but I think we'd better seal this end off. It's going to head back to that underground bachelor pad and climb up through the well. We need to destroy the thing, then we can see about the valuables."

"We don't need to explode," Bobek said. "Make sticks sharp, put the points at the hole. If that thing tries to come out, it stabs itself."

"Very sensible," Sax said, because it was. This Bobek chap was all right. Four men stayed behind to perform these offices, cutting down dead limbs and sharpening the ends to long points of the type preferred for slaying vampires. Meanwhile the rest of the party, Sax not in the lead, scrambled up the rock at the margin of the swamp and began the hike overland through the darkness, back to the cavern.

III

They had sealed the entrance to the crypt behind them, which was only sensible, as their activity might have attracted attention. It only took one curiosity seeker to spoil the whole thing. Now the question was whether to open it and attack the vampire, or have done with it and leave the thing in there, perhaps delegating the destruction of the monster to the authorities. But in those days, in that part of the world, there *wasn't* an authority to deal with this: the Communists had forbidden the Church from any presence behind the Curtain, so there wasn't any infrastructure in place for such a mission. Anyway, Sax was in danger of losing his shirt on this one. The more entities that got involved, the less of the profits would go to him.

So he pretended to be in charge, and called for the men to get their shovels ready—a shovel was just an ax with the blade sideways—and be prepared to hack the thing if it came through. They were eager to comply, because their fear had turned to excitement—this was a hunt now. These men were on the cusp of a new society, the burden of Communism thrown off. They would be free to prosper. They sure as hell weren't going to let a giant, scorched frog stop them from getting a head start on the prospering bit.

Two of the biggest lads pried the slab of stone aside. The stench of roasted meat wafted out of the gap. Their prey was inside. They shone their lights in and saw no sign of the monster, but there wasn't much of a view down the narrow entry passage, so the bolder of them scrambled through the gap, armed with shovels and crowbars. Sax hadn't made any suggestions since he recommended they open the entrance. The rest was the men acting on their own initiative. Which suited Sax fine. He was less worried about the vampire than he was about how he was going to keep his own crew from killing him and taking all the treasure away. The men he trusted, the ones at the trucks, didn't expect to see him until morning anyway. By then, the vampire might be dispatched, and Sax along with it, both bodies chucked down the subterranean well.

He was fretting about this when the fountain of blood sprayed out of the entrance to the crypt.

There hadn't even been a cry of fear. One moment, the men were chattering excitedly, jockeying for a view into the tomb; the next, they were lurching back, blinded by jets of gore spewing through the gap. Then the slab itself shook, struck furiously by something behind it. It cracked, and the top half teetered. A second blow and the stone fell apart. The monster crawled through.

Had the men stood their ground as they had at the swamp, all might have ended sooner and better. As it was, the thing sprang out—its hind legs were phenomenally overdeveloped—and took two men down like wickets. It locked its jaws on one of them and took away fifteen pounds of meat, organs spilling from the crater, the man's cries of agony cut short because he was drowning in his own blood. Then the thing sprang again, caroming off the ceiling of the cave, and crushed a third man to the ground. They all heard his bones snap like wood. It was each man for himself, fleeing and stumbling up toward the mouth of the cave with the electric torches making more confusion than light, whirling around, catching glimpses of pandemonium.

The monster was a mass of roasted black flesh splitting apart to reveal white tissue beneath, all sauced liberally with blood, human and vampire. One of its eyes had burst, leaving behind a crater the size of a grapefruit, but the other saw only too well in the darkness.

Sax was escaping like the others when the monster picked him as a target.

It leapt at him, and he saw it coming and threw himself to the ground. It missed him but landed heavily six feet away. It opened shark-wide jaws—and its enormous tongue shot out. The thing was like a glistening white sledgehammer and moved far more swiftly than Sax could react. He twitched out of the path of the hideous organ, but it struck him high up on his thigh. There was another woody *crack* and a fireball of pain blasted through his body, as if someone had fired a rocket launcher at his balls. His leg wasn't merely broken; it was crushed.

The vampire's tongue retracted into its bulging throat like an eel into its burrow. The creature backed up, perhaps seeking a better shot at him. Sax found one of the lamps had been discarded beside him; in desperation he aimed its light at the monster, trying not to vomit from the pain as he kept it fixed in the beam. It might spoil the thing's aim.

"Kill it!" he cried, and struggled to remember the Czech phrase despite his scrambled mind. "*Zabít zvíře!*"

It was the light that saved them. The monster was nearly blinded as it was; the glare finished the job. He kept his torch on it no matter which way it dodged, and then more beams of light joined his, and a rock sailed out of the dark and struck the creature. Cornered, it snarled and raged but made no further attack. The men hurled stones at it, pry bars, anything they had. Then they rushed in with their shovels. It took over an hour, but the men were able to render the thing incapable of defense, smashing its bones, crushing its head; then they chopped it to bits. By dawn, the monster was completely destroyed.

When Sax's most trusted men came to see what was going on, two hours after the deadline of first light had passed, they found Sax and the other wounded lying in the grass outside the cave, having been tended to with what limited medical knowledge the group possessed. Sax, although delirious, knew the job wasn't finished. Before he passed out, he directed his team to gather the remains of the monster in buckets and bring them along.

The treasure they raised from the swamp was much older than the legend of Prince Křesomysl. It had been an ancient hoard even then, treasure of Celts and Romans. They found enough of it to fully justify the expense of the adventure, if not the cost in human life. Four men died, and Sax and two others were so badly injured they were despaired of for weeks. But they all recovered, and Sax walked with his cane for the first time, making it into an accessory his many admirers found impossibly sexy. In fact, the period of convalescence lost him a good deal of weight and added some character to his face, so he came out ahead in the looks department.

Archaeologists were still working the underground waterway as late as the turn of the century; the monster had been hiding his treasure in its nooks and fissures for half a millennium, and a great deal of it had washed into the swamp and been carried improbable distances by the currents there. Sax made no claim on anything other than what his crew was able to carry out before the police arrived, which amounted to almost six hundred pounds of gold. It was worth three hundred and eighty dollars per troy ounce at the time. And some of the pieces were of such extraordinary workmanship they commanded much higher prices than the standard valuations.

To sweeten the deal, the Vatican hadn't been able to make any claim on this treasure, thanks to godless Communism having shut down its local franchises. Enough of it made its way into museums that Sax never felt particularly guilty about what was, if he dared use the word, outright theft. Besides, he wouldn't ever have to work again, not for five lifetimes.

His retirement lasted five weeks. But he vowed he would never, ever have anything to do with vampires again, and that resolution lasted much longer.

Present Day

12

FRANCE

It had only been a few seconds since the team had turned to him, expecting to hear about his own exploits in vampire hunting. The memories had blazed through his mind in a sort of snapshot flash. He decided against mentioning the Czech vampire. Instead he drew a breath, held it long enough to study the glass of wine glittering in his uplifted fingers, then spoke.

"I could tell you of my adventures," Sax said. "You may have heard some of them. Brother Paolo has heard all of it; I'm the talk of the Holy See. However, suffice it to say I got into this business for the worst possible reasons, and out of it again from sheer, unalloyed cowardice. As is obvious from your presence at this table, I have returned once again to the unpleasant work. The reasons why are mine to know. There is wealth, I think, if we succeed. Great riches. There will be a certain amount of glory, as always when a coven is revealed and its constituent monsters slain. I don't care about any of that. I'm far too rich and old and repulsive."

There was a chuckle around the table at this, although Gheorghe started looking around at the furnishings as if to determine if he could lay his hands on any of the wealth without dealing with vampires. Sax continued, putting his glass on the table and staring at it as if to summon visions from its depths.

"I was telling Paolo a few days back that there would certainly be bloodshed, pain, tears, and death. This isn't some mindless creature huddled in a cave, looking out at a terrible modern world it cannot comprehend. This is a being of sophistication, means, and cunning. And it has human confederates. Anyway, this topic is somewhat more depressing than it needs to be. I'm here because this thing needs killing. After that, I expect to get paid."

The others nodded. Fair enough. Sax had stated his position, warned them of the dangers, and not made a fuss. If he awoke in the morning and there was nobody left but Paolo, the others having slunk away in the night, so be it.

With that, he told them the story of the auction, the murder of his night watchman and the theft of the ormolu clock, and of some of his subsequent research; he left out any unflattering details but gave them all enough information so he wouldn't have to explain himself later on when it might be inconvenient. There were no interruptions.

The evening wound down after another hour. To Sax's amazement, Rock insisted on washing the dishes. Sax offered him his apron, but Rock smiled that away. He did a proper job of it, his fingers agile although they were the size of carrots left in the ground too long. He hummed fragments of a tune Sax almost recognized. It might have been Coltrane's *A Love Supreme*.

Min tried to drag Nilu back up the hill. Nilu resisted, yanking her arm out of Min's grasp. Min scowled at her, then at Sax. The meaning of the look was clear. *Do something.*

"I have a suggestion," he said to Min. "I'll keep watch on our young friend here tonight. You get some rest. Deal?"

"No. She is where I see her."

"Look, Ms. Hee-Jin. I have been around, as should be obvious. I am experienced in these matters. You need rest. This young woman is not going to kill me in the night, because these rugged gentlemen will be all around. I can't use you in the course of my operation if you're not in peak condition. So go get some rest."

Without further comment, Min went out the back door and through the yard past the barn, and trod up the hill, her breath surrounding her head with plumes of vapor in the light of the new moon.

"Bed for me," Sax said. "You'd better come along," he added when Nilu sat back down at the table, hands folded in her lap. She looked terribly alone and hopeless. Paolo, Rock, and Gheorghe settled down in the living room area of the cottage to shoot more bull. They'd crawl off to their various beds when the excitement of the occasion wore off.

Sax felt crushingly weary. It came over him without warning. Something to do with Nilu. This poor girl dragged into a madhouse on the far side of the world, sick with a disease she didn't understand, feeling all the terrible things Sax remembered from when he was ill himself. She would live or die; there wasn't much Sax could do about that, except keep Min from killing her prematurely. He understood it was not within his power to influence that outcome. What he hated was knowing about it. This was something that intersected with his own life. He had breathed the same air as Nilu. He had admired the gleaming blackness of her hair and smelled the sour smell of her unwashed body. He couldn't help himself. He felt responsible.

Nilu followed Sax into the big house next to the cottage and up the creaking stairs. He drew a steaming bath in the *salle de bain* shared by the four bedrooms and switched on the heated towel rack because it also warmed the room nicely, and the night was chilly. During this process, Nilu sat on the side of the bed in the smallest bedroom, her skin sallow brown against the white quilted coverlet. She must have been intolerably cold in the night at that miserable desolate hospital, Sax thought. He didn't have clothes that would look any good on her, but he did have some things that might fit, up in the attic closet. It was the only room in the house with a working lock: when he rented the house in the summers, he didn't want silly children locking themselves in bedrooms. But the attic closet was to ensure his own personal effects didn't leave with the guests.

Nilu spoke perfectly good English, Sax had gradually determined. It was just that she didn't speak. So he explained she should get in the bath and have a good soak. He told her he had endured something like what happened to her, and how awful he felt for some time afterward. Nothing like a tub to make the aches and pains go away for a while.

"I have never had a bath before," Nilu said.

"Surely you've bathed," Sax replied, not knowing what this setback might mean. Sax hadn't been to India in thirty years, but he recalled they had hot and cold running water in those days.

"In a bathtub," Nilu said.

"Ah." Sax understood. Sluice baths and showers, but not bathtubs. He ran the water hot and deep, struggling to operate the supernumerary mock-Victorian taps. Although on his knees, he slipped and plunged his sleeve into the water. Nilu laughed. It was a quick, merry one. Sax got back to his feet, knees crackling like fireworks, and fixed her with his best *queen of the world* arched eyebrow. Nilu had one hand pressed over her mouth, but she was still smiling and her eyes glittered with mirth.

"You laugh, but I am made of sugar. I melt in water," Sax said, and exited the room.

Nilu demurely shut the door behind him, and a minute later Sax heard her sloshing about. He ascended the steep attic stairs, found the light switch after much groping of walls, located the key to the closet on top of the beam where he left it, and found the clothes he'd been thinking of.

Then he sat on the frail spindle chair outside the bathroom door, cradling his chin in his palm as if with toothache, trying to stay awake. He didn't want to leave Nilu in there unattended in case she fell asleep. Eventually he rapped on the door with his fingernails and then looked in. She had fallen asleep but hadn't drowned.

When she emerged, Nilu was wrapped in a white Turkish-towel robe of hotel caliber—in fact it came from a hotel, one of the small crimes with which Sax spiced his drearier moments while traveling. Standing there in the bulky robe with a sheet of wet hair spilled down her back and her bare brown feet on the tile floor, the girl looked vulnerable and beguiling.

Sax presented her with the clothes—a pink T-shirt with Moominpappa on it, faded overalls of the farmer type, a thick cotton roll-neck sweater, and a pair of frayed espadrilles with straw soles. It wasn't much of a look, but Nilu almost wept with gratitude.

"Thank you, Uncle," she said. Sax was well pleased. *Uncle* was an honorific in India. That she hadn't been alarmed when he looked in while she soaked was an honor as well. Up to a point. In India, men were forbidden from seeing an unmarried woman in *déshabillé*, especially in the intimate quarters of a bathroom. That was where Sax's particular category of man came in. In India, there was a caste of "third gender" people: homosexuals, eunuchs, transvestites, and all the rest of the glam-rock crowd. *Hijra* was the word, if Sax remembered correctly. *Hijras* enjoyed special privileges to go along with the abuse, beatings, fear, and rejection that occupied their days. One of these privileges was to be considered harmless around young women.

Then again, perhaps she just didn't give a damn. Once you were bitten by a vampire, rules of decorum seemed pretty trivial.

• • •

At some time between midnight and dawn, in that long, dark period when only the slow turning of the moon reminds one that the night will ever pass, Sax woke up. He hadn't been sleeping well in any case. The mattress was too soft, the moonlight getting in around the curtains, and besides, his mind was swarming with schemes and outcomes, and he was desperate to get moving—to get to that jail cell in Germany and speak with the hapless burglar. At last he sat up in bed and blinked weary eyes.

There was something in the room with him.

A shape. Dark against the dark wall, something there, human in outline but shrouded, a widow beneath the veil. Sax's flesh crawled. His heart thumped like it was rolling down a corrugated roof. The shape was alive, swaying ever so slightly, a shadow with a will of its own. Then it began to move. Sax's bedroom door was ajar, the crack between door and frame a thin black stripe on deepest gray. Someone had come into the room.

He'd been a fool, of course. The vampire knew he was in Europe. It would be searching for him. It might have found his farm in the countryside. Why not? Vampires did have their familiars, and they were always watching. Too late for precautions now.

Sax shifted his weight. His cane was propped up against the nightstand by his head. He might be able to deliver a painful blow to the dark shape that swayed toward him through the gloom. Club it, shout for help, and if Rock was a light sleeper, Sax might be able to fight off the ripping teeth long enough for help to arrive.

Then the shape stepped into a ribbon of moonlight. It was Nilu. Her face was wet with tears, the point of her chin puckered with suppressed grief. What Sax had taken for a black veil was simply her hair, fanned out across her shoulders like the Virgin Mary's wimple. She was clad in one of Sax's old Regency nightshirts from his Colin Firth period.

The girl crawled onto the bed next to Sax and shook with silent sobs, her back to him. He said nothing, but threw his side of the coverlet over her quaking body. He kept his hand at the base of her neck for a long while, a chaste sort of reassurance. Eventually she slept. Sax lay on his side of the bed, feeling the sheets grow cold, and did not sleep again.

By dawn, Nilu's health was failing.

In her sleep, she had begun to shiver, then broke into a sour, cold sweat. She twitched and writhed, murmuring in scraps of argument with imaginary interrogators. Sax saw by first light that her skin had gone from brown to greenish, the difference between "olive skin," as the phrase is understood, and the actual color olive. He rose without disturbing her further, dressed inattentively, and padded downstairs.

There he found Min asleep in one of the living room chairs facing the stairway, a cleaver across her knees. Her eyes opened the moment he put his weight on the top step. She watched the space behind him. When she didn't see Nilu, she rose to meet him. Min could have used a bath as well, Sax noticed. Her clothes were positively waxy. Her hair had separated into little flat spikes.

"She's very ill," Sax said. "I need you to take care of her until we get back." He hoped that giving Min nursing duties would help keep her from killing Nilu instead.

"She was in your room," Min said.

"Yes, and she didn't bite me," Sax said. "Don't let her die."

"Where are you going?" Min gnawed the side of her thumb, scowling up at Sax. She looked taller than she really was, probably because she gave off such ferocious vibrations. Sax saw her knuckles were pale with scar tissue, presumably from punching anvils or whatever it was martial artists did instead of developing meaningful relationships. Sax observed her and considered his answer.

"Germany," he said at last. "Not far. Paolo and myself. We shall return this evening, late. I can't tell you more than that, but I will once we get back."

Min nodded and returned to her chair and closed her eyes. Sax put the kettle on, judged it was too early to make phone calls, and went to wake up Paolo instead. Despite his checking on Nilu, getting Paolo moving around, making tea, and looking at e-mail on the tiny smartphone Sax had never properly mastered, it was still too early when he started making his calls. The sky was washed pink and yellow over slate. The horizon glimmered white, turning the trees along the hills into inky ciphers.

Abingdon answered the phone on the fifth ring, his voice muddy with sleep.

"Oozat?" He coughed into the phone.

"Asmodeus Saxon-Tang," Sax said, and waited. There was a long pause.

"Fuck me, mate, what dost this fucking ringaling portend?" Abingdon was delighted. Sax could hear it in his voice, genuine pleasure. Gratifying, of course, especially at 6:53 in the morning. There was a muffled female voice in the background on Abingdon's end of the line. Abingdon said something back that Sax couldn't make out, and then his attention was back on Sax.

"Abingdon," Sax began, as if to remind his listener who he was. "Still bucketing about on horses, shoving bits of wood at your enemies, and so forth?"

"Living fucking history, that is, princess." Abingdon was a rugged, active man. A professional jouster and blacksmith, he worked the circuit of European history–themed events. Sax had seen him in action, clad in jingling hauberk and plate and a great heavy helmet on the back of a big, wild-eyed horse, charging down the muddy tilt. He could handle a twelve-foot lance like it was a pencil. Biceps like pumpkins. He didn't just shatter lances and hack his way through exhibition swordsmanship, either: when he wasn't in the arena, he was making iron candlesticks and swords and flails in his portable forge. Tourists loved it. Steel weapons for the gents, huge sweating muscles in a leather apron for the ladies.

Abingdon and Sax had met some years earlier when Sax needed someone who could replicate metal alloys no longer manufactured in the modern world. Abingdon, in addition to being a drunken, sword-swinging medieval womanizer, was also in possession of a doctorate in archaeometallurgy. He could duplicate, in somewhat safer conditions than the original artisans, authentic mercury-vapor ormolu. He could craft wrought iron, rich in manganese, to precisely duplicate late-Roman artifacts, or make ingots of the strange metals developed quite by chance while alchemists pursued their dream of turning base metals into gold. Sax called him every couple of years to repair or duplicate some damaged piece that would otherwise have little place in the world, for all its antiquity.

"The thing is, I wonder if you're free the next week or so?" Sax said.

"I'm on the job, mate," Abingdon whispered into the phone. "Got a bird here."

"You can't shag all week, though, can you?" Even as Sax said it he knew it was a stupid statement. *Of course* Abingdon could shag all week.

"Been reading my diary, me old ginger beer. Right," Abingdon said, resigning himself. "Your stuff's always interesting. I could use a few quid, it being the off-season for the old pleasure fairs, and my tackle could likely use a drying out. What, pray tell, 'ave you fucking got?"

Sax got off the phone grinning. He liked Abingdon. A hale fellow such as they didn't often make anymore. He would have been a rock star, back in the day. Gotten into fistfights with Roger Daltrey and run fancy automobiles into hotel swimming pools. He did pretty well regardless. Abingdon was probably the only metallurgist with groupies.

Sax handed the phone to Paolo, who was still groggy.

"Ring up your chaps back in Rome and tell them we need access to this prisoner in Germany. Tell them it's a matter of his immortal soul or whatever you need to do. No later than three this afternoon."

Paolo dialed the number. "*Ciao*, Fabrizio . . . ," he began.

Sax went out to check that the barn was arranged for Abingdon's arrival.

The weather remained overcast and grim across all of northern Europe. It was getting chillier each day. Paolo steered the rental car through a colorless landscape from the farmhouse to the private airfield at Lemberg; the plane Paolo had chartered for them was waiting on the tarmac. It would have been a six-hour drive to their destination, and the flight took less than two, so it was well worth the Vatican's money, in Sax's opinion. He disliked small aircraft and wore earplugs to reduce the din of the engine.

The Cessna made its way across the tip of the Vosges Mountains, then over the Rhine Valley and through rough air above the Odenwald range. Then they descended, Sax feeling bilious with airsickness, along the top of the Ore Mountains to an airstrip outside Chemnitz, Germany. Sax had forgotten just how lumpy Germany could be, a mass of mountains and valleys in the southern half. It was only the north that was flat, those vast plains draining into the North Sea.

They hired a taxi to take them to the *Stadtgefängnis*. The taxi driver beguiled his passengers for the entire trip, complaining that

Mercedes's quality had gone down so much he was now driving Opel cars exclusively. Paolo seemed interested in the conversation and the two Europeans discussed cars until they reached the street that ran along the frontage of the prison. Then the driver became serious, all but doffing his cap. He might even have done so if he had been wearing one. A man in the habiliments of a priest arriving at the gates of a prison spoke of bad luck for someone on the inside.

There was a delay of almost an hour inside the facility, which had the crisp, prefabricated ambiance of a modern airport, only with fewer windows. Guards in severe uniforms marched in and out of the waiting area armed with paperwork to be filled out in triplicate. Phone calls were made. Superiors summoned. Throughout all this, a man in urban camouflage sat at a desk and ignored Sax and Paolo with a display of total indifference that must have been agony to keep up. An Italian priest and a mid-Atlantic *schwuler*: Was this evidence of the new liberality of the Church, or could this be a *gleichgeschlechtliche Partnerschaft*?

A guard in black trousers and white shirt emerged from the secure part of the building and, having checked their identification, ushered Sax and Paolo within.

They walked down noisy, echoing corridors with bright light and not a single fleck of dirt or chipped paint or any other evidence of use; they passed through an armored door, then a slightly less sterile corridor, and finally entered the place of imprisonment. Here the cell blocks looked far more like those everywhere else in the world: built to withstand constant abuse, and constantly abused. The acoustics were terrible.

The guard led them along a passageway with a clear acrylic partition that divided it from the cell blocks, on two levels, to the left; on the right was a wall of concrete block with slit windows high up near the ceiling. At the end of the passage was a further heavy door, but this one stood open, and another guard sat on a folding chair on the threshold. This one stood up and took over escorting duties, while the first guard returned the way they had come.

Beyond the door were six cells. Two of these cells were occupied. The guard led his charges to the one on the right, opened a small grille set into the porthole in the door, clicked his heels, and returned to his folding chair.

"Right," said Sax. "You speak better German than me, Paolo, so you do the talking." There was a terrible stink coming through the window from the cell. It smelled like human dung. Inside the cell was a man wearing hospital-style scrubs. His red face was a mindless blank, eyes bulging and yellowish with bright blue centers. His pupils were constricted to pinpoints. This was Jakob Bächtold.

Paolo spoke to the inmate. It took some time to get the man's attention, as he was studying the surface of the cell wall, tracing imaginary routes with a fingertip along the seams of the concrete. Sometimes he would look around the room, wonderingly, like an infant. His mouth was constantly working, chewing on unintelligible words.

Eventually Bächtold turned to the cell door and, seeing Paolo in the window, lunged forward. Paolo involuntarily jerked backward. The guard stood up. Sax shook his head: *it's all fine*. Bächtold's breath huffed through the porthole; it stank of ulcerated teeth. He pressed his face to the wire.

Paolo translated Sax's questions into German. Who hired him to steal the candelabra? Where was he to bring it? Why were the other things found but not the candelabra? Again, who hired him to steal the candelabra? Why? The same questions, over and over, all with the same result: vacant mumbling.

Paolo was starting to sweat. He did not like being so close to the eye-rolling imbecile on the other side of the door. Bächtold was gazing around at invisible flies. *Just like Renfield*, Sax thought. This gave Sax an idea.

"You're going to ask him some different questions," Sax said quietly, twisting his eyes toward the guard to indicate Paolo should be discreet. "This may get a reaction. Keep with it if it does."

"As long as we can get away from here," Paolo said.

"I thought you Christian-charity types loved going to these sorts of places," Sax said.

"I get claustrophobia," Paolo said. He made the admission sound like a confession.

"Ask him this. Ask him what the vampire did."

Sax heard Paolo's Italian-accented German clunking along for a few words, then the word *vampir*, and in the next instant, Bächtold went berserk.

He screamed, gobbets of saliva spraying through the window. *"Blutsauger kommen für mich!"* Then he leapt into the air and began hurling himself around the cell, clawing at the walls. Amid his high-pitched shouting Sax caught a few words he recognized, *stein* being one of them, but most of it was such a cacophony it was all he could do not to run away. The guard rushed to the cell, pressed a button on a small electronic box on his belt, and flung the cell door open. Seconds later, he was joined by four more guards, two of whom grabbed Sax and Paolo. The rest rushed into the cell and the shrieking, struggling Bächtold went down beneath them, flailing with such mad strength the guards had to beat him into submission. Then the scene was out of view to Sax, and he was trotting down the hall after Paolo with hard guardsman's fingers dug into his shoulder. Two minutes later, they were back in the waiting area, panting with fear and exertion.

Blutsauger kommen für mich! Bächtold had cried. Sax knew what that meant, more or less.

The bloodsucker is coming for me.

Once out on the street again, following a reprimand from a senior administrator of the prison with no neck, Sax's hands began to tremble uncontrollably. Paolo sucked in deep drafts of cold air, letting them out in white plumes that drifted halfway down the block before they faded from sight.

"Quickly," Sax said. "Before you forget. What was he saying?"

"The warden? He's very upset with us disturbing his prisoners. He says a man of the cloth—"

"Yes yes yes. No. The madman, Bächtold."

"Oh," Paolo said, and for a terrifying moment his face went Bächtold-blank and Sax thought he actually had forgotten. But Paolo was only organizing his jumbled thoughts.

"He said the blood drinker was coming to get him—" Paolo began.

"I got that bit. Then he said something about *stein*?"

"Ah. That's 'stone' in German," Paolo said. "He said, 'She will come down from the stone of murder.' She is the master or mistress, and he is the slave, and she will come down for him from the stone of murder and suck his blood."

"And?" Sax said when Paolo failed to continue.

"I don't know! I was very frightened when he started to shout. I am the weakest servant of God, an unworthy man only," Paolo added. Then, to Sax's astonishment, Paolo dashed a tear from his eye with the sleeve of his black jacket.

"You're a berk and an idiot," Sax seethed. "A cretin. He did all that shouting and you can't remember it? What a balls-up. This is what comes of trusting a priest."

"I am not really a priest."

"Worse yet. Let us proceed to plan B, because you are certainly a fool."

Plan B was a terrible waste of time and wasn't much of a plan at all. Sax wished to go through with it primarily because it was a way of punishing Paolo, which wasn't really anything to do with Paolo but rather was a way for Sax to channel his own frustration that the magic bullet had turned out to be a squib.

They found with difficulty a place to rent yet another car, put it on the Vatican tab, and left Chemnitz approximately four hours after they'd arrived. The city was one of those places that had been bombed unrelentingly during the war, and consequently the entire core of the town was overtaken by slabs of dull concrete architecture, steel-and-glass office boxes, and all the aesthetic ills to which East German territory had been heir, relieved by outlying neighborhoods of red-roofed or slated structures from a time before explosives could be dropped from the sky. The landscape was bitter, leafless, and sere with frost, but attractive in its forms. There were low, wooded hills and distant gray pastures and a broad, flat river not yet frozen.

Sax was not setting out entirely blind. He had in the calfskin notebook his lists, his cross-references and provenances, and scattered points of information. He had a sheaf of documents from Eric at the Louvre. The details of the Interpol bulletin were useful as well. He started with that.

Aided by a petrol map from the nearest filling station and the GPS unit mounted on the dashboard, which Paolo could not operate but, for reasons mysterious to himself, Sax could, they found the site of the robbery—a local Great House that had been turned into a museum for tax purposes. They didn't go inside. It was just a place to begin, a way to make physical the origin of the crime.

The house stood by a tributary of the larger river in a flat piece of ground. The property had a brick gated entrance but no wall; the gate was just a bit of pomp. The house itself was a pastiche of medieval styles, all lead-framed windows and rustic plaster, the sort of thing rich people whipped up in the nineteenth century to give themselves airs.

"The break-in occurred there, on the water side," Sax said, reading from the bulletin. "Now, we know something else, which is that the criminal, that chap we just visited, got caught in . . . ah, damn, I've lost my place. Hang on . . . in Schönbrunn. So that's our next destination, if it's not too far away. I should have done this before—but I was so certain we'd get something from Bächtold."

Sax phoned back to the farm in Petit-Grünenwald. Rock answered. Sax explained that their mission had come up against a minor obstacle and they might be detained in Germany a day or two; meanwhile, please stand by. He explained who Abingdon the metallurgist was and what to expect when the man arrived.

"You'll have a great deal to discuss, I'm sure," Sax concluded. "Abingdon is also a warrior, although his specialty is combat prior to the year 1600. Is Nilu still alive?"

"She's hanging in there but she doesn't look real good. I was talking about the hospital, but Mad Min says no way."

Sax made a low noise in the back of his throat. "She's right. Hospitals don't know anything about what she's got. They'd kill her without fail."

"Didn't Paolo say there's a Catholic hospice where they can treat her?"

"If you try to take Nilu there, Min will kill her. Trust me on that," Sax said, and with a few further words of instruction, ended the call. He knew Min's type. All vampires must die, and also all people connected to vampires—even their infected victims, who could themselves become dangerous.

Sax settled in for the drive, Paolo conscientiously piloting the car along at precisely the speed limit, to the irritation of the German motorists who kept passing them flat out. It was approximately forty kilometers to their destination. They could make that, even at Paolo's pace, in less than an hour. Which would give Sax that long to figure out what they should do next. He hadn't a clue.

They'd been driving for twenty minutes when, with a great rush of noise, Sax's left ear finally popped, the pressure equalizing with the sound of a huge, wet kiss. He'd been more than half deaf in that ear since the small Cessna got to cruising altitude. As if his ear was the key to all Sax's discomforts, the faint queasiness that had also dogged him vanished, his mood improved, and he became hungry. They stopped at the nearest *Mittag-Haus* for lunch, and Sax once again encouraged Paolo to gluttony, this time with *Sauerbraten mit Spätzle*.

They emerged into the wan afternoon sunlight. At that time of year in Germany the sun never properly got started, ascending only halfway into the sky at midday before beginning its long, slow decline into night. It was cold and the wind was picking up, blustering in from the northeast. Sax took a look at the wire stand laden with touristic brochures set up outside the restaurant door; antique shops often advertised in this way, and thus he could see what sort of rubbish the lesser merchants were peddling. He studied the brochures—and then all the remaining hair on his head stood straight up.

"Paolo," Sax said, snatching up one of the pamphlets.

"*Sì, signore*," Paolo said, his voice strained by the freight of food in his stomach.

"What did Bächtold say about a 'stone of murder'? Was that *exactly* what he said?" Sax had his auction face on, betraying no special interest in the colorful accordion-folded slip of paper before him.

"Ah, he said," Paolo said, struggling to recall despite the influx of calories fuddling his brain, "that 'she will come down from the stone of murder.' Like that."

"Did he by any chance," Sax said, speaking with great care, "use the exact word *Mordstein*?"

"Yes. *Yes*. That is precisely what he said," Paolo replied, brightening. Sax thrust the brochure into Paolo's hands.

"Only Mordstein isn't a stone," Sax said. "It's a castle."

• • •

They drove straight to the castle Mordstein, not a long journey. Sax was nearly hysterical with excitement and kept demanding Paolo go faster, pointing out each time they were passed by another vehicle the relative age and infirmity of the driver. Paolo was patient.

Sax eventually burned himself out and slouched in silence, glaring at the brochure that listed the scenic castles of Lower Saxony. The thing that struck Sax as most bizarre was that Mordstein had a visitor's center. If that were true, it would be the first vampire's lair ever to feature a gift shop.

He speculated that Mordstein was only the drop-off point for the stolen goods, and Herr Bächtold had had his simple mind destroyed there in the parking area by vampiric telepathy, such as he had himself experienced when he encountered Madame Magnat-l'Étrange. In that case, Mordstein itself would be another dead end. The monster could have been anywhere at all, certainly nearby, but thoroughly concealed. There were a thousand noble houses and castles and caves and secret places all through this region. Mordstein wasn't suitable. Vampires didn't hide in plain sight. It wouldn't work.

But it *would* work.

The entrance to the property was off a secondary road; there was a gray stone wall that split the landscape and vehicles entered through a quaint medieval gatehouse with turrets and drawbridge. Looming up above them across leather-colored fields was a range of jagged black-forested hills amongst which a black river snarled. The road wound through fallow ground, then entered the eternal shade of the trees and made its pilgrimage by serpentine ways amongst the ruins of what had once been a village, the structures collapsed and mossy, nothing left but green stone.

Then above the hills came glimpses of their destination. It was something from Grimm, a place of lost children and talking wolves.

There above the spines of the trees loomed a crag of stone that jutted up like a monstrous black jawbone crowded with rotten teeth. It was clad to the shoulders in a carapace of shaggy black evergreens with the look of gallows crows clutching a tombstone, but the final eminence, rising up at a sickening height above the forest, was a riven claw of stone atop which hunched Schloss Mordstein.

The castle sprang from the brow of the cliff in spires of black slate and frost-colored stone, the bulk of its carcass a single square keep, narrow and tall. Bristling from this vertiginous finger of masonry were turrets, and pressed close around it were battlements thrown up to expand its size and defensive capabilities over a thousand years of warfare, until the entire summit of the mount was covered in fortifications like mussels clinging to an icy rock. Even the cliffs were pressed into service, scored with hewn steps that tottered down sickening steeps to lesser structures, slate-roofed blocks that pressed their bellies to the precipice and hung above empty, wind-screaming space.

"It looks," Sax said, when they left the car for the "photo op" spot marked by a signboard, "like the place all the gargoyles in Europe came from. They flew out of those slit windows and spread out and perched in the night on all the high places, and when the sun came up, they turned to stone."

"Shut up," Paolo said.

Sax shot a look at his companion to see if he was joking. He was not. Paolo understood the gravity of the situation. If the vampire was up there on that spur of rock in the sky, they would need an air force to invade it and an army to occupy it. What they had was a soldier, a burglar, a psychopath, and a false priest. Sax didn't even enter into the equation, or rather, he certainly didn't plan on doing so. Nilu might make a good excuse: he could claim he needed to keep an eye on her while everyone else scampered around up above doing aerialist tricks against the icy blowing sky.

• • •

When they reached the castle, there were a few dutiful Germans wandering around looking at things, but it was not a peak day for tourism in general, being freezing cold with a wind that worked its numbing fingers around one's neck.

The tourist destination was not the castle itself, the tower on the crag, but rather the later, more fairy-tale-looking revetments that had been built at the foot of the cliff several hundred years after the original fortification was complete. This knightly retreat, in addition to the fortifications that secured the lower slopes, had a fine manor at its center with elegant windows, decorative chimneys, and plastered towers with oxblood-colored half-timbering to offset the severity of its walls of stone. It was charming yet imposing. It looked, Sax thought, like an excellent spot for one of Jean-Marc's luxury hotel projects, if he had still been around.

This lower portion of the Castle Mordstein was where visitors came. There was no hotel, but a restaurant, a shop for souvenirs and books, and an interpretive center had all been fitted into the manor house's ground floor. As noted on quaintly lettered notice boards in the gift shop, to the fortress on the crag, the *große Schloss*, there was no access. It was strictly *Privatgrundstück*. Not that many would care to visit. From the foot of the cliff it rose up so steeply and high that it appeared, through an optical illusion akin to that seen at the base of skyscrapers, as if the lofty towers were perpetually toppling over onto the lower part of the castle, or *Unterschloss*, and the viewer would soon be crushed beneath tons of brutal rubble.

Paolo took many pictures with his phone. Then, while Sax browsed the gift shop and purchased everything he could find that contained information about Castle Mordstein, Paolo wandered away from the prescribed paths and got a sense of the off-limits portions of the castle.

As he later reported to Sax, he found a gravel road for employees to enter from the back by the river, and a footpath that twisted its way up the forested slope that appeared as if it would eventually connect with the ridge from which the crag rose. Each way was heavily signposted with warnings to turn back: *Betreten für Unbefugte verboten* and all the rest of it.

The lower slopes were steep but not impassable. Some distance down the gravel road there was a fork and a second road turned off beneath the trees, but where it went, Paolo didn't know. There was an enormous signpost at the fork that read *VERBOTEN* with skull and crossbones and a drawing of large rocks falling on a stick figure.

On his way back to the parking lot, he had been discovered by a man in blue coveralls pushing a barrow; the man told Paolo he had gone to the wrong place, go back. Paolo mimed having to urinate, and shrugged and kept on walking. The man in coveralls didn't pursue the matter. Security, it seemed, was informal, driven less by secrecy than insurance liabilities. For his part, Sax was impressed when he heard of Paolo's improvised dishonesty. It gave him hope for the monk.

As Paolo was rejoining Sax in the parking lot, he had seen a very handsome red-haired woman staring at him from atop one of the fortification walls. She wore a down parka with her hair flaming out of the hood and her eyes were definitely upon him. It was no wonder laymen were always getting in trouble, Paolo admitted—the world was a teeming sea of attractive women with bold eyes.

They drove over the last little hill before the French farmhouse. The car's wheels rumbled on a cow grate and woke Sax, who had dozed off again; he blinked and looked around him at the darkness and said, "Back already?" and propped his cane between his knees. Home at last. One of his homes, anyway.

It had been, by Sax's standards, an extremely busy day. The return trip from Castle Mordstein had been unremarkable, but it was a great deal of traveling, and the plane back to France had been buffeted with stomach-churning turbulence. Paolo turned the nose of the car into the farmyard, which was outlined by hedges and a low wall of rubble. The headlights swept over these details and just as quickly forgot them, and then they were pulling up in front of the barn. There was much activity there. Light shone through all the gaps in the walls, and the doors, partway open, embraced a glare of bright, hot color.

"Our metalsmith is here, I suspect," Sax said, and made a noise of satisfaction in the back of his throat. He thanked Paolo for driving, by which he meant, *Thank you for putting up with a crotchety old man all day*, but which he couldn't possibly say as it would diminish his carefully cultivated image as a crotchety old man. Then he got out of the car with his cane in one hand and his sack of guidebooks in the other, and hobbled toward the barn.

As he approached the barn, Sax heard the bellowing *whoosh* of the portable forge Abingdon took with him to all the festivals, clanging steel, and laughter. He smelled hot iron and the stink of bituminous coal smoke. For a grand moment he felt like the general at the head of an army, about to set off on a campaign that would be written in history books. Then a human outline appeared in the doorway of the barn, a woman's silhouette, and she emerged from the hot brightness into the cold blue moonlight and Sax's bubble of good spirits burst and disappeared.

13

FRANCE

Paolo's eyes fairly sprang from his head. The most beautiful woman he had ever seen in his life had just stepped from within the barn doorway and put her slender arms around the old man's neck.

"Hello, Uncle Sax," she said, and smiled.

Emily had arrived at the farm that morning, just before noon, at the same time that Sax and Paolo were touching down on the airstrip outside Chemnitz five hundred kilometers to the northeast. She had with her an old-fashioned and impractical box suitcase of canvas and leather that Sax had given her for her tenth birthday, as well as a proper Cordura nylon roll-aboard thing without any charm. She was dressed in navy wool peacoat, roll-cuffed jeans, and paddock boots, her hair an explosion of black curls held behind her ears with a red cotton paisley-printed headband. When she opened the door and called into the *maison de maître* to see if anyone was in, Emily was startled by the sudden appearance of a short Japanese-looking woman only partially concealing a big carving knife against her side.

"Who are you?" Min asked in her toneless suspicious voice.

"I'm Saxon's niece," Emily said, using the semiformal version of Uncle Sax's name because it sounded more important.

Then Rock emerged from the back of the house, where he and Gheorghe had been watching *le foot* on television. He took one look at Emily, still in the doorway blocked by the small but feral Min, and did a double take.

Emily caught the reaction. A lifetime as a biracial woman had taught her that most people automatically put her in whatever category suited their prejudices—she was high yellow to ill-disposed black people and an octoroon to ill-disposed whites. But Rock smoothly offered to take Emily's suitcase, apologized for his inability to speak French, asked her if she knew any Arabic, and when she replied she was American, he asked her if she'd like a cup of coffee, because he had made some.

So far, so good. Then Gheorghe had emerged from the back of the house in socks and T-shirt. He saluted Emily with the beer in his hand.

"I'm Emily Saxon," Emily said, introducing herself to everyone at once. "I'm Sax's niece from New York."

"So he is not the only surprise in Saxon family," Gheorghe said.

Rock shook his head. Emily ignored the remark and squinched up her eyes, unsure how to pose the question uppermost in her mind. "Are you— Look, this is going to sound stupid, but are you—the vampire-hunting team?"

A couple of hours later, right around the time Paolo was translating Sax's question that would drive Herr Bächtold to scream and claw at the walls of his cell, Abingdon arrived in his converted bread truck with gaudy paintings of hammer and anvil on one side and a knight *à cheval* on the other. In this vehicle he traveled the festival circuit; kept his forge, tools, and armor safe; and often as not, slept in the back. Or didn't sleep, but reclined, indoctrinating a fair disciple into the mysteries of the metallurgist's hammer, as he put it. Abingdon was composed of lean, raw muscle, his fair skin always chapped with wind, sea, sun, or sheer diabolical heat from the forge. His shaggy red-blond hair looked like flames. There was an impressive white scar across his forehead from side to side where the edge of a shield had struck him during a melee before a cheering crowd. His heavy-lidded eyes and easy smile got him into endless trouble, and he didn't want it to end.

Abingdon instantly made friends with Rock; Gheorghe didn't altogether trust him—or anyone—but he knew a fellow rogue when he saw one. The difference between Abingdon and a clever grifter was primarily his doctorate, and he didn't hang the diploma in the back of the old bread truck. Still, they had something in common, as Gheorghe often went on the continental circuit himself, to fairs and festivals, performing as part of a troupe of jugglers and acrobats. He was a skilled but indifferent performer, being more interested in what opportunities for larceny were available in whatever town hosted the event.

It became evident within an hour or two that Abingdon had his own sort of criminal career, but it only involved women. Picking the locks to their undergarments, stealing within, and escaping with their hearts was his modus operandi. He tried it with Min first, as she helped Abingdon and Rock unload the bread truck, transporting his gear into the barn. She was invulnerable to masculine wiles, having buried her need for intimacy alongside her family.

Emily was next. She flirted with him while he assembled his portable forge, but she, too, was inaccessible. She found him very attractive, but must, with New York caution, have known the difference between very attractive and too attractive, and Abingdon was right on the line. She preferred the clumsy but sincere passes she got from her economist colleagues.

As it was, there was a great deal of banter, some coarse double entendres, a lot of lifting and hauling, and by late afternoon they were out of beer and there was a fully operational blacksmith's shop in the middle of the barn. The forge was designed to vent without sparks, but one never knew; Abingdon would have preferred to set the thing up outdoors, but the weather didn't look very promising, and if he burned the barn down, it was only Sax, after all. He'd be forgiven. What Abingdon really wanted to know was if Sax would forgive him for slipping his gorgeous young niece the Abingdon Knob.

Once the forge was arranged, he brought out his metals: sheets, bars, and rods, as well as glass jars full of powders and shavings that glittered in many colors. He had a safe bolted into the floor of the bread truck containing gold and silver as well.

"Fucking alchemist, me," he explained to Min, and winked, and she thought there must be something in his eye. He had his attention back on Min now because she was attractive in an ugly-sexy kind of way and because Emily had gone into the *maison* to see about the mysterious Indian woman lying in bed with a fever.

Once Emily set eyes on Nilu, she didn't leave her side again for hours, until the sun was long down and Nilu seemed to fall into a somewhat more restful sleep than the eye-rolling, thrashing state in which she had spent most of her day. Emily had initially asked Min what was the matter with Nilu; Min said, "Vampire bite," and left the room.

At that moment, Emily's trip to see what her mad uncle was doing had lost its whimsical flavor. For the first time, the truth of the matter hit her, almost a physical blow. Here was a *real* victim.

Her original concern had been for Uncle Sax's soundness of mind. She was genuinely concerned. He'd told her the story of the vampire-slaying hammers with such conviction. It was obvious he thought it all to be true. But it couldn't be. It was preposterous. She'd almost believed him for a while that afternoon. He was a persuasive man. But the hard light of day soon put her to rights. Vampires didn't exist.

Then she noticed he was scuttling off to unnamed appointments when they were scheduled to have tea together. She'd visited his flat and found a notebook lying open on the coffee table he hated; she caught a glimpse of timetables and flight information intermixed with phrases like *VAMPIRE ALLOY* and *Mercenary? Bring weapons.* He'd seen her looking at it and tossed a volume of Tom Poulton drawings on top of the notebook to conceal it. *She* might not have believed his story, but it was clear her uncle did. And it looked very much as if he intended to do something about it.

Then he'd announced he was going to his place in Alsace-Lorraine for a few weeks, don't wait up for him. Typically he'd have told her all about his plans as he was making them. This time he'd hidden them from her. Something was very much up, and she suspected it was senile dementia. Why not drop in and make sure he wasn't wandering around in his bathrobe eating soap? It couldn't hurt. Emily had always sworn to herself she'd take care of him. Nobody else was as close to him as she was. He could afford the best old-age care, but there should be somebody to see it was done properly, and that he was allowed to keep his dignity as a human being. Maybe it was time to begin that care.

So she booked herself a flight to France and discovered her uncle had indeed assembled a band of colorful misfits for whatever quixotic adventure he had in mind. But he himself was nowhere to be found. She had passed an entertaining hour or two amongst them before any-one mentioned there was a sick woman in the house. They seemed rather matter-of-fact about it. Mercenary, in a word. Like it had said in Sax's notebook. She thought she'd better go have a look. Even as she entered the bedroom in which Nilu suffered, she had still believed it must be a hangover or the flu.

Then she realized the girl was near death. She could *feel* it—something uncanny in the room, like possession, like ghosts. The vampire thesis abruptly gained a deal more credibility than it had enjoyed before.

She sat on the edge of the bed and took Nilu's cold, wet hand. The air left Emily's body. She had to tell herself to breathe. There were no marks on the sick girl's neck, no double punctures of mortician's wax with artful droplets of blood running from them as in the glorious old vampire films Emily had watched on cable when she was small (not at Uncle Sax's place, though, because he possessed no television).

But did vampires really bite people on the neck? Did they fear garlic, or crucifixes? Suddenly the vague pop-cultural creature with a red-lined cape and swallowtail coat became absurd. She had come here not expecting there would be anything real about it. Even meeting the team, she had thought it must be one of those strange experimental theater happenings that had been popular in the early 1970s when drugs were no longer enough and people required scenery and role-playing before they could get off. She should have known better. After all her smug self-satisfaction that she alone understood her uncle best, she had, in this time when he was most serious, most earnest in his entreaties, failed to take him at his word. He would be terribly hurt by that. He would know. Her mere presence, after all his dire warnings, would be enough. *Even you*, he would think when he saw her: *even you*.

Emily stayed there by the bed and thought things over. It began to seem more plausible. Rock brought her tea at intervals during her afternoon vigil; she expressed some of these thoughts to him, although not her concerns about Sax's feelings being hurt. Nobody would believe it was possible to do.

"Yeah, vampires," Rock replied when she asked if it was true. He spoke more quietly than usual, sitting on a petite chair beside the bed. Both of them were looking at Nilu. "I saw my first one in that border fight with Iran nobody wants to talk about. We blew up this old ruin and there were tunnels under it. I went down in there with a team of three. The other cats bought it one by one, and there was no way to figure out what was killing us. It was like a shadow came to life. Backup couldn't get to me by the time I was alone, because we didn't have radios, because we were never there, you understand."

Emily shook her head. "Am I living in a world full of people who know vampires are real, and somehow I just missed it? This is hard for me to—"

"I think about half the people on earth who have ever seen one and lived to tell about it are right here on this farm. You're in rare company."

"So why are you alive?" Emily said, bidding him finish his story.

"Well, I'm down the hole alone with this thing, right? So I said to myself, 'If you don't live, nobody's going to know what killed you.' And for some reason, that bothered me a lot. I guess I was just feeling sensitive that day. So I decided to keep a grenade in my hand with the pin out, and if the thing got me, obviously I'd let go of the grenade and we'd both go to hell together.

"When the thing finally showed itself, it was in this underground room with a well in the floor. It came after me and it was like—I mean, I pride myself on a certain level of physical fitness. But this thing picked me up like it was my grammy when I was three years old. But it didn't look like my grammy much. I don't know if you know about vampires. I guess not. Did you know they take the shape of their prey? Happens real slowly. Couple hundred years, they start looking like what they eat. For a long damn time, this one had been living on spiders."

Rock stopped speaking and stared down at Nilu. He was rubbing his forearms as if it was chilly in the room, shaking his head.

"But you survived," Emily prompted.

"It was about to put the bite on me with this—I guess it was its mouth—so I stuck the grenade in there and when it let go of me I shoved it down the well. That worked pretty good. I quit the soldier business as soon after that as I could, and decided to take up gardening or something, but here I am. You get bit by vampires more ways than one. It's like there's something crawling under your skin, you know? You got to dig it out."

Emily had no idea what to say to any of this. It was insane, like learning magic was real. But then, what was electricity? What was gravity? Just magic with a name. She sought for something to say but only nodded.

Rock left the room, his mood now subdued by memories. Emily's thoughts returned to her uncle Sax.

She had only one defense against the hurt she knew he would feel. In her suitcase, as a kind of rabbit's foot to bring luck—or so she viewed it at the time—she had brought along Simon, the vampire hammer. It was her ticket to the show. That might be something to mollify Uncle Sax. At least it showed she was listening, if not altogether believing. But the people she found herself amongst were the real thing. Vampire hunters. She hadn't entirely believed it when they were assembling the forge down in the barn, but she did now. They all seemed indifferent, that's what it was. That was the thing that made her a convert. None of these people were acting phony-tough or talking up the strange nature of their mission—they were just doing what needed to be done, as if it was painting a fence or planning a ski trip.

Emily's head whirled. She hadn't realized until this moment just how much she *hadn't* believed her uncle was really on a vampire-hunting mission. That there was a woman in the bed beside her sick with something unknown to modern medicine was not proof enough. So many things went misdiagnosed. During her watch over the woman, she had asked Rock why they didn't get her to a real doctor. Rock had shrugged and said, "Hospital's no good for what she got," and moved along with his day. Then Emily had seen something that cemented the truth of the situation in her mind.

Because there, in the pretty bedroom with small blue flowers on the white wallpaper, Emily had noticed—sharing a doily with a carafe of water—the sharp wooden stake that lay on Nilu's bedside table.

"Uncle Sax," Emily said, and hugged him. He felt terribly old and tired. His eyes were hopeless when he looked at her, and his arms remained hanging at his sides.

"What were you thinking?" he said, and trudged toward the barn to greet Abingdon.

Sax went to bed as soon as he possibly could. That left Paolo to explain to the group what had transpired in Germany that day. As Nilu was in Sax's bed for the duration, soaking the mattress with sour sweat, Sax moved himself out of the *maison* and into the cottage. The farm was now fully occupied: Rock, Paolo, and Emily had the remaining bedrooms in the big house, while Gheorghe and Sax had the two bedrooms in the cottage, Abingdon happily slept in his van ("If one of those blokes snores, my door is always open," he pointed out to Emily, in case she couldn't sleep), and Min was bunked up in Château le Tétanos, the concrete fort up on top of the hill.

Sax lay in the bed beneath the low-beamed ceiling of the cottage's attic, and stared at the knots and fissures in the massive timbers. They reminded him of the cracks in the ugly rock upon which squatted Castle Mordstein.

Sleep would not come for Sax. He wished his brains would stop shouting at him, but there it was. Sleep seemed to have lost interest in him. He had gotten all these young people together, his beloved Emily had shown up out of the blue, they were saddled with a woman from the other side of the world who would soon be dead from vampire bite, and they had spent a fair amount of Vatican money. It was all for nothing.

Castle Mordstein could not be entered by stealth. His team could probably get helicopters with Roman assistance. Sax was sure the Pope would have his own fleet of them, and the Swiss Guards might dress up in fifteenth-century costumes but they were crack soldiers; they were bound to have fighter jets and tanks and all sorts of things. The problem was, you couldn't lower a bunch of men on ropes into a castle in the middle of Germany and have it go unnoticed, least of all by its occupants. The German authorities might even get interested. But a full-scale assault had never been his plan. Vampires were solitary creatures, and this one, from what Sax could gather, was alone, without its mate—probably brooding over his remains, as they liked to do.

Although if by chance it was the same vampire Min had seen spirit away the Russian fiend in Mumbai, all bets were off. The creature might have been assembling its own team, somehow. Rare as it was amongst vampires, highly monogamous as they were, she of Castle Mordstein might have taken a new lover. Particularly if she'd killed her old lover. In that case they were up against two of the beasts. But Min had told him what she'd done to Nilu's attacker. Sax had no reason to doubt the clinical description of the violence Min had performed on the creature; it was the longest speech she'd made since he met her, delivered while she stood in the doorway of the bedroom looking at Nilu's feverish body.

Assuming Min's inventory of wounds was accurate, she'd left the Russian in a terrible state. So one powerful vampire and one weak vampire might be in the castle. That still fell within the outer limits of Sax's original plan. But he had imagined the fiend would be holed up in some more conventional fastness, such as a château or mansion. They liked their comfort and they preferred splendor. It was the usual thing for vampires to do, if they had their wits about them. The diseased ones, like the specimen Sax had dispatched during his midlife crisis, would live in whatever primitive conditions they found, as long as there was only one way in and out.

But here was a very clever vampire indeed, and it was living more like an eagle, hidden up there on its rock in the sky. One way in and out there, certainly. A postcard Sax had bought featured an aerial photograph of the place. A thin ridge of rock ran up to the summit of the cliff, and that ridge had been carved just flat enough on top for a cart track. On either side of the track was a plummet to oblivion of between three hundred and eight hundred feet in height; the entire peak of the rock was similarly defended by cliffs.

The best you could hope for at any point around the castle perimeter was to fall sixty or seventy feet, survive with shattered bones on some ledge on the cliff face, and die of exposure a few hours later. The castle had been so thoroughly expanded out over the summit of the mountain that there was, furthermore, no small margin to creep along, looking for a climbing route up the masonry; in most places, the walls actually overhung the rock beneath it.

There might be secret passages. Sax was sure there would be. Vampires loved that sort of thing, and the knights of the thirteenth century wouldn't have settled up on a crag like that without leaving themselves an escape hatch somewhere below. But he didn't anticipate they would find it. There might be a cave or tunnel entrance inside the lower castle or by the river somewhere, even submerged beneath the water. It could take years to search the whole mountain. And the vampire wouldn't merely stand by and wait for them. It would respond to the threat of human curiosity, the trait of mortal men that had killed more vampires than bravery.

Sax tried and failed to clear his mind. He wondered what Gheorghe thought of all this. That young criminal knew vampires existed, but he might never have come up against one as formidable as this. Sax could hear the Romanian in the next bedroom rolling around, thumping his pillows. He probably wasn't used to a good bed. Or he might himself have been sleepless, torn between the desire to steal Sax's silverware and run for it, and his interest in seeing where this mission led.

Sax studied the beams and tried not to think about vampires and castles that couldn't be invaded, but the impossibility of a stealth approach to the place taunted him. His plan, his entire scheme, revolved around recruiting a few people who were very good at sneaking and killing. Find an undefended window, a faulty latch somewhere, slip inside the grand old house in dark of night, locate and destroy the vampire, and by dawn have half the furniture out on the lawn waiting for the removal company to come and truck it all away, that overpriced clucking ormolu clock included. As it turned out, they would need siege engines, aerial support, mountaineers, and a good deal more courage and ingenuity than Sax had found in himself over the decades.

On top of everything else, Sax brooded, he was afflicted with gas, probably from the German cabbage at lunch. As the flatus wafted around the room, he wondered if that might be an approach: gas the castle from below. Fire canisters of nerve gas up in through the few windows of the main keep and kill or stun whoever was inside. Then they could raid the place from the narrow road that led up the ridge, no need for climbing cliffs and so forth. Straight up the cart track to the top and in through the front gates. Although gas wouldn't necessarily work on creatures that breathe only once per minute. If you wanted to kill a vampire, it typically had to be done face-to-face.

Then a glimmer of understanding shone out in the darkness of Sax's brain. He had an idea.

It was a stupid, bad, awful, wretched idea.

It taunted him, turning cartwheels and jabbering at the edge of his conscious mind, like an ape just outside the ring of firelight in some prehistoric contest between proto-man and his simian relatives. He shied rocks at the idea to make it go away, but it would not. At last, exhausted, Sax allowed himself to acknowledge the inspiration. He invited it into the firelight. He looked the thing over. It was just as terrible as he had thought. Better to pack everything (and everyone) up and go home, leaving his slain night watchman unavenged, his clock unreturned, his latest fortune unmade, his reputation lost. The monster could continue its filthy work and someday, in the blink of an eye in vampire time, Sax would die, and he would not have done the one good deed he was called upon to do. The monster would never know nor care.

Sax fell asleep dreaming of it. First, before he would even mention his latest inspiration, they needed to get up close to the castle and study it, looking for some forgotten way to get in. If their reconnaissance turned up no possible route of assault, however, there *was* another way.

Sax had, some time back, thought of using human bait. If there was no other means to storm the castle, that might very well work.

But there was only one person Sax could use as a lure: it would have to be himself.

In that case, all he had to do was walk through Castle Mordstein's front door.

• • •

There was frost on the ground.

Sax awoke the next morning and rose from bed less by act of will than by erosion. He resumed staring at the knotholes in the beams overhead, watching the square of sky framed in the roof window brighten, then, as if the sun sensed his mood, it grew steely and dim. Sax first allowed one of his thin white legs to dangle over the side of the bed, and then, after an interval, he threw back the covers on the upper half of his body. After further concentration of will, he was able to get his second foot beside the first, and then it was the work of only a few minutes or a quarter of an hour before he was sitting upright. By the time he had showered, shaved, and dressed to something like a reasonable standard for public appearances, then tottered on his cane to the big house, where the kitchen smelled like breakfast, the meal had been over for half an hour.

There was some coffee left. He poured a cup black and hot as a *Macumbeiro Baitola*. Back out in the barnyard he picked his way across cinder-hard earth with the frosted fields around, the whole world blanketed in a skin of glinting ice that coruscated like ground glass, the steaming coffee held before him a torch in the gloom, a source of heat rather than light.

In the barn, he found things were proceeding according to plan, if not the plan he had now constantly on his mind. In addition to the metalworking gear, Abingdon possessed a chemistry lab built into the bulkhead between the cab and cargo sections of his van; it was mostly small glass cylinders containing acids, as Sax recalled. There was an acid to dissolve everything.

In Sax's pocket, he had a small buff envelope. This he gave to Abingdon after the morning's greetings were exchanged. Everyone but Emily and Paolo was out there in the barn, staying warm by the forge, their breath pluming in the frosty air. Presumably the monk and the niece were tending to ailing Nilu; Sax had heard their voices upstairs in the big house. To the others, Abingdon was delivering an impromptu lecture on alchemy and what a lot of good science came out of it, if not the actual secret to turning lead into gold.

"I have the specimen, young man," Sax said once the greetings were dispensed with. He handed Abingdon the envelope. Inside was a scrap of the silver from the hammer, Simon, that Sax had given to Emily. He'd cut it from an unobtrusive spot inside the eye through which the handle ought to pass. There was a rime of iron oxidization on one side of the silver, so he imagined there ought to be sufficient metallurgical data available from that to sort out the composition of the thing. Abingdon began his work with the chemicals, his little ceramic workbench set up on the fender of the van. It was essentially a sophisticated tea tray. The others were curious, and Sax wanted more time to think before he relayed his plan, so he explained what Abingdon was up to.

"That silver was amalgamated, if that's the word I want," Sax began.

"Only if it has mercury in it," Abingdon remarked.

"Alloyed, then," Sax amended, "assuming it is an alloy and not pure silver they used back during the twelfth century, when it was all the rage to go on crusades and sack Jerusalem and that sort of thing. Made there in the Holy Land. I cannot say what they would have used for fuel in those days, or the construction of the crucibles and whatnot they would have employed, so that bit is rather up to you, Abingdon."

"No worries, dearest," Abingdon said.

"Right," Sax said, pleased despite himself. *Someone* called him dearest. "This specimen comes from one of the twelve hammers called the Apostles. I believe you, Min, have a copy of one of these hammers in your little ditty bag."

"It doesn't work," she said, as if Sax had personally written the warranty.

"Yes, I know it doesn't work," Sax said testily. Homicidal maniacs were not just dangerous; they were tiresome. "Please listen, young lady. Whatever happened to your Confucian sense of deference to the older authority figure? It's a disgrace. Now, the reason these modern hammers don't work has got to be something to do with the metal. Everything else has been tried. Exploding tips, stainless steel, platinum, great wicked knives that spring out of the sides—disgusting things. Sometimes they kill the vampire and sometimes they don't. Usually they do not, which isn't a suitable outcome for anyone involved. Vampire blood is highly reactive and full of all sorts of nastiness, so it's bound to get fizzing with the right ingredients thrown in; that's the way I see it. That ingredient must be in the silver of these old hammers. Which is where Abingdon comes in."

"Just one of the places I come in, but it will do for a start," Abingdon said, swishing the piece of silver around in a slender flask. The liquid it was swirling in stank of industrial smoke. "There's two variables, really. What's in the silver, and what's in the iron. Three variables, if you include the idea that they might have dipped these fuckers in poison. But what I'm doing here is to get this bit of metal to come apart into its constituent elements. Then we can get things sorted."

He set up a gas burner with a wire rack above it and fetched out more chemicals and vessels, ready to begin the analysis.

"This would be easier in a laboratory, but it's not necessary. This is called assaying, and it's been going on since ever somebody figured out how to make a realistic-looking fake of silver or gold out of something cheap. Pony-fucking Mongols could do this—nothing personal, ma'am." Abingdon winked at Min. "Anyway the steel core is easy enough. They would have mixed iron, charcoal, and glass, then cooked them up over a charcoal fire. Gives your steel lots of lovely carbon, that does. The vessels they used would have been crap sandy-clay ceramic, it being that part of the world. The iron ore would have had some cobalt, some zinc, depending where it came from. Other impurities. But not much. I don't see how that would make the difference when it came to punching holes in vampires."

Now Abingdon was decanting another liquid into the vial. It stank like horse urine and bleach. Abingdon cautioned Rock to stand back, as the enormous man was crowding in to see what was going on. "Nitric acid, mate. Burn a hole and stain you yellow at the same time. The old acid test, this. I've got sulfuric acid here, too. We could make a jolly batch of nitroglycerin."

Sax felt faint. It came over him in a rush like the tide at Mont St. Michel. He leaned heavily on his cane, thinking it must only be the smell of chemicals, but the feeling didn't lift. It progressed to an unpleasant tingling in his hands and wrists, and his legs felt distant and numb. Perhaps he was having a heart attack. That would take care of having to march up to the vampire's front door and say hello.

Min was the only one who observed Sax's distress and she didn't remark upon it. She watched him for a few seconds beneath lowered eyelids, then turned back to the chemistry lesson.

Sax tottered back to the house. He might just need to eat. Paolo was sitting in the kitchen, alone at the square table with the frayed white linen cloth. He was turning a coffee mug slowly in his hands, studying it, but his thoughts were elsewhere.

"Homesick for the old Holy Roman Empire?" Sax asked, and sat heavily beside him. He'd lost his own coffee cup somewhere.

"It is not easy to be apart from the life I know," Paolo said. "Much is going on."

"Much is going on in your well-shaped skull, or in the world?"

"Everywhere," Paolo said, and sighed mournfully.

"You're not getting ill, I trust," Sax said, after Paolo lapsed back into his mug-turning reverie.

"No," Paolo said. "I think I am not."

"Then you're worried about Nilu, upstairs? I asked Min about her. Apparently she's been in the Indian motion pictures. She's a dancer. They do these musical numbers in their movies, you know, very colorful, and whenever someone wants to make an emotional point, they start singing and dancing. It's a clever shorthand; it's a way of externalizing the inner thoughts and feelings of the characters. Falling in love, and so forth."

Paolo said nothing. He had stopped rotating the mug and was now trying to line up the handle so it pointed straight at the sink faucet opposite. Sax decided to change the subject. He was out of his depth.

"I'm going back to bloody Germany," Sax said. "With Masters Rock and Vladimirescu, and possibly Ms. Hee-Jin, if I can persuade her not to attempt to kill the vampire ahead of schedule. I haven't decided. The point is this: we have to do some reconnaissance. You will be here with Abingdon, Emily, and the ailing dancer above. I want you to develop, to the best of our existing information, a complete picture of Castle Mordstein. I want maps and elevations. I want the whole damn thing on a great big board when we get back. And most of all, I want you to use the power vested in you as a man of the Church and keeper of mortal souls and whatnot to fix a damn sharp eye on Abingdon and make sure, above all else, he doesn't lay a finger or anything similar on my niece. Am I clear?"

Paolo didn't respond. Sax backed up and tried again.

"Paolo, I'm going to write a list. Do what's on it. I'll be back in a couple of days."

Now Paolo turned to Sax, hearing him, and his fine black brows developed squiggles of concern.

"You're leaving me here?" Paolo said.

"Yes," Sax said.

"Please don't leave me here," Paolo said, and gripped Sax's arm in both his hands.

"I'm going to need some things delivered," Sax added, ignoring Paolo's entreaty. He rose to his feet and retrieved his cane. "I'll make a list of that as well. So many lists to make, so little time. You keep an eye on that eroto-maniacal swine Abingdon. I'd trust him with my life, you understand? But not for five minutes with a woman. And especially not my Emily."

14

GERMANY

The castle stood against the sky like an iron spike driven through a sheet of steel. Sax shivered in the cold, his back against the reptile bark of a spruce tree. He stood between Rock and Gheorghe, both leaning against the tree to stabilize their hands; they were surveying the castle through binoculars armored with camouflaged rubber. There wasn't anything Sax needed to see—if they found an ingress that didn't involve the front door, it was good news. Otherwise, he had his suicidal plan to fall back on. What Gheorghe and Rock were looking for were subtle things that never would have occurred to Sax to seek, indications of where and how the castle was inhabited.

"There's a cable of some kind on the northwest corner," Rock said. "It's anchored at the top and goes down to the rocks and then it's stapled, looks like, and I can't see where it goes from there."

"Would it take the weight of a man?" Gheorghe said.

"Not mine," Rock said. "There's something else on top of the tallest tower, the flat one with no roof. I can't see what it is. We're on the wrong side of the castle."

Gheorghe pointed at something lower down in the structure. "You can easily see there is waste pipe there under edge of the stone where is the box that comes out," he said.

Rock didn't see it, and Gheorghe picked up his clipboard and drew in red pen where the pipe was located on a simple drawing of the castle. Rock compared the drawing to the castle and then spotted the pipe.

"Looks recent," Rock said. "Sewer pipe. Do vampires shit?"

It took Sax a second to realize Rock was speaking to him.

"You mean literally?" he said.

"Yeah. Would a vampire need to install a potty in its bedroom or anything?"

"They're like reptiles or birds," Sax said. "They excrete waste, but only one kind. Out their, ah, bottoms."

"They do not pissing?" Gheorghe said.

"Only out the back," Sax said, and Gheorghe laughed his clacking laugh.

"No shit, Sherlock," Gheorghe said.

They resumed their study of the castle.

By the time the sun was going down behind the clouds, they had made a circuit of the fortification that covered most of its exposure on the southern and eastern sides. Although the area was accessible to tourists, they took care to remain out of sight, keeping to the trees and rocks. Nobody would mistake them for sightseers. There were a few minor blind spots they hadn't been able to examine, but located in places of such terrifying inaccessibility that they'd be of no use in any case. Gheorghe made drawings from several angles. He'd added in red lines wherever there was some element to suggest a modern addition or inhabitation.

They had already seen a trend: the improvements were very carefully done, nearly invisible. This could be a matter of the structure's landmark status; the authorities never wanted the character of such places changed, which was reasonable enough. But there was a hint of stealth about some of it. The drainpipe had been painted in alternating strokes of color to match the stone around it. There were a number of modern windows set deep into openings; the window frames had been painted dark gray, effectively rendering them invisible.

As the daylight faded, they discussed their results over ready-made sandwiches and beer from a local Spar supermarket, sitting in the camper van Sax had hired. They wouldn't be sleeping in it, but rather at a nearby motel; however, the van was good cover for their purposes. If anyone did notice them, and questioned their activities, then the van, sleeping bags, and hiking gear inside it would make it perfectly clear they were ordinary outdoors enthusiasts. Even Sax. He was an old, sedentary outdoors enthusiast.

The consensus was the lower floors of the castle were empty, mostly disused, while the upper floors showed signs of at least being properly weather sealed, if not inhabited. But although they waited and watched until late in the evening, no lights came on in any of the windows. There *was* light within the castle, but they couldn't see where it was coming from. It was somewhere inside the mass of turrets that jutted from the keep, shining up into the low clouds, throwing thin rims of light on the towers and roofs. It might have been some kind of mood lighting, a Make Our Castles Ominous-Looking program enacted by the German government, or it might have been shining from a big skylight or a series of spotlights. The effect was strange, however. There was not a single illuminated window in the outer walls.

This suggested the castle was only being used, or lived in, at its inner core.

The lower castle, at the foot of the cliff, enjoyed a decorative lighting scheme of blue and green up-lights on the castle proper, and oblique lighting to rake the grounds and pop the forms and textures of the scenery into relief. The effect was what the travel books would call "magical," especially taken in context of the frowning cliff that leapt up above the castle with its freight of stone at the summit needling the belly of the clouds.

They had parked the camper on a forest road that ran along the ridge opposite the castle, so Sax and the others could see down inside the defensive walls as the employees, numbering half a dozen or so, closed the visitor center down. It was early evening when they switched on the atmospheric lighting, an hour later when the last tourist vehicle rolled out of the parking lot, and an engulfing black night surrounded the castle when the employees switched off the interior lights and closed the front and back gates. They scattered to their cars in the small employee parking lot next to the access road Paolo had discovered.

A significant moment punctuated this part of the vigil. Rock had been watching the employees file through the back gate with his binoculars when he said, "Man, there's a fine redhead down there."

Sax urgently grabbed at his binoculars, but by the time he had them focused and figured out how to aim them in the correct direction, she was concealed inside a sporty late-model BMW that contrasted with the older, more staid cars driven by the other employees. Gheorghe had made some remark about Sax's sudden interest in girls, then laughed, *ha ha ha ha*, like a rusty water pump. Sax shoved the binoculars back into the cleft between Rock's immense pectoral muscles, then scrambled clumsily over the top of the ridge, cursing and snagging his clothes on branches, to watch the headlights from the various cars wend their way through the forest valley beneath the cliff.

The BMW turned off in the opposite direction at the fork Paolo had seen. The headlights rose up onto the hillside at the foot of the cliff, zigzagging around hairpin bends, and then the car's taillights replaced the headlights and it disappeared between two eminences of rock higher up on the slopes.

"Did you see where that car went?" Sax asked.

"All we gotta do is follow the road," Rock said. "You want to do that tonight?"

Sax considered giving up for now. The road would still be there when they got back, after all, and they could stay up late the next night following a good long sleep-in. He was exhausted all the time now, Sax was sorry to observe. His old body just didn't have what it took. The enthusiasm in his brain, the leaping excitement, even the constant trickle of fear that ran through him like ice water from melting snow at the thought of his Very Bad Plan, while they energized his mind, could not keep his body going.

"I'm getting very bloody old," Sax said out loud, which was another sign he was getting very bloody old. He hadn't meant to speak. "This redhead," he added, changing the subject, "she was attractive?"

"I mean it was a long way off, but yeah," Rock said.

"I'm concerned she might be one of the vampire's familiars."

"I'll keep an eye out for her."

"I'll keep out my pecker for her," Gheorghe said, and laughed, and then, when Rock failed to join in, he added, "You know is pecker, right? Is a word you use for the *pula*. The Johnson? Hahahahaha."

Still nobody laughed.

While they waited for a suitably late hour, Rock and Gheorghe discussed possible points of entry into the castle. They sat up front, Sax lying on the bench seat in back. Sax had not yet told anyone what his real plan was, so the rest of the team was working under the assumption that they would have to mount some kind of ingenious burglary-style assault on the fortifications. He hoped they'd find a way. Then he could forget his awful plan. He called the farm on his mobile phone to check in.

"Are you staying warm, Uncle Sax?" Emily asked.

"Yes yes yes. Has Abingdon tried anything with you?"

"You mean like mating?"

"If you must put it thus."

"Yes he has, Uncle Sax."

"And?"

"And he hasn't succeeded. Anyway, what business is it of yours? You have enough to worry about. What I'm worried about is this woman Nilu. She's terribly sick. She needs some kind of medical attention right away."

There was something in her tone of voice that sounded like apology. Sax started with that. "Why do I have the feeling you've already dragged a doctor into this?"

"Not just any doctor, Uncle Sax. This one is from the Vatican. Or next to the Vatican. Paolo was trying to explain his sort of enclave thing isn't actually on Vatican property—it's across the street or something? He's very sweet, you know. Paolo's like a—well, like a saint, as they say. He's been feeding Nilu ice cubes for hours now, just to keep her hydrated."

"Yes yes yes yes yes. What about the doctor," Sax said, his impatience growing rapidly.

"Well, he's one of the same brethren or brothers or what have you as Paolo is, from the same sect. He's a vampire doctor. I mean, he treats vampire victims. He'll be here any minute now."

Sax considered the ramifications of this. The more involvement the Church had, the more of the spoils of war they could claim. They would get a bigger piece of the action, which meant a smaller piece for Sax—which, if he was going to risk everything and die, hardly seemed appropriate.

But then again, if the castle was impregnable, it hardly mattered, did it? He wasn't going to get anything at all, and neither was the Vatican. So the joke was on them. Much as the joke would probably be on Sax when the vampire tore him apart and it turned out there really were pearly gates in the clouds and Saint Whatsisname at the concierge's desk sent him down the back staircase to hell with a pitchfork up his bum.

"Uncle Sax? Are you still there?"

"Make sure Min tells the doctor everything she knows about the vampire that bit the girl, will you? And make sure Paolo doesn't try to get Nilu back to his hospice place, wherever that is, because Min won't put up with it. The last thing I need is a fight amongst ourselves."

"Understood. How's it going there?" Emily asked. Somehow the way her voice brightened, the hint of admiration in it that Sax found so alarming, made him hesitate. He wanted to tell her the thing might be impossible, regardless of whether anybody stole his stupid old clock or killed his night watchman. People got murdered all the time. Just as senselessly. He had the whole argument laid out. But it was like so much burned newspaper in his mouth. The words were gone.

"It's going quite well," Sax said.

He got off the phone as quickly as he could.

Sax would not have thought he could sleep in the cold van, lying with a sleeping bag thrown over him, knees hooked up, one arm twisted around behind his head for a pillow. But he fell into a doze without knowing it, and dreamed of the castle, and the redhead, and Rock chasing first her, then Sax, along the battlements with the sheer cliff below them, stark naked, a purple-black *pula* the size of a moray eel projecting from his groin, Gheorghe's laughter, *Hahahahaha*, in his ear.

When Sax awoke, the van was moving, jolting along the forest road, heading down the ridge toward the castle grounds. It was midnight.

"We could not get you to awake," Gheorghe said when Sax came up between the front seats for a cup of coffee from a flask.

"I'm old, that's why," Sax said, scalding his mouth.

"Man, I hope I got your kind of snap when I'm old," Rock said, and clapped Sax on the shoulder with a hand the size of a tractor seat. "Hell," he added, "I hope I'm around next week."

At Sax's direction, Rock turned onto the narrow way that led along behind the lower fortifications. They took the fork of the road partway up the hill, along the same route the BMW had taken. There was no indication it was a private road, and the surface was blacktopped and in reasonable condition. They were certainly within the grounds of the castle, but the camping gear provided a plausible excuse for being there, if they were apprehended by the police. Sax found he was rehearsing what he would say to the authorities in his head. *These are my sons*, he would explain, introducing his companions. *Different mothers.*

Rock steered the van across the grass of the fields by the road and parked it beneath the trees, well out of sight. It was not obviously concealed, merely hidden; that was the effect they wanted. Gheorghe decamped immediately and stood in the dark, testing Sax's fancy set of night-vision goggles. Rock hauled out his backpack, relaced his boots, and wished Sax luck while he waited for them to return. He warned Sax to turn on the heat once in a while so they didn't return in the morning to find him frozen to death.

"Should we synchronize our watches or anything?" Sax asked, suddenly realizing he didn't want to be alone. The nose of the van faced the lower castle, and up above the windshield in the dark sky was the upper castle on its crag. Sax didn't want to look at them.

"One minute this side or that side of the hour won't make any difference," Rock said, and again clamped his massive hand on Sax's shoulder. "We volunteered for this, man. Whatever happens next, remember we chose to do this."

"It's your funeral," Sax agreed.

Rock winked and made an imaginary pistol of his fingers, shooting Sax in the chest with it. Then he slid the side door of the van shut, closing out the frigid night air, and his huge frame was hustling double time across the frozen field after Gheorghe. Their shapes merged for a brief moment with the gravel road, reappeared silhouetted dimly against the field on the other side, and then they were gone beneath the trees that covered the hill.

Sax settled in, wearing all of his newly purchased cold-weather gear: hat, gloves, jacket, silk drawers beneath moleskin trousers, and a pair of boots that looked like running shoes. It was all horribly unstylish but warm: gloves, boots, and jacket all filled with those thin miracle insulations that take the place of a mattress's worth of eiderdown. They'd bought these things immediately after they rented the camper in Chemnitz.

Eventually the patient, inexorable cold got through the clothes, and Sax pulled a sleeping bag up around him. He didn't feel like sleeping anymore. The silence and chill seemed to press up against the camper with a palpable mass, as if he was not parked under some trees in Germany, but rather at the bottom of the Arctic Ocean.

He felt the presence of the vampire. Even if it was thousands of miles away, it left a kind of psychic stink behind. Sax wondered how the others were getting along.

He checked his watch, a gold manually wound Vacheron Constantin from 1954, a sound article. The timepiece had originally been given to Peter Fonda by Marlon Brando. Fonda himself had handed it to Sax during the filming of *Easy Rider*; he'd been doing a scene involving a costume watch, and neither of them remembered it until the mid-1980s, when Sax was clearing out one of his many wardrobes and found the timepiece in the pocket of his old fringed and beaded deerskin jacket. After all that time, Fonda said, the watch had chosen its master. Sax could keep it.

It didn't run particularly well in the cold. Sax had forgotten that.

His companions would be somewhere well up that precipitous road with its hairpins and switchbacks, probably not even short of breath because they were both fit, active men, which Sax regarded as a kind of rebuke. He hadn't been fit or active even when he was fit and active—that is, not like these men were, who scaled mountains in the dark. They had those veins on their forearms that radiated out from the inside of the elbow, an effect Sax always admired but never achieved. Sax found he was thinking of men's arms without the slightest tickle of erotic impulse; he didn't know if this was because of his advanced age or because the cold had reduced his penis to the size of a caraway seed.

At three in the morning, Sax dozed off for a while, a drop of liquid dangling from his nose. He awoke disoriented, the windows of the van opaque as candle wax. Something had jolted him alert.

He wiped at the condensation with the corner of the sleeping bag. It was frozen. He had to fish out a credit card from his wallet to clear the glass enough to see. Nothing seemed to have changed in the landscape, except the moon was peeping through the clouds at intervals now, casting ghosts of light down across the hills, throwing silvery highlights and crisp shadows across the scarred face of the cliff.

Sax strained his eyes into the darkness, trying to discern anything that might have been the cause of his awakening.

There was a sound. It was faint, at the top of the register he could hear, like the squeal of automobile brakes somewhere far distant.

Then he saw lights up under the cliff. They appeared in pieces, as if the beams had shattered in the cold and now the fragments were tumbling down the mountain. After a few minutes they resolved themselves into a pair of vehicle headlights moving through the trees along the hidden road that zigzagged down the slope. The vehicle was moving as slowly as a man could walk, and Sax wondered if it represented a search party looking for his companions. If so, the search team might see the camper, even at a distance. It was not intended to look like it had been parked to avoid detection. Now Sax thought that was a bit too clever. They should have hidden it thoroughly and covered it with branches.

There was a pair of binoculars tucked up on the dashboard. He retrieved them, cleared the condensation off the glass again, and watched the headlights. It was not a satisfactory arrangement. And he couldn't hear. But he also couldn't figure out how to lower the windows without turning on the engine, which Sax thought might be the swiftest way he could possibly devise to call attention to himself. So instead he popped the sliding door open in the side of the camper.

Cold air rushed in. As chilly as it was inside the camper, it was far worse outside. Then the small store of heat inside the camper was gone, and the whole world was equally frigid. Sax began to shiver. He jammed the binoculars against the doorframe and kept them stable enough to watch.

The headlights were halfway down the hill now. Sax could just make out the small figure of a man walking along between them, in front of the vehicle, which he discerned was some kind of medium-weight truck with a big box on the back. With the door open, he could hear, too. Tiny snatches of voices, shouting. Not in alarm, but calling to be heard by someone distant. He could hear the clashing of the gears as the truck kept its speed low on the steep grade. Then he heard the shrill noise again. It wasn't brakes. It was some kind of whistle, brandished by the man on foot.

Sax took his eyes from the binoculars. The rubber cups of the eyepieces were freezing his face. He massaged some life back into his eyelids and was about to resume his vigil when he saw another man loping across the dark field, chased by a scudding patch of moonlight.

Or at first it *seemed* like a man.

But the figure was moving far too fast for that. He was running at the speed of a horse, in great bunching strides that sometimes used not just his legs but his arms, hunched, apelike. As swift as the silent figure was, he could not outrun the moonlight, and as the pale photobathic rays swept over him, Sax saw it was not a man at all.

It was a hunding. The debased form of the vampire—no less deadly, but certainly more beast than man. Not anything like the Czech monster, which had strength but no wits. These were cunning hunters.

The thing was big, pale, its shoulders matted with fur or bristles that stood erect. Its torso was long and deep, its chest not broad but keeled like a dog's, and its limbs hinged differently from those of a man. Its arms were long in the wrists and short above the elbows, and it ran on its toes with its heels halfway up the calves of its legs. The head that projected from the long, thick neck was man-shaped, upright, but the nose and jaw projected past the sloped forehead. Even at a distance, there was no mistaking the thing for human, now the light was upon it. The moon hid its face again and the monster was an indistinct, lunging shadow once more, charging across the frozen meadow.

Sax's blood stopped coursing. He was terrified. The creature was half a kilometer away, and yet Sax's mind could imagine it scenting him and turning in its tracks, eyes glinting green, and devouring the space between with powerful strides. It could, too. Those monsters were impossibly swift. Then it would tear out his bowels and suck the still-pumping blood from his liver, draining him while he struggled and screamed and eventually died.

All of this was thirty seconds away, if the monster sensed Sax's presence. But it seemed intent on the truck up the mountainside, its course straight ahead. The creature galloped across the gravel road, paused to thrust its head into the grass and smell where Rock and Gheorghe had been a few hours before, then probed the air with its nose, searching. The trail was cold. It galloped onward and was lost under the trees a few moments later. Sax heard branches breaking. The thing was clearly in a hurry, abandoning its native stealth.

Sax eased the side door of the camper shut. The latch fell into place with a clap like a hammer. Sax cringed as he depressed the locking button. When nothing responded to the noise, he went up to the forequarters of the van and locked the front doors. Not that it would keep him alive for more than a second longer if a hunding decided to attack, but there was some pathetic reassurance in door locks. Although they came from the same poisoned flesh as vampires—both were the same, in different phases, depending on their prey—hundings wouldn't pause to listen to a fellow's last words or give him a chance to talk things over. They were only in it for the kill.

Sax scraped the glass again to give himself a view of the hill and watched the headlights descend the twisted road. The man was still walking in front of it. Sax tried the binoculars again. The man should be dead, if there was a hunding around. Sax found the truck's lights, twitched the focus lever, and saw something he didn't know was possible. The man was, indeed, confronted by the hunding, there in the down-raked headlights of the truck. Sax's view was partly obscured by trees in the foreground, but he could not mistake the white, shaggy back of the beast.

The man was barely close enough for Sax to discern his features as well. He wore a black hat pulled low, and there was a dark scarf wound around his face to the eyes. He was otherwise clad in a long, gray coat that reminded Sax of Paolo's cassock. In his hand was something Sax at first took for a wreath, it being quite distant, even with the binoculars; however, when the man uncoiled the object and began slashing at the hunding, Sax understood it was a bullwhip. The monster crouched and threw its claws up over its head and was driven by the man around the side of the truck. Then the creature jumped up into the truck's enclosed back and the man swung a heavy door shut upon it, closing the hunding in. Sax had never seen anything like it. And he wondered with dread if his companions were still alive out there in the cold night.

Sax spent the hours until dawn slowly freezing. He never turned on the heater but bundled himself up like a silkworm. His extremities lost sensation and he had to force his fingers and toes to move at intervals; otherwise, he feared, he might lose them. His ears and nose ached with the cold and the van's windows were so thickly iced that even the moonlight could barely penetrate.

He did not sleep again, but breathed into his gloves and wondered if he was the only man left alive out of his party.

What would he do? He couldn't drive the camper. He could call Paolo, of course, on his mobile phone, but it would be hours before the man could show up. He did not dare call Gheorghe or Rock, because the last thing they would need, if they were hidden in some crack in the rocks with another hunding prowling around, would be a ringing phone.

There might well be another such creature. Sax had watched the truck make its way down the hill and saw, just before it reached the flat ground, a second monster lope its way along the tree line. The performance by the man with the whip was repeated. The area must have been infested. Sax was convinced there must be another one on the roof of the camper, salivating with desire to rip out his guts. It could also be the scraping of a low-hanging bough of the tree under which the camper was parked, but Sax was *certain* it was anything but that. After several hours during which the noise on the roof failed to change in rhythm or intensity, Sax decided it might possibly be a mere twig. But he also didn't relax, because that's what a hunding would *want* you to think. Only a twig! And then the claws like steak knives would rip into your guts and the thick white fangs— He forced himself to concentrate on the dark landscape before him.

Eventually the cold was too much. Sax was preparing himself for death, having grown apathetic and fatalistic, his eyes leaking tears that froze on his lashes. His shivering had become continuous and convulsive, expanding and contracting in waves of intensity.

Then there was a noise outside the van. Chewing, sax thought, the crunch of tusks on bone. It came closer, and he hoped he could freeze to death in the next ten seconds or so, but he didn't. The crunching resolved itself into footsteps on icy grass. He heard voices. A moment later there was a banging on the side door of the camper.

"Let us in, man, my nuts are gonna fall off," Rock hissed, and Sax fumbled for what felt like half a minute before he got the lock up and his companions tumbled back inside the van.

As they drove around the back of the range of hills, the van's heater blasting at full force, the men discussed the events of the night so far. Sax described the hunding; Rock and Gheorghe had heard the things crashing through the trees, at least three of them, probably more, but never saw one. They believed Sax without question, however. They had listened to the panting and snarling of the monsters and smelled a glandular stench like that of a badger or skunk in the air as they passed by on the slope. The men had taken refuge amongst some rocks on the mountainside when the truck approached, and what with all this activity they remained in their hiding place until it was time to either move or die of the cold.

They never dared take a look at what was going on, even after a long interval when the truck was a couple of curves below them, because every time they stirred, it seemed, another one of the unknown animals would come loping past. The truck was long gone when they finally agreed it was time to move, and they had confirmed what they suspected: there was only one way up to the castle on this side of the mountain, and that was the road. So they didn't climb any higher but made their way straight down the steep hillside, convinced they were going to be ambushed at every step. But it seemed the business with the truck had left them entirely alone.

It remained only to examine the far side of the castle, the north face, and then they would be out of things to do, unless they could figure out some way to sneak inside the castle for a look around. Sax nixed that idea. Once inside, they were finishing the job. You didn't poke around in a vampire's lair—you went straight for the vampire. Otherwise, at some point, you'd have your back turned. Sax was terribly disappointed about the inaccessibility of the fortress, however. It meant his terrible plan was more likely to be the *only* plan.

Somehow, though he racked his brain during every spare moment, he couldn't come up with any solution that didn't involve his direct, central participation. There wasn't any other way, or he most certainly would have embraced it.

This was it, then. He had only two choices: be slaughtered on the threshold of the monster, or cancel the entire operation. So in truth he had only one choice, because there was no way he could walk through that portcullis into the vampire's fortress. The caper was not happening. He would already have confessed to Rock and Gheorghe that he couldn't go through with his plan, except he hadn't told them his plan, and he lacked the bravery even to admit the whole scheme was already a bust.

His own failures of courage just cascaded outward in endless folds and permutations until Sax was sure there was no less valiant creature in all the world. And it could have been avoided if he hadn't long ago allowed his greed to overmaster his terror and set his foot for the first time inside a vampire's château. He might have been like every other old queen peddling vintage knickknacks in the world but for that one failure of cowardice; now here he was, much more sensible, much less able, and certain he was not going to make the same mistake again.

Sax considered the possibility that there wasn't anything in the castle—no vampire, no hoard, no clock. According to the gift shop guidebook on the history of the castle, Mordstein had been cleaned out by American officers at the end of the Second World War, its contents bound for Wolfsburg by train. But of five boxcars, only one arrived, having been attached to a different engine from the rest. The rest were considered lost treasure, and constituted one of the mysteries of the postwar period.

Sax made phone calls while they circled the mountain, keeping his fingers on the many strands of web that stretched out from where he was to assorted schemes and operations around the world. The detective working on Alberto's murder at the warehouse wasn't available—it was nearly nine p.m. in New York—but the sergeant on duty told Sax they had a suspect, completely crazy, who had left fingerprints at the scene, a known professional thief from Newark who appeared to have lost his mind. Sax thought that madness would resemble what he'd seen in the prison in Chemnitz. And he had received a message while his phone was off during the freezing vigil: Abingdon had called to report his metallurgical research had yielded a formula for the hammer silver that was extremely high, oddly enough, in sulfur, which ought to have turned it black, but there was also a lot of lead in the mixture, which might isolate the sulfur. Abingdon did not know. Sax called back.

"Christ, man, it's two in the bloody morning," Abingdon groaned down the line.

"There's no time to waste," Sax said. "I need you to use that formula and make me some hammers, first order of business tomorrow."

"How many do you want?" Abingdon asked, now fully awake and interested.

"Oh . . . a dozen, I should think," Sax said.

It occurred to him to call Paolo and ask him what he knew about hundings, but things were complicated enough as it was. It would be the bloody Ordine dei Santi Contro l'Uomo Lupo getting involved next, if he wasn't careful. And if he woke everybody up at this hour, they might panic.

Then Rock announced simply, "We're here."

They were in the hills behind Castle Mordstein. The final leg of the route they'd taken was hardly a road, designed only for access to a handful of prewar holiday chalets tucked away in the trees. They didn't look like they'd been occupied for decades. As the headlights swept over them, there was a mournful aspect to the cottages with their drooping eaves and rotting gingerbread trim, the unpainted wood dark brown and silver, the shingles on the roofs as mossy as river stones. They seemed to mourn the children who had played amongst them, then went to war and never came back.

Sax remained with the vehicle as before, alone with the empty chalets and the black trunks of the trees and the brown corpses of the summer ferns.

The other men set off at a brisk pace up the rocky slope of the nearest hill, Gheorghe leading with the night-vision goggles. They would quickly scout the lower part of the cliffs there, then get out before dawn came. If the werewolves were back in the forest, both

Gheorghe and Rock had guns with hollow-point bullets, something Gheorghe had gotten hold of on his way into France, by means Sax did not wish to know about. The problem was that hundings, being made of the same material as vampires, were extremely difficult to kill. They could shoot the things and stop them for a moment, but they would continue the attack as long as they could move their limbs.

Sax waited in the icy dark inside the van, afraid to turn on a light or run the heater, trusting instead to his thoughts to occupy him, and his three pairs of socks to keep him from losing any toes. An hour before dawn, Sax was in an exhausted doze when he awoke to the sound of small stones rattling down the slope to his right, pelting off the roofs of the chalets. Then Rock and Gheorghe came rushing to the doors, shouting for Sax to get them open. They leapt inside and Rock scratched at the ignition keyhole, his cold fingers not up to the fine motor control required.

"We gotta get the fuck out of here, man!" Rock yelled, apparently at his own useless fingers.

"Allow me," Sax said, and guided the key into the slot. Rock cranked it over and gunned the engine and shoved the gas pedal to the floor. The camper lurched forward and he snapped on the headlights and in that moment there was a shape in the beams, a man, but not a man. Sax saw the thing rushing at the windshield, a long gray coat flying up around it like bat wings, its one eye a glistening marble, the other eye socket empty, the light finding nothing but gristle within. Its face was a scarred and festering mass of wreckage, lipless, the broken teeth snapping, and then the thing slammed into the camper and Rock almost lost control of the wheel, fighting it from side to side as the impact flung the machine heavily toward the trees on the margin of the track.

Gheorghe's door scraped noisily along one of the trunks and the mirror flew off the frame and then Rock had the van jolting violently onto the road and it was moving fast, now, and Sax looked out the rear window but did not see the thing they'd rammed in the glow of the taillights.

"It's gone," he said. And at that moment the fist slammed into the roof above his head, buckling the sheet metal, and Sax threw himself on the floor. The monster was on top of them.

Gheorghe shouted a continuous stream of Romanian, rummaging in his backpack, throwing things around in his haste. Sax was making a high-pitched sound like a goat trapped in a cistern. A bloody-fingered hand crashed through the window of the sliding door above Sax's head, showering him with crumbs of safety glass. The thick, raw fingers snatched at the air, trying to get into Sax's hair. The monster was going to pull him out.

Rock slammed the van from side to side, trying to shake off the creature on the roof. The hand stretched for Sax, and Sax shoved himself across the floor of the van and now he could see up and the thing's single, lifeless eye was fixed upon him, that ruined, scabby jaw gaping, upside down because it was leaning far over the roof to get at him.

There was a bang and a bright flash and the monster was gone in a whirl of gray fabric. Rock kept the pedal down and drove them out of the forest at a speed that had surely never before been attempted on that neglected road.

"The *Rusă*," Gheorghe said, when he had his breath back. "Min's Russian." He shoved the big .45 automatic into his backpack.

Sax got himself onto his knees and tried not to throw up. His heart was slamming against his ribs at a tremendous rate and there were purple and green zinnias blossoming and vanishing behind his eyelids. He sucked for air and after a long minute had some oxygen back in his racing blood and he began to feel like he might survive. The wind was howling in through the broken window, bringing on its wings a blast of polar ice. Sax spat a fragment of glass from his mouth, coughed, and at last answered Rock's repeated demands to know if he was all right.

"No, I'm not bloody all right!" Sax barked. "Bloody *vampire* attack, in case you didn't notice."

"*Acela a fost un vampir foarte furios*," Gheorghe muttered, and crossed himself. This irritated Sax. Childish mock-religious gestures weren't going to help anybody.

"Speak English, you berk," Sax said.

"I say," Gheorghe said, turning around in his seat, "that was one pissed-off vampire."

The strangest thing they had seen on their exploratory mission, Rock said once they had reached their hotel, was a helicopter. "On top of that real tall tower with the flat roof. This vampire travels in style."

"Really," Sax said, "a helicopter."

"Harrison Ford has his own helicopter, man."

"That explains it."

The narrative continued. Rock and Gheorghe had made it as far as the bottom of the cliff, a scree of large, broken boulders that had fallen or been thrown down over the centuries to form a moraine along the foot of the mountain. Gheorghe thought they might be able to ascend to the ridge from there, but Rock didn't want to take the chance at night. They wouldn't be able to use a route on that side anyway, simply because it didn't connect with anywhere they could keep a vehicle. It was no good for getaway purposes. They had argued at that point. Gheorghe was an opportunist. He liked to strike when he saw the chance, and this felt like a chance to him. Rock insisted they stick to the plan. They were in whatever the opposite of a hurry was. Voices got raised, Rock admitted.

It was unprofessional. They had failed to keep their situation in mind. Then pebbles began to shower down from above, and bits of stone, and it hurt, so they scrambled out of the way and shone their high-intensity flashlights up the cliff face. That's when they saw the monster coming down at them, headfirst, clinging to the rock by jamming the toes of its boots and the tips of its fingers into cracks in the stone. It moved at terrifying speed, half falling, half clinging. They wasted precious seconds just staring at it, the hideous purple mess of its face coming closer and closer.

"How did you know it was the Russian?" Sax interrupted.

They were sitting in Sax's hotel room, heads close together, passing around a half-liter of brandy. All three men were hunched forward with their elbows on their knees as if planning a prison break under the watchful eye of the guards. Their voices were low: The walls have ears. And also it was five in the morning.

"I know it was the Russian because of his boots were Russian," Gheorghe said, as if that was conclusive. But it *had* to be him—Yeretyik. Min said she'd blown his face off. The description certainly fit. And it meant nothing that he was well enough to descend cliffs with his bare hands—vampires healed much faster than men, especially if fed copious amounts of fresh human blood. But why was the mystery vampire, the female, helping the Russian to get well? Why had she rescued him in India? It could be love, Sax knew, but that was such a rare thing amongst vampires. They liked their lovers dead, so they could dwell on the good old days without having to deal with them in the present. Yet he was there, defending the castle on her behalf. For that matter, Yeretyik had sought Nilu as a victim. So did he plan to switch genders? Was the mystery vampire a lesbian? Did vampires swing both ways? Maybe orientation didn't matter to a creature that could be male or female according to its nibbles.

And did all of this have something to do with the ormolu clock? Sax wondered. After all, it had once been owned by a Russian, although how a ballet master tied in to the whole business was beyond him. Then there was poor murdered Radiguet, the French writer, who had at least *known* the ballet master, and was slain by such a fiend. He might somehow fit in as well. It was mysterious and disturbing to Sax. He felt like a child stirring the black waters of an *étang* with a stick, watching the rotten things swirl up from the bottom, emerging indistinctly through the murk, becoming clear for a moment just below the surface before sinking again into the mire.

Rock and Gheorghe swapped back and forth to finish narrating their adventure: they had bolted at the same time, the vampire descending the cliff, and when they ran, the monster leapt into the air and crashed down through the trees. It had missed Rock by inches and hit an actual rock instead, which slowed it down considerably and gave them time to flee through the darkness, running pell-mell down the treacherous slope in the pitch black with their lights whirling uselessly in all directions.

They couldn't believe the thing could move at all. It had fallen sixty feet and it was in rough condition to begin with. But move it did, and gathered speed as it went. By the end, both men were screaming for air and not so much running as hurling themselves down the rugged hillside through the trees, and then they saw the roofs of the chalets and a moment later, the van beyond them, and Sax knew the rest.

"She knows," Sax observed when the tale was told and they had sat in silence for a while.

He sat back and drummed his fingers on the arm of the upholstered chair. Rock was seated on the bed. He fell backward and let out a long breath and stared at the ceiling with his fingers laced across his chest. Gheorghe was in the desk chair. He put his elbow on the glass top of the desk, then pressed his fist into the side of his jaw and sat there with his pale skin and the dark circles around his eyes lending him the look of a silent film star posing for a photograph.

"She knows we're here, and she will not sit back and wait for us to return," Sax went on.

Things had become urgent. The game had come to them.

Sax wasn't ready for it. The Russian, Yeretyik, added a dangerous twist to things. The vampire had a watchdog. And literally so, in the case of the hundings. They'd been gathering the things up in that truck. Why? Yeretyik should not have had to defend the castle himself. Surely half a dozen savage, murderous creatures with no regard for their own lives would make a wiser home security mechanism than a wounded lover? Could it be that the vampire had *wanted* them to go out exploring, and corralled the werewolves for that very purpose, knowing the men would be watching? Sax's mind was bursting with questions.

"Why," he said, when the others had watched him silently for several moments, "were the hundings called off?"

"I've been wondering that," Rock said. "We were *that* close to getting killed tonight. If those things had been out there, we would've been fucked."

"This vampire"—Gheorghe pronounced it *yemp-year*—"has an army. That is new."

"Ye-e-ess," Sax said, drawing the word out long and worried. "Sometimes they work in pairs, when they're not killing each other. This one has not only got its lover with the missing face, it has—what, six, at least, sort of henchmen in the form of the hundings. I can't believe I just used the word *henchmen* in earnest. But they are. A pack of vampire dogs, if you will. So she's got a whole gang of monsters at her back, plus her human familiars. I wasn't anticipating that. One rather hopes for the solitary creature."

"I about shit myself back there, running through the woods," Rock said. "I was so scared, I was like a little baby. That ugly fucker came after us like the motherfuckin' Terminator, man. You add a couple werewolves to the mix and I'm going home with my pride busted but my ass intact, you follow me? 'Cause this is just a job."

"It *is* just a job. I think . . . we're going to have to call it quits."

Sax hated to say the words.

Even now that Rock had given him the opportunity to bail out of the entire scheme with his dignity intact, Sax still somehow hoped the others would come up with something. That they would catch a break for being the good guys. Anything. There was nothing, however. They were three marked men who had fled a monster and lived. They weren't vampire hunters or anything else except fools.

"Quit the job?" Gheorghe said.

"Yes," Sax said, and hung his hands between his thighs, head down. He felt the tiredness of an old man again. He wanted suddenly to retire to Miami Beach. He wanted to have a pool boy and a pool, in that order, and never purchase or sell another fine object of any description.

"We cannot the job quit, Saxon." Gheorghe's voice had lost its laughter.

"Watch me do it," Sax said. "I quit. So does he. You quit too, right, Rock?"

"Yeah. Fuck it. I quit. I'd rather fight the fuckin' Red Guard. They can't move that fast."

Gheorghe was shaking his head now. The gallows smile came back on his face. "You do not get what it is, gentlemen," he said. "We cannot quit this game. This vampire, she knows who we are. She has seen us now. We shoot boyfriend in his head some more, probably not happy for that. I think we are, so to say—fucked in our bottoms."

"One of her minions," Sax said, amazed he was using the word *minions* so soon after using the word *henchmen*, "raided my warehouse, you know. She already knew who I was. And yet she allowed me to live."

Gheorghe was no longer smiling. "She allow you to live because then she had object. She want clock of yours, got clock. All done. Kill only man between her and clock. Watchman, not you. Now you are make her not safe, you understand? You are the threat. Now the watchman is you."

He was right. Sax saw it.

"I'm not between her and anything, though, right?" Rock said.

"I think," Gheorghe said, "boyfriend is problem there. You and me, he not like us anymore."

"Damn."

They were silent and the dawn came up and they said nothing and did nothing except watch the light behind the curtains grow brighter.

They couldn't even turn back now. The fight was on.

Sax wished he had a better plan. Rock's eyes closed and he breathed deeply, arms crossed on his chest like a dead man at a wake. Sax and Gheorghe stared into the carpet.

"I'll tell you what," Sax said, breaking the silence. "I think Paolo is going to get us out of this. He's got a whole army of his own, you know. These fellows are highly trained. They can come bomb the castle or something. The Vatican. Make itself useful for once."

Gheorghe snorted. "Why they do not already come? They know where is the vampire now. They only need to make it dead."

"Well . . . ," Sax said, not realizing it was a rhetorical question.

"Because," Gheorghe went on, "is political problem. Catholic Church never invade anybody for many years. They come with bombs and soldiers, all of a sudden, right? Suddenly not neutral. Is at war with Germany. Not good thing."

"Damn," Sax said.

Gheorghe was right. The Vatican would never have let an amateur get this far if they had any choice, but they didn't. It had been the same each time. Sax did the dirty work, or got his people to do it, more accurately, and then Rome came along and mopped up the gravy as a privilege of the Church.

"So we're just stuck fighting this vampire on our own, is that what you think?" Sax said.

"I think that, yes."

"Right," Sax said, trying to think what to do next. His latest plan was to change his name and hide in Venezuela. Then Rock spoke. He had not been asleep.

"I say we get ourselves back to France and hole up in your place for a while and figure out how we're gonna proceed," he said. "If this vampire has a grudge, I don't want to be sitting in a hotel room when she decides to do something about it."

The camper van was destroyed.

It had been merely damaged the night before. Gheorghe's door had been dented in, the paint all along the passenger side was ruined, the wing mirror and door handle gone. The roof was buckled. The side window was broken. That was bad enough.

They had made it easy for the vandal, parking the camper behind a rubbish skip to avoid unnecessary questions about what had happened to it—so the working-over had been done unobserved. It was thorough. Now the van sat on four burst tires; every window had been pushed in—not smashed, but crushed, probably to avoid making enough noise to attract attention in the parking lot. Not only were the tires and windows destroyed, the interior was torn to shreds, the seats reduced to twisted wire and chunks of foam, the steering wheel uprooted, the dashboard split and bent. Nothing was left.

The finishing touch was a spray of reeking, semifrozen liquid shit that spattered the detritus on the floor. It looked like the vehicle had been abandoned for six months in the worst neighborhood in Detroit.

"Man," Rock said.

"Vampire, you mean," Sax said. "Yeretyik did this, mark my words. That's vampire poo."

"The rental is on your credit card, right?" Gheorghe said.

The towing service arrived swiftly. They decided to say the vehicle had been stolen. No sense trying to explain they had partially wrecked it in the night and someone else had finished the job. Sax and Rock got a lift with the tow truck driver to the rental car place, where they recognized Sax—he had been their best customer all week.

For Sax's part, he hoped the people at the rental place were impressed by the variety and quality of his lovers. He'd shown up with the gorgeous Italian dressed as a priest, then the desperate-eyed Romanian, and now this enormous black American who looked like a professional athlete.

They didn't remark upon it, but handled the paperwork and insurance and provided a new vehicle with consummate professionalism, and assured Sax there was no difficulty with the stolen and destroyed van. These things occur. He couldn't believe they were letting him off the hook.

Rock drove Sax back to the hotel in the newly rented sport-utility vehicle and they loaded their gear into the back. Then Rock started driving to nowhere in particular, as long as they were moving. There was some argument as to what to do next. Sax's authority was thoroughly undermined. He wasn't the boss anymore, now that the job was off the track he had intended. The impetus was on the vampire's side. Whether Sax or Rock decided what to do next, it hardly mattered. Even if he knew what he wanted done, there wasn't any reason to accept his authority.

He'd known there was a danger of this. The team was necessarily composed of loners, brought together for a purpose interesting enough to keep them working in concert. Now that things had gone wrong, they were loners again, each scheming to ensure their own best outcome. Gheorghe was all for melting into the scenery. Give up their old lives and find something else to do that wouldn't attract attention. They could just slip away, one at a time, in some busy place.

"They can smell you, man," Rock said. "You can lose a human tail. Get lost in a crowd. But you can't shake a thing that just has to put its nose up in the air."

"So I will change my smell," Gheorghe said.

"I been wanting to suggest that for days," Rock said.

"It doesn't work, Gheorghe," Sax said. "Perhaps for you, but not for me. Without the life I have waiting for me back in New York, I'm nothing. I'm already dead. And as for you, I was told by Paolo that there was a plea bargain involved in your participation on this mission, set up by his people with the cooperation of the international courts. So you would be going back on a deal with one of the most powerful and extensive organizations in human history. That would take some very serious disappearing, vampire or no vampire."

Rock had his own idea, also shaped by his way of getting through life. He was a soldier, a man who balanced strategy with direct action. "What I'm thinking is we got this vampire's attention, right? So maybe we're the bait in the tiger trap. We get Paolo and them to hook up with some serious firepower—I know some people that would kick ass in this situation—and kind of ease on over here with us and hide in the woods. We make ourselves obvious, they come after us, and our backup lights them up. Vampires may be immortal, but they're not invulnerable, you dig the distinction there? Can't die, but if you're in little inch-long pieces, it don't matter."

"That was exactly what I did last time," Sax said. "It's a lovely way of dealing with a single monster. You just have to make sure you collect all the bits and dispose of them properly so they don't grow back. We have a different circumstance here. This vampire is not going to do its own attacking. It's a thinker. It will use its understudies to attack from behind. What happens when we have an army hidden in the trees and it goes 'round one at a time and kills everybody and we're standing there with our trousers down waiting for the gunfire to begin? We'll feel pretty foolish, is what, and then we'll still die."

Sax realized they hadn't heard his original, terrible plan.

"I didn't tell you this before, because I was not altogether convinced I could go through with it. But I have had, in my longanimous way, a scheme that has been brewing. It is not a good scheme, because it involves me being anywhere near the danger zone. I confess that was my primary reservation."

Rock pulled the vehicle off the road into a petrol station and turned all the way around in his seat to face Sax. His height was so great that his head nearly touched the ceiling; a shadow from the light reflected off the ground outside had formed above him, narrowing to a dark point that hung above his head so that he became a glowering exclamation point looking at Sax.

"If you got a plan, old man, now would be a goddamn good time to mention it," Rock said.

"Three days ago would have been a good time to mention also this plan," Gheorghe added, all but fingering an invisible dagger.

"It's not a good plan," Sax observed. "Stupid, in fact. This was my earliest idea, from when I first won the loathsome clock and suspected I was up against something inhuman. I was thinking I would get the Vatican's help to determine who the vampire was and where she is, and more or less give her a ring on the telephone to offer her my services as an expert in securing sound articles."

"You'd offer to work for the vampire?" Rock said, his voice flat.

"Precisely. I offer to procure for the vampire any further articles of furniture or objets d'art she might require. Get better prices than she was, at a modest commission. And I was going to offer to sell her a particular ormolu clock, which was an item I know she greatly desired."

"That's the worst plan I ever heard," Rock observed. "Bullshit, even."

"Yes. I'm not finished," Sax said. "A bullshit plan. But you see, that was only part one. In the second part, I collect a few items for her, pack them up, and send my removals experts to deliver them. These experts would in fact be a crack team of vampire killers—yourselves—who kill the vampire while it's cackling over the clock and so forth, and once that's done, in we go to loot the place. You know the way vampires are—they gloat terribly. You can often get them while they're gloating."

"*We* were the delivery people?" Gheorghe said.

"You didn't think *I'd* risk showing up in person, did you?" Sax said, indignant. "But as I said, that was only the first version of my plan. It gets worse."

Rock shook his head. "Now, hold on. That sounds like a pretty damn good plan. Why don't we—"

"Because she had her people *steal* the beastly clock before I could make the offer, is why. There went my leverage, and my night watchman, a fellow named Alberto. Her hired burglar killed him."

"She should have used me," Gheorghe said. "I would only stun him on the head."

"Very humane," Sax said. "Stop talking nonsense. Plan B was no better than plan A. It was plan B we were here to explore. I didn't mention the details because unfortunately it involved my personal participation. I was going to go up to the castle—"

"You personally?" Rock said.

"Me personally, yes. I told you it wasn't a good plan. Hence the *B*. I was going to toddle on up to the gates, knock knock knock, hello, I'm Asmodeus Saxon-Tang the antiques dealer whose night watchman you slew and whose ormolu clock you absconded with, and I would like the clock back, please."

There was a silence that curled up like cigarette smoke into the air between them. Traffic rumbled past on the road. Motorists came and went, rubbing their arms as they dashed through the cold to their cars. It was ordinary life in Germany outside the windows of the SUV, but it had the quality of a movie projected on a screen. Nothing seemed real.

"And?" Rock said.

"And," said Sax, "while I'm talking to the vampire, you lot set off the explosives, rush in, and kill it."

"You make the joke," Gheorghe said.

"No," Sax said.

"What explosives?" Rock said.

"The details weren't fully formed in my mind. I was thinking some sort of mixture of TNT; liquid diallyl disulfide, which of course is a distillate of garlic . . . and roofing nails."

They had no plan, and therefore, no purpose in Germany any longer.

They didn't know how to keep safe. Staying in hotels seemed like suicide, after the destruction of the camper. The vampire had either hunted them down by smell or somehow gotten hold of their itinerary. The latter possibility worried Sax the most. He had been calling the farmhouse at intervals, spelling out what they were doing to keep that blasted Emily from worrying about him.

This vampire was clever, and not the recluse Sax was expecting. She had something like a social life, what with all the hundings, the human familiars, and the Russian Yeretyik hanging about. She clearly knew about Sax and had been several steps ahead of him the entire time. He'd been played, in fact, for a fool. The creature must have been allowing him to get close, poke around her lair, just for the sheer sport of it. Something to occupy her time. It was not at all out of the question that she had put a tap on the telephone at the farmhouse and was listening to everything Sax said.

When Sax relayed this line of thinking, all three men were of one mind: they were damn well not getting back into a small airplane destined for a known airfield where an ambush could be arranged. Sax had the brilliant idea that they might drive all the way back to France. It would take the rest of the day, and they could come up with a new plan while they drove. Rather than sit at a restaurant where they might be observed, gripped by paranoia as they were, the men decided to grab lunch at a Nordsee restaurant, specializing in take-out fish items; Rock and Gheorghe had been happy to go to the McDonald's down the street because then they didn't have to get out of the vehicle, but Sax could not stoop so low. He made Rock go inside to pick up the Nordsee order, however. The entire world was swarming with hidden Russian vampires with ruined, purple-scarred skulls waiting to get him. He didn't dare get out of the vehicle.

They ate and drove and the air in the SUV was overheated and stale and Gheorghe began a campaign of silent, aggressive flatulence, after each episode of which he would laugh his hahahaha mechanical laugh, and then Sax and Rock would smell it a few seconds later and there would be much complaining and rolling down of windows to let the freezing air blast the stench out. So they were never entirely warm. The trip would take them five hours at a good pace. They were heading back to the farm in Petit-Grünenwald, tails firmly between their legs.

15

France

Paolo was in love with Emily.

He didn't want to admit it to himself. There was too much going on—the world had crowded in upon him too suddenly. He knew what he was experiencing was simply temptation wrapping itself around his cerebral cortex and squeezing—the devil, if one wished to put it in those terms, using the tools at his disposal to capitalize on Paolo's weakened state. Paolo didn't entirely buy the concept of the devil as a cloven-hoofed entity that personally moved in people's lives; God was that way, but God was the creator. The devil was just a character, a personification of certain immutable problems in human nature.

It had been easier for Paolo to ignore the sudden blooming of this emotion inside him while he was in charge of Nilu's care. He had focused on that project with desperate attention, keeping the poor suffering girl drinking water, and when that failed, melting ice into her mouth. At last, overriding Sax's orders in the name of saving a life, Paolo had called Fra Giuseppe in Rome and begged him to come at once. Now that brother Giu was in the *maison de maître* with his thin, pimply assistant, Fra Dinckel, tending to the victim, Paolo had been consigned to ice-fetching duty. He had time to think about his emotional state again. Fra Dinckel was an officious youth, evidently delighted at the opportunity to stand over someone on death's doorstep and look pious and disappointed. His job was to read from the Bible in Latin, which he did in a high, reedy voice with a German accent. It was like listening to a fly trapped in a bottle. Paolo couldn't stand to be in the room for long.

Fra Giu was tireless. He was plump, silver haired, with a nose that looked like something to be stored in a root cellar for winter stews. His hands worked swiftly, feeling for the hidden wounds upon Nilu's neck. Paolo had not been able to find them, but Giu did. At the base of the throat, on the right side. He had asked Paolo if by any chance the girl was baptized; Paolo did not think so. Fra Giu had frowned with his short, thick eyebrows folded in half over his eyes. He was trying to save someone at a great disadvantage, as her soul was already in hock. That was how he put it: *dato in pegno*. He assembled a breathing apparatus, regulator, tubes, and mask, and installed them on a tall oxygen tank that was parked on a trolley by the bedside.

Satisfied Nilu was getting some proper air, Giu rummaged in his doctor's bag, an orange nylon thing with a hundred compartments filled with modern medical supplies as well as stoppered jars of ancient remedies, herbs, and poultices. He took out a black pouch containing four small vials and one large one. He began mixing these powders in a saucer, dropping in small measures of water to make the stuff into a paste. Paolo knew what that was: a silver acetate solution in the big bottle, assorted sulfides and salts in the others. Some combination of them would soften the vampire's adhesive saliva seal on the neck wound.

Lovelorn Paolo was now starting to wonder if the devil was amongst them. In the clanging of Abingdon's hammer on the forge in the barn, he heard the sound of *il diavolo*'s cloven hooves ringing on the frozen ground. The sulfurous stink of the smoke was the very reek of hell. The Bible seemed to be coming to life all around him, his fevered imagination finding similarities between his present circumstances and the book that formed the foundation of his life. It was everywhere: even in the unfamiliar words mumbled and moaned by Nilu in her delirium, a tangle of Hindi and Malayalam and English, he heard the Confusion of Tongues that beset Babylon. Yet he bathed her brow and prayed for her.

Now Fra Giu used cotton swabs to dab his mixture on the place he had located on Nilu's pale greenish-brown neck. He warned Fra Dinckel to get back and bade Paolo come with a towel to receive the discharge in it. Giu saw Emily in the doorway. She had been watching, arms folded across her breasts.

"Do you know," he said, "every vampire leaves behind a discharge in its victim? It keeps the other vampires away. It says, *I am taken*. Tastes like the *escremento* to other fiends. That discharge, it must come out. You do not wish this thing to see."

He looked at the open doorway behind Emily and tried to shoo her away with his eyebrows.

"You want a little privacy?" she said. Her voice was music to Paolo.

Emily wished them luck and went downstairs. She wasn't interested in the gruesome side of things.

Paolo tried to occupy his mind with the struggle to save Nilu, but his thoughts would always double back to Emily when he wasn't paying attention. They would start giggling and pointing and whispering about her again. Certain instructive passages from the Song of Solomon kept invading his mind's eye: *Thy navel is like a round goblet, which wanteth not liquor: thy belly is like an heap of wheat set about with lilies.* Other lines as well.

Paolo dragged his mind back to the present. He held a white bath towel cupped around Fra Giu's hands against Nilu's neck. Fra Giu muttered a prayer and Paolo joined in. Dinckel's voice rose higher and higher, chanting from the Book. Giu had the correct mixture at last, he thought. It stank of onions. He warned Paolo to be ready and with the swab painted the liquid onto the wound, and now at last Paolo saw it begin to open.

It was like a small smiling mouth, bloodless folds of skin parting. Giu kept swabbing, each stroke of the cotton tip dissolving the salivary glue another few microns deeper into the wound. And then he was through, and the pressure of the blood beneath did the rest of the work. A jet of foul, gelatinous liquid the color of liver spurted out with stinging force into the towel and spattered the men. It stank like urine and pumped and foamed, shooting in loops and gobbets until the towel was streaming and Paolo had to fold it around itself and toss it aside and put another one in its place. When Fra Giu thought enough of the stuff had spurted out, he sealed the wound with a clamp resembling an eyelash curler. He left this device in place and began to assemble an intravenous drip, hanging the bag from the finial of the lampshade on the bedside table.

"Saline and holy water," he said.

Paolo took the rancid towels into the bathroom and ran water over them in the tub, once he figured out how to operate the complicated old-fashioned taps. Then he washed the slime from himself and went downstairs with much trepidation.

There was beautiful Emily, so American in her straightforwardness, but never bold like her uncle. She was so tempting! He tried to concentrate his thoughts upon the gory spectacle he'd witnessed upstairs but it was useless, as if he had been drugged so he would only think of this woman. It put Paolo in mind of Proverbs 5, which said,

My son! to my wisdom give attention, To mine understanding incline thine ear,
To observe thoughtfulness, And knowledge do thy lips keep.

For the lips of a strange woman drop honey, And smoother than oil is her mouth,
And her latter end is bitter as wormwood, Sharp as a sword with mouths.
Her feet are going down to death, Sheol do her steps take hold of.

"Sharp as a sword with mouths," he said out loud. Emily looked up from her book of vampire lore. There was a collection of them at the cottage; she'd previously assumed they'd been left by a morbid houseguest.

"What?" she said. "How is Nilu?"

Paolo wanted her with an ache he felt in his guts. He was out in the world, soaked in it with all these delicious dinners and comfortable beds and women sleeping in the next room with their smooth brown limbs thrown across the pillows, and the influence of such immersion in the world was getting to him, like salt water blistering the skin after a day at the ocean. His defenses were for the first time in his life (or since he was a teenager, at least), being tried—and they were worthless.

"She will live," Paolo said. He filled a couple of ice cube trays with water and shoved them roughly into the freezer. Then he threw some clean dish towels over his arm, found some shallow bowls in a cabinet, and carried them upstairs.

Emily allowed herself a slight shrug. He was gorgeous, Paolo was. But a little remote. *Must be the celibacy*, she thought, and returned to her book. He was dotted with bloodstains, she had noticed. She hoped Nilu was going to be okay.

Outside in the barn, Min watched the Englishman laboring at his forge and found herself thinking hazily about taking him for a lover.

It would be an act like exercising or sharpening a knife: something pleasurable and straightforward, without further baggage. And he was obviously one of those horse-cocked Europeans they joked about back in her home country. He was just an erection with a man standing behind it. It might be interesting, difficult as it was to find anything that diverted her besides her chosen mission in life.

The old *dongseongaeja* Saxon-Tang had asked her if she was one of the people who had lost everything, and he had said it in a casual way that was not unsympathetic but that made Min feel like she was ordinary, somehow. Like he knew many such people. Nobody had ever spoken to her like that before, not least because she would break their arms. He was a strange one.

Her thoughts swept back to a time years before when another stranger appeared in the remote Korean countryside where her family was staying for the summer holidays, her parents, both university professors, having an entire month to spend as they wished.

It was a monster, and yet it had appeared to be a man. It had spent some time with them, becoming friends. Vampires often did, savoring their prey.

Then one night it had arrived unexpectedly as Min's family was getting ready for bed. It had brought with it a false vampire that strained against its collar on the end of a leash. The false vampire was a victim the monster allowed to survive, so infected with the vampire's alien biology by repeated feedings that it had developed the thirst for human blood itself. At first, the vampire kept its crazed disciple lashed to a post in the main room of the cabin; the vampire had then fallen upon her parents, whose efforts to resist were like the struggles of children in a flood, and it sucked the blood out of them until they were helpless and weak, barely alive.

Following what must have been a program of entertainments in its mind, the vampire next unleashed the screaming madman upon Min's sister, three years younger than her, and Min herself, both of whom had been cowering in the corner; they struggled to get away but the man bit Min's sister to death. It took fifteen minutes with blunt human teeth. The vampire watched with fascination. Min had seen its face, the pleasure there. Then, weary of the evening's amusements, the vampire capriciously broke the spine of the false vampire, pulled out his heart, and forced the trembling organ between Min's jaws. Then the vampire tore Min's parents to pieces and left.

Min was suddenly seething with fury. This was what happened. One minute, she was watching Abingdon at his forge, seeing the nicely defined muscles in his sweating back and the big red-skinned arms hammering hot metal bright as sunset into crisp shapes, letting the man charm her. The next minute she was thousands of miles away and fifteen years younger and witnessing the slaughter of her family once again, every blow, torn screaming mouths vomiting rubies, and the rage rushed up like magma in the marrow of a volcano and mixed with the fear and everything was smoke and heat and cinders. Suddenly Abingdon was just a man making weapons, which was all she required. All else was superfluous. Love was nothing. Pleasure was nothing. Even Min herself was nothing, except that she killed the evil in the world.

Nilu went through five bags of saline. Soon she would be switched to glucose because her body had no fuel in it. Over baguettes filled with meat, cheese, tomato, and butter, Fra Giu explained to Emily the meaning of the procedure they had just performed. The infection was a parasitic organism, after a fashion. The ugly clotted muck that had poured out of Nilu's wound was the product of the vampire's biology: it was attacking and colonizing her blood, which is considered a kind of tissue from an anatomical standpoint. It was anchored at the inside of the bite wound. That was how vampires worked: each one had an adhesive saliva that sealed the wound after drinking. No other vampire's saliva would break the seal; it was a delicate chemistry. And if a different vampire opened a new wound on the same victim, the blood would taste foul because of the infection. However, the parasitic colony in the victim's blood made it more readily digestible by the vampire from whom the infection came, and was even involved in vampire reproduction. Nilu was two days away from becoming so infected she would be forced, if she had any strength, to begin feeding on blood herself.

Emily was disgusted by all this. She didn't touch her food.

Abingdon, eating heartily, told them he had a good batch of silver alloy to match the sample from the hammer Simon in his crucible, and had begun shaping a new set of hammers on the forge, beating the metal rather than casting it because he lacked the equipment to make the molds. They discussed names for the new hammers. Fra Giu had some saints in mind, Fra Dinckel his favorite popes. Abingdon wanted to name them after his favorite women, and Min didn't care. Paolo declared the hammers should not be named. It struck him as too much like idolatry.

Emily thought Paolo had become unreasonable in the last few hours, very prickly, and he kept getting biblical without warning. A far cry from the charming, relaxed man she had met yesterday. Rather than risk his disapproval, Emily did not suggest the names she'd thought of, which were a combination of Santa's eight reindeer and the Marx Brothers. She liked the abstract idea of plunging a hammer named "Harpo" or "Blitzen" into the heart of a vampire.

"Did you feel the erotic charge in that room?" Fra Giu said, surprising everyone.

"You mean sexual energy?" Fra Dinckel said. "No."

"I don't suppose you would," Fra Giu joked, and laughed at himself, nudging Fra Dinckel in his bony side. "But in truth. One of the side effects, so to say it, of vampire infection is the victim gives off clouds of something like pheromones. It makes them seem very attractive to the opposite sex. Everyone here will be feeling it. I myself had quite an *erezione*."

"What?" Paolo gasped. He looked like a man who had just found an electric eel in his bath.

"Yes, it's true," Fra Giu said. "They do not much discuss this in our order, of course, because of the confusion it might cause for some of the monks. And you trained in operations, not special medicine. But it is true. In that room above, I was overwhelmed with desire for the sick girl. It was madness. I have not felt such urges since ten years ago in a similar case."

Here he smiled at Emily, bowed his head, and placed one hand on his heart.

"With apologies to you, mademoiselle, for my frank speech, but I am speaking now of medical matters, not genuine lust. You understand."

"Yes, of course," Emily said. There was nothing *of course* about it, but she didn't know what else to say. She'd felt it herself.

Fra Giu continued. "That is why I opened the window, although it made the room cold. Our minds would become clouded. That is the nature of the disease. It makes the uninfected person crave to be near the vampire, and when at last the victim can stand it no longer, he or she attacks and feeds on the victims close at hand. Again, something to do with the vampires, an *effetto collaterale*—side effect. The vampire itself can give off a powerful chemical that makes human beings go mad with desire, a psychotic response similar to the experience of heroin introduced into the bloodstream. The sound of beautiful music, bells, such colors as the real world does not have in it, and at the heart of it all, the vampire. That is why these creatures are successful feeders upon any species and any individuals. The influence of the poison is nearly irresistible."

"My uncle survived a vampire attack. He told me about it," Emily said. "He heard bells and saw a golden light, and strange colors. You know what saved him? The vampire was a girl, and he doesn't—well, you know. He doesn't go for women in that way. So the spell kind of broke."

"It was far more than that," Fra Giu said. "Your uncle is a man of hidden strength—strength beyond reckoning, in a way. It is also his weakness. He refuses to be a victim. That's why he survived the attack. That's why he's here. He won't tolerate the vampire taking his watchman's life, or stealing his clock. Paolo told me the whole story," Fra Giu added, interrupting himself. "He thinks your uncle is a very worthy man. But a man that delights in throwing temptation in people's ways."

Here Fra Giu fixed a peculiar look on Paolo, and Paolo blushed and looked down at his half-eaten sandwich. Emily wondered what was going on there.

"But Uncle Sax," Emily said, "is the opposite of that. Not the temptation part. He's all *about* temptation. I mean personality-wise he's a total victim. When I was a girl, he was always getting robbed by someone he'd—he'd met, you know, I mean he'd wake up with no money and that sort of thing. And he always complains his clients are ripping him off and everything. Really."

Fra Giu looked very amused by this. "It's a role, I tell you. He plays the victim part. He never paid for the, ah, for the favors he received from the wayward youths. But he left his purse of money where it could be taken."

"He's not like that," Emily said, realizing he was exactly like that.

16

France

The *maison* was warm and comfortable looking after the long drive through cold darkness with the sky shaking its black fists over the landscape, threatening storms. As Rock turned the car into the farmyard, rain spattered down, tossed by the blustering wind. There was going to be a hell of a downpour soon. Emily was standing in the doorway of the *maison*, for some reason. It took Sax so long to unfold himself from the backseat of the SUV that Rock and Gheorghe had already scattered by the time Sax had his feet on the frozen dirt.

Emily had thrown on a jacket by then, and helped haul Sax up by the wrists. As she guided him toward the house, Sax reminded himself for the thousandth time to get gravel laid down in the courtyard. He never would, of course, because he never had. Gheorghe urinated extravagantly around the corner on the wall of the cottage, decorum not being amongst his talents, while Sax limped inside.

Emily gave Sax a squeeze and he felt for a moment as if he was home.

"I've been so worried about you," she said.

"Don't stop now," Sax said, "being worried. Dear niece, please go and round up the crew. I have a report to make."

Everyone was there. This gathering of souls was so interesting, so rare, Sax hated to break it up. Nine extraordinary people present, not including Nilu, who was of course upstairs quietly surviving in the best bed. Sax had been to gala balls with five thousand guests at which there were not ten people worth talking to; this was a special group.

The kitchen of the *maison* was humid, the air fragrant with old cooking, the liquid dark outside the windows throwing back reflections of himself and the others like underexposed snapshots of the occasion. It was raining with increasing force outside, and the panes rattled with the suck and push of the wind.

Sax looked around the room at his companions. Emily leaned her rump against the island in the middle of the cooking area; Paolo inclined his shoulder against the fridge a few feet behind Emily, his black-furred arms folded. The others—Min, Abingdon, the monks Giu and Dinckel, Rock, and Gheorghe—were arrayed in a manner reminiscent of Jan de Bray's 1675 painting *Governors of the Guild of St. Luke*. Direct, expectant stares, with here and there a questing glance between them. Sax finished his inspection of the troupe and thought it was a pity they hadn't gotten together for some more realistic purpose. He might have enjoyed himself.

"So we're back from our reccy of Castle Mordstein," Sax began, and quite poorly. Obviously they were back, or he'd be speaking on the telephone. Get on with it. "And—well, it's impregnable."

"That's what they said about the Queen Mother," Abingdon remarked.

"What I mean to say," Sax said, "is the situation stands as follows. Were we to pursue our intended course of action vis-à-vis this vampire, with regard to liberating its property and so forth—and of course avenging its various wrongdoings, obviously—we would all be slaughtered. Here are the obstacles: First, the castle itself can only be assaulted from the air, and even then, it's unlikely we'd make it inside. Second, it's not one vampire. It's two vampires, half a dozen hundings, and God knows how many sort of Igor types running around going 'yes, master' and strangling people in their sleep."

"What are you saying?" Emily asked, because she wasn't required to be polite.

"There has been a change of plans," Sax said. "The whole operation is off. Sorry, but no dice, we're done, we fuck off out of it at first light tomorrow."

There was a silence as enduring as Gibraltar.

"I apologize," Sax amended, "for the unfortunate choice of words. I mean to say 'pack up tomorrow and depart forthwith.'"

"What you mean *depart?*" Min said, her voice simmering low.

"*S'en aller.* Quit the premises. Abscond, skedaddle, bugger off, leave." Sax felt a fine hysteria building up. He terribly disliked having things not go his way. Disappointing people was not his strength, despite long practice. He wished now to shrivel up and hide in the corner, but the business must be concluded. "I'll see that those of you who entered into this project with expectations of compensation are remunerated appropriately, of course."

"Bloody right," Abingdon said, not meaning it.

"My price goes up after what happen," Gheorghe said, meaning it.

"You are making a joke, yes?" Paolo said.

"I'm not joking," Sax replied.

"We quit? *Ci fermiamo al progetto?*"

"If your Leaping Monks of the Righteous Order of Tooting Flamingoes want to assault the castle, be my guest. I told you what we saw. It pains me to admit I am defeated. But we were nearly killed. This is a consortium of monsters we're up against, not one isolated crank stuck in the seventeenth century. She has a *helicopter*, for Christ's sake."

"We have helicopters," Paolo said. He just wasn't getting it.

Sax looked around the room, growing desperate. Emily was merely confused, but Sax saw Min, Gheorghe, and the other two monks were not well pleased. Now the scene looked rather more like Tintoretto's agitated 1570 version of *The Last Supper.* Fra Giu stood up and placed his palms on the table, leaning across it toward Sax.

"You do not the decision make for stopping this job," he said. "There are forces at your back. We need this creature to be destroyed. But we cannot do it with ourselves because of the political situation and the nature of the Church in modern Europe. We cannot, you understand me? But every day that passes, that monster is kill more and more of the people. That girl upstairs is a heathen, but her soul is worth more price than anything you can take from the world. How many more souls?"

"Don't get biblical on me," Sax said. This wasn't going at all well.

"Uncle Sax, nobody got hurt, right?" Emily said. She had a proper direct way of thinking, bless her. Sound mind, sound body. The rest is décor.

"Other than hypothermia and a few bruises I'd say we all survived," Sax said. "And we used up all the luck we'll ever have. Listen, people. I'll pay you, I'll write a letter to His Holiness the Pope on my personal stationery. The whole bit. But one thing I will not do is go back to that castle, and none of you are going either. Not on my watch, anyway. You god-fearing celibates can organize your own picnic."

There was a brief silence while this news soaked in. Rock ended it. "I'll go pack up my gear," he said, and turned to leave.

"Chickenshit," Gheorghe said.

"Say what?" Rock turned about a quarter of the way around, like a partial eclipse, his expression bemused, eyes fixed almost dreamily on some distance that only he could see. Sax recognized the look. He was making an effort not to blow his stack, as the kids used to say.

"I say you are scared like baby," Gheorghe elaborated. "The big baby jungle bunny."

Sax pressed his fingertips into his eyelids, trying by force of will to make time speed up so that, in the next three seconds, it would be a week later and he could open his eyes in his place in New York City and go back to hating the Wolfgang Hoffmann coffee table, which was really all he was good for anymore.

"Gheorghe," Sax said, when time failed to accelerate, "please don't use racial epithets."

"It's okay," Rock said. "I'm here in a professional capacity. If the mission is canceled, so be it. We'd need a platoon."

Sax was grateful for Rock's self-control. It must have angered him, however, because he stepped outside. A rill of cold, wet air made its way through the kitchen.

"I'll walk you home," Abingdon said, and followed Rock outside.

Although Rock outwardly showed no emotion, when he closed the door behind them, it shook the entire house.

"Min?" Sax said, because Min was visibly trembling, her fists clenching and unclenching.

"You make vampire go free?" she said, composing her thought with care.

"It's not my favorite idea," he said. "I mean for one thing, it knows who I am. You have the advantage of anonymity. But if you want to scale the battlements on your own, be my guest. I'll give you a map."

Min threw her head around at the entire crowd, furious. Her mouth worked on foreign words that wouldn't come.

"Everybody can go fuck you!" she barked, and stomped outside after Rock, probably heading back up to her stronghold on the hilltop to pack her meager belongings. It was raining needles. She'd be half dead of the cold before she got there.

"I think you are making a mistake," Paolo said.

"I didn't *ask* you," Sax observed.

"I know something about these things, even if you do not trust me."

"Don't trust you?" Sax was nonplussed. "Of course I trust you. I just can't bear to see you killed."

"You don't bear to see him killed," Gheorghe said, "because he is so pretty."

"Yes," Sax said. "He's lovely."

"But is okay me and Negro baby get the death. That is fine with you."

"That," Sax said, with exaggerated patience, "is why you are here."

"Okay," Gheorghe said. "*Vechiul meu prieten, un poponar laş.* Does he suck on your pee-pee also?"

Paolo lurched upright from his slouch against the fridge and stepped past Emily, suddenly angry. Sax had never seen him angry.

"You do not speak that way in front of a woman," Paolo said.

Gheorghe smiled. "One woman, the rest girls," he said, his hands at his sides, fingers outstretched with palms forward, in the pose that meant *take a swing at me*. Sax saw what was happening. Gheorghe was frustrated because the mission had failed, so now he was going to insult everybody until he got a big reaction. Then there would be a fight, and he could divert his frustration down that more familiar channel, and at least *he* would be satisfied.

"One woman, three castrati, and an old faggot, I think you meant," Sax said. "Get out now, Gheorghe. Nobody here is going to fight you. Just leave." Sax went to the door and placed his hand on the doorknob. Gheorghe detached himself from the wall and sauntered with consummate insolence across the room. He winked at Emily.

"Don't you wink at me," Emily said.

Paolo advanced halfway across the room, and Fra Giu stepped between them.

"Paolo, this is not seemly," he said.

"This man is a disgrace," Paolo said.

"You are lucky, boy," Gheorghe said. "If you went to the castle, you make wet in your pants and cry."

Paolo surprised Sax when he didn't respond to Gheorghe, but instead pointed an accusatory finger at Sax.

"You have no right," he said, "to keep me from what needs to be done. I'm not a Greek statue for you to look at, Sax. Do not think I haven't noticed. I am a professional. This is my job. You insult me and you insult the order."

"Oh, come off it, you ravishing Roman reprobate. I'm running this thing. You want to take your lads for a butcher's holiday in Germany, that's no longer my business. It's not like you've suffered, have you? I've fed you well. You've been making googly eyes at my niece ever since she arrived—"

"Uncle Sax!" Emily interjected.

"Oh, Emily, don't be Edwardian," Sax snapped. "You're the one that showed up uninvited and threw Paolo off his game in the first place. You were never supposed to be here, that's all, and you've made things more difficult altogether. I cannot thank you for it."

Emily was stunned by this. Her mouth hung open but no sound emerged.

"Right," Sax said, turning to the monks Giuseppe and Dinckel. "Anyone else want a go before we retire for the evening?" He knew he was behaving abominably—he'd taken the insult-slinging role from Gheorghe and done him one better, going after anybody the Romanian had missed. But they didn't seem to *understand*. It wasn't just because of cowardice on his part that he'd canceled the operation. Rock had said as much—it was clearly suicide to proceed. And now they were all looking at him as if he'd spoiled somebody's birthday party, rather than kept them all from dying horrible, unnatural deaths.

Sax was angry and upset and he wanted everyone right there with him. That was all there was to it. To signal the end of his remarks, he wheeled around, stuck his finger in Gheorghe's chest, then opened the door and pointed out into the yard. Gheorghe turned to leave but remained in the doorway, letting the wind and rain get in. It was getting wetter by the minute outside, and cold enough that it might turn to snow.

"Will you please go," Sax said. Gheorghe continued staring into the weather, apparently having forgotten everyone.

"That clock of yours," Gheorghe said at last. "Gold with a blue middle?"

"Forget the clock. What do you care about the clock?" Sax said.

Gheorghe pointed out the door.

"It is here."

Everyone crowded in the doorway to see for themselves. Sax switched on the floodlights he had installed along the eaves of the house for summer parties. The courtyard glittered with the impact of the smoking rain.

There was the clock, a pompous little folly in gold and porcelain with a pompadour of stiff yellow curls above a white face, standing on its four slender legs in the middle of the frozen dirt and the rain and the cold night wind. Sax's first reaction was to run outside and bring it in so it wouldn't get soaked—the clock represented the single most overpriced object he had ever purchased. And besides, it was his, and it was back. He wouldn't let it out of his sight again.

That phase of his response took all of a half second. It was followed by a tremendous sense of dread. If the clock was here, it had been delivered by his nemesis. Somehow Sax didn't think the vampire had sent it by Deutsche Post. She was out there, or her servants were.

"I think I'd better close the door," Sax said, and did so, crowding everyone back.

"Do not you want stupid clock?" Gheorghe said. He hadn't yet realized what its presence meant.

"We have a problem," Sax said, his voice unnaturally calm. He did not feel calm. "Let's move away from the doors and windows. I think we need to think what we're going to do."

"Rock has so much weapons," Gheorghe said. "He's there. I get him."

He reached for the doorknob and Sax caught his wrist.

"Gheorghe," Sax said. "If that clock is here—"

Emily was moving toward the window to look out at the clock. "The vampire is nearby, isn't it," Emily said. She was shivering.

Sax motioned to Paolo. "Get her away from there," he said. Paolo grabbed the back of Emily's blouse and pulled her into the middle of the kitchen. "Can someone," Sax continued, "please call Rock on his mobile phone? I'll call Abingdon. Min hasn't got a phone but she may already be dead, crossing that field."

Sax let it ring. Abingdon didn't answer. The vampire might have gotten him while he was walking over to his bread truck. Sax dared to get close to the window to look outside—he vividly remembered the Russian's ragged fist coming through the window of the camper van, and expected another grab at any moment—and saw Abingdon's truck standing by the barn looking perfectly normal. There were lamps lit in the cottage as well, the small windows spilling honeyed light through the slashing wind and rain. Rock might be in there, oblivious to the danger, or he might be dead.

Paolo was sensibly turning out the lights around the *maison*.

Sax got Abingdon's automated message, waited for the beep, and said, "Don't go outside, the vampire is here." Then he ended the call. What a strange world, that with a piece of technology like the mobile phone he was leaving a message to warn a fellow forty feet away about a vampire.

Fra Giu had his own mobile out: "I called the order in Roma. Four hours away most soon, even in the swift helicopter. They are coming. When they can, here be they will."

Sax was grateful. It was far past time to be sensible and let the professionals deal with the situation. He had never felt more amateur than he did now. Fra Giu suggested Fra Dinckel get Emily upstairs, and they went; Gheorghe stood beside the living room drapes, concealed by them, looking into the farmyard through the gap in the curtains.

The house was tragically insecure. At least they were inside a building, which was better than being inside, for example, an old bread truck; but the house was defenseless without its heavy shutters drawn shut. These were dogged back against the exterior walls, so that was that. Sax had a suspicion there were eyes watching him out there in the darkness beyond the panes.

"I gave to Emily a cooking knife," Paolo said. He was standing in the darkness beside Sax, in the kitchen, where there was a view of the cottage.

"We might be safer if we can get over there," Sax said. "It's got hardly any windows and only two great heavy doors."

"I think the vampire wants us to go out in the yard," Paolo said. It had been less than four minutes since Gheorghe had first seen the clock. A blast of cold air suddenly rushed around the house.

"Gheorghe, don't!" Sax shouted, but he was already speaking to an empty dining room doorway. Gheorghe had run out into the yard. With the house dark and the exterior floodlights burning, he was like a mime on a stage in a dark, wet theater. He had his head tucked down into his shoulders against the stinging lances of icy rain, but he moved with speed and grace. His course took him past the pathetic little clock, which did not appear to notice him. He ran to the SUV and threw himself inside. Nothing leapt from the darkness beyond the glistening farmyard wall. Nothing changed.

"What the hell is he up to?" Sax muttered.

Paolo slammed the French doors in the dining room shut. The floor was already wet. He jammed a chair up under the door handle. Outside in the SUV, Gheorghe was rummaging around for something. Sax saw him in silhouette behind the streaming glass of the vehicle's windows. He found what he was looking for: the handgun he'd shot the vampire Yeretyik with.

"I give us ten minutes," Sax said. "Unless she's just toying with us."

Paolo blew through his nostrils by way of response, a noise of disbelief.

"Maybe," he said.

That was when Sax saw it.

First the green discs of the eyes, then the white, wet flesh looming out of the darkness beyond the wall of the yard. A hunding.

"Aieee," Paolo said, under his breath. "*Mio Dio.*"

"You're in for it now," Sax said, deeply angry not at Paolo but at the huge, pale creature stepping into the light of the yard. "A piece of the action like you wanted."

One by one, the others saw the creature. Emily made a sound in her throat like an antique telephone disconnecting. She was too frightened for words. Fra Giu muttered a prayer. The thing outside was maggot colored, covered in straps of thick muscle, its claws and fangs like something from a child's drawing, huge and gleaming. The heavy bristles on its back looked like cactus spines. Its eyes never left the group inside the *maison*.

There was a *crack* and a flash of light and a black hole appeared in the monster's chest. The creature recoiled and leapt back into the shadows and Gheorghe rolled his window up in the SUV. At least, Sax thought, he'd seen the thing in time. But the Romanian was now well and truly trapped.

"We need to do something," Sax said. "Get more knives."

Emily appeared at his side.

"For God's sake, woman—" Sax began, and then stopped, and instead of speaking he threw a quaking arm around her, pulled her to him, and clutched her tight.

"Emily, I'm sorry about this," he managed to say at last. He turned back to the kitchen window. Gheorghe had a second gun in his hands now. It must have been the one Rock had brought with him to Germany.

"I have the hammer you gave me," Emily said.

"What?" Sax wheeled on her, his old eyes lit with energy.

"Simon. I brought it."

"Why didn't you tell me?"

"Because it was a ridiculous thing to do," Emily hissed, angry and ashamed and afraid all at once. "It's in my suitcase under the bed. Should I get it?"

"Foolish girl!" Sax hissed, frantic.

Fra Dinckel descended the stairs now, his eyes bulging almost out of his head, the massive Bible clutched to his chest.

"We heard a gunshot," he said.

Paolo spoke to Fra Dinckel in rapid Italian and pointed at the ceiling. Emily's room was above the kitchen. Fra Dinckel put his Bible on the kitchen table and ran up the stairs with his thin-soled Italian shoes slapping.

The hunding was there again, moving along behind the wall of the yard. The wound in its chest issued a red river of blood and the lashing rain diluted the blood and kept it flowing, its intensity of color shocking against the pale flesh. The creature slunk behind the cottage. Rock must have heard the shot from inside. He knew that sound well. He would be alert to danger, if he was still alive. Sax hoped so.

The hunding emerged on the other end of the cottage, by the entrance gate of the yard, and went down on all four legs. It kept low, the rear bulk of the SUV between itself and Gheorghe, who was in the front seats. Sax saw that Gheorghe was aware of the monster's position. He was up on his knees on the passenger seat. The Romanian wasn't wasting another shot. He kept the gun trained on the beast but did not fire, allowing the monster to come closer.

The hunding looked around at the *maison* and its green-glowing eyes fixed upon Sax, visible in the kitchen window by the floodlight that reflected from the wet, icy ground. When the monster locked eyes with him, Sax shrank. He was so very frightened. *Little pig, little pig*, he thought. *Mine is a house of straw.*

Paolo took Emily by the shoulders and got her well back from the window, but she had seen enough. She was as terrified as Sax. Then the hunding's eyes turned back to Gheorghe, Sax dismissed for now, and the thing drifted closer to the SUV, water streaming from its sparse fur and glistening in beads on the coarse bristles of its shoulders.

Sax was watching Gheorghe as intently as the monster. The man was up to something. Sax tried to will Gheorghe to stay calm, to stay where he was. Sax could not hear the sounds of the tableau but saw it all in pantomime. Gheorghe used his elbow to pop the latch handle of his door and put one foot down onto the wet ground, keeping the mass of the vehicle between himself and the lycanthropic thing that had hunched, arms back, head low, ready to spring, at the sound of the opening latch. Rock appeared at the cottage door, shotgun in hand.

Rock was shouting to Gheorghe, who shook his head. The hunding gathered itself low for the spring—and Gheorghe fired both guns. The monster leapt not at Gheorghe but sideways, out of the line of fire, and Rock shot at it as well. The thing was hit, but it did not flee now. It sank low on its front legs and tried to push itself up but lacked the strength. It was snarling, teeth bared.

These things didn't fear injury, because they could survive almost anything—but their boldness got them badly hurt. At least it might be out of commission. Then they could finish it off. Rock fired another round from the doorway and Sax saw a halo of dark blood jump up from the hunding into the spotlights. Again Rock was shouting to Gheorghe. Gheorghe tossed the wet hair out of his eyes. There was a filament of rainwater streaming from the end of his nose.

Rock fired the shotgun again, and in that moment, Gheorghe made his move, running with his shoulders turned at right angles to his path, firing the guns in his hands. A wild bullet shattered one of the windowpanes to Sax's left; he and Paolo and Emily hit the floor, scrabbling in a cascade of broken glass.

"We need to get to safety," Paolo said.

"Brilliant," Sax said, and lifted his head up to see out the window set in the kitchen door.

Only a second or two had passed. Gheorghe was still moving. He was almost to the cottage doorway when the second hunding appeared.

It lunged out from behind the corner of the building, just beyond the front door, and Gheorghe all but ran into its arms. The beast caught him around the neck with one of its thick limbs, and with the other it reached up and stripped open the man's belly. Gheorghe's guns flew from his hands. His mouth was stretched open in a tortured scream that Sax could hear through the window. A tangle of entrails spilled out of his body, then the blood poured forth, and the monster thrust its huge paw inside Gheorghe's abdomen and ripped out his lungs.

Sax must have made quite a sound himself, because Paolo came forward and clapped his hand over Sax's mouth and dragged him away from the door, their shoes slithering in the broken glass. They reached the foot of the stairs, Emily following, bent double to keep out of sight. Fra Dinckel was at the top of the stairs, holding the hammer in his hands.

"It has no handle," he whispered.

"Break a bit off that bloody chair," Sax said. In his fear and anger he wanted to lash out, and he had always disliked the chair at the top of the stairs. He'd been meaning to get rid of it for years. Let it suffer—it wasn't a hunding, but it was something. When Fra Dinckel just stood there and did nothing, Paolo rushed up the steps, then smashed the chair over the stair railing, which was not at all what Sax had in mind. No sense breaking *everything*. But then one of the long uprights of the chair back came free and Paolo shoved it through the eye of the silver hammer Simon with its sharp tip shining even in the semidarkness.

A length of broken chair leg clattered down the stairs, split along its length: it could pass for a wooden stake, Sax realized, and snatched it up. It would not make much of a weapon. Maybe he could stab *himself* with it before they got to him. He saw in his mind a flash of Gheorghe's screaming face as the entrails tore free from his body. It was almost beyond Sax's ability to imagine surviving now. The flowers were blooming behind his eyes again. He felt faint. If he hadn't been sitting on the floor he would have fallen. Fra Giu was beside Paolo at the top of the stairs now. He placed a hand on Dinckel's shoulder and the younger man jumped with fright.

"Go with Nilu," Giu said, and tossed his thumb over his shoulder at Sax's bedroom door. Dinckel scuttled away into the darkness.

"What is happening?" Giu continued, seeing the look on the others' faces. "Did someone—"

"Gheorghe," Sax croaked. "He's done."

"There are two wolf men," Emily whispered. "One is wounded. They killed—" She didn't say it. Too much to encompass in words.

"There could be as many as six," Sax said. "We saw them being loaded into the back of a truck at the foot of that bloody castle. That's what was happening—it never occurred to me. They trucked them here, and released them as soon as we got back."

Sax cursed himself. In hindsight, if he had only paused to consider it, shouldn't this have been obvious? What *else* would the vampire have been up to? He was a fool, and now there was another dead man. But it was time to act, not utter mea culpas.

"How do we kill them?" Emily asked, like a child wanting to know how to stop the rain.

"We can't. Not six of them. They're just as tough as any man-shaped vampire, and stronger. The only advantage we have is they're stupid. But they have all the instincts you can get. So we're in real trouble—"

Emily interrupted: "If we were up in Fort Tetanus on the hill, we could lock ourselves in and wait for help."

Sax shook his head. He was sweating. But he had an idea, a plan as bad as any he'd ever devised. "Yes, but we're not up there, we're down here in the airy-fairy farmhouse, all windows and doors, and they can walk right in here and play football with our livers. So instead—"

"Don't lose your head," Fra Giu said. He was shaking now, too, his back to the stairway wall.

"I'm not," snapped Sax. "I'm just telling you what we're dealing with. I suppose you know it all, with your precious team of crack vampire-slaying monks. Listen to me! You know what we have to defend ourselves? We have fire. They hate fire."

"What fire?" Paolo asked.

"I mean let's get a bloody fire *going*," Sax said.

Fra Giu went down the stairs and peeked out the dining room window beside the French doors.

"They're still out there. They're trying to get into the cottage," he said. Then: "*O Gesù benedetto.*" He had seen the remains of Gheorghe.

"Can you see Abingdon anywhere? Or Min?" Sax was gripping his wooden stake with such convulsive force that his hands ached.

"Only those things."

Sax started to move. He crossed to the dining room and knelt by the liquor cabinet. A dozen bottles in there, half empty, things tenants had left behind. He pulled out the most flammable stuff. Vodka. Whiskey. Liqueurs.

"Help me," he said to Fra Giu. "Tablecloths in there."

Fra Giu pulled a stack of neatly folded white tablecloths from within the sideboard and threw them to Sax.

"What do we do, make torches? Surround them with fire?" he asked. Sax was pouring the liquor over the tablecloths, making acrid, dripping sponges of them.

"We surround *ourselves* with fire," Sax said. "Look, I've a kind of a plan but it's not very good. We might have very little time before they attack. We need to move. Spread these wet cloths out under the windows and doors, will you? Now-ish would be best."

Fra Giu did as he was told, taking a couple of fragrant, sopping tablecloths into the kitchen. Paolo grabbed the next couple and spread them out along the foot of the French doors, twisting the cloths along their lengths as if he planned to knot them together for an escape rope. Emily pulled down the curtains above some of the back windows and piled them on the windowsills. Sax poured liquor over them. Fra Giu returned with olive oil and splashed that around as well.

"How are we going to escape the fire?" he asked.

"No idea," Sax said. "We'll have to do something with the girl upstairs. Carry her."

"You'll have to do this," Giu said to Paolo. "Move faster than me."

Sax brought a bunch of wax tapers and a box of matches out of a kitchen drawer. "Light these candles, please. There's a gas lighter in that drawer there. Quickly."

Fra Giu took a bundle of white candles from Sax and lit them. Sax realized his plan was moving almost *too* fast. Safer to light the candles after they were in position. It didn't matter. He stuck one of the tapers in a water glass and placed it at the foot of the kitchen door, surrounded by a rumpled-up tablecloth soaked in whiskey. The candle flame flared and crackled as if hungry to reach the spirits evaporating all around it.

Emily made a noise—a sob, a gasp of terror. Sax couldn't tell. But he looked at her sharply, and she sucked whatever it was back inside herself, squeezing her eyes shut for a moment.

"I'm getting light-headed from all the alcohol," Emily said. "I'm going upstairs to tell Mr. Dinckel what's happening."

Paolo set up a pair of candles in the dining room in the same manner, placing them in glasses so the long wax cylinders teetered at an angle over their top lips. If somebody made a mistake now, the whole place would go up in flames and drive them outside, if anyone could even make it through the flames to begin with. Sax was sweating so profusely that a fat droplet of perspiration extinguished the candle he placed under the window at the far end of the kitchen. He fumbled out his matches and relit the candle. A fragment of burning match head spiraled down onto the floor beside the vodka-fuming cloth bundled at his feet. Sax jerked back. The alcohol didn't catch fire. He sank to his knees. Fra Giu appeared at his side.

"Okay, you make a good plan. If they come in, the candle falls, the fire comes. Good plan."

"Yes, well it's missing the bit after that," Sax said curtly, and forced his rusty knees to bear him upright again.

Paolo was watching the yard from a few feet inside the kitchen door. They were all keeping well away from the candles.

"There is a third creature outside now," he said. "It's looking at us."

"Get away from the light," Sax hissed. He doubled over to get himself out of sight as much as possible and made it to the stairs. Fra Giu followed him. They went up. It was dark. Fra Dinckel came to the bedroom door, his wide eyes glittering.

"Emily?" Sax whispered through the bathroom door.

"Just a minute," she said from inside.

She came out wiping her eyes. Sax suspected she'd just had a fit of tears, the remainder of the panic she'd first shown downstairs. Typical of her to require privacy for that.

It was wholly dark now except for the light from the yard. The rain drummed on the roof and the exterior lights made snakes of reflected water writhe over the walls. Thunder rumbled deep in the bones of the house, too far away for the crack of sound. Sax went alone into Emily's room and looked out into the yard.

He saw the three hundings now. One was on the roof of the cottage, almost level with his eyes. It was watching the *maison* but it was not looking at him. Could it leap as far as the window at which he stood? He didn't think so, not quite. The other two were circling the cottage, pacing counterclockwise, studying the windows and doors, ignoring the *maison*. Rock had attacked one of their own. They wanted him first.

The cottage was a strong structure with very few openings in it, being constructed according to the needs of impoverished eighteenth-century peasants. The big house was as insecure as a china cabinet, all bourgeois glass and delicate woodwork, not stout timbers and stone. Rock might survive by sitting tight; the monsters would slink away at daybreak. By that time the *maison de maître* would be an abattoir of blood and destruction, or a blazing funeral pyre.

Then Sax saw the situation change, and after that it all happened at a ferocious speed. The hunding on the roof abruptly raised a foreclaw and slammed it downward and Sax saw it had found one of the skylights, both of which were big enough for the creature to shove its bulk through. It tore the broken plastic shell from the frame, then wrenched the frame out of the roof and shoved itself head and shoulders into the opening. At that moment, it was framed by a flash of light as if someone had just taken a photograph, but it couldn't have been that, because the monster's head vanished in a fountain of brains, blood, and bone, its severed mandible whipping through the rain like an obscene fang-studded boomerang. The monster convulsed and its limbs went stiff and it rolled, blood spewing from its ragged neck, off the cottage roof and onto the hood of the SUV below. *That* would stop it for a few decades.

At that moment, there was a metallic *clang* from across the yard and the back door of the bread truck flew open. Abingdon leapt out. Sax was both exhilarated and terrified.

Abingdon was clad in a suit of medieval armor and held a broadsword in his gauntleted hands. His body and arms were encased in the fluid coat of mail called a hauberk, and there was a shining gorget at his throat. He wore a helmet with an iron nasal that came down between his eyes, and his arms were further bound in steel vambraces with bat-wing hinges at the elbows. It made a strange contrast to the faded blue jeans and engineer's boots below. Abingdon charged, and one of the other hundings was caught off guard. It had been crouched over the corpse of its headless companion when Abingdon emerged from the van. Now the monster turned, leading with its head, gathering its mass low to pounce—Abingdon swept the long, flashing blade of the sword in a low arc and cut off the monster's face. Sax could see into its sinuses and the empty half-sockets of its eyes for an instant before the blood came pouring out and the thing went berserk, hurling itself around the yard. If Abingdon had ignored it to attack the remaining creature, he might have survived.

As it was, he ran after the thing to finish the job, hacking at its limbs. The yard was awash in blood. Abingdon himself was painted red from head to foot, and Sax thought he was seeing the real chivalric ideal of battle with dragons brought to life. Emily was at his shoulder now. Some instinct told him to propel her away from the window. She resisted but stepped back.

The third hunding came up behind Abingdon and he swung around and severed its foreleg at the elbow joint. At that same moment, three *more* of the monsters came hurtling out of the darkness beyond the farmyard wall and fell upon Abingdon at once. He did not strike another blow, but was ripped into thirty-pound chunks in a matter of seconds, the coat of mail torn to heavy rags that trailed in the blood-slimy yard. The white rain poured down and hit the dirt and sprayed back up crimson.

The monsters turned to the *maison* as one. It was time to finish things.

"They're coming!" Sax shouted, his voice unexpectedly loud in the silent house. Glass broke downstairs. Sax squeezed Emily's arm. Then he slammed the bedroom door and twisted the key in the lock. He didn't know where anybody else was. They were going to have to live or die according to their individual wits and fortunes. It always came down to that eventually, whenever men squared off against vampires.

There was a *boom* below the floor and something crashed to the ground and broke, then everything was smashing below them, the floor-boards jumping beneath their feet. Smoke curled up through the floor and the boards became hot.

"I wish you hadn't come," Sax said. Emily didn't have any words. She threw an arm around his shoulders and took the wooden stake from his nerveless fingers and held it like a dagger. Sax felt so old and helpless and, worst of all, stupid. He had caused all this. Every ounce of blood and scream of agony was his work. He still had the lees-end of a bottle of vodka in his hands. He wondered if he shouldn't offer the poor girl a drink.

He heard gunshots. There was an explosion. Human screams.

And then the flaming hunding came crashing through the door.

The oak panels shattered like glass, long staves of broken wood flying into the room. The creature was wreathed in fire, its white flesh splitting, blackening. It howled and Sax could see the heavy sawing teeth behind its fangs, the ridges of its hard palate, the vulval anatomy of its throat, all illuminated by the flames that wreathed its head.

Sax's time had come. He threw Emily aside, not consciously to save her—it wasn't possible—but because, perversely, he wanted her to live a second or two longer than him, so he wouldn't have to witness her death. She tumbled against the bed and the monster lunged at Sax. He struck at the thing from instinct, reduced as he was to a frightened ape incapable of conscious thought, and the vodka bottle shattered in its teeth. White fire filled Sax's vision, there was an intolerable weight upon him, and Sax knew nothing, felt nothing, was nothing.

Rock had requested some special equipment from the Holy See when he accepted the vampire-hunting job but hadn't brought the stuff to Germany for the recon mission. He had been very glad his duffel bag was in the cottage in Petit-Grünenwald, however, when the monsters came. Wouldn't have done him any good in the back of the SUV. The shotgun proved most effective. He had come up with an innovation that would later go on to become a standard item in the antivampire toolkit. The shells of the ten-gauge shotgun he'd ordered were loaded with a mixture of silver .00 buckshot and granulated sulfur, all suspended in a matrix of gelled garlic oil. He had based this formula on anecdotal evidence of what worked best on vampires; there was no science to it. But it did work. Something about sulfur and silver at the same time had a hell of an effect on vampire tissue. Add to that the allium oil and it was like hitting the monsters with a hand grenade full of razor blades.

Rock killed the one on the roof about the same time that Min was strapping on her weapons up in the *petit ouvrage*. When Abingdon was dying, she was halfway down the hill from the fort. If she'd been any sooner, the three hundings that had been lying in wait would have pulled her apart. As it was, she saw them go over the wall a few seconds before she reached it herself. The Englishman was already dead. She remembered the value of caution, and so lived, throwing herself down behind the wall they'd just leapt over. She saw the things gather, sending signals with their eyes, their heads heavy and swaying on thick, bristling necks.

Min was soaked through already, only outdoors for forty seconds in a driving rain so cold it was like whips lashing her skin. She had to blink to keep her eyes clear. Seconds passed. Then, in a burst of muscular force, the monsters rushed the *maison* as one, hurling themselves through windows and doors. Fire leapt up everywhere at once. The hundings were blazing scarecrows of light in there, and Min knew there was no point rushing in after them. She wasn't going to die in a fire. She was going to die in combat. It wasn't just caution that held her back: she wanted a specific vampire. These dog-faced shape-shifters were nothing to her. Yeretyik was her quarry.

Min kept behind the wall and watched for a few seconds more. It was pandemonium in the house, every door and window alight with flames. The monsters were howling and screaming. She heard human voices upstairs. Min realized she had an opportunity to improve her armament: she had her own war hammer in hand, but it was of the wrong alloy. What she wanted was one of Abingdon's specimens in the barn. She scanned the perimeter of the yard and saw no further creatures hidden in the shadows.

She threw herself across the wall and dodged inside the barn, ready for an attack. It was vacant and dry in there.

She found the hammers laid out on a workbench by the forge, eight beautiful silver weapons with wicked, flanged points, two fitted with handles. She took both of these and stepped back outside and the first hunding was just coming out of the house as she emerged from behind the bread truck. It was in flames, its flesh black, scored with rivulets of white and red. The rain was putting the fire out. Clouds of steam leapt up from its scorched hide.

Min took three strides, dropped one of the hammers, and with both hands swung the other up over her head and had the great satisfaction of looking directly into the hunding's eyes as she brought the hammer down. It entered the monster's neck at the base of its skull, severing the spinal cord, and there was a stench like vomit as the silver alloy ate into its flesh. The creature collapsed but was by no means dead. It was paralyzed.

There was a double explosion off to the side, coming from the cottage. Min wheeled around and it was Rock there with a shotgun in his hands. Min yanked her attention back to the house and saw another hunding fall limp and heavy through the window frame between living room and kitchen. Blood poured out of its chest in a stream the diameter of Min's wrist. Rock ran to her side. Another of the things came crashing through what was left of the living room's French doors, one of its arms on fire, but otherwise unhurt; Rock shot it in the head and Min charged forward and hammered it in the heart.

This put her close to the house when the next one emerged, its head framed in a mane of blazing curtain fabric. The thing did not see her but tore at the burning shroud around it. Min was mad with bloodlust by now and no longer cared if she lived or died. Only if the monster died.

She struck it in the rib cage with the hammer and broke the handle. The hammer remained in its chest. The monster swung its claws and hit her across the right side and sent her tumbling through the air. She felt her flesh part on the hard dirt as she landed. Min forced herself back into action, ignoring the pain coming from wounds so deep she could feel the coldness of the rain inside her muscles. She found the second hammer lying in a heap of Abingdon's guts. She picked it up. There was the Englishman's head, parted from his shoulders but still in the helmet, his face slack and doughy, looking up at the rain that fell on his open eyes. There was a powerful explosion inside the house that sent shards of glass and stone and wood whistling through the air and Min was thrown off her feet again.

Min heard more blasts from the shotgun, then looked up and saw a flaming planet falling from the sky. No. A hunding, its head a fireball, hurtling from an upstairs window. It hit the ground and she crawled toward it.

Rock was there first. He pressed his weapon to the crackling head and fired. Min tried to hammer the thing, but she couldn't lift her arms. She fell down and let the rain mingle her blood with the monster's, and all the blood flowed past her and ran down the yard toward the lane. She let it. It had been a good battle.

Sax was unconscious for half an hour. When he awoke, he was in the cottage, not the *maison*. It was no longer raining. He recognized the lamp over the dining room table. He was lying directly beneath it. He sat up, and his head flared with pain. It had taken quite a knock. He couldn't remember anything about the final confrontation in the bedroom.

Emily's face loomed into his vision. *One mercy*, Sax thought. *She's alive.* Although he couldn't remember exactly why, he had somehow thought she was dead. She smiled and touched his cheek. So she didn't wish him dead or curse him for the disaster. Who else was still alive? Sax looked around, his every move sending pain through head and body.

Min sat on the table beside his legs, and Fra Giu stitched up several deep gashes in her side. The lowermost wound wasn't yet sewn up and Sax could see a white rib in there. It made his gorge rise. He moved to get off the table. Emily tried to stop him, but he made it to an upright position. Rock was at the window over the sink with his glorious shotgun in his hands. Firelight flickered and leapt on his face from outside.

"Is it over?" Sax croaked.

"We won on points," Rock said.

Rock told his side of the story first: How he had been stuck in the cottage unable to help, pinned down because he knew he was asking for what Gheorghe got if he set foot outside. He'd heard the noise on the roof, killed that hunding, and after that he just kept shooting whenever he had the chance. Min told her part of the story almost backward, picking up from where she joined the fight with Rock and filling in what happened before that when prompted by Paolo. Sax noticed Fra Dinckel was not amongst them but that Nilu was lying on the couch in the living room. A big Welsh dresser had been pushed in front of the picture window there.

"Fra Dinckel, God rest him," Paolo said, "one of those things came upstairs and it was covered in fire. It came straight to the bedroom. All of us were there, my brothers and Nilu, and the monster came in. Fra Dinckel took the oxygen tank and hit it in the head and he"—here Paolo acted out the action, throwing his weight back and forth, arms in front of him—"he run like this and crash into the monster and the air is coming out and they go down the stairs and the cylinder exploded, boom! And blew up the whole place. Big fire. But it also put some of the fire out, because of the push from the blast, you know?"

"And you got out that way? Because the fire was out?" Sax said.

"No, the fire was still very big. But the whole inside of the house fell down on the middle, do you know what I mean? The floors came down."

Emily cut in with an explanation. "The bearing wall down the middle," she said. "It collapsed, and the floors went like this"—here she made a level surface of her hands, then dropped them in the center—"so we just climbed out of the wreckage and we were already downstairs. Nilu was still in bed."

"Ridiculous," Sax said, as if they'd all been let down by this one stroke of relative good fortune.

"Yes," Paolo said. "Poor Fra Dinckel. But he was a brave man. Now three of the hundings, they are still in the world but they are badly injured, one of them very much so. May be that we find them. Somebody finds them, not us. My people will come."

"Has anyone," Sax said, now that his brain was working again, "considered the possibility that there might still be two human-type vampires out there? That the hundings could yet regroup? We are by no means out of danger."

"We were talking of that subject when you came awake," Fra Giu said. "Our reinforcements are some hours of time away. But your niece tells to us that there is a fortress upon the hill."

Sax had an idea. It was a mad idea, and he didn't think it would work, but they were all dead if they didn't do something quickly. Right now, the vampire's forces were scattered and her current plans foiled. Before she had a new plan was the time to act. The SUV was still working, just a little worse for the wear what with all the explosions and hundings falling on it. But these were cosmetic considerations. Sax suggested they all drive on up to the fort and spend the time there, where it was chilly but absolutely impossible to break in. No danger of assault once inside. This suggestion was met with universal approval. Everyone was utterly dispirited. They had suffered defeat after defeat and only just barely scratched out a draw on this occasion, losing in the process Gheorghe, Abingdon, and Fra Dinckel. They had fought amongst themselves while the monsters were at the peak of their powers. They had lost everything. Even the ormolu clock, which lay smashed and blood-soaked in the dirt.

It would never cluck again.

They took relays out to the SUV. The rain was already frozen on the ground, and everything appeared to be coated in black glass. The ferocious clouds were lifting up over the dark hills. It was painfully cold, but the storm had passed. While they went back and forth from cottage to vehicle, Sax had the opportunity to speak to Rock alone concerning an additional aspect of his plan. He wanted to be discreet about it.

Rock saw the wisdom of Sax's idea and agreed to it. He relayed the idea to Min, who was extremely stiff on one side but otherwise couldn't have been readier. The entire party was crammed into the vehicle. Rock drove. Paolo was in the passenger seat, shotgun at the ready, with Fra Giu, Emily, and Min in the backseat; in the cargo area at the rear, Sax was cradling Nilu across his lap.

Nilu was semiconscious and hadn't any idea what was going on. She seemed to think she was on a carnival ride at a Holi festival and all the colors were so beautiful. There would be shadowy figures moving in the colors, Sax knew.

The track to the fort was greasy and wet but the ground still frozen, and they made it up the hill without getting stuck. Everyone piled out as fast as they were able, Paolo and Fra Giu carrying Nilu, Emily supporting her uncle. They got the key into the lock on the big iron door and went inside the *petit ouvrage*. It would do. Not a pleasant place, but a safe one.

Min had previously made herself a kind of nest in the topmost room, the one with the machine-gun tower projecting from the peak of it. It was the room they entered with the key. Sax's suggestion was well received: a little more discomfort was nothing compared to knowing they were safe from attack. Emily, limping heavily because of a cut under her big toe, sat on the skeleton of an old bunk bed that once supported a mattress. There were a couple of electric battery lanterns for light. Paolo and Fra Giu got Nilu arranged on a pile of sleeping bags.

It was then that the exterior door clanged shut again and the key grated in the lock. Paolo and Emily rushed to the door, Emily's toe leaving crescents of blood behind her.

"Uncle Sax!" she shouted, and opened the tiny hatch set into the door at eye height.

"Sorry, dear girl," Sax said through the hatch.

"What are you doing?" Emily already thought she knew. Sax only confirmed it.

"We're just popping off to Germany," he said. "Back tomorrow evening, but don't wait up for us."

Paolo rapped the door with the flat of his hand. "Let me go as well."

"I'm sorry, no," Sax said. "I have grown very fond of you, young man, and I will not see your life thrown away with all the others because of my blind incompetence."

Paolo hung his head. There was a finality in the old man's voice that wasn't something argument would change.

"Go with God," Paolo said.

17

FRANCE

It was an hour and twenty minutes later when they heard the heavy thud of rotor blades beating the frigid air outside, and Paolo and Fra Giu began bundling Nilu up for the journey to the hospital. The Ordine dei Cavalieri Sacri dei Teutonici e dei Fiamminghi, Special Branch, was an hour early, and not a minute too soon. As the helicopter powered down above them on the hilltop, Emily banged on the door to let them know the fort was occupied. After all, the order would only have landed there because it was the most open ground. It could otherwise be hours before they even realized the *petit ouvrage* existed.

Uncle Sax, while a bastard, was not a fool, Emily was pleased to note. He'd left the key in the other side of the door. It creaked around and the door shuddered open and the brethren got Nilu into a fireman's lift. Just then a long white hand came through the door and caught Emily by the front of her shirt.

"Only you," the vampire said, and pulled her outside with the ease of a child selecting a doll from a toy cupboard.

The door banged shut behind her, and a minute later the helicopter was rising into the night again, clattering away eastward, toward Germany.

18

Germany

The castle gates were open. Sax had suspected they would be. If the vampire's minions destroyed them, there was no need for security. Nobody else was trying to get in. But if they failed, and Sax and his people survived to reach Mordstein, the fiend didn't want them running around loose. *Come into my parlor, said the spider to the expert in antiques*. She could easily slaughter them in her lair.

Sax, Min, and Rock went inside.

It was like walking through a dark city deserted in the predawn hours. The ground was flagged with stone, and walls of the same stone rose up on all sides, five times the height of a man, so that there was never much sunlight in its maze of damp streets. The only light came from Rock's flashlight and occasional industrial-style fixtures bolted into the walls at knee level to illuminate the paths. They walked beneath the pointed arch of the gatehouse, then found a small square of open space, its margin of high walls pierced with slits for archers at the top and fringed with a roof of blue slate. Narrow stairs rose steeply up the walls on both sides, unprotected by railings, connecting the square below with the uppermost battlements that overlooked the cliffs. Sax couldn't have mounted those stairs if his life depended on it. Too high, too steep, and too narrow. The flights ascended in opposing directions so that a right-handed attacker coming up would always have his sword arm against the wall, regardless of which side he took.

"Where the men?" Min asked, pausing to inspect the battlements above them.

"I don't think she'd have guards about the place, do you?" Sax said. "What would the point be?"

"But people must come up here sometimes," Rock said. "Curiosity seekers and whatnot."

"Think about it," Sax snapped, and kept on marching.

"Right. Duh," Rock said, after a pause. "She eats them."

They passed beneath a second Gothic arch, this one carved with serpents and armored men. It adorned an inner gatehouse, with the iron fangs of the portcullis jutting down from the underside of the arch. Sax remembered the vicious gateway of spears he and Gander had faced in the château long ago. If there were traps, this time he would walk straight into them. Beyond the bastion of high walls before them was the tall wedge of the keep, bristling with spires. Atop the tallest one, the thick cylindrical tower that was older than the rest of the fort, was the red helicopter. Its rotor blades drooped around it like the wings of a sulking dragon.

"She's home," said Sax, indicating the aircraft.

Sax wondered if the vampire was watching them. If she had her hands on the controls of hidden mechanisms to crush them. She might have anything installed in this lofty prison: trapdoors in the floor to precipitate them a thousand feet to their destruction on the rocks below, or great piles of stone to dump into the narrow streets of the castle upon their heads, or simply a pair of massive gates like the portcullis that could be dropped at either end of one of these passages so that they would be trapped there and would die of exposure in a day or two.

"Cameras," Rock said, and indicated a small box mounted on an arm up under the eaves of one of the walls. It was thirty feet above their heads.

"How very modern," Sax said between his teeth. If he was going to die—and with every step they took, it became more certain—he was, just this once, going to behave with dignity. The absolute shame and humiliation he'd suffered back at the farm, while it did not qualify as suffering in the same ghastly way that Gheorghe or that ululating young monk had experienced it, was almost the worst thing Sax had ever experienced in his life. He had never quite seen the power of shame before. His entire existence, all seventy-odd years of it, Sax had courted disgrace. Yet he had never gotten used to the agony that came along with meeting it. He would rather die than be humiliated. He knew that now.

They passed along a series of short alleys that turned each time to the right, again putting an invader at a disadvantage with his sword; Sax realized if the plan was symmetrical, the castle's keep stood at the center of what was essentially a gigantic swastika. He returned to his inward brooding. Rock and Min were watching for trouble—leave them to it. Better if he could enjoy the onset of senility while he still had the chance, lost in his self-loathing for the last time.

Sax had spent, he had to admit to himself, every moment of his waking life on a campaign to look good in front of other people, to use his weaknesses as strengths. Even going so far as to not once, but twice, and now three times, confront vampires—and he'd faced other horrors as well. It was a preposterous overcompensation. He was a coward, so he occasionally did something that appeared to be brave—but invariably did it with as little courage or grace as possible, running for his life at the soonest opportunity.

The first time he'd stalked a vampire, he had not known he was doing so—nor the dangers he confronted. He'd been abjectly humiliated by his own total failure of courage in the matter. The *second* time he had chosen a far lesser monster to confront and *still* was humiliated, and damn near lost his leg. Now here he was at an advanced age, tottering along like some gray Dorothy in a deserted Emerald City on the way to confront the Wizard, who he knew was something far worse than a man behind the curtain. Even as he made his way through that cold castle, doing this very brave thing for which there would almost certainly be no living witnesses, he suspected he was only doing it to salvage his pride.

Min and Rock by unspoken agreement took up positions in front of Sax and behind him, switching periodically, keeping their eyes fresh as they watched for anything at all besides stone and moss. They were at the base of the keep. It rose up, despite the already immense height of the rock upon which they stood, to what appeared an equally great height. Sax did not dare look up at it for fear he would develop vertigo and fall down. If he was going to walk to the gallows, he wanted his steps to appear firm. Sax was confronting his oldest enemy, he now understood. And his oldest enemy was not the vampire. It was himself.

They circled the keep and found the entrance. It was not an imposing door, although there was a time-effaced shield above it carved into the stones of the wall that was grand in scale and fierce in workmanship, despite the softening that centuries of harsh weather had brought to it. Two tiny windows, a foot tall and ten feet deep in the masonry, looked like the blinkered eyes of a deformed skull surmounting the doorway. Which meant they were walking into a toothless stone mouth. A cheerful thought, Sax mused, and went in first. He paused on the threshold. Only an hour until dawn. The urgent drive through the night had taken them four hours, Rock keeping the accelerator to the floor except at the border crossing, where they didn't want to look like fugitives. Sax wished there was some truth to the idea that vampires couldn't live in daylight. In fact the only thing it did was give them sunburn.

"Remember, caution is the best weapon you have," he said, and meant it. "She's got cameras and things, but they're nothing. Her real weapon is sheer bloody ruthlessness. She won't have a submachine gun or anything like that. They never do. She'll wait for us to do something stupid, and then we're for it. Do you understand?"

"Yeah," Rock said. "I'm definitely feeling mortal as a motherfucker right now."

"Min?" Sax said. There was a look in her eyes he didn't like. In her mind, she was already fighting. That was *exactly* what the vampire would want. Precipitous action. Haste. There lay destruction. Min made a guttural noise in response to Sax's question, but he needed her to say the words.

"Min. Repeat after me. I will not take the bait. You understand what bait is, yes? Like for a fish?"

"I know what is bait," she said. Whatever Sax had to say, she was going to do what she was going to do. She had her hand pressed to the wounds in her side, Sax noted.

"Rock, will you please take the lead? And Min, after me." He could at least slow her down.

Sax went inside. There was a naked electric bulb overhead in a fixture that dated, Sax estimated, from the 1930s. Before the war. Rock's head hardly cleared the steel light shade as he squeezed past Sax, filling the corridor that led into the keep. There were further lamps suspended at intervals from an armored cable stapled to the ceiling.

They proceeded into the bowels of the castle, which was silent, cold, and still. They moved as fast as they dared, meeting no obstacles or opposition. There was no furniture in any of the rooms that opened out from the corridor. This was the lower part of the castle that had been uninhabited, according to their reconnaissance; these rooms would once have been crammed with fighting men and their families, the floors covered in rushes, furnished with simple pieces hewn from the wood of the local forests. Some of the chambers would have stored food, arms, and fuel for fires. The fortress had always been isolated and ugly, but it had once been bursting with activity as well, a kind of robust life that was not lonely.

Now it was a dead shell. The thresholds of the doors and the steps in the spiral staircases that rose up in niches on either side were worn concave by centuries of constant use. Few feet had disturbed the stone since the vampire came. Sax wondered when that was. A hundred years? Two hundred? Was Shakespeare alive when this place fell victim to the monster, its squires and pages taking ill, its knights and ladies at last hastening out of the halls rather than sicken and die themselves? Were there false vampires, screaming and biting until dispatched with crossbows?

She was waiting for them in one of these rooms, smiling that mirthless grin that vampires wore.

They came to a steel door, of modern manufacture. There was a security system mounted within it; Rock pointed out the pattern of bolt heads where the electronics would be fixed inside the panel.

"The spider's lair," Sax muttered.

"It's probably locked," Rock said. "We haven't got cutting gear. We'll have to go back."

"*Ya-gol*," Min said, and grabbed the handle of the door. It swung open on well-greased hinges.

"This is too easy," Rock said.

"Of course it is," Sax whispered. "She's expecting us."

The door let into a short hallway, fifteen feet deep, the thickness of the bearing wall through which it passed. No secret passages here:

This was solid rubble laid for strength, not subterfuge. The hallway was of smooth stone, like the parts of the castle through which they had already passed, but there was no dust here. Min forged ahead; Sax and Rock followed. No door at the far end of the hall. They reached the opening without being killed.

Beyond the hall—riches.

They had found the vampire's hoard.

The narrow way opened out into the great hall, the core of the keep, six-sided, its walls plastered and figured with scenes of pageantry and pleasure. The frescoes had been rendered at least a thousand years ago, judging from the technique and the costumes of the subjects. The colors were faded but still warm. The walls rose up, punctuated by iron braziers to hold bundles of rushlights, to a gallery that encircled the room, with a deeper choir for minstrels at one end and the massive chimney at the other, beneath which was a hearth that could hold an entire tree, if one wished to burn it. The walls continued upward to a ceiling of immense beams, jointed together like a wagon wheel, their surfaces covered in heraldry and notchwork. The shields and devices of hundreds of knights had been painted there, forming great flowers of intricate and warlike design that gleamed starry in the lofty shadows. The bones of the room had gone unchanged for a millennium at least. But time had not stood still. A collection had been assembled.

The enormous volume of space was crammed with masterpieces of every period hanging over the frescoes on the walls. The stone floor was scattered with carpets of exquisite design, deep and fine. There were sculptures for which the Louvre would sacrifice half its icons, and artifacts of exquisite craftsmanship—from the entrance, Sax's eye picked out an elephant howdah that must have been fifth century, now resting on the floor with pillows beneath its canopy and heaps of leather-bound folios beside it, a kind of reading niche. So many of the things were in immaculate condition. They had been removed from the world when they were young and slept here ever since, untouched by time. Half the treasure appeared to be forgeries, they were so perfect. The furniture, of every period, looked as if it should still smell of shellac and paint.

Shimmering silks, Chinese and Japanese, were thrown carelessly over the arms of chairs and sofas. Sax could see something that looked very much like a robe of the Han Dynasty, but even with a vampire, it was hard to imagine such a thing in private hands—it was twenty-two centuries old, tossed across the seat of a Roman backless couch, itself probably from the second century AD; the only reason he recognized the style of the piece was because there was a reconstruction of one in the Metropolitan Museum of Art. This one was original, and far finer. Such objects no longer existed.

Sax's mouth was dry, his heart batting like an exhausted moth. The wealth was beyond estimation. His own warehouses were nothing but trinket shops compared to this.

He forgot where he was, and what peril lay somewhere behind these walls, and he staggered, leaning heavily on his cane, across the sward of carpets. He passed a William & Mary gateleg table laden with porcelain: The table alone was worth sixty thousand dollars, and it bore a careless arrangement of Kangxi vases in blue and white, each worth seventy thousand, beside a couple of big Qianlong famille moon flasks, their colors as delicate as springtime, for which Sax could easily get seven hundred thousand the pair, if he could bear to part with them; and next to the table stood a Japanese Imari lantern in porcelain and gilt, five feet tall, a mere trifle worth something like thirty thousand until you threw in the First Dynasty Egyptian crown sitting atop it, the value of which was incalculable. Sax felt as if his sanity was at stake now. That was the freight of just *one table*. There must have been forty such tables scattered around the great hall, not to mention the shelves and cabinets and curios, each one stuffed with priceless artifacts to which he would have very dearly loved to have given a price.

Sax was transfixed.

"Get back here," he heard a voice say from a great distance.

"What the hell are you doing?" the same voice said, now in his ear. Sax was confused. He turned and saw a vast man with a frightened face atop a neck almost as large in diameter as the Ming Dynasty Longquan celadon garden seat upon which he abruptly sat down. *Rock*, Sax recalled. His name was Rock.

"I'm sorry," Sax said. "I lost my head." He waved his cane around at the splendors in the great hall. Rock didn't see what he saw.

"It looks like Jay Z's crib in here, man, and that's cool, but I didn't come this far just to get killed in an attractive environment, know what I'm saying?" Rock lifted Sax up and hauled him bodily back to the doorway. Sax wiped his eyes and shook Rock off once they were back in the doorway, where Min was covering the way out with her own shotgun. Sax observed she was sweating profusely, and blood dappled her bandaged side. Rock was always perspiring; Sax was under the impression Korean women never did. Then he realized he was sweating, too, and mopped his face.

"You don't realize what you're seeing, I think," Sax said. "The ransom of bloody Zeus in Olympus. This makes King Tut's tomb look like a box lunch. I forget our business, however. I see no evidence of our hostess anywhere. But that might be what we want, over there."

Sax indicated the enormous fireplace. Beside it was built an elevator in the early Art Deco style, brass and chromium tubes framing thick glass ribs that formed the car. It was designed to rise up in the open air to the heights of the great hall; at the very top, there was a hole framed into the ceiling. The rails on which the elevator ascended continued on up above.

"She's waiting for us up there?" Rock said, not sure if he was asking or making a statement.

"She wouldn't want a gunfight down here, I assure you," Sax said, and hobbled around the perimeter of the room, discretion at least dictating they stay in the shelter of the gallery above. He tried his best to ignore the items of interest they passed, and made it all the way to the fireplace before he came to a halt, frozen in place.

"Not again," Rock said.

"I know her. I've met her," Sax said.

He felt a kind of fear that was new in his experience. It came from far away in his own past, mocking him.

He had *always* survived at the pleasure of this monster. He just hadn't known it until now.

There was a magnificent painting on the chimneypiece above the hearth, its frame a vast rococo fantasy in gilt and plaster, later than the artwork within. There was no mistaking the hand of the master who'd painted it. It was a biblical scene, deep shadows and soft natural light with the figures emerging from the darkness. Plain, honest faces, and proud kings.

It was Caravaggio's lost masterpiece *The Magi in Bethlehem*.

Sax had spent some time talking to the woman who claimed to own it, one drunken night in Paris in 1965. She was pale and attractive and she had a long German title after her name.

He was, he now understood, about to meet her again. Edie Sedgwick would not be attending this time.

Sax paused at the door of the elevator and looked back.

"We're coming back down," he said, with genuine resolution in his voice. "We're coming back down and taking all this. Mine. Every single bloody bit of it. *Mine.*"

. . .

The elevator rose with perfect smoothness. There was a plate on the frame that read *G. Eiffel, 1922*. Only the best for this vampire—and the great engineer had died the following year.

Min had taken the stairs, although limping; Rock was with Sax, shotgun trained on the elevator door. Sax was trembling, but the cosmic pitch of fear he had experienced on the way into the castle had been replaced by something more like the doomsense of the condemned man. It was a chilly resignation he felt, almost of already being dead. This was not a castle perched atop the mountain—it was his tomb.

He had already been sentenced to this death in 1965, when the vampire had conversed with him, and Andy Warhol and Charlie Watts and all the rest of the fascinating people had been there.

She had chatted with Sax particularly, of course, because he was an unscrupulous sharpie in the matter of furniture and antiques, and that was something she needed to get her patrimony back. In 1965, it had only been twenty years since her hoard was piled into boxcars and sent down the railway. She had probably been considering Sax as a confederate to help get the stuff back.

A week later, Sax played his part in the destruction of the vampire Corfax in the Loire Valley. This creature would have decided against requesting Sax's services at that time, of course. And she might even have thought, *Someday when he's old, I'll lure him here and destroy him.*

That day had finally come.

The elevator stopped moving, the door folded back, and before them was the secret lair.

They were in the room above the great hall. It was the summit of the castle, beneath the peak of the tallest roof. It had once been five or six stories of private chambers, composed of board floors laid across the beams that spanned the space. The boards were long gone, and now it was just a single echoing volume beneath the peak, crisscrossed by massive timbers where the levels had been.

The steep angle of the roof was duplicated inside the enormous chamber, giving it the aspect of a natural cavern; there were thousands of whispering bats in the highest rafters to lend vitality to the effect. The air stank abominably of bat urine and dung and noxious chemicals. Sax knew bats were supposed to be useful, but he hated all of those small hairy creatures—bats and rats and mice. Horrid wriggling things with tiny teeth and knobby claws like miniature human hands. He hated rats the most, ever since he met them in a tunnel in 1965 while fleeing for his life. He'd attempted to make it into a proper phobia, but it had always remained simple loathing.

There were two levels remaining in the vast chamber. Sax and Rock stepped with care onto the lower level, the floor that was also the ceiling of the great hall below. Above them was a rectangle hanging in space thirty feet above, the second level, suspended on the beams with a twenty-foot margin of open space around it on all four sides, accessible only by a single iron catwalk from the narrow parapet that circled the wall at the same height. It was an island in the air.

The floor under their feet had been paved with linoleum. The walls at this level were clad in sheets of white glass or plastic, lit from behind, so that their pallid light cast angular shadows in unnatural directions. The stone walls emerged above the upper catwalk encircling the room. Dr. Caligari would have loved it.

What most struck the eye, after the sheer height of the room, was the mass of equipment that formed a labyrinth inside it: hulking iron cabinets, studded with rivets the size of mushroom caps, covered in dials and meters and huge levers from which mighty rubber-clad cables and coils of copper tubing ascended. From the walls sprouted mazes of pipe and plumbing. There were pyramids of fuel and chemical drums, some modern, some so old the metal was blistered and sweating. There was a great humpbacked machine with masses of copper wire wound around a core inside it, a generator of some kind, from which ran cables thick as pythons. Amongst the runs of plastic-clad wire, there were benches littered with handmade brass instruments. Everything was a combination of antiquated and modern science, flung together according to need.

Of the vampire, there was no sign.

"You understand what's next, traditionally speaking," Sax murmured. "We wander around until we find what she wants us to find, and then she appears behind us without warning, makes a speech, and kills us both."

"I got that," Rock said. Sweat was running in gleaming cords down his skin.

"So if we're going to do her in, it's got to be while she's making the speech," Sax added. It sounded rather silly to mention it at this point. "Be on the lookout for something to distract her."

"What if she doesn't make the speech?" Rock whispered.

Sax considered it. "Then shoot me first, will you?"

"I surely will. You got me into this," Rock said. He might have been reconsidering his role in the mission, but it was too late to turn back. They advanced around the laboratory, keeping beneath the ring of walkways on the wall above, their backs to the translucent material that covered the stone walls. There could be no attack from behind that, at least, because there was nothing behind these walls except a thousand-foot drop.

The visibility within the laboratory was poor. It was all in glimpses, seen through Expressionist juxtapositions of technology from the age of steam to the present day. Ahead of them, a spiral staircase in perforated iron rose up to the catwalk. Sax and Rock, moving slowly sideways as if traversing a ledge, reached the stair without incident, and then it was time to make a decision. If they went up, they were entering the trap of all traps. If they did not, they were in a waiting game with a creature that had nothing but time.

"You stay here," Sax whispered. Or rather, his voice was so faint it *sounded* as if he was whispering. In fact he couldn't have spoken any louder if he'd tried. The fear inside him had adhered to itself and accumulated into an icy ball. He felt as if he were physically filled with snow. He was trembling, his system most of the way to shutting down. It was only will that kept him breathing and moving.

Rock was circling away now, eyes on the upper reaches of the chamber, and in a few moments, he was lost to Sax's sight amongst the machines. Sax turned his own eyes upward and ascended the iron stairs, one halting step at a time. It was an exhausting journey. He would have had difficulty with the climb even without the burden of dread he was hauling up with him; the open lattice of the iron stairs promoted vertigo, and the entire construction shook slightly with every step, swaying.

Now he could see the tops of the infernal machines arrayed on the lower level, marvels of technology laden incongruously with mountains of guano, corroded where the polyuric bats in the rafters had voided down for many decades upon them. Now he could see into the aluminum races that bore the thick bundles of modern data and power cables. He began to grasp something of the plan of the space, how the passages between the machines all converged upon a central mass, like the densest part of a city skyline, clustered with strange engines and ducts and pipes that rose up to meet the suspended island above.

Then his eyes were level with the floor of the upper platform. He saw the three-inch thickness of the boards, the ebonized beams as big around as the belly of an ox, freighted with bat shit like a fall of heavy stinking snow. The pipes and cables and tubes rose through the floor to meet in a strange tower in the center of the platform.

Sax's legs were trembling with the effort of climbing the stairs. He resisted the urge to look down. In his coat pocket he had the only weapon he'd been able to convince himself to bring, the ampoule of silver sulfide suspended in acid that he'd liberated from amongst Abingdon's effects. He was of two minds how he would use it: he could, of course, dash the stuff in the vampire's face. That seemed a very poor plan as it would likely infuriate the creature rather than kill it, thus hastening Sax's own demise. His only other idea was to swallow the stuff and hope it killed him before the vampire did. He was beginning to wish he'd brought a firearm, a stick with a point on the end, or even a hat pin. Anything weaponlike, rather than this little bit of glass with a stopper in it, no larger than a roll of quarters.

Sax placed his foot on the catwalk. It made a soft but unmistakable clang, and he closed his eyes in repentance and put his weight on the fragile bridge across the open air to the heart of the laboratory.

She was there.

He saw her now that she moved, in the middle of the web of technology she'd woven for herself. She was looking at him.

The creature was just the same, her platinum hair piled high, her figure as long and thin as a fashion illustration, and somehow as unlikely in proportion: her legs seemed never to end, her head was suspended atop a neck so long it appeared too frail to support it. She was wearing a white laboratory coat; on her it was elegant. She stared, and that joyless smile was on her lips.

Sax could see there were several monitor screens behind her, one of which was divided into eight sections, each showing a different black-and-white image from around the castle. Min was clearly visible in one of the octants, moving carefully up a wooden stair that would once have been the only way up into the attic from the great hall. She was favoring her injuries. The vampire had been following their progress, as Sax knew she would.

There was a tank behind the monster, a great long thing of murky glass bound with bronze hoops. Inside the tank was what appeared to be blood, dark and ropy with strands of coagulation. Something humanoid floated inside it. The tank was mounted on chains. Sax saw that the chains rose up to a system of pulleys under the roof. There was a panel there mounted on rails, probably to open the roof to the night sky. That must have been the source of the mysterious light they'd seen.

Sax felt himself falling, although he wasn't, and the sensation was so vivid that he reached out and took hold of the thin iron railing along the catwalk. He was experiencing a particularly pure form of panic that left the nervous system in a continuous state of anticipating death, of which falling is the most oft-experienced.

Sax wondered what he should do. Had he come here of his free will, or was this all the outcome of some subtle chemistry of mind control, at which vampires so excelled? Could the seeds of this moment have been planted in his mind by the monster half a century before? He felt he should say something.

"I've come about the ormolu clock," he said, because it was true.

"You have grown old, I see," the vampire replied.

Her accent was Germanic but there were other things beneath it. Over the centuries she had spoken many tongues, adopting and discarding them as a mortal would fashions in clothing. Sax had, he suddenly realized, walked halfway across the catwalk. She was already exerting her influence. He was no longer in proper control of his perception of time. He would have to be very careful if he wanted to live long enough for Rock or Min to get a shot at her. And he didn't want to get so close that he became a human shield—not so much because it would force his companions to hold their fire, but because it probably wouldn't. His mouth was so dry his tongue felt like a flap of suede. Seconds were passing.

"You know we're here to stop you," he said. It was a ridiculous thing to say.

"You're here because I need fresh blood for my work," the vampire said. "You're all B-positive, which is what I require."

"We have the same blood type? How can you know that?" Sax was bewildered. What work was she talking about? "I don't even *know* my blood type."

"I have access to information, Mr. Saxon-Tang. Unlike you, I have moved with the times. Amongst my people, it is a fatal mistake to dwell in the past. Our great flaw. That is why you were able to destroy my sister."

"Who?" Sax heard a rushing in his ears, and his skin felt terribly hot, although inside himself he was freezing. He clutched the railing with both hands, and found even then he was creeping closer and closer to the vampire.

"Corfax. You killed her the same week we met. That is when I decided you were not a suitable business partner."

"Business partner," Sax repeated. "Yes, I thought as much. But I didn't know vampires had sisters." A drop of sweat fell from his nose and he saw it sparkle away past the catwalk, through the reeking air, and into a heap of bat excrement far below. Golden light flickered at the margins of his sight. He heard a tinkling of bells or silver coins in an endless cascade.

"Sisters or brothers, it can change," the vampire said. "But *blood*."

"What's your name?" Sax asked. "Your real name."

This question surprised her, broke her concentration. He felt an easing of the relentless, gravitational pull that had been drawing him toward her. The bells and warm golden light faded from the world.

"No one ever asks this thing." The vampire considered it. "Innin En-Men-Lu-Ana-Ni," she said, the syllables loose and wet as stones in a river. "Sumerian, because you are interested in the past. My husband ruled for millennia."

All around him was bathed in molten, gentle gold. Sax's ears rang with the pleasure of tuneless music like the laughter of bright waters.

"Rubbish," Sax said.

Again he felt the pull of the vampire slacken. She was, it seemed, susceptible to surprises. She must have thought humans so predictable after thousands of years. His last defense, then, was to be unpredictable.

"You dare much," the vampire said.

"I dare ask," Sax said, feeling almost amused by his own performance, "what's in the tank thing there behind you? It must be frightfully important. All these pipes and tubes and so forth—everything in this whole laboratory seems to converge on it."

The vampire looked away from Sax, turning her eyes to the tank. When she broke eye contact, Sax almost fell down, the relief was so great. She had been sucking his mind dry, somehow. Sax had an unpleasant feeling he already knew what the oblong vessel was. He'd seen something like it before.

The box was the length of a man, and there was something inside its red, slimy depths that threw the dim outlines of a humanoid form against its thick glass flanks. Under different circumstances one might mistake it for a strangely constructed coffin.

"En-Men-Lu-Ana, my husband," the vampire said. "His time has come again."

"But that looks more like that Russian bloke with no face," Sax observed. He *knew* he recognized the shape inside the glass coffin.

The vampire turned back upon Sax and immediately he felt the weight again, despite the pleasure of his senses bathed in beautiful light and sound, his nerves splashing in the warm pool of delight—there was a weary price for the sensuality of it, as if his pockets were filled with wet sand, pulling him down. And not just down, but forward. His shoes were at the edge of the catwalk, he discovered. He would step onto the platform next, and into her arms after that.

"You must have wondered why I required the ormolu clock," she said.

"Not really," Sax said, because the opposite was true. Her attention flickered again. He clutched at the instant of relief.

"During the war—"

"Yes yes yes yes," Sax said, suddenly impatient. His head was throbbing. Vampire or not, he was tired of this interview. Another power trip, like all such petty displays he'd endured over the years. She was just a bloodthirsty version of old Pillsbury, the apostolic protonotary diocesan priest back in New York. For all her murderous power, just another puffed-up Napoléon. He wished Rock would fire his little popgun or Min would attack her with the hammer. Anything to take the pressure off his mind.

His fear was now veined with irritation. That was good. It took the edge off. He found he was not advancing anymore. He remained where he was on the catwalk, albeit hanging on to the railing with both hands. Before she could speak again, Sax took up the narrative.

"I know all about the clock. Did my research. This castle fell to the Allies in 1947. You'd run off somewhere because that's what vampires do, bloody cowards. They packed up all your bits and bobs and took them away by locomotive. But they didn't put all your things on the one train. So you went and took everything back except for one boxcar that got away. And in that car was the bric-a-brac you've been buying back or stealing all this time. Including that wretched old clock."

He found he was able to move his feet. He shuffled them backward, away from the vampire. Sweat poured down his spine. The monster stared at him, her eyes drawing him toward her once more, and Sax thought he was resisting, but he was not.

He was suddenly standing on the edge of the vampire's platform again, his feet on the bat-beshitten boards. The Turing engine in his brain had an idea it wanted to share with him. A good idea that might buy him some time, or even tip the balance of power. Unfortunately the idea involved his standing right where the vampire was. He thrust his hands in his pockets.

"That tells you nothing," the vampire said, her voice thick with menace.

"You mean in terms of your motives?" Sax said, his voice unnaturally light and cheerful. He felt like the lead actor in the final performance of a long-running play, trying to keep his mind at once on what he was doing in the present and at the same time experiencing the end of an era represented by all that had gone before. The character he'd played for so long, this Asmodeus Saxon-Tang, was about to cease to be: He was about to leave the role. Time to go off-script again.

"I don't care what your motive is," he continued. "Vampires don't interest me that much, to be perfectly honest. I only like your taste in furniture."

She hissed at him, and her slender throat swelled with veins that writhed across each other beneath the skin. Sax might have overplayed his hand. He didn't think he could get to the coffin before she got to him, if it came to that. He shuffled another step forward, as if compelled, although he no longer felt the hypnotic pressure to advance.

"There's no need to get upset," Sax said. *Noël Coward could not hope for a more deadpan delivery*, he thought. He might even die with a modicum of style, at this rate. He'd die alone, anyway; his companions had apparently taken the opportunity to quit the premises. They should already have attacked. "Suppose you tell me," he continued, "why on earth *you* should be so interested in that silly little clock."

The vampire seemed pacified by this. Her throat lost some of its bulging anatomical detail. She began to pace, not in steps that were obvious to the eye, but drifting from side to side. As she did so, she drew nearer Sax. There were several routes besides the direct one to get to the glass coffin. They were longer. But if bloody Rock would oblige him by condescending to fire a few rounds at the creature, Sax thought, he might just possibly have a chance of getting at it. He promised himself: if there was a gunshot, he would run like the wind for the coffin, not just stand in place and hoot like a forlorn owl.

His fingers were clenched around the ampoule in his pocket, so tightly he was afraid it would shatter. But he could not let go.

"When En-Men-Lu-Ana died, I took his heart," she said. "With its *Herzblutkammer*."

"Your sister had her own lover in a box like that one," Sax said. "You probably killed your boyfriends around the same time, am I right? And you regretted it. So you decided to reanimate old Be-Bop-A-Lula there in Yeretyik's body, poorly as it is. That's why you saved him."

The creature was growing distant, reaching into the past, which was just as Sax hoped she would do. Vampires were only vulnerable when they waxed nostalgic. He suspected the inevitable monologue was coming. He prayed it was.

"En-Men-Lu-Ana's heart was like a seed, dry and still, waiting to be planted in soil of flesh. To bloom. I was away when the soldiers came," she said, not to Sax but to infinity. "One of my familiars hid the precious heart. The familiar died defending my treasures and had no chance to tell me where the heart was hidden. When it was not discovered, I knew it must be amongst the things stolen from me by the so-called Allies. *Your* people," she added, as if, when she killed Sax, it would be in response to the indignities of the postwar period in Germany. "I was sure he had hidden it within one of the candelabra," she continued, "those ridiculous things with the sea god on them. But I was mistaken. The clock. It was in the clock."

"Another five hundred dollars and I would have dropped out of the auction, you know," Sax said.

"The girl is sorry she did not outbid you," the vampire said, and the smile came back, revealing those perfectly even teeth. Vampires didn't have elongated canine teeth, as Sax well knew; if anything, the canines appeared short. Their teeth were used to cut, not to stab; they met against each other like the blades of surgical scissors. He could almost feel the thin white edges slashing through his old flesh. It was coming, and he had made no progress toward his goal. He shuffled another couple of steps toward the vampire—toward the coffin.

"So you plucked out old Yeretyik's heart and stuck your boyfriend's in the body?" he asked, knowing damn well that's what she had done. He only wanted to keep her talking.

"And then I ate Yeretyik's heart," she said. The dreamy look had gone from her eyes. She was back in the present.

He had a strong feeling the vampire was almost finished with its speech-making. Sax supposed it was some kind of desire to connect with any other living thing that made them want to talk to their prey. Or it might just have been part of the hypnosis. They expended no effort they could avoid, did vampires. Lazy creatures. In fifty thousand years, mankind had risen from a hairless ape with a good throwing arm to master of the entire planet. What had vampires done? Fought amongst themselves and killed people. They didn't even have their own art. They took everything from humanity, except humanity itself.

Sax was ten steps from the glass coffin now, and five steps from the vampire. She had stopped her drifting. Her throat pulsed and swelled. She was controlling her appetite, but not for long.

Sax thought he could hear a clock ticking away his last seconds.

No, that was his heart, battering the inside of his ribs, looking for a way out. He wondered if he could manage a feat of unexpected athletic prowess but didn't expect so. He didn't think he'd accomplished anything so far, except he was arm's reach away from a slavering monster with the face of a goddess, the strength of a lion, and the compassion of a bone saw.

The vampire was about to attack.

Rock shouted, "Get down!" and for lack of a better idea, Sax did.

The gunshot was a hot wind that scorched past. Sax saw white particles of flame struck from the handrail of the platform as he dropped, and beyond in the same instant there was a great crashing of glass and metal and sparks poured down from inside the cathedral of fierce machinery that rose up around the glass coffin. The vampire was instantly in motion, seeming almost to vanish as she leapt from the platform toward Rock, who was positioned behind one of the metal boxes full of electronics down below.

The vampire hit the box, buckling the lid, and sent a haze of bat droppings into the air; she had covered the distance at twice the velocity she could have achieved by falling, propelled by muscles like spring steel. But the collapse of the box threw her from her trajectory and Rock was able to hurl himself aside before the steely crooks of her hands could rip out his heart. He rolled and got out of sight in the maze of apparatus on the lower floor. The vampire screamed and went into the hunting pose Sax had seen amongst the hundings, head down, weight distributed on three limbs, one hand lifted up and back, fingers extended like knives. She could throw herself with immense force in any direction, and that one hand was coiled to strike. Rock had as many seconds to live as it took her to locate him.

While Rock distracted the monster, Sax for once fulfilled a promise to himself. He got to his feet and made the last few steps.

Now he stood above the coffin. It was open at the top, and a stench of rotting fish rose from the liquid inside. He had the vial of silver sulfide in his quaking hand, the stopper out, the slender cylinder of glass tipped so that a droplet of the liquid within stood on its lip, a bright bead.

"I have a question," Sax said, his voice as loud as he could make it, which wasn't much. But the monster heard him. Her head screwed smoothly to an unnatural angle over her shoulder, eyes fixed upon him; Sax remembered how the vampire in the château, this one's sister, had moved its head in a similar fashion. Now he saw the family resemblance, beyond the pallor and cruel, lifeless eyes. He found himself afraid to continue speaking, but as he had her attention, he might as well get on with it.

"I'm guessing your boyfriend's heart is in this glass coffin here, stuffed inside the Russian, am I correct? A sort of heart transplant."

Sax knew as little of what he had in his hand as Abingdon had told him: it contained silver and sulfur. And he knew that the liquid it was suspended in was highly concentrated sulfuric acid. He didn't know what the stuff would do in a coffin full of bloody vampiric slime, but he expected it would be unpleasant.

The vampire slithered smoothly as a marionette operated by an expert puppeteer, in apparent defiance of gravity, until she was standing atop the crushed cabinet below him. Her knees were bent. She could spring and it would be all Sax could do to decant the ampoule before she tore him in half. Possibly he wouldn't even manage that much. She was *snarling*, Sax realized. Like an animal. Words failed her. Then she found speech.

"Do not," she said. There was nothing else. Sax hadn't thought about what he would do next. At the moment he tipped the liquid into the glass coffin, he was going to be torn to bits. He would never find out if his gambit had been successful. Still, what else was there? He was down to the last speech in the last scene of Asmodeus Saxon-Tang's illustrious life, himself starring, and then the lights would go out and the final curtain would fall and the lead actor would be dismembered by a supernatural monster. He tried to think of something clever to say. Nothing came to mind. He opened his mouth, preparatory to dumping the vial into the coffin, trusting that *something* would occur to him—but it was the vampire who spoke, instead.

"I have your niece."

Sax did not poison the thing in the glass coffin after all.

The vampire saw his hesitation and smiled in cruel triumph.

It was over.

"I have his niece," she said again, loudly, to the entire laboratory. "The one called Emily. She has a wound on her foot." Now Sax could see Rock from his vantage point; he had been working himself into a firing position with the vampire as exposed as she was. And then Sax saw Min, too. She was stealing along the perimeter wall of the lab, the silver hammer in her hands, shotgun slung over her shoulder, like a shadow that had taken on life, slipping from cover to cover. Sax did not think the vampire could see Min.

"I'm sorry, come again?" Sax said. He must somehow have been misunderstanding.

A shot ripped the air. Tufts of cloth flew from the sleeve of the vampire's laboratory coat and she hurled herself forty feet up and across the airspace, alighting on one of the dung-caked beams before she launched herself again and landed on the platform behind the equipment to Sax's left. There was a scuffling sound. She was descending under the platform, beneath Sax's position.

"I have her here," the vampire said, her voice echoing from somewhere below, out of Sax's field of vision.

"What the fuck do we do?" Rock hissed at Sax from his hiding place. Min was relentlessly circling toward the vampire, still flitting between the shadows.

"Can you see her?" Sax said.

"I can't see dick," Rock said.

Sax carefully uprighted the ampoule of acid, knowing a single spilled drop would precipitate chaos, and stepped away from the coffin. It was a fatal mistake, and he knew it. The vampire was tricking him, and he would be killed like a fool, the same way her victims for twenty or fifty or a hundred thousand years had been killed. But for all her cunning, how could she know Emily's name, and know of the injury to her foot? Who could have told her? Had it been said on the telephone that the vampire might have tapped? His mind was churning and coming up with nothing but froth and confusion. He leaned over the railing of the platform, knowing he was already dead, tricked, and an idiot, in reverse order.

But Emily was there below, in the grip of the fiend, both of them perched on top of the generator. She was pale and shivering, holding herself. Sax saw why. The vampire had pulled her out of a walk-in freezer of the type used in supermarkets and butcher's shops. Fog flowed out onto the linoleum floor from inside the freezer. Of its interior, Sax could only see an oblique slice, but it was enough. Hanging there upside down, rimed with frost, their long hair trailing, were the naked corpses of a redhead and a blonde. The brunette would be there, too, he expected. Probably others as well. Emily was more frightened than himself, Sax saw. And colder. His heart contracted at the sight. This was his doing. She was going to die because of him. The vampire was *touching* her. That was the end of anybody.

The vampire was looking up at Sax with her black shark's eyes. "Come down and I will allow her alone to live."

"I don't believe you," Sax said.

"Uncle Sax?" Emily said. She was disoriented, probably hypothermic. What was about to happen to her might not even hurt too much, if she was numb with cold.

Sax backed away from the edge of the platform, moving closer to the coffin full of vampire remains. He was confronted with a simple dilemma. The vampire was appealing to hope, an emotion she could not feel or understand. But she knew how to manipulate it. It was a tool with which they often lured their prey to destruction. If Sax imagined Emily could survive, he was falling prey to hope. In that case, they would both certainly die. If he gave up hope, then paradoxically there might *be* hope. He was so old and confused. He needed dinner and a nap.

"You and your servants come out, and this one alone shall live," the vampire declared.

Sax needed to let Emily know he was about to do something, and that she should be prepared. But vampires could read human intentions in even the most oblique speech. So nothing he could say would prepare Emily without alerting the monster. In reality, there was only one thing he could do, for terrible or worse.

"No," Sax said, and unceremoniously dumped the vial of acid into the bloody mixture within the vat.

The acid sank beneath the surface. Yeretyik was in there, his mutilated head a shadow beneath the bubbling surface of the mire.

There was a sound piercing Sax's brain. It came from everywhere, a single, deafening note like an air-raid siren. For an instant, he thought nothing was going to happen in the vat. The mixture of silver sulfide and acid just fell into the liquid, leaving a small twist of iridescent color on the surface that took on the graceful, swirling pattern of an acanthus leaf.

Then a large, oily bubble rose up from below, bearing with it the stench of a thousand open graves. The bubble burst and a puff of putrid brown smoke rose into the air like a miniature mushroom cloud. Then the entire platform lurched sideways, and the vampire Innin En-Men-Lu-Ana-Ni was there beside him, her eyes white bulging globes of polished stone with pinpricks in them, her jaws gaping crocodile-wide so that Sax could see all of her teeth and the glistening violet flesh at the back of her throat. The ear-shattering noise was coming from those jaws.

The monster had a split-second choice: kill Sax or rescue the thing from within the now-boiling glass coffin. After an instant of hesitation, she thrust her claws not into Sax's chest—but into the coffin.

She dragged up the cumbersome, flopping corpse within, huge gouts of bubbling gore spilling down over the sides of the glass box and hissing on the boards of the floor, and the scream that poured forth from her maw ascended to the edge of human hearing. The vibration sent up clouds of dust. Every surface in the laboratory appeared to smoke. A great swarming mass of blisters rose up where the acid had touched her like blackflies on meat, and then slabs of flesh peeled away and there was a foul brown smoke and the bones of her arms were turning black even as the corpse she clutched to her chest became a vast, suppurating pudding of decay, its skeleton disarticulated, and it poured from between the twitching black bones of the vampire's fingers.

The heart of her lover En-Men-Lu-Ana fell to the boards. Sax saw the thing was beating, even as it blistered in destruction, blackening and swelling, and then an impossible amount of inky fluid poured from the organ, the *Herzblutkammer*, the fifth house of the heart, vomiting forth its essence.

Now the platform was tilting. Sax tumbled to the edge. The vampire had nearly unmoored it when she ascended. Sax was clinging to the rim of the floor. The black slime of the long-dead monster's heart was streaming across the platform toward him. His foe, with her arms reduced to smoldering black splinters from the elbows down, was no less deadly. She crouched to spring upon him. He was a dead man, and she would grow new arms, but at least he'd pissed her off. That wasn't nothing. Sax consigned himself to death and although he was mortally afraid, there was at the core of his turbulent emotions a kind of white, clean peace, like a fleck of diamond. For all the suffering he had precipitated, it was repaid.

Then Min attacked. There was a rapid *clang-clang-clang* as she ran the length of the collapsing catwalk, leapt, and flew over Sax's head. He saw her there, eclipsing the lamps that hung above them, her legs stretched out like a hurdler's, arms raised over her right shoulder with the silver hammer flashing.

The hammer came down and struck the vampire full in the joint of neck and body, and the shrill whistle of her scream stopped, leaving behind the ringing of half-ruptured eardrums. A pair of twisted black bones thrust through Min's chest and emerged from her back, all that was left of the vampire's arms. They retracted, then emerged again through fresh flesh, and then the bones pumped in and out like jackhammers, ripping dozens of holes through Min's vital organs. And yet Min kept pushing the hammer down, jamming it toward the vampire's heart, and with the last of her hate-fueled strength, she twisted the weapon and the bright blades tore and a geyser of rotten vampire blood hit Min like a fire hose and drove her into the air. She pirouetted without grace or direction and crashed across one of the aluminum panels that formed shit covers for the workbenches below. The cover collapsed and Min, lifeless, tumbled to the linoleum in a slush of chemicals and guano and broken glass.

Sax saw the vampire's face. It was not white now but red, and her eyes were white voids in the blood. The creature rose again, a stream of blood jetting from its chest, and took two lurching steps toward Sax.

Huge hands dragged him over the side of the platform. Sax found himself borne to the floor below in Rock's arms; the man had climbed up the heaps of equipment to rescue him. The vampire was above now, the stream of blood narrowing to the diameter of a long, thin rope, then a string, then it was only beads spilling through the air. Sax felt the foul stuff splash his face. It didn't matter. The monster toppled and fell, its eyes empty now, and crashed to the floor, facedown.

Rock pulled Sax to his feet and propped him against one of the machines.

"Right back," he said, and ran off through the maze of equipment. Sax found that he could move. The ringing in his ears was persistent, throwing his internal gyroscope off so that the world seemed always to tilt left or right but never remained properly level, and his legs felt like a pair of overripe bananas, but there was nothing for it. He had to get going.

The Emily-freezer he'd seen was off to the right somewhere. He hauled his wobbly frame along, grappling with pipes and benches and cabinets to keep himself afloat. He got lost for a few precious seconds in the tangle of gear beneath the platform. Steaming brown-black goo was leaking through the floorboards overhead and he thought he'd better not get beneath it. Even liquefied vampire was probably toxic. He saw Min's broken body a few yards away in a puddle of chemicals and shattered Pyrex, and he wondered if she had experienced the same tiny but durable core of peace when she faced death. Sax hoped so. There was hope. Even for the dead, who are beyond hope.

Sax worked his way around the warren of scientific apparatus and found the freezer. The door stood open and there were dripping icicles forming in the entrance. Inside he could see the three familiars, the blonde, the redhead, and the brunette, hanging inverted from meat hooks in the freezer ceiling. There were others on the floor, frozen in a heap in the back, a woodpile of limbs. He didn't see Emily. He felt some sympathy for the lost souls in there, seduced and destroyed. His opponent in the auction had seemed hard as nails in New York. Now she was just a terribly dead young woman, her cynicism gone. And the redhead—she was the very one he'd seen at the train station.

Sax left the freezer behind and continued rummaging around for Emily, and ultimately tripped over her. She was sprawled beneath a dented-in cabinet that was intended to hold flammable liquids but had disgorged shelves full of tinned cat food instead, hundreds of cans in every flavor. Sax shuddered to think what the vampire had used the stuff for. Maybe she had the bats trained. He rather thought, however, it was more in the nature of a snack, like his pâté de foie gras back in Manhattan.

Sax knelt. The vampire must have flung Emily aside when it leapt back up onto the platform; Sax could see that the monster had driven herself straight up through the three-inch planks that composed the floor, heaving them aside in her haste to stop him pouring the acid in the coffin. It had upset the entire platform, causing one of the massive beams to fall from its socket in the wall where it had been fast for some ten centuries. The thick planks and the machinery atop them had slumped down after the beam and it all now rested on several old iron boilers that had been crushed out of shape but seemed to be bearing the weight.

Sax heard tremendous crashing and banging about. It wasn't the floor coming down. It sounded like metal, hollow. Fuel drums. Rock was doing something. Sax could now smell kerosene, even through the stench of the bat droppings and the vampire sludge. He had a feeling his time was limited.

Emily was unconscious. A thread of blood leaked from beneath her hair. She was cold to the touch. Sax lifted her arms and pulled and Emily inched out from beneath the cabinet, but his strength was not altogether up to the job.

"I'll get you out, dear girl," Sax said, but didn't believe it.

Emily's eyes fluttered and she drew a broken breath of air and rolled on her side, head lolling, to look up at Sax. Her eyes flew wide with the return of full consciousness.

"The vampire," she said.

"Dead," Sax said.

He felt a tap on his shoulder.

"Help me with her, man," Sax said, and turned to find it was not Rock who was behind him.

It was the vampire, the crimson mask of blood on the demon face stretched into rubbery folds by the extension of her jaws.

Sax had time to utter a single word, which disappointingly was *gosh*, and then she threw the bone stumps of her arms around Sax's shoulders, her head sprang forward, and although he got his own forearm up in time to defend his neck, he couldn't stop the razor-edged teeth sinking into his chest. He felt the blood pouring down his body, but the vampire didn't suck out his life. It didn't even attempt to jam its teeth in further.

Instead the thing recoiled, gagging, clawing at its mouth with the twisted black bones, retching and falling to its knees. Sax knew what had just happened.

"Your sister bit me years ago," he gasped, collapsing onto his side. "It gave me a nasty flavor."

The vampire was exhausted. It crawled across the floor toward Emily, but with the sluggishness of a cold reptile. The bones projecting from its truncated arms scratched and scraped on the linoleum. The chest crater where the hammer had gone in dribbled blood, but there was no pressure behind it.

A river of diesel fuel poured fragrantly around Sax's feet and soaked through Emily's shirt and made her find the strength to rise. Her bare feet must have stung abominably.

The vampire was some three or four yards away. Sax was bleeding profusely and there was a flap of what had to be his skin hanging out over the torn breast of his shirt; beneath it was a material that looked like prosciutto but was probably his pectoral muscle. He considered fainting dead away, which would relieve him of the bother of having to survive anymore.

But Emily said, "Help me up," so Sax did.

He dragged her away from the vampire, which splashed now in the growing flood of spilled fuel. They found the outer wall and followed it around interminably, both of them weak as newborns, until the elevator was before them, and they got into the car, and Sax wondered if the power was still working. Then he saw Rock, who tossed one of the big fuel drums aside and strode toward them, grabbing the shotgun from the floor where he'd dropped it.

"You got fucked up pretty comprehensively," Rock said, seeing the curtain of blood streaming from Sax's chest.

"On me it looks good," Sax said, and wondered if it was at all witty. But the delivery wasn't quite there, because the pain in his chest had finally arrived with a ten-piece mariachi band and he was losing his ability to endure.

"Okay, you two get out of here fast as you can. Min's gone. I'll follow you once I light this place up," Rock said.

Sax felt a renewed energy. This was all wrong.

"You can't do that," he said.

"That vampire is still alive. We let her crawl around, she will find a way to get herself back in action. You know it and I know it. And that thing up above, too. And she might have more hundings locked up in the goddamn basement. Only one way to sterilize this place and that's to burn the mother down."

"Rock, listen to me," Sax said, his voice sounding like it was coming from a telephone held five feet from his ear. "Downstairs, that room we went through? It contains probably one hundred million dollars' worth of art. Or ten times that. You can't even put a price to it. There's another hundred million dollars in artifacts, and several thousand objects of literally incalculable worth. There are things down there, masterpieces that will enrich humanity for the rest of time."

There was diesel fuel getting into Sax's wound. The sting of the oil was almost worse than the pain of the injuries itself. Emily was sagging badly. There wasn't any time to argue.

"Old man," Rock said. "This stuff in here been lost to mankind for hundreds of years, am I right?"

"Thousands, some of it." Sax was fading.

"It's just gonna be lost some more, is all. Think of it that way. 'Cause I am not leaving this castle until there's nothing left."

Rock hit the DOWN button and gave Sax a gentle push. Sax fell into the elevator.

"Don't do it," Sax said. The car was starting to move.

Rock smiled. "Bat shit and diesel, man. Think about it. Fertilizer bomb. You think it's gonna make a noise?" Then he laughed, and tugged the elevator door shut, and was lost to sight as the car descended below the level of the floor.

Emily had to drag Sax bodily out of the great hall filled with priceless treasures. He reached up to the Caravaggio. He felt the brushstrokes, those tiny hard feathers of paint daubed on by the hand of one of the greatest artists who ever lived.

There was a heavy *thud* and the entire castle shook. Dirt and dust spilled down from the ceiling. Objects rocked on tables and in cabinets, disturbed in their sleep. Sax could hear after the explosion the thin rattle of the glass in cabinet doors, the cabinets themselves of incredible value, the objects within beyond price. Emily pulled him through the trove.

There was a second explosion and an iron chandelier fell from the ceiling, whirling down through the soaring airspace, crashing brutally into a handsome belle epoque vitrine, probably by François Linke, which contained a selection of violins. Probably all Stradivari. It didn't matter now. They were reduced to splinters.

There was a third explosion, and without warning, a huge timber in the ceiling split in half and Sax saw a mass of laboratory equipment slide into the gap that appeared in the floorboards overhead. Flaming fuel poured through the opening and spilled down into the glorious profusion of man's works below. Sax could not look. He turned away and obediently followed Emily, who had regained much of her strength if not her agility—she was limping extravagantly—to the corridor that would lead them outside.

Sax did not look back again into that chamber of wonders. In fact, he discovered he could not see properly, and he wondered if his eyes had been injured. Then he knew what it was: he was blinded by tears.

One hand pressed to the terrible wound in his chest, Sax hobbled double time down the maze of corridors, following Emily, his hand in hers. He had almost lost her, the person whom he valued most in all the world. An immense, rumbling blast shook the floor with such violence they were thrown off their feet. Emily pulled Sax up. The corridor filled with choking dust and an acrid smell of carbon smoke. Stones fell from the walls. There was a continuous, grinding vibration, an earthquake, and even as they ran, the castle felt as if it were changing shape. Gravity began to play tricks. The highest tower of the great keep must have been collapsing, and with it would come down most of the rest.

They came to an intersection where their own footprints already marked the floor, Emily's right big toe leaving the distinctive blood marks. They'd gone in a circle. Sax was completely winded, so he stopped and bent double with his hands on his knees, gasping in lungful after lungful of the dust-thick air.

"Uncle Sax, the Russian carried me straight down from the helicopter on the roof. They shoved me in that horrible freezer. I've never seen the rest of the castle. I'm lost."

"I'm sorry, I wasn't paying attention. We go," he said, coughing and clutching at the gelatinous wound in his chest, "straight on, then take a left and an immediate right. There will be a long passageway. At the end we go left again, and the exit will be at the end of that. It's not too terribly far. Run."

"Run without you?" Emily said.

"Yes, go on. I'm done," Sax said. "Take my shoes." His spirit had been broken when the tower collapsed on all that human glory in the great hall. The future contained nothing worth living for. He had destroyed it all by his own infernal meddling.

"Uncle Sax, knock it off. You're just tired," Emily said. She used such a patronizing tone of voice that Sax became annoyed, and when he became annoyed, he wanted to live again. If only so he could bear a grudge.

"Right," he said, and started to follow her again. The smoke was getting thicker in the hallways. Something crashed down nearby and shook the floor. Sax was dizzy. He placed his hand against the groaning wall.

"Just weary," he said. "I'm coming along."

There was a noise issuing from behind them, the way they had come.

"Do you hear that?" Sax asked. It was a squeaking, scratching sound. As if a hundred rusty bicycles were approaching, dragging straw brooms.

"What is that?" Emily heard it, too.

"I hear," he said—for he recognized the scuttling sound and knew it must be (as his mind was on, having recently mused upon his fear of rats, rats) rats—"rats."

"Rats?"

"Rats. Lots of rats."

They tried to run, but loped and staggered and lurched along instead. There was a hot, ashy wind blowing now from behind them; there must have been a raging fire back there.

They went as fast as they could but the rats were much faster. A tide of the things, the color of filth, came rushing down the corridor, from wall to wall, a foot deep, boiling like sewage. The rats flowed over them, leaping onto their clothes, tiny scratching paws tearing. Emily danced and screamed as they scrabbled over her bare feet. Sax fell and threw his hands up over his face with his knees drawn up to his chin, and he would have screamed if he could have opened his mouth but he dared not. He was buried in rats, buried beneath their squirming, rushing, screeching thousands, his wounds nail-dug, his hair tangled in braided tails and wriggling limbs. It was a foretaste of hell.

Then the animals had passed, and the corridor contained only himself and Emily and a strew of twitching, crippled rats that had been mangled in the stampede.

Emily was still on her feet, making a strange *eep*ing noise in the back of her throat. She picked Sax up and threw her arm around him, and they kept on going along the route Sax described.

By the time they emerged from the keep into the cold dawn air, they could hear the roar of the flames devouring the castle, advancing through the corridors like an all-consuming army. They made their way through the twists and turns outside the keep, and went beneath the inner gatehouse. Sax looked back. The great jutting fortification was gone. A pillar of flame tossed its shaggy head and roared where the keep had been, a triumphant fire dragon devouring its kill. Only the lesser tower atop which the helicopter had landed was still there. And even as they watched, the fortification slumped on its inward side, lost its shape, and plunged into the blaze. The helicopter fell after it and was consumed like a brittle insect.

The sky was murky with first light, the glow of sunrise a wound in its belly. A mighty black fist of smoke rose up against it. Sax and Emily kept on moving, and five minutes later they passed beneath the portcullis into the road, and were no longer within the walls of Castle Mordstein.

They were met by the men of the Ordine dei Cavalieri Sacri dei Teutonici e dei Fiamminghi, Special Branch, Fra Paolo at their head.

The monks were all clad in cassocks and combat boots, strapped with bandoliers of ammunition, and laden with guns. On the narrow track was parked a Centauro wheeled tank destroyer and a field ambulance. It looked as if they'd gotten permission to invade Germany after all. At least fifty monks were standing there behind Paolo, who had been on the verge of advancing into the castle when Sax and Emily came reeling out of the gates. Sax collapsed and had to be carried to the ambulance. Paolo threw his arms around Emily, not caring how it looked to the rest of his men. Then he tenderly guided her to the medics as well.

Inside the ambulance, however, it was Sax's wounds that made Paolo weep. Emily kept herself out of the way while a monk examined her injuries; for his part, Paolo sobbed, his tears falling on Sax's face, and held his hand and made everything difficult for the medical crew, most notably Fra Giuseppe, who was bustling around with his usual unflappable efficiency, minus the chanting from poor deceased

Fra Dinckel. Another monk was handling that chore, and he had a faint voice and besides was up in the cab where they couldn't hear him anyway.

"Latin," Sax croaked. "It's all Greek to me." Then he finally did faint, and properly, too.

19

NEW YORK

Sax had never so intensely looked forward to spring. He wanted to have done with the cold, harsh winter that had finally broken over the world. No more mountains of frozen garbage, no more filthy snow piling up around Gramercy Park. And with spring came his opportunity to get out of the accursed wheelchair.

His health had not been good after the vampire had bitten him, of course, because anytime a deep, diseased bite wound is trodden upon by ten thousand rats, the injury will tend to get infected. But in addition, there had been vampire-related complications. He now had the saliva of *two* vampires in his system. This caused a certain amount of unpleasantness that eventually landed him, upon Paolo's insistence, in the Ordine dei Cavalieri Sacri dei Teutonici e dei Fiamminghi's hospice in Nimes, where he found himself one of only four patients in an eighty-bed ward.

One of the other inmates died of injuries received when excavating a cellar hole in northern China that turned out to be the resting place of a nasty, subnormal ghoul; another one, a child of eight years, survived the injuries incurred when she was bitten by a hyena-shaped hunding in Tanzania. The girl was very cheerful about the whole ordeal and when she went home, Sax was lonely and bored. The remaining patient in the ward was Nilu. The order had transported her from the remains of the farm in Petit-Grünenwald to the hospital, and she had recovered steadily. Fra Giu's field bloodletting technique was apparently impeccable. But Nilu was very quiet.

Paolo hung about to keep him company when he could. They had long conversations about anything except vampires. Paolo told Sax of the aftermath of the adventure. Castle Mordstein was ruined, and even the lower castle was badly damaged by the tons of rubble that had fallen over the cliff. The official story, as disseminated by the authorities, concerned an electrical fire that had consumed the luckily uninhabited landmark. The monks, reduced to fire-control duty, later examined the wreckage and found a few articles of astonishing worth that had survived the inferno, although they found far more evidence of things lost forever. They never found any corpses. The destruction had simply been too complete. And there was no way to shift all the rubble, because there was nowhere to put it.

Nilu gained strength. Eventually she began to speak. Sax learned she was worried because she had no future.

"That monster took my life away," she confessed to him one evening.

"I know the feeling," he said.

"I have lost my dreams," she added. "I still have nightmares, but I do not mean those dreams. I mean my hope for the future."

"It's not as bad as all that," Sax said, flapping his hand as much as the intravenous drip would allow. "You're young and beautiful, and very special things happen to people who survive vampire attacks. Once the vampire is destroyed, you get a whole new life." He couldn't believe he was saying this. It sounded like he'd break into song next.

"The monster killed my *aatma*, my soul."

"That, young lady, is the one thing they *cannot* do. It's what they hate most about human beings, I think. We have all the soul in the world and they cannot extinguish it. That's why vampires don't make art, write music or poetry. They can't mourn their dead because they are never properly alive. All they can do is exist. They can't *be*. Not like us. Not like *you*. You'll see."

The following evening, Nilu picked up the conversation again. "I have been thinking about what you said. You are correct, I still have my soul or I could not grieve." But her delicate features were furrowed with worry.

"You can tell me anything, you know," Sax offered. "The only secrets I can't keep are my own."

"I can't go back into making films," Nilu said, after a long, thoughtful pause. "I don't know what to do with myself after this. I care nothing for my ambition any longer."

"Ah," said Sax, and felt the old mercenary spirit rise within him. "They haven't told you, I take it, about the hush money."

"Quiet money?"

"Money to be quiet, precisely. You see, the Vatican keeps an insurance account against such situations as yours. They'll pay you an annuity of something like twenty-five thousand euros a year for the rest of your life to remain silent about your ordeal. Don't take their first offer—it's always terribly low."

Nilu nodded thoughtfully, and thereafter her spirits improved. Money might be the root of all evil, but it's also the source of most meals.

Nilu, in turn, had touched on something that gnawed at Sax himself.

His own fire had gone out. He wasn't interested in antiques anymore. Something inside him had broken. The acquisitive urge was gone. As she improved, Sax was failing.

His business, in any case, did well enough without him. Word had gotten out that he'd nearly been killed in another one of his shadowy escapades. It gave him tremendous cachet. Many of his clients thought he was secretly breaking up the last of the Nazi hoards. Others believed him to be a spy along the lines of Jim Thompson—the CIA agent, silk merchant, and man of the world who lived in Thailand and one day disappeared in the Malaysian jungle. That was closer to the truth: Sax had known the man, and he knew what had happened to him. Vampires, of course. Thompson wasn't an ordinary CIA agent, after all. A bit of the special branch himself. And a very fine decorator. Sax still had a small Cambodian bronze from him.

In any case, nobody believed Sax's story that he'd fallen down a manhole in Paris, although they were amused by the double entendre. But they couldn't visit him at the hospital, either. So he became despondent while the vampire fever gradually overtook him, his health failed, and he came to understand that he was going to die, not in a spectacular show of destruction, but in bed like the old desiccated trout he was. Nilu was well enough to walk, at last, and she came around to Sax's bedside on her last day and put her hands on his feet and lowered her head to them and said, "Thank you, Uncle," and then she was bundled off back to India. Sax wept deliciously with self-pity that day.

Sax's condition steadily worsened. Weeks crawled past with no improvement. He was isolated. Emily was busy at home, Paolo away on some business for the order. Sax's only company was the funereal monks who worked at the hospital. Then Paolo returned with Fra Giu. Sax found he was ridiculously happy to see the young man again, although he didn't like the worried look in Fra Giu's eyes. There was something on Paolo's mind, but he didn't mention it until the older monk was out of the ward.

"How is your niece?"

"Emily? Haven't you spoken with her?"

"I've been busy," Paolo said, and reddened. Sax realized the two of them had never been at his bedside at the same time, like Superman and Clark Kent.

"If you can face vampires, surely you can talk to an American woman without my assistance."

"I nearly— The temptation. I can't," Paolo said. "I haven't recovered yet. Please convey my best wishes to her."

"Tell her yourself," Sax said. "She said she's coming here soon."

"I am ashamed."

"Did you make advances upon her?" Sax asked, highly amused despite the discomfort of his fading health.

"No, I did not," Paolo said.

"You probably should have. I'll convey your apologies," Sax said. "But only if I don't die first."

Fra Giu later explained to Sax that he didn't need to die, but he might very well die, and what first needed to be done was a proper bloodletting. It was the same procedure done on Nilu, but with a much better transfusion system and sterile conditions. Sax had a 50 percent chance of surviving, depending on how much of the infected vampire matter was in his bloodstream.

"I've been infected since nineteen hundred and sixty-five, mate," Sax complained. "There's more vampire junk in me than in Nosferatu's underpants."

Emily arrived two days later, three days before his procedure was to begin. Paolo was conspicuously absent, although he had not returned to Rome.

"You look awful, Uncle Sax," she said, and took his cool hand.

"I like the scar," he said.

She had a little half-moon-shaped scar on her cheek, gained at some point during the excitement at Mordstein. It gave her a rakish look, Sax thought.

"How's Nilu?" he asked when Emily failed to speak again. Sax had a terrible feeling she was choked with emotion. Even Emily, at last, was letting him down with this sentimental rubbish.

"She's good," Emily said. Her voice was husky, a lot of sadness shoved down inside it. "She's back in Mumbai and apparently instead of being in trouble, these guys put out some crazy story that got her a lot of good press. Have you seen her?"

"Not recently," Sax said. "She was just a skinny green thing when she left here. Why?"

Emily smiled. "Overnight she's the most beautiful woman in India, they're saying. She's becoming a star. I brought you a magazine with her picture in it, but I left it in the taxi."

"I'm glad for her," Sax said bitterly. Nilu's fears had proven unfounded. The strange attraction that vampires possessed could be passed on to their victims, if the victims were attractive enough to begin with. People wouldn't be able to take their eyes off her now. Sax had enjoyed some of that effect himself, once almost getting David Bowie into bed, although Bowie was resolutely heterosexual despite the whole *Hunky Dory* thing. So Nilu had gotten something from her brush with destruction after all.

He was glad for her. But Nilu's plight had nothing to do with Sax. He was responsible for the deaths of his watchman and his team of experts. Abingdon, Gheorghe, Min, Rock. Even to some extent the girl who had failed to win the ormolu clock at auction. The bitterness Sax couldn't erase came from knowing that he himself had once again survived death, as others had not—others to whom he owed a great deal. He was not at peace with that. An old man sending younger people to die. It was rather too much like being a white-whiskered brigadier in some forgotten war, issuing vainglorious orders to get virgin youths slaughtered before the Turkish guns. And he was bitter for himself as well.

The thing he cared about most in the world was Emily. But after her, he cared most for what was beautiful and old and rare, the lovely works that time could not defeat (unlike himself, he thought sneeringly). And yet, despite his love, he had personally caused the destruction of more such treasure than his mind could grasp.

He'd seen everything all at once, in one place, a magnificent collection tens of thousands of years in the making within his grasp. And it had all been wrecked. Destroyed by his own ambition. What was the point of shining up some old bit of seventeenth-century lumber when he had seen before his eyes an Egyptian throne upon which Cleopatra most probably reclined? Nothing could compare to what had been lost.

"You know, Uncle Sax," Emily said, breaking into his reverie, "economics is boring after all the excitement. I can't settle down."

"Terrible thing," Sax said. "I find I've lost my interest in antiques, too. Perhaps we could switch careers."

Sax smiled at her, but his eyes were dim and full of sorrow and her own smile faded away.

"Don't give up," she said.

"I'm glad you're alive," he said.

They bled him white, and the horrid, fibrous mess that shot out of his veins was the worst they'd ever seen. It even had some subtle anthropomorphic features—the vampire Corfax had busily been regenerating herself inside Sax's bloodstream, although he would have died long before she was able to take any useful form. It would have killed him, eventually—not old age or cancer or anything respectable. Fra Giu told Sax there had been a foot-long, slender structure in there that represented the rudiments of a spinal cord in his pulmonary artery. Once they'd run a few rounds of fresh blood through him, they went in with one of those tiny cameras on a fine cable and discovered what looked like a small blister inside the third ventricle of his heart. They went in with another cable and snipped it out. Fra Giu was delighted with this discovery.

"*You* would have become the vampire, you see," he explained. "*You*, of all the people!" The portly monk laughed then. Sax couldn't join in because his chest was a mass of tubes and it wasn't the least bit funny. He was declared a well man again, if weak, and indeed he felt healthier than he had in ages and ages.

"That's how they reproduce," Paolo had mentioned to Sax in his worst bedside manner one evening. "Infect the heart, my friend. In a hundred or two hundred years, there would be a whole new creature inside your coffin that looked like you but was a vampire. Very *striminzito*, puny, you know how I say. That is why the ancient Egyptians made the mummies. The cremation and embalming has made vampires almost extinct."

"Infection of the heart," Sax said.

"Yes," Palo said, and sighed that melancholy sigh. He hadn't entirely recovered from his own infection of the heart. The only cure for what Paolo had, Sax thought, was marriage, which also boasted a 50 percent survival rate.

Sax was abominably weak, and after Emily had gone, he spent another month in the hospital.

It was three months from the day in December when he'd stumbled out of the castle to the day they stuck him in a wheelchair and let him roll himself around.

A week later, he was back in New York. It was the beginning of April, and spring hadn't yet asserted itself. Finally, in mid-May, the winter packed up and went home, and Gramercy Park began to reach for the sunlight again.

Sax was on his feet after that, stumping around his apartment with the help of an aluminum-frame walker with tennis balls on the bottom of the front legs. Pillsbury paid him a courtesy visit some days later and stayed precisely one hour too long, having been at Sax's place for one hour and three minutes. The bulk of the conversation was Pillsbury telling Sax how extraordinary it all was, as if he didn't believe a word of it but was too polite to say it directly. After the visit, it being a pleasant afternoon with the last of the snow gone and all sorts of tulips and daffodils and crocuses bursting out of the flower beds, not to mention the blooming magnolia tree just opposite Sax's window with the white and pink blossoms, Sax decided to get his key and descend to the street and drag his remains across to the park, where he would sit on a bench until his ass fell asleep. That would occupy half an hour of his time.

He was approaching the gate when an enormous black man with a beard and an ex-military parka approached him from the opposite side of the street, jaywalking diagonally to intercept him.

Sax had the usual reaction of a white man of a certain age: at first he was afraid, then ashamed of his fear because it was based upon racist stereotypes, then afraid again because that was just how people got mugged, by trying to pretend there wasn't a threat; by the time he'd gotten through it the man was before him. It was Rock.

"I . . . I thought you were dead," Sax said.

Rock put an immense arm around Sax's shoulders and pulled him close. "Glad you made it, old man." He was laughing.

Sax was in shock. He had grieved for Rock, as for the others who had died.

"Still getting over it?" Rock said, and gave the walker a gentle shake that nearly threw Sax into the traffic on East Twentieth Street. "Sorry I couldn't stick with you to help you out, but that place took some exploding. I guess you saw that."

"It was a thorough job," Sax said. His face felt strange, somehow tight. He realized he was grinning. "By God, it's good to see you," he added, and put his hand partway around Rock's wrist. "A real pleasure."

"Listen," Rock said. "I gotta go. Things going on as always, right? But I got something for you. I was on my way to the exit in Castle Skeletor with all this fire and shit raining down and I went through that room full of goodies, the ceiling coming down, and I remembered how you were so hot for all that stuff in there, so I took a chance and grabbed a couple things. Had to be portable. Anyway, consider this a memento."

Rock reached into his pocket and pressed something hard and cold into Sax's hand. Sax turned it over and his eyes fell upon a diamond. It was heavy, the largest gem Sax had ever seen in person. But it was not the extraordinary size that struck him. He *recognized* the stone. It was well known but had been lost for centuries.

"I had it checked out by a guy," Rock said. "It's real."

"Did he tell you its name?" Sax asked in a dismal croak.

"Nah," Rock said.

"Let's sit down. Just for a minute."

Sax let Rock into the park, where there were some children playing and fiercely attractive mothers watching them. The martinet who oversaw the place must have been out of town, Sax thought, or she'd have run everyone out by now. The sun was low in the sky and the warm day would soon give way to a cool evening. But the last of the daylight was ideal for basking in. The two men went slowly along to an unoccupied bench and sat down. The stone was in Sax's pocket now; it seemed to give off radiation, exciting his nerves.

"Did your chap offer you a price for it?" Sax said.

"Yeah. A million bucks."

"You could get sixty million from the right collector. Minimum."

"Thought you'd know something about it," Rock said, and laughed. "Man, you know some shit."

"As do you, though it's different shit. More useful, certainly. Look, Rock, can we get a coffee somewhere? I can't tell you how happy I am to see you alive."

"I don't know what you're talking about. You *didn't* see me alive."

"Are you on a secret mission or something?" Sax was intrigued.

"I'm working for some people, let's just say that. All anonymous. If they saw me hanging with anybody—"

"Understood. Let's just talk about this little bit of stone, then," Sax said.

"I thought you'd like it," Rock said.

The diamond was back in Sax's hand, although he shielded it from curious eyes. He felt an enormous greed well up inside him. A familiar greed. He had missed it.

"I must tell you," Sax said, "this appears to be the Great Mogul Diamond, young man. Uniquely shaped like a beehive. Mined in 1650, stolen in Persia in 1747, its owner assassinated—Persia is where that witch in the castle happens to be *from*, incidentally. Coincidence, I'm sure. The real Great Mogul has a couple of documented flaws visible with the naked eye, which I can't help but notice are in this object here."

Sax had this single, precious object, this glittering eye torn from the monster's lair, worth more than everything he'd ever bought and sold all together at once, worth ten times more than the entire château of the vampire Corfax, alias Madame Magnat-l'Étrange, including buildings, grounds, contents, and all.

He felt that burning desire, the acquisitive Gollum-like lust for precious things, and even as it rose up in him, it was fulfilled, his great thirst quenched with a single chunk of shining, water-clear carbon. He had forgotten the thrill of avarice, living as he had lately been without that eternal want that had driven him his entire life, even to the brink of destruction. It was as if Rock had handed him his purpose again. His reason to exist.

"Anyway, a little something to remember me by," Rock said. He had his arms stretched along the back of the bench. They spanned it. In that moment, as clearly as if a bell had rung, Sax had an epiphany.

"Keep it," Sax said.

Sax tucked the enormous diamond into the breast pocket of Rock's jacket.

"No, I can't, seriously," Rock said. "Don't be modest. I got a few little things for myself out of the same box. I'm hooked up for retirement, let's say."

"Do you remember," Sax said, "you said that great hall in the Castle Mordstein looked like somebody's crib?"

"Jay Z's crib," Rock said. "Yeah."

"I procured most of the antiques for Jay Z's crib."

"You're shitting me."

"I shit you not."

They sat in companionable stillness for a few minutes, watching life unwind before them in the park. The mothers called their skylarking children; the shadows were long. It would be time for everyone to go home and eat and be together. Sax was himself looking forward to a dinner with Emily that evening. They saw each other more often since the curious events of December, both of them grappling with the uneasy, shared feeling that their ambitions in life had been false, and everything they had accomplished was of little meaning—antiques and economics were cultured trades, comfortably respectable ways of frittering away the few decades that were theirs to spend in a world of cruelty and hidden wonders that could only be found outside the bounds of civilization.

When you stare into the abyss, the abyss stares into you.

Sax thought he understood that better now. He'd gone out into the darkness and fought monsters on the edge of the abyss, or at least he'd been near to the fighting, with the abyss exceedingly close at hand as well. Either way, he'd stared into the abyss, and it had looked back at him, and he had seen *himself* with the eyes of a creature that might have come into being before man discovered fire. What he had seen was a vain, fleeting, grasping little person, ruthless in pursuit of his petty ambition, but ultimately pathetic. And that was how he had been able to defeat the vampires.

He'd seen it then, as the castle fell in flames. He had somehow made his hunger for acquisition into the entire meaning of his life, of more value even than life itself. So when the vampires looked out from the abyss and saw Asmodeus Saxon-Tang, they saw a wretched, insignificant mammal with the hoarding instinct of a hamster and the plumage of a bullfinch, and underestimated him—not Sax personally, for it would be difficult to underestimate him as a human being, he thought. What they had underestimated was the epoch-making greatness of his greed.

It was the *greed* that made him formidable, Sax now understood, and it had died when the vampire's treasure was destroyed along with the monster. It had died because he would never again come near so vast a fortune in material things. Nothing could ever fill that void. Without his all-consuming avarice, Sax was just another ordinary old man.

Sax and Rock left the park, and Rock went his way up the street with his hands in his pockets and, no doubt, a large diamond in one of them.

Sax inched his walker down the sidewalk past the park, along the fence of iron staves, and was sorry to have discovered his life had no meaning anymore. On the other hand, now he could come up with a new meaning to put into it. Something he chose. A refreshing thought, and one he would share with Emily. She would think he was terribly clever for having come up with it.

As Sax made his way to the corner, he saw an attractive platinum-haired gentleman in trench coat and homburg hat, very chic, on the opposite side of the street. The man looked vaguely familiar and seemed to take an interest in him, smiling slightly. But that couldn't be right; Sax was eminently uninteresting now. So he glanced over his shoulder, to see if the man was looking at someone else, and there was no one. When he turned back, the man was gone—nowhere to be seen.

A brief chill slithered over Sax's bones.

He had been wondering lately if the reason no other vampire had attacked him in the intervening forty years was because of the infection he carried from the vampire Corfax. If that was true, now he was fair game.

Sometimes, he thought, as he hobbled across the empty street, *the cure is worse than the disease.*

ACKNOWLEDGMENTS

I am indebted to many people who directly or indirectly assisted in the creation of this work. Here are just a few of them. To my ofttimes wife, Corinne Marrinan Tripp, I owe the greatest thanks, in this and all things. Mr. Buz Carter lent his ear, and Dr. Paolo Focardi his accent; I am indebted to Nirmitha Iyangar for help with Hindi, Cris Oprea for the Romanian obscenities, and Prathima Bangalooru for her research assistance in London. New Yorker supreme Mr. Harry Segal, as always, was my key to that great city.

Many thanks to the tireless Ed Schlesinger for editing this one, our third together (more than a quarter of a million words combined), and to my glamorous agent, Kirby Kim, for selling it to Ed, and for selling all my manuscripts, despite my constant efforts to write unsalable books. And let us not forget the folks who make novels seem like professional work, at least to the casual reader: the jacket designed by Jason Gabbert; the whole thing art directed by Lisa Litwack; the proofing, queries, fact-checking, and general right-making by Sarah Wright. Let us not forget the publishers—Louise Burke and Jennifer Bergstrom—and the people who market and do publicity: Liz Psaltis and Stephanie DeLuca, respectively. It takes a village to make a novel. I'm the village idiot.

I also humbly thank the research staff of the New York Public Library and the staff of the Archivio Segreto Vaticano at the Città del Vaticano, who clearly thought I was pulling their legs with some of my questions. To them I confess I lied about having the PhD. *Meā culpā, meā culpā, meā maximā culpā* and all that.

Ben Tripp
Prague
February 2015